KT-220-019

NORTHLAND

TIDERICE

RAZOR Mts.

SKULL KINGDOM

KIERLAK DESERT

Skull Mt.

Knife Edge Mts.

River Lethe

The Lazareen

Anatcherae

Malg Swamp

TAUPO ROUGH

The Slags

Stridegate

Rampling Steep

KLU

Valley of Shale

The Spikes

BONE HOLLOW

Jannison Pass

PARANOR

Hall of Kings

VALLEY OF SHALE

Hadeshorn

Dragon's Teeth

Kennon Pass

Moutians of Runne

Varfleet

Tyrsis

Southwatch

Rainbow Lake

Patch Run

Mist Marsh

Leah

BATTLE MOUND LOWLANDS

LOWLANDS of CLETE

PREKKENDORRAN HEIGHTS

PLATEAU

Dechtera

Wayford

R A B B   P L A I N S

Rabb River

Storlock

Chard Rush

Pass of Jade

Pass of Noon

Silver River

UPPER ANAR

REACH

DARKLIN

Grimpond

Rooker Line

Hearthstone

Culhaven

The Wedge

Capaal

Cillidellan

LOWER ANAR

ANAR FORREST

Toffer Ridge

OLDEN MOOR

Maelmord

Heaven's Well

Greymark

HIGH BENS

Dun Fee Aran

Stern

ANAR

N
W   E
S

CHARPENTIER

THE DEFENDERS of
SHANNARA

TERRY
BROOKS

THE SORCERER'S
DAUGHTER

www.orbitbooks.net

ORBIT

First published in Great Britain in 2016 by Orbit

1 3 5 7 9 10 8 6 4 2

Copyright © 2016 by Terry Brooks

Map copyright © 2012 by Russ Charpentier

The moral right of the author has been asserted.

All characters and events in this publication, other than those
clearly in the public domain, are fictitious and any resemblance
to real persons, living or dead, is purely coincidental.

All rights reserved.
No part of this publication may be reproduced, stored in a
retrieval system, or transmitted, in any form or by any means, without
the prior permission in writing of the publisher, nor be otherwise circulated
in any form of binding or cover other than that in which it is published
and without a similar condition including this condition being
imposed on the subsequent purchaser.

A CIP catalogue record for this book
is available from the British Library.

HB ISBN 978-0-356-50223-6
C format 978-0-356-50222-9

Printed and bound in Great Britain by
Clays Ltd, St Ives plc

MIX
Paper from
responsible sources
FSC® C104740

Papers used by Orbit are from well-managed forests
and other responsible sources.

Orbit
An imprint of
Little, Brown Book Group
Carmelite House
50 Victoria Embankment
London EC4Y 0DZ

An Hachette UK Company
www.hachette.co.uk

www.orbitbooks.net

For Kelly & Michael

RENFREWSHIRE COUNCIL	
198079121	
Bertrams	24/05/2016
	£20.00
CEN	

I

NONE OF THE FEDERATION SENTRIES SPARED more than a passing glance for the gray-robed pilgrim as he wound his way through the isolated watchtowers that bracketed the road leading up to the east gates of Arishaig. None of those who occupied the towers and could look down on all who passed; none of those stationed to either side of the gates themselves, armed and ready to act to defend the city should a threat present itself. Not even any of those standing atop the walls overlooking the approach, all of whom had the longest span of time and clearest opportunity to observe him.

He was beneath their notice.

He was ragged and sweat-stained, and while he walked steadily enough, there was an air of weariness about him that confirmed his visible circumstances. Others traveling the road passed him by easily, and none of them paid him but a moment's notice, either. The pilgrim was hooded, so it was impossible to see his face within the shadows of his covering—not without making an effort, and no one felt inclined to do so. He was just one more visitor to the Federation Capital City, one more visitor come to view the most wondrous Southland edifice constructed in the last fifty years.

Indeed, the city of Arishaig frequently astounded the men and women of the Four Lands. Rebuilt after the demons of the Forbidding had burned it to the ground, it was nothing if not formidable. Constructed to withstand any attack launched against it—whether by demons and dragons or things more fearful still—Arishaig had become a fortress that defied all attackers. Its walls soared hundreds of feet high and were thicker than the tightened formation lines of a shield-and-spear rank. Its battlements were studded with flash rips and rail slings loaded and ready to release, all mounted on swivels that directed fire accurately and broadly. Airships were situated on elevated landing pads in each of the four corners of the city proper, with flits and skiffs and other assorted quick-moving fliers readily available for the use of First Response—the company formed years earlier to serve as an initial line of defense against all assaults on the city.

Within, an inner wall shadowed the outer, and within both rings the entire population save those engaged in labor on the outlying farms worked and resided. Five million people lived within Arishaig now—and some claimed there were even more. Even the bulk of the Federation army was housed and trained inside those walls. And at its exact center, the Phoenix Tower—symbol of a Federation city raised from the ashes of the old—towered above all, rising more than thirty stories into the clouds. The Coalition Council occupied it. The Federation government's offices, living quarters, healing centers, education adjuncts, and food storage warehouses formed a compound more than a mile square.

All this awaited the traveler in the gray robes, but he kept his eyes on the road ahead. He already knew what lay within. He had passed this way before.

A flurry of skyward motion, coupled with the sound of expended power from diapson crystals exploding through parse tubes, caught his attention, and for a second he slowed. Ghost Flares roared overhead, the fastest of the airships, looking like naught but black shadows as they flashed past. All eyes turned skyward to watch. Even the gray-robed pilgrim paused.

But only so he would not attract attention by choosing to move while the others stood still.

At the gates, he waited in line for permission to pass. Others crowded ahead of him, and he let them do so. *Patience in all things,* he reminded himself. When it was his turn to approach, he did so almost reluctantly, his robes dragging on the ground, his head lowered.

The soldiers judging the merits of those seeking admission barely looked at him. "Name?" said one.

"Raushka." His voice was as weary as his look.

"Home?"

"I am from Sterne."

"Business?"

A moment's hesitation. "I seek medical care."

Now the soldier looked up. "What sort of medical care?"

"Surgery to repair flesh damaged in a fire. I require a reconstruction."

Another soldier stepped forward to join the first. Both peered at him questioningly. "Where were you burned?" the new man asked.

"My face."

The soldiers exchanged a glance. "Let me see," said the first.

The pilgrim hesitated. "I would advise against it."

"Fellow, we are soldiers," said the second. "What we have already seen would turn your innards to jelly. Let us be the judge of what we can and cannot stand to look upon."

A long silence. "As you wish."

He lifted his head slightly and pulled back the hood. The soldiers' faces turned ashen. People around them gasped and flinched back. One woman turned her head and vomited. The pilgrim stood without moving, his face and head exposed, his eyes—or the one eye that remained—fixed on the soldier who claimed to have seen the worst of everything.

"That's enough," the soldier said, shaking his head in dismay. "Cover yourself."

The pilgrim did so, again assuming a slightly bent position so that his face retreated once more into the hood's shadows.

The speaker took a deep breath. He didn't even bother looking at

his fellow. "If there is help for you here, it surpasses any form of healing I am familiar with. Go on, now, and find it if you can."

The pilgrim moved on, into the shadow of the gates, into the
throngs that crowded the streets beyond. Behind him, there were
mutterings and exclamations, oaths and wardings. Everyone was unsettled by what they had seen.

Just as the pilgrim had intended.

When the door to his shop opened an hour later and the pilgrim
walked through, the old man who was the shop's owner and sole oc-
cupant glanced up in the manner of the soldiers at the gate, but was
quicker than they were to revise his level of interest. The pilgrim was
not who he appeared to be; the owner recognized this at once. It was
his business to deal with men and women who specialized in deception and trickery, and he knew this one. So instincts honed on a thousand such encounters kept him from being caught off guard.

The gray-robed horror approached the counter and stopped. He
did not look up. He did not lift his face into the light. "You have what
I ordered?"

"I do," the old man replied. "Do you wish it now?"

"In a minute. Tell me, is your business much improved since leaving Sterne? Is it not doing better in Arishaig?"

The question seemed innocuous, but no question asked by this
man ever was. "I am content."

"You traffic in so many wondrous things. It must be easier finding
them here, in such a large city."

"It is easier, yes."

"And you remember it was I who sent you here? I who told you to
leave Sterne before the unfortunate events involving the Red Slash?
You remember this?"

"I could hardly forget. And I will always be grateful."

"Opportunities abound?"

"They do."

"But where there are greater opportunities, there are greater temp-
tations, as well. Opportunities present themselves—opportunities

that require acts once believed unthinkable. What does it matter if you commit a small betrayal when doing so might result in the acquisition of a considerable fortune?"

The old man went cold. "Such acts serve little purpose if you are a dead man. It is much better to stay faithful to those who have been faithful to you."

The pilgrim laughed softly. "I would expect you to say as much."

"Is there some reason you think I have deceived you?"

"None. I ask only to reassure myself. If you were to lie, I would see it in your eyes. Why don't you show me what you have been holding for me?"

The old man took the pilgrim into the back of his shop. This establishment was much like the one he had managed in Sterne—small, cramped, and shabby, filled with this and that—a place where no discernible order or purpose revealed itself to any save himself. He still mostly provided information and access, although now and then—and for his better customers—he also provided supplies. He had done so for this man, this monster.

The back of the store was much like the front, although so crammed with boxes and crates that almost no open space was available. The two of them barely found room to maneuver as the old man released the spring catch hidden in the wall behind the false crate and pulled out the garments hung within.

"You may try them on here, if you wish," he offered.

The pilgrim lifted his head far enough that his distorted features were revealed. The old man shuddered inwardly but kept from showing his horror. "An imaginative disguise," he managed.

A thin laugh. "Not a disguise, exactly. More a reordering of flesh, blood, and bone through a careful employment of magic. I wished to look a certain way and I found the means by which to do so. I took no chances of discovery."

The shopkeeper bowed in acknowledgment. "Very clever."

"I will need a basin filled with hot water, towels, and a mirror." The pilgrim's face lowered once more into shadow. "Can you provide me with these?"

The old man beckoned. "My apartment is next door. Come."

They went outside. The old man locked the door to his business behind him, then walked a dozen steps to another door. A stairway took them to an upstairs hallway. His was the second door on the left. He unlocked it and they entered. Once inside, he started to lock the door behind them when the pilgrim stopped him.

"Go back to your shop and wait for me there. Leave the key to these rooms. I will lock up when I am done and return the key before leaving."

Bowing, the old man did as he was ordered. There was never any question of doing otherwise. He left the apartment, went back down the stairs, and returned to his shop. He took a few minutes to close up his hiding place in the back room and reseal the false crate front. Then he waited, occupying himself with cataloging the cost of his services and watching the clock on the wall tick slowly toward the new hour. He was not afraid of this man, but he was wary. It did not matter that he would never betray him. If the man even suspected he had, he would be dead. There was no predicting a man like that. He would rest easier when this business was finished.

He did not have to wait much longer. Approximately thirty minutes later, the shop door opened. The man who entered was garbed in black robes of fine quality, with silver embroidery woven into the edges of the sleeves. A patch was sewn into the breast panel over his heart—an insignia well known throughout the Four Lands. It was called the Eilt Druin and displayed the image of a hand holding forth a burning torch. It could be found on the robes of all members of the Fourth Druid Order.

The face of the pilgrim had changed yet again; now he was someone else entirely. The shopkeeper did not know this man, and he thought it would be best if he forgot him right away. It would be best if he took even the memory of that face to the grave with him.

"Excellency," he said instead. "Always your servant."

The other man made no response but merely handed back the key to the shopkeeper's apartment. The old man took it and pocketed it. The man who pretended to be a Druid then handed him a fistful of credits—far more than the shopkeeper had expected for his services.

"Remember this," the man said. "I always reward those who serve me well, and I always find out about those who don't."

Then he turned and went through the door, his black Druid robes billowing out behind him. The old man walked to the doorway and watched him go. Even after the stranger was gone, he waited almost an hour, just to be sure. Then he closed up his shop and retired to his apartment. Once there, he counted out the credits he had been paid and swore he would never do this again.

But he was lying to himself; he would always do whatever this man told him to.

Because it was never a good idea to say no to Arcannen Rai.

2

LEOFUR RAI STOOD AT THE PARAPETS OF THE INNER walls of Paranor, staring out over the miles and miles of deep woods that surrounded the Druid's Keep. She studied the emerald canopy with intense concentration, as if she might find something that was hidden. Then, pushing back from the walls, she began wandering the ramparts, looking at her feet as she walked, wondering where she was going—not here specifically, of course, but in the wider course of her life. She remained unsure, even after a year of searching. An entire year spent living in Paranor.

Paxon had brought her to Paranor after they had lived together for a time in Wayford—an arrangement arrived at spontaneously and with considerable misgivings on her part. She could still recall the night he appeared on her doorstep after a five-year absence. He had looked so desperate, so lost, that her heart had broken for him. At the time, she had been convinced that he was never returning—that he had chosen a different path from the one she had once imagined they would take together, and there was nothing she could do about it. So it was a shock that he had found his way back.

A shock that, after it lessened, would arouse suspicion, regret, and deep uncertainty.

But she had taken him in. Her feelings for him were still strong enough that she was not prepared to cast him out, so she had brought him into her home and into her life in less than a week. He was damaged, she knew, and needed time to recover. He had left the Druid order. He was thinking of abandoning his post as the High Druid's Blade. What happened to him when he faced the sorcerer Arcannen in the city of Sterne, and thereafter when he searched for—and found—the strange boy who had inherited the magic of the wishsong, had undone him. He was still Paxon, but hollow and directionless, and believed she was the true north that might lead him out of the wilderness.

The love they found grew slowly but steadily. The seeds had been planted even before his return. Like flowers buried in fertile soil, love had broken through and bloomed into something amazing. She had doubted it for a time, wary of such miracles, but in the end had given herself to it readily. He wanted her; he needed her. He was where he belonged with her. She could feel it in his words and actions. But would it last? She couldn't be sure. She only knew it was worth finding out.

Then, inevitably perhaps—when he had come all the way back from his dark uncertainty—he had decided to return to Paranor. Perhaps only for a while, perhaps never again as the Blade, but Chrysallin was there, and he could not let his sister stay longer without him. He was afraid for her. She was vulnerable without his steadying presence—something the Druid order might try to take advantage of.

It was her voice, of course. The power of her voice was enough to destroy someone as powerful as the witch Mischa—now, *there* was magic the Druid order would love to get its hands on! If Chrysallin could be persuaded to use it for their purposes . . .

But of course, it wasn't that simple. Chrys had suffered a breakdown during her battle with Mischa and had blocked out all memory of what had transpired. She had no idea that she possessed this power, no hint she had inherited the fabled wishsong from her Ohmsford ancestors.

Leofur turned, looking away from the forest and down into the south courtyard where the gardens flourished. Chrysallin sat amid a profusion of colors and scents, her eyes closed, her hands clasped loosely in her lap, meditating. It was Leofur who had taught her this technique.

As she watched Paxon's sister, Leofur took note of her stillness, her calm. And her thoughts returned to her own lack of both.

It had been a hard decision to come north with Paxon, yet she had done so anyway. She had valued her independence in Wayford, where her home and her friends were, but none of these was as important to her as Paxon. He had told her he would have understood if she had chosen to remain behind. He would come back to visit her, he promised, if she decided to stay. But he must leave no matter what her choice, because he feared for his sister and could not bear the thought of losing her again.

So Leofur had decided, following the path that would keep them together, believing their time as a couple had not yet played out. But she had asked him of their future together, seeking a commitment to buttress her decision. Would he become her life partner? Would he commit to doing so right now?

He said he would.

So resolved, they had returned to Paranor, where both were received warmly by Isaturin, Ard Rhys of the Fourth Druid Order. Perhaps he dissembled, but she thought not. Paxon was reunited with his sister and reinstated as the High Druid's Blade without equivocation. Leofur herself was given leave to pursue any course of study or action she wished. It was all she could have hoped for.

But what surprised her—and what in the end made all the difference—was the friendship she had found with Chrys.

It was an unexpected discovery. At first, the two had circled each other like wary cats, each knowing the other held an important place in Paxon's life, yet neither willing to yield ground. But once the sizing up was completed, Leofur had found herself drawn to Chrys more strongly than she had expected, and they quickly bonded. In part, it was because Chrysallin filled a void. As Paxon's duties called him away from the Keep for increasingly longer periods of time, Leofur found herself missing the sheer need for her company he had displayed in the early days, and his sister proved an unexpected substitute. But in larger part, it was because Arcannen had scarred both of them permanently. Both had suffered at his hands and were trying to find ways to heal.

Of course, Chrysallin had been more than a little wary when Leofur had first revealed that she was Arcannen Rai's daughter. But whatever awkwardness this might have caused was quickly lifted when Leofur explained what her father had done to her in her early years, and how they had been estranged ever since. The fact that Paxon had chosen her as a life partner provided further proof that any relationship between father and daughter—save for the inescapable biological one—had long since vanished.

In addition, Paxon was eager for Leofur and his sister to be friends, and had asked Leofur to do what she could to help Chrys come to terms with the wishsong magic. Because she was her father's daughter, Leofur might have some knowledge and understanding of Arcannen's skills that would help Chrys to develop a mastery of her own. After all, Paxon had come back to Paranor intent on revealing to his sister the truth about her dubious gift, and to help her find a way through the doubt and fear that might arise with the knowledge. And Leofur was in a unique position to help with this.

Once Chrysallin had been provided with the full story behind her encounter with Mischa, Leofur stepped in to offer what help she could. Paxon arranged for a Druid who was a skilled practitioner of mental projection—a form of magic not so different from the wishsong—to work with Chrys on the practical aspects of mastering its power. Leofur chose to teach Chrys what she knew of developing control over her emotional and mental stability—a skill she'd learned when her own life had become so unpredictable. She started with meditation several times a day, and employed a regimen of sleeping and eating that should mitigate any stress. She helped Chrys come to terms with the aftereffects of Arcannen's damage by detailing her own experience. She encouraged Chrys to take long walks, to take up crafts and pastimes that would relax her mind while occupying her hands. But mostly, she made herself available as a confidante.

All of which had led to the breakthrough they had been hoping for. By now, Chrysallin Leah was using her gift regularly and with increasing control, despite the fact that she was still learning.

Leofur stood on the wall for a moment longer, studying Paxon's sister, admiring her slender form, her poise and beauty. Chrys was no longer the gawky young girl she had been when she'd first encountered Arcannen Rai. She was three years into her womanhood now, fully grown and undeniably striking, with classic features, huge blue eyes, raven-black hair, and a dazzling smile. She was gaining maturity with the passing of every day, and while Leofur believed herself reasonably attractive and certainly more mature and experienced than her friend, Leofur knew she was not Chrys's equal.

How could she be, when Chrysallin Leah had such unlimited potential as a future member of the Druid order?

As if reading her thoughts, Chrys looked up at her and waved, climbing to her feet. It was time for their walk.

Leofur went down the stairway to the courtyard and stood waiting on her friend. As she did, she cast her mind back to an earlier time, to Wayford and her now shuttered home—to her life as a tradeswoman and salvager. Then she was on her own, her past an open secret to those who knew her, her future defined mostly by the work she was doing. She remembered how she had learned to be self-sufficient, to need only her own presence to feel complete.

And it had all been enough until an emotionally battered and terrified Chrysallin Leah had appeared on her doorstep, and everything had changed in an instant—because then Paxon had come, too.

I do love you, she said to herself. She wished she could say it to his face—but, as always, he was off on a mission for the Druids instead of here, at her side.

It was hard to have him away so often. Was it any wonder she was not sure of herself in the way she once had been? Here in this distant part of the Four Lands, what was she, after all? The daughter of a fugitive sorcerer hunted by everyone from Druids to Federation soldiers to Elves and Bordermen, who had caused death and destruction on a scale that dwarfed that of entire armies? The life partner of a conflicted Highlander who believed his destiny was to confront and do battle with her father? The close companion of a young woman who commanded ancient magic? All of these? Did she belong here at all, an outsider who on the face of things was accepted but who in the looks and silences of others felt herself under constant scrutiny?

Her uncertainties were legion, but she kept them under tight control because she knew, in her heart, that—whatever else she was—she was still Paxon's true north and Chrysallin's closest friend.

A bold assessment, this last. Would the role of Chrys's best friend not better belong to her brother? Yet Leofur didn't think so. Paxon answered to a higher calling as the Ard Rhys's Blade, the protector of the Druid order. His duties and obligations did not permit him to be as physically or emotionally close to Chrys as he needed to be. Not in the way Leofur believed necessary, and not in the way Chrys required in order to heal. Leofur might be the true north for Paxon, but she was also the rock to which Chrysallin clung when the worst of her doubts surfaced. It was a great and terrible responsibility for Leofur to assume, but one that kept her anchored to Paranor when the urge to flee back home loomed strong.

So she forced herself to smile as Chrys arrived and greeted her with a hug.

They passed through the gates and moved onto the meandering paths that wound deep into the forests surrounding Paranor. Every day they took this walk, finding their way to new places, exploring the world beyond the Keep—and giving Chrys fresh opportunities to practice and test the wishsong's magic. Today was just another day. Sunshine dappled their shoulders and backs, and a soft breeze brushed their faces. All around them, birds sang and darted through the trees.

Once, this wouldn't have been the case. Once, wolves and the ghosts of the dead prowled these woods. There were centuries when Paranor sat empty, and centuries more when it was nearly so. A Druid order the size of the current one had not survived the fall of the Keep in the days of the Warlock Lord. But the ghosts and the wolves and the silence had vanished, and now there was life everywhere.

"You worry about your father, don't you?" Chrys said to Leofur, after long minutes of silence had removed them from the shadows of the walls. "You think he will show himself soon."

Leofur looked at her. "How do you know I am not thinking of Paxon?"

The other woman grinned. "When you think of Paxon, you have a different expression."

Leofur blushed. "Then I am entirely too transparent. Yes, I am thinking of my father. My instincts warn me he is going to resurface. His history suggests it, and I am sure he wants still what he has wanted all along—to gain control over the Druids and their magic. He wants recognition and power, and he won't quit until he either has achieved his goal or is dead."

They walked on in silence, the Keep now lost in the tangle of trees behind them. "I hope Paxon is all right," Chrys said quietly.

Paxon had departed for Arishaig two days ago, a key member of a Druid delegation tasked with finding common ground between their order and the Federation. Save for the tribal factions of the reclusive Gnomes, all of the remaining populations had begun to cement relationships that could transcend the ancient, arbitrary boundaries that once had divided them. An acceptance of both magic and science required that everyone do better at working together and spending less time emphasizing their differences. The conclusion of the War on the Prekkendorran and the subsequent defeat of the demon hordes let loose from the Forbidding had left everyone weary of fighting and anxious for peace.

So this meeting between the Druids and the Federation was a necessary first step toward improving relations, and Paxon Leah was attending as the leader of a Druid Guard who would act as the protectors of Paranor's official delegation.

Leofur's father would love to disrupt such an event, but he was wary of Paxon, having twice faced him and been defeated. Arcannen was no fool; he would be hesitant about going up against the Highlander a third time. Besides, no one had seen or heard from him since the night he had destroyed the Red Slash and killed the young Druid Avelene before being driven off. Most believed he had gone to ground and would stay there. Even though Leofur wasn't one of these, she didn't want Chrys to think otherwise.

"Paxon will be fine," she said. "Come on, let's concentrate on your lessons. Why don't you try something new with your magic today? See if you can find a different way to make it do what you want."

So, for a time, Chrys attempted various techniques to make the magic respond as she wished. She understood the principles behind using it well enough. It was the concentration and the sustained effort at shaping it that proved difficult. Mostly, when she struggled, it was because she could not keep focused long enough or implement her imaginings sufficiently to achieve her goals.

This morning, she tried bringing flowers to bloom from the still-closed buds in which they germinated. A simple enough task, and she had done it before. But on this occasion she succeeded only in wilting the plants. She tried it over and over, and each time she failed.

"Wait a minute," Leofur said finally, aware of her friend's frustration. "I don't think you are approaching this the right way. Making flowers bloom doesn't mean anything special to you."

Chrysallin looked confused. "What do you mean?"

"For magic to work, it has to come first and foremost from the heart. It has to be connected to your feelings, your desires. My father once told me that magic responds best when the emotions that fuel it are strongest. So try to do something that really *means* something to you. After all, that's why it is called the *wishsong*."

They walked on a bit farther, Leofur glancing skyward as a pair of tiny yellow finches flew over. "I know," she said. "Try calling those finches to you. Summon them with your magic."

They stood in place as Chrys began to hum softly, drawing the magic up from within. She found the music in her mind as she improvised from her memory of dozens of different birdsongs. Her voice shaped a call—a series of soft chirps followed by a whistle. She started and stopped, clearly unable to decide if she was taking the correct approach, but she went back to it in seconds, starting anew and keeping control of her emotions.

Slowly, she steadied, and her song rose into the air, loud and clear.

Leofur had no idea if Chrysallin sounded anything like a real finch, but she didn't interfere with her friend's efforts. The sounds were melodic and bright in the forest silence, and suddenly birds all around began calling back.

"Chrys . . . ," Leofur said, glancing around hurriedly.

A chill ran down her back. Birds were flying at them from everywhere, swooping through the air and landing on nearby branches, sending back their own calls, bright and eager. There were handfuls at first, then dozens, and finally hundreds. Leofur flinched in spite of herself as some flew dangerously close. Would they attack? She glanced at Chrys and found her in something resembling a trance, her eyes closed and her head thrown back as she gave voice to her improvised song.

"Chrysallin!" she whispered urgently, wanting the other to see. "Look!"

The other girl responded, opening her eyes to find hundreds of brightly colored birds flying past, sweeping and fluttering and singing. Her face lit up with pleasure. "Oh, Leofur!" she gasped, and quit singing.

Instantly the birds disappeared, scattering in all directions once the spell was broken.

Leofur started laughing. "Look what you did! Shades!"

Chrys embraced her excitedly. "I just sang like I remembered birds could sing! I wasn't even trying all that hard. I was simply . . . letting go."

Leofur hugged her back. "Now remember how you did it. Remember how that felt the next time you use the magic. You did something important just now! Something wonderful. I'm so happy for you!"

Her friend was crying, unable to steady herself, and Leofur sat her down on the woodland floor and held her. This hadn't been all that difficult, but every accomplishment brought her a step closer to mastering the magic.

Chrys drew back finally, her face wet. "I'm not even sure what I did, Leofur. I don't know if I can repeat it. I don't have any idea at all what a finch sounds like—"

"No, Chrys," Leofur interrupted quickly. "You're missing the point! It doesn't matter what a finch sounds like. You wanted to call birds to you, and you fashioned a song that did so. You brought hundreds of them! Your magic was doing more than you expected! Can't you see?"

They began laughing, and finally Chrysallin nodded in agreement. "I do see. It's good, isn't it? I did call all those birds. I used my magic to bring them to me. And I didn't hurt anyone! I wasn't afraid, and I wasn't unsure. I knew I was using the magic in the right way."

They hugged again, and Leofur whispered, "Remember this day. Remember how it began. You made the magic work like you wanted it to, Chrys. Really work."

Then she was crying, too.

They walked on after that, but Chrys did not want to use the magic again right away. Mostly, they talked about what other uses they could find for it. Chrys wanted to try summoning other creatures, particularly butterflies, even though she had no idea how to do that. But having summoned birds with as little intent, she was confident she could do the same with butterflies. Or dragonflies. Or even small animals.

Leofur thought she should try her skills on controlling the elements—earth, wind, fire, and water. From what Paxon had told her, that was the traditional use of the wishsong, and Chrys should attempt to learn what her ancestors had managed to achieve. Leofur firmly believed that Chrysallin should always try to exceed her perceived limits. Why not push against the resistance that had held her back for so long? Why not make sure she had broken through her emotional restraints for good?

"Oh, I don't care what I do next," Chrysallin gushed finally, "just so I do something! Just so I keep trying new things and not worrying about what they might do to me. I'm not afraid anymore, Leofur! I know I can use this magic safely. I know I can use it and not hurt others!"

"Just keep that in mind. You have the ability to master it and keep it from mastering you." Leofur paused. "Wait until you tell Paxon about this!"

They had wandered much farther away from the Keep than they had intended, and quickly turned around when they realized. Still talking about Chrys's breakthrough and arguing about which way to go next, they walked back through the deep woods, absorbed in their conversation. The day remained sunny and bright, but inside the forest it was heavily layered with shadows and very still.

In the trees around them, the birds had stopped singing.

Leofur noticed first. She stopped talking, motioning for her companion to do the same, and listened. Everything had gone still. She forced herself to keep walking, even though her instincts told her she should run. Chrys glanced at her, then looked around in alarm. She sensed it, too. Someone or something was out there, hidden in the trees, in the shadows, watching. "Leofur?" she whispered.

Leofur shook her head and kept walking. There was nothing to do now but keep moving. Whoever was out there would reveal themselves when they were ready . . .

A whirring sound broke the stillness. Webbing flew into her face, and something hard struck her head, and she tumbled into blackness.

Time slowed.

Time stopped.

She was drifting again, far away somewhere, untethered to any sense of place or time. When consciousness began to return, it did so slowly. It seemed as if she were being dragged upward from a deep hole toward a sliver of light.

Then she blinked and her eyes opened. She was lying on her back in the forest. Her head throbbed, but whatever had wrapped itself around her and struck her was gone. She reached up and felt the bruise above her temple and pulled back quickly.

Chrysallin, she thought.

She forced herself into a sitting position and looked around frantically.

But she was alone.

3

DEEP WITHIN THE PHOENIX TOWER, IN QUARTERS designated for use by members of the Coalition Council and their families and staff and visiting dignitaries, Paxon Leah stood motionless in his tiny bedroom and considered the day ahead. He was dressed in his regular working uniform—leather belt and boots and lightweight, durable forest clothing, colored green and brown, all of it overlaid by the familiar black-and-silver cloak that indicated members of the Druid Guard. He wore his sword strapped across his back, its black handle protruding over his left shoulder and within easy reach. He should have no need of a weapon in the Coalition Council chambers, but as lead protector of the Druids in the delegation, he must always be prepared.

He looked at himself in the wall mirror and saw a man as rough-hewn and shaggy as his clothing. Long reddish hair and the beginnings of a beard, sun-browned skin, eyes that were a startling blue, and features that were chiseled and sharp—all of it made a map of his years. He should have shaved and considered dressing up a bit more, but that wasn't who he was. And it was a bit late to try to change his habits now, especially given the nature of his work. If Leofur were there, she wouldn't advise him to alter his appearance to please others. So in her absence, neither would he.

He tightened the long knives he wore strapped to his lower body—one to his waist and the other to his right thigh. They were partially concealed by the cloak, but he could get at them easily enough. He considered again the possibility that weapons might be needed. Was there any reason to think an attack would be made on the Druids within the Federation Capital City, especially when they had been guaranteed safe passage? And after so much effort had been expended to bring this meeting about? He couldn't imagine the Federation breaking its word—not with its Prime Minister so eager to have them come to Arishaig to discuss how the two powers might better cooperate in their efforts to fashion a stronger guarantee of continued peace.

No one wanted another Prekkendorran.

And no one wanted a repeat of what had happened when the Forbidding collapsed and the demons escaped.

There might be differences between the Druids and the Federation regarding the proper place of magic and science in the world. There might be disagreements about which should be cultivated, expanded, and used to further the aims of the various governments. There might be suspicions and dislikes and even outright hostilities from time to time, but no one wanted it to come to war.

Which didn't mean it wouldn't, unfortunately. Not while there were insurgents and firebrands to lead them. Not while the Gnomes remained war-like and the Trolls drew lines in the sand. And especially not when there were dangerous sorcerers like Arcannen Rai still loose in the world, just waiting for a chance to stir things up.

Paxon couldn't help himself. He was always alert to the possibility that Arcannen would make a fresh appearance. He kept himself ready for that moment, knowing it would happen eventually. Hard life lessons and painful experience had taught him that you could never take anything for granted where the sorcerer was concerned. Others might behave in rational ways and display some measure of caution and common sense, but not Arcannen. Nothing he did ever followed a recognizable pattern. All of his appearances had been unexpected and violent, tailored to further his goal of destroying the Druids. Men and women had died as a result, several of them Druids, and two of them his friends. Each time, Paxon had come close to putting an end to Arcannen, and each time the sorcerer had been just a little bit quicker.

He would try again. He would keep trying until he had finished what he had set out to do.

Which was why Paxon was prepared for it here, just as he was prepared for it in every other situation where the Druids under his protection might be at risk. It might seem as if nothing could go wrong within Arishaig's walls, for who would dare attempt anything here in the heart of the Federation? But Paxon was not taking any chances.

He had asked Isaturin if it would be possible for the Druids not to sit together during the conference, but Isaturin had said they must. He had asked if body armor might be worn, but that was rejected out of hand, too. He asked if, just this one time, the Druid Guard might carry flash rips, even though it was forbidden to Druids and those in their employ while without the walls of Paranor. Light, deadly, and easily employed, the flash rips were swifter and surer than the blades and bows the Trolls were normally permitted.

Again, Isaturin said no.

So here Paxon was on the morning of the first session of the Assembly with no real protection for his charges other than standard weapons and his sword. Oh, there was magic, of course. But save for Miriya, none of the Druids in attendance was a warrior, and none had extensive training in the use of magic for defense. He had almost decided to ignore the Ard Rhys and equip the Trolls with flash rips anyway, but in the end he had decided against it. The Trolls were loyal to a fault. They would reject anything not specifically approved by the Ard Rhys himself.

I should have brought Leofur, he thought. *She, at least, would have come armed and ready. She would have brought her Arc-5.*

He pictured her with the big, long-barreled flash rip hybrid, its diapson crystals sufficiently powerful to blow out a wall. It was almost bigger than she was, yet she carried it with ease. He smiled, thinking of her hefting it—a formidable figure. Her presence now would have helped tremendously.

But Leofur was back in Paranor, doing what he had asked her to do, protecting and mentoring his sister. Helping her find ways to come to terms with the magic of the wishsong.

He regarded himself once more in the mirror, took a deep breath, then went out the door into the residence hallway. A single floor of rooms had been given over to the Druid delegation for its personal use—a readily defensible place in which no one outside their order was allowed without permission. It contained bedrooms, a kitchen and dining room, and a reception area where all of them were to gather this morning before going over to the council chambers.

Paxon walked down the hallway toward the designated meeting area, nodding to the Trolls who patrolled the floor in a steady crisscross pattern. Nominally, he was in charge of the guard and held absolute authority over them. But early on he had decided the order of command needed tweaking, so had given responsibility for overseeing the guard to a Troll captain named Netheren. The Trolls knew who Paxon was and respected his position as the High Druid's Blade, but they responded better to one of their own. He just wished he could make better use of their presence in this situation.

He had passed several doors when the one in front of him opened and Miriya stepped into view. "Well met, Paxon Leah."

"Morning," he said, falling into step beside her. "Sleep well?"

She shrugged. "My bedmate saw to it that I did." She cocked an eyebrow at him. "I'll bet you miss yours!"

He made a rude noise. She knew the answer to that well enough. "Is Karlin still sleeping?"

"Already up and gone. She likes to rise early and meditate. Says it loosens up her cognitive powers. Gives her better use of the sight."

Karlin Ryl. A seer with formidable skills, tall and willowy, with skin as smooth and black as ink. She was a rare breed of magic user, everyone agreed. Almost none among the Druid order possessed the sight, so she was esteemed for her gift. Of course, there was the problem of recognizing what she saw for what it was, but all seers suffered from the same dilemma. How did you interpret visions of things that hadn't come to pass when sometimes they were so foreign as to be unrecognizable?

Miriya brushed back her short-cropped blond hair and rolled her powerful shoulders. "I prefer exercises in sets of thirty for waking my cognitive powers." She grinned at his look. "You doubt me? Don't. Loosening up my muscles always focuses my ability to reason. And don't say you don't know what I'm talking about. You must experience the same thing when you spar with old Oost."

Oost Mondara was his Dwarf mentor and trainer in the use of weapons—in particular, the magic-infused Sword of Leah. Given centuries ago to his ancestor Rone Leah by the Druid Allanon, after the latter had dipped the blade in the deadly waters of the Hadeshorn to instill in it a new form of magic, it had been passed down through the centuries to finally end up in Paxon's hands. Ironically, it was his first encounter with Arcannen Rai that had revealed the sword's incredible power and led eventually to his becoming the Ard Rhys's Blade.

"I might characterize training with Oost in somewhat different terms," he replied, "but I take your point. Tell me how you see our chances in winning over the Federation today."

"Good." She gave him a look. "They want to find common ground as badly as we do, and there are places where we can do that. Agriculture, roadways, airship travel routes for trade and passenger service, the education of the young." She paused. "In everything save defense and weapons, I would guess. In that, each will want to go a different way."

"Magic and new science."

"It can't be helped. Our history is too deeply embedded to allow for anything else. You know how the Federation feels about us, and us about them. The Elves don't like the idea of an alliance with the Southlanders, either, but they'll support whatever we decide ... I guess."

He wondered about that. On the surface, maybe, but the Elves were independent-minded and headstrong, the curators and protectors of the magic they had brought with them out of the age of Faerie. They were suspicious of everyone, even the Druids, but the Southlanders especially. There was too much history between them that couldn't easily be set aside. There had been too many wars with the Federation, too many betrayals, too many situations in which the Southlanders had failed to come to the aid of the Elves when it was needed. Callahorn and the Borderlands were another matter, but then they didn't see themselves as a part of the Southland or the Federation, either, and they had allied themselves with the Elves repeatedly over the years.

"I worry about Isaturin," Miriya said suddenly, lowering her voice.

Paxon looked over. "What do you mean?"

She shook her head. "I'm not sure. Something about him bothers me. He's too eager for this. He wants it too badly. It will be his legacy—and a good one, if he can manage to achieve it—and that means something to him, something more than I think is healthy for what's likely in store."

They were almost to the reception area. "He's not blind to that," Paxon said. "He'd not trade away anything that the rest of us didn't believe was wise. He'd not sacrifice our place in the Four Lands as collectors and keepers of magic." He paused. "Do you think?"

She didn't answer, for they had reached the reception area and found everyone but Isaturin present. Old Consloe, bent and worn but possessing a wealth of information about Druid history and acquisitions, sat alone in a corner, reading. Darconnen Drue, a skilled orator and debater who would carry the argument for the mission when they reached the Assembly floor, was talking with Karlin Ryl, holding forth at the center of the room. Cresson Oridian, a Southlander by birth and once a Federation official and member of the Coalition Council, stood looking out the windows at the gray skies beyond.

Adding in Isaturin and Miriya, there were six Druids under Paxon's protection. A sizable responsibility.

The Trolls that made up the Druid Guard were clustered in a tight knot by the door, talking among themselves in their harsh, guttural language, their dark, nearly featureless faces inscrutable. Netheren looked up, then away again. Paxon and Miriya slowed and paused, glancing about at those gathered.

"A fine delegation for a good morning's work, don't you think?"

Isaturin had come up behind them so quietly they hadn't heard him approach, but both nodded in response.

"Are we ready, then?" Paxon asked.

"Ready as we can be." Isaturin moved past them, headed for the door. "Time to go," he announced to the room. "The Coalition Council Assembly is on the second floor. Let's keep together, please. Remember our intentions and plans, and good luck to all of us!"

With the Trolls leading and Paxon Leah trailing, the members of the Druid delegation went through the door, speaking in lowered voices, and started down the stairs.

The delegation selected by the Coalition Council to represent the Federation was already seated and waiting when the Druids entered the Assembly. From across the room, Fero Darz looked up, noting numbers and faces, doing a quick head count and at the same time taking each delegate's and guard's measure. It was his job to do so. As commander of the newly minted Ministerial Watch, he was Paxon Leah's counterpart. In the wake of recent events—among them a series of attempts on the lives of council members and government officials—the Watch had been formed to provide personal protection for both. Most of these incidents had not amounted to much, and almost none of them ever had a realistic chance of succeeding, but a small chance was still a chance. The odds of success didn't change the fact that the attacks had happened, and those threatened were anxious to prevent them from happening again.

Darz was smart and poised, an accomplished Federation army commander with more than twenty years of service. His appointment had come at the suggestion of the Prime Minister himself, who liked to remain involved in matters of personal security. The Ministerial Watch was a hundred strong—a sizable number of soldiers for such a limited usage, but no one wanted to take chances by cutting corners. Darz had parceled out the roles for his command early, to make certain they were kept active. Idle soldiers were all too likely to grow careless. He formed a unit for protection of the Prime Minister himself, a series of units for other members of the Coalition Council

when need or prudence dictated it, a unit for investigation and inter-
rogation, one to manage paperwork and supply orders, and a handful
of others to accompany delegations on long journeys outside the
Southland borders. He'd been tinkering with the format ever since,
but overall it seemed to be working well.

His gaze shifted back across the aisle to find Paxon Leah, and he
nodded companionably. They knew each other from previous encounters while carrying out their duties, and they shared a mutual
respect that in other circumstances might have led to friendship.
Paxon was an honorable man—rare in this business of protecting
others at the risk of your own life—and Fero Darz liked to think of
himself as honorable, too, though he hadn't yet been tested as the
Highlander had. Darz was a career soldier who did what he was told
and tried to make the best of the things he didn't much care for. His
position as Commander of the Ministerial Watch gave him measurable autonomy in carrying out his duties, which was fortunate. He
liked being in control, and liked being responsible for his own life
and the lives of those under his command. If something went wrong,
at least he knew who to blame.

But Paxon? He was a horse of a different color, and something of
an enigma. He was relentless in the performance of his duties at
Paranor, the inheritor of a magic said to be so powerful that he had
twice fought the sorcerer Arcannen to a standstill. Most men would
have been dead after the first encounter; that he had survived two was
remarkable. Yet his life history and particularly his disappearance a
year or so ago into the wilds of the Westland suggested he was not
entirely satisfied with the direction his life had taken. There were rumors, of course. There were always rumors about these sorts of things.
People said he lost his nerve when the Druid he was protecting was
killed atop the Horn of Honor in Sterne. Others claimed that he lost
his sense of purpose when he failed to stop Arcannen. Or that he lost
his faith in himself and his cause. There were as many speculations as
there were men and women willing to make them.

Fero had investigated all of this because one wanted to know as
much about one's counterparts as possible. Everyone involved in service to the governing bodies of the Four Lands spent a fair amount of

time investigating everyone else, always looking for secrets to uncover, for weaknesses to exploit, for an edge in potential dealings
down the road. But there wasn't much to report about Paxon Leah. It
was said he had taken a life partner, but no one seemed to know who
she was. He had a sister, but no one had seen her in quite some
time—or at least no one who was willing to talk about it. Since there
was no history of deceit or treachery and no indication that Paxon
had ever been anything but honorable, Fero felt reasonably confident
that no bad intentions were driving the Druids during this meeting
with the Federation.

Which didn't mean he intended to leave anything to chance.

"We are all set, Commander," his second-in-command, Serge
Baliscom, said quietly, coming up beside him. "We have armed
guards at every door to secure the Assembly, and we have patrols in
the halls beyond. We have soldiers at the back of the room, as well—
just in case."

Darz glanced down to the open Assembly floor. A wide oval table
had been placed at its center with chairs provided for the Prime Minister and his associates on one side, and the Ard Rhys and his Druids
on the other. Farther back, space had been provided for soldiers of
the Ministerial Watch and the Druid Guard.

All were now in place. "Have I missed anything?" Baliscom asked.

Darz took a moment to consider. "I want no one to be let in or out
unless I approve it. If anyone leaves, they are to be accompanied by
one of our men. No exceptions. These rules apply to everyone from
this moment on."

"Yes, Commander." And Baliscom moved off, leaving Darz to his
thoughts. He watched Paxon surveying the room while the members
of the Druid delegation began the tedious process of offering formal
greetings to their counterparts, accepting glasses of cold ale from service staff that appeared with trays. He surveyed the room a final time
while the delegates exchanged small talk or studied notes, waiting for
the Prime Minister to open the negotiations.

Everything seemed to be sufficiently locked down. Everything appeared to be just as it should.

So why did he have a nagging feeling that maybe it wasn't?

4

ACROSS THE ASSEMBLY CHAMBER FROM FERO Darz, Paxon was conducting his own survey. While the members of the delegation continued their small talk prior to the beginning of negotiations, he checked out each of the guarded doors, the soldiers down on the floor along with the Druid protectors, and Fero Darz himself. The only oddity was the behavior of the latter. The Commander of the Ministerial Watch seemed uncomfortable, shifting about and frowning, casting glances this way and that. This made the Highlander nervous. He supposed this was just the way Darz behaved when he was on alert, but the extent of his agitation was troubling. Paxon's own examination of the room had not revealed anything out of place, but he was experienced enough to know you must always be prepared for the possibility that you still might miss something.

He almost left his post to confront the other man, but at that moment the Federation Prime Minister rose to begin his formal comments. He seemed much older than Paxon remembered, even though not much more than two years had passed since they'd last come into contact. But time weighed more heavily the older you got. The Prime Minister was well into his eighties, and the lines and hollows on his face gave testament to the stress and burden of responsibility he had weathered.

"Friends, countrymen, and guests from the esteemed and highly talented Fourth Order of Druids. Welcome all! It is a momentous occasion that brings us to this table, and a formidable task that we have chosen to undertake on behalf of the people of the Four Lands. This day marks the beginning of what I hope will become a new era of cooperation and understanding between us. This day, I believe, marks the first of many that will be remembered years from now as the end of enmity among all Races and Governments, and the beginning of a new brotherhood."

Well spoken, Paxon told himself. At the same time, he was thinking, *But they are only words.*

The welcoming speech continued, the Prime Minister warming to his subject and doing his very best to describe the euphoria and excitement he felt at the future he envisioned. Paxon should have been more encouraged, but mostly he felt the same lack of interest such speeches always seemed to generate. He wished he could feel differently, but experience said otherwise. Politicians were adept at making everything sound positive, but the results so often failed to live up to expectations.

He glanced several times at Fero Darz and caught glimpses of a similar reaction.

Then Paxon turned his attention to the others in the room. There were varying expressions on the faces of the delegates, most of them impossible to read. The Federation soldiers looked bored. Since the Trolls never changed expression, it was hard to tell what they were feeling. Paxon kept his place several feet behind Isaturin, but he was beginning to wish he could walk around a bit. Isaturin made his remarks quickly, then the delegates moved on to a discussion of specific issues. The Prime Minister and then the Ard Rhys would suggest a subject, and a discussion would follow. Much was said, but not much was decided. Agreements to strengthen trade routes and share information on methods of mining ore and on planting and irrigating crops came quickly enough, but that was about it. Everything else provoked heated discussion and impasse after impasse.

The morning dragged on.

It was nearing midday when an adjournment for lunch was announced, and the negotiations broke up long enough for serving staff to bring in platters of food and pitchers of ale. Paxon took the opportunity to walk across the floor and up into the raised seats of the forum to exchange greetings with Fero Darz.

"You're looking good, Paxon," the other declared, exchanging a handshake. "Does your life go well?"

Paxon nodded. "Well enough. How do things stand these days in the Ministerial Watch? A little more settled?"

"Settled and mostly quiet. I have the men and women I want serving under my command, I have a budget I can live with, and I have autonomy in my work. Mostly. I listen to the Prime Minister and the senior army officers, and ignore everyone else."

Paxon glanced around. "Don't take this the wrong way, but are we safe enough in here?"

"You ask this for a reason?" The other's smile did not reach his eyes.

"When I was looking over earlier, you seemed upset about something. Irritated? Dissatisfied? Am I wrong?"

"No, but you can't always read my mood from my face. I wasn't upset exactly. I had one of those uneasy feelings people like you and me get all too frequently in our profession, as if something was amiss. I couldn't identify what it was or even if it was real, but it was there. That's what you saw. I don't like mysteries."

"Nor I. Like you, I looked everything over, but I didn't see anything troubling. You've got the room locked down and well guarded. Everything looks good. This is all rather boring, actually."

Darz grunted. "Might be all the talk, talk, and more talk. Worst profession in the world, being a politician. Too much of what you rely on is your own hot air. It makes it harder for you and me to keep our eyes open like we need to." He glanced around. "I have to get back to work, but I'm glad to see you looking so well. Now go on back to your side of the aisle. We don't want our employers thinking we're too friendly."

Paxon grinned, they shook again, and the Highlander walked back down to the Assembly floor and over to the food trays. He was about to take meat and bread for a sandwich when he glanced back at Darz and saw him climbing the Assembly aisle steps toward the doors directly behind him, the urgency in his movements unmistakable.

At the top of the steps, the doors stood unguarded.

It was right after Paxon Leah had departed that Fero Darz realized what was bothering him. When assignments for security were handed out prior to this gathering, he had hand-chosen all of the personnel. He wanted to be certain of the people he had working with him while the negotiations were ongoing. He wanted to be able to trust everyone who would be representing the Federation during the days ahead. The people he had selected were well known to him, and most had been tested on other occasions and proven reliable. As a matter of course, at the beginning of the morning while everyone was getting settled, he had scanned the faces of his guards to be certain they were all in place. At the time, everything had seemed fine. But still something had felt vaguely wrong. It was a subconscious recognition, the sort where you see it without at first realizing, the lingering sense of things not being quite right.

Now he knew why.

One of his guards was missing, and the doors right behind him were not secured. There was no one guarding them at all.

He started up the aisle at once, calling to Baliscom. They were within a dozen steps of the top when a long wail rose out of nowhere, a deeply chilling sound.

Heads turned, searching for its source.

Then a dark shadow appeared—something that was not much more than an amorphous blob suspended against the ceiling thirty feet up, swirling like smoke stirred by intense heat. There were shouts and cries from those watching. Everyone took a step back but otherwise remained frozen in place, waiting to see what was happening.

From across the room, Paxon Leah shouted, "Get them out! Get everyone out!"

It took Darz a moment to realize the Highlander was shouting at him.

But by then it was too late.

While most were still watching the shadow expand and contract like a living, breathing organism, the doors behind Darz and Baliscom flew all the way open and a creature out of everyone's darkest, most terrible nightmare entered. It resembled in parts a cat and a wolf, and yet was neither. It was entirely black, its lithe, sinuous body sleek and elongated, as if it had been stretched out of shape. There was an opaqueness to it that did not reflect but absorbed the light, suggesting more emptiness than presence in the space it occupied. Its muscles flexed, ready to propel it forward. It crouched, eyeing the creatures in front of it with yellow orbs so bright they seemed to glow. It sniffed the air and made a keening sound—deep and mournful, matching the one that had come from the shadow on the ceiling seconds before.

Down on all fours it went, swinging its flat head from side to side, a hypnotic movement that held everyone frozen in place.

Everyone except for Darz. Delay now would be fatal. "Guards!" he screamed. "Weapons up! Fire!"

Flash rip charges exploded across the room and slammed into the intruder. It shuddered and seemed to shrink into itself in response. Darz waited for it to go down, but the creature just shook itself and lunged, coming down the aisle directly toward Darz and Baliscom. The latter had his flash rip out of his holster and was firing wildly, but he only managed three shots before the creature was on top of him, tearing and ripping with teeth and claws. Baliscom died screaming, unable to save himself. Darz was already backing away, yelling to his men, repeating Paxon's warning—knowing it was too late for his second-in-command, but maybe not for the delegates, his primary responsibility. Even though it was probably pointless, he drew his own weapon to try to get a shot at the creature's head.

But the creature was too quick for him.

It dropped Baliscom's lifeless body and was down the stairs and into the knot of delegates clustered behind the oval table in one shadowy flash of movement. Federation soldiers and Trolls from the Druid Guard were attempting to herd the delegates from the room, but most were frozen with fear.

Darz saw Paxon's sword gleam brightly, the fire of the Druid magic forming green snakes along the length of the blade. If Federation science couldn't stop it, maybe . . .

But Paxon could not seem to get himself into a position to do anything. He was blocked by the milling delegates and guards, and even shouting at them and trying to shove them aside wasn't getting him any closer. The shadow that had been clinging to the ceiling had begun to spread, engulfing the entire chamber. The screams and cries of those trapped within rose to a new level, and a surge of bodies flooded toward the exits.

Then the creature leapt, and the killing began.

Paxon was trying to fight his way through the fleeing delegates. He shouted at them to let him through, brandishing his sword to emphasize the urgency, but they paid no attention. He didn't blame them. Like himself, they didn't know what they were up against. But one thing he did know—flash rips didn't affect this creature. He had to hope Druid magic would kill it, because otherwise they were all doomed.

Miriya and Isaturin must have been thinking the same thing. Instead of fleeing with the others, they had turned back and positioned themselves between the creature and those fleeing it. The thing was still busy tearing apart the guards who had tried to stop it and so for a moment paid no attention to the Druids. It had already caught three of the Federation delegates, including the Prime Minister, and savaged them so badly there was nothing left but body parts. The Prime Minister's head lay off the one side, eyes open and staring. Of the others, even less remained.

But there was no time to dwell on that as the creature turned on the Druids. Both Isaturin and Miriya had conjured separate forms of magic to ward off or disable it. Both were trained in defensive magic; both were skilled and capable wielders of elemental power.

Yet neither stood a chance. The black thing went through them as if they weren't even there, ripping apart their magic-induced shields with such ease that Paxon felt his heart stop. Then the creature brushed them aside, barely slowing as it did so. It had no interest in them, Paxon realized. It was after the three Federation delegates who had escaped it.

Now it was his turn to hold it off. He had finally gotten through those charging up the aisle and he barred its way, heart hammering, the power of the Sword of Leah thrumming in his arms and body. As the creature launched itself, he swung the blade with such force that, had it connected, he would have cut the creature in half. Green light flared and the snakes raced up and down the metal edge like sunlight on moving water.

But his blow missed entirely.

The creature went past him so swiftly that he found nothing but air. One black arm caught him a glancing blow, the force of it throwing him backward into the Assembly seats.

Then it was on top of the delegates, hauling them in like fish in a net. One, two, a third, they seemed to explode with the fury of the attack, limbs separating from bodies, blood flying everywhere in red showers. The hapless men and women died almost before they knew what was happening. A few screams, a single cry for mercy, and then they were gone.

Abruptly, the creature was standing alone in the midst of the Druids and a handful of Troll guards. The entire Southland delegation and most of its protectors had been destroyed. Not one of the former remained alive, and besides Fero Darz only two of the latter. Those three stood on the far side of the Assembly floor, staring in horror at what had happened, no longer sure what they should do. Paxon, Miriya, and Isaturin were all pulling themselves back to their feet, trying to recover sufficiently to help their fellows.

The Druids and Trolls of Paranor stood scattered about the aisle steps, only scant yards away from a monster they had no chance against.

Only Karlin Ryl seemed able to act. She moved a few steps closer to confront the beast, standing before it like a slender reed in a strong wind and speaking softly to it, lips moving and hands weaving— a kind of soothing action that might have calmed an animal of rational thought. But was this thing even capable of thinking rationally? Paxon feared for Karlin as he watched her trying to communicate, and he heard Isaturin cry out in warning.

"No, Karlin!" It came out as a howl, long and sharp and unmistakable. "That's a Sleath!"

But if Karlin heard or understood, she did not react. She continued her efforts, and indeed the black thing seemed to be listening to her with an almost hypnotic intensity, its posture becoming less threatening. For just a moment, Paxon thought maybe she'd be able to do what the rest of them could not.

Then the moment was gone. The creature threw back its head and wailed. The sound was terrifying as it rose to a feverish pitch. The shadow that had preceded its appearance and turned the room from day to night dissipated completely, and the chamber air cleared. Paxon struggled up and started forward, intent on reaching Karlin before the creature could turn on her.

Yet in the next instant, the creature began to break apart into tiny fragments, like ash flying up from a fire. These whirled wildly before descending in a rush on Karlin, engulfing her momentarily and then passing through her and disappearing entirely.

A stunned silence followed. For a few endless seconds, no one said anything. Eyes scanned the room, wanting to make certain it was gone. Hearts and breathing steadied and slowed. Memories engaged, as everyone called to mind that all those lying dead about them had been alive only minutes ago. Shock said this wasn't possible, but experience assured them it was.

"Paxon!" Fero Darz called from across the room. "I want everyone to remain where they are until I've called in new guards and had a chance to examine the room thoroughly!"

Isaturin spoke instead. "I see no reason for us to remain in this room, or even in this city. That was a Sleath, Commander! A thing of magic. A terrible, dangerous conjuring that only a handful could have managed. I intend to take what measures I must to protect my people. We will speak of this another time!"

"Ard Rhys!" Darz shouted, his voice raised in anger now. "Did you take note of what happened to that thing? Did you witness exactly where it went after it broke apart?"

Paxon knew where this was going. The black creature had passed through Karlin Ryl before disappearing. And wasn't it strange that the creature had killed only the Federation delegates? Wasn't it odd that it had left the Druids unscathed? There was no mistaking it. Whatever had actually happened, that was the appearance. And Isaturin might well be right about the nature of the beast. Arcannen Rai sprang to mind as one of the few who could conjure it, but strong magic was not solely the province of the sorcerer. The Ard Rhys and a few other Druids had such magic at their command, as well.

Isaturin seemed to realize the problem, too, but his mind was made up, perhaps in no small part because of the obvious danger in waiting around for others to decide his fate.

"We will return to our home, Commander. When all this is sorted out and you have need of us again, we will meet. We have our resources, too, and we will do our best to find out who is responsible for what was done here. But it was not our doing, nor was it in any way carried out with our knowledge or approval."

Only Fero Darz was no longer listening. He had leveled his flash rip at the Ard Rhys and called for his surviving soldiers to do the same. Weapons pointed, they squared off against the Druids, holding them at bay.

"Fero, please don't do this!" Paxon begged him.

But the Commander of the Ministerial Watch had witnessed the death of the entire Federation delegation and two dozen of his own soldiers and been powerless to stop it. He was not likely to cede power of that sort again without trying to dredge some small measure of redemption from his self-perceived failures. Not when those most likely responsible for what had happened were standing right in front of him.

What Fero didn't understand was that he had no real power to cede when it came to detaining the Druids, and it took only seconds for Miriya to whisper the words and make the subtle gestures that caused the flash rips to turn so hot, all three men dropped them instantly.

"We're going now," she said quietly, giving Fero Darz a meaningful nod. "Please don't try to stop us."

The Commander of the Ministerial Watch attempted a shout for help, but a second gesture from Miriya left him sprawled unconscious on the floor with his companions for company.

"We will have to move quickly," Isaturin advised. "We won't have much of a head start, and few will be willing to help us. Paxon, take the lead. Get us out of this city!"

When Fero Darz came awake again, the Druids and their protectors were gone, Paxon among them. He rose slowly, foggy-headed and lethargic, but burning with anger. He knew what he had seen. That black thing might have appeared from nowhere but it had gone straight into and then through the young female Druid before disappearing. And though all the members of the Southland delegation lay dead, no Druid had been touched. The evidence seemed conclusive that the Druid order was somehow involved. Darz could not provide a motive for what had happened. Why would the Druids agree to come to Arishaig solely for the purpose of killing members of the Coalition Council? But that was what had happened, and the reason for it could be determined once the offenders were in custody and could be questioned.

He pulled himself to his feet and, with only a glance at the two still-unconscious members of his command, started for the doors to the Assembly. Isaturin had seemed confident they could escape Arishaig with ease, but Paxon was smarter than that. He knew how pursuit could cut off almost any escape if one knew what one was doing—and Fero Darz did.

The Druids might have gotten away momentarily, but he would have them in the end.

5

THE DRUID DELEGATION ESCAPED THE BUILDING
without trouble. No one tried to stop them. No one even
spoke to them.

They even escaped the compound, although by the time they were
clear and making their way through the streets of Arishaig, alarms
were beginning to sound. They came in the form of shouts and cries
accompanied by the deep ringing of a gong that was clearly meant to
be a call to action. Paxon was not sure what it was intended to accomplish, but if nothing else it generated a fresh sense of urgency.

He was leading the way at this point, and it appeared that the effort
to get free of the walls of the city had fallen entirely on his shoulders.
Neither Isaturin nor any of the others was making any attempt to offer
advice on routes of escape, so it was clear that the responsibility was his.

It was not going to be easy. They were perhaps a quarter mile
from the gates and hemmed in on all sides by hordes of people
crowding the streets, most of them now pausing at the sound of the
shouts and the gong, trying to determine what was happening. At
the very least, patrols would already be hunting for them. If they
evaded those, they would still have to find a way through the gates,
which would be either closed down entirely or carefully monitored.
It would be bad enough to try to get through that obstacle alone. But

with nearly a dozen Druids and Troll guards in tow, it seemed almost impossible.

Paxon began to panic as the enormity of what was at stake seized him. But then he steadied himself. His training was too thoroughly ingrained to be abandoned at the first sign of trouble. He knew the drill. One problem at a time. One step at a time. Don't try to do too much or think too far ahead. Stay in the moment.

The first thing they had to do was to get rid of the Druid cloaks and guard uniforms, which were immediately recognizable. In ordinary clothes, they would draw less attention and could move more freely.

Right, he thought. *Seven men and women, and four Trolls. Who would notice that?*

He began scanning the streets, searching for a clothing shop where they could find what they needed. At the same time, he kept watch for Federation soldiers. He glanced once or twice at Isaturin, but the Ard Rhys seemed lost in thought and didn't look back.

He found a shop quickly enough. A sign in the window said it was closed, but one of the Trolls broke the lock and opened the door just by leaning against it heavily. A few heads turned, a few passersby paused, but no one said anything or stopped. It was like that in cities everywhere, Paxon thought. Everyone minded their own business. No one wanted trouble.

In seconds they were inside with the door closed behind them.

"Cloaks and broad-brimmed hats," Paxon told his charges. "Anything that will hide who you are. We don't have time for a full change of clothing. Just cover your Druid garments. Leave your cloaks behind."

Isaturin and the others did not argue. They found what they needed and were out the door again in minutes, looking like ordinary citizens now. Even the Trolls, with their size and bark-like skin, could pass. With their bodies covered and their faces shadowed by the hats, only their size suggested their true nature.

They were walking again, with Paxon setting a quicker pace. They could not sustain this for long, however. Already, old Consloe was beginning to show signs of tiring. He was too old and physically weak to be able to keep up with the rest of them, but there was no other choice. They couldn't afford to slow down, and trying to hide from Fero Darz in Arishaig was suicide.

Paxon pondered Darz's certainty that the Druids had been involved in the killings, and again found himself unable to dispute the conclusions the other had drawn. He wished it were someone else hunting them—not just because he admired Darz and thought of him as a friend, but because Darz was very good at his job. He had a gift for anticipation, and he would surely put that gift to use here. So Paxon was going to have to do something drastic to throw Darz off their trail.

"Aren't we going in the wrong direction?" Isaturin asked finally. "It seems we're heading toward the east gates. Shouldn't we be going north?"

Paxon shook his head. "Darz will expect us to take the shortest path out of the city. Most of his efforts will be concentrated on the north gates."

"He's trying to out-think our esteemed Ministerial Watch Commander," Miriya offered. "This is a chess game, High Lord."

Which it was indeed, and Paxon was not at all sure he was the better player. "There's also a private airfield near the east gates," he added, glancing back again at a faltering Consloe. "Nach! Help our friend," he ordered, motioning to one of the Trolls.

It wasn't his place to order them about, but considerations of that sort had no place in their present circumstances.

"How do we get through the gates?" Miriya asked.

"Maybe we won't have to. Maybe we can fly over them." Paxon shrugged. "All we need is a ship."

The vessel they had arrived in was housed inside the Council Headquarters, and thus effectively lost to them.

"Or several ships," Miriya added, "if they're small, to carry us all."

Paxon nodded. "But I prefer large. One that comes with flash rips and rail slings."

"And speed," she added. "Lots of speed."

The wind had picked up, blowing grit and debris in sharp blasts. The group walked with heads down and collars up. It helped that everyone they encountered was doing the same. Eyes were averted for protection, and no one was paying much attention to their little band.

In the cross street directly ahead, a squad of foot soldiers appeared, calling out to be let through, shouldering aside all who stood in their way. There were a dozen, maybe more. On their way to the east gates, Paxon presumed. He wished they had been a little slower coming. He wished now they had tied up Darz and his companions.

"Look!" Miriya breathed.

Overhead, a formation of Ghost Flares and transports appeared, flying toward the east wall. A sizable command—more than Paxon cared to go up against, even with Druid magic and his sword to aid him. He felt a fresh twinge of doubt about their chances of escape. Their options were too few and their enemies too strong.

"First Response," Paxon whispered to himself. Now there was fresh cause to be concerned. The Federation unit responsible for the safety of the city had been dispatched to deal with them.

He slowed. Darz would block all the gates and seal them off. As furious as he was certain to be after his failure to prevent the Druids from leaving the Coalition Council compound, he wouldn't think twice about inconveniencing travelers for as long as it took to correct that mistake. The chances of getting through the gates or even managing to commandeer an airship from one of the private airfields had dropped to almost zero.

He held up his hand and directed the others into an overhang fronting a leatherwork kiosk, out of the dust-filled wind.

"We have to change our plans," he told them. "We have to go back."

"Back?" Isaturin echoed. "Back to where? Are you serious, Paxon?"

"Indeed," Miriya agreed. "What brought this on?"

A few others voiced similar comments. All of them were distressed at the prospect of returning.

"Just listen a moment," Paxon said, quieting them. "Those were First Response airships heading for the east gates. More will have been dispatched to the other gates. Those soldiers have a lot of experience with enemies trying to get into or out of the city, and that's how we will be seen. As enemies. Fero Darz will try to find a way to shut down every exit he thinks we might attempt to use, so we have to do something he isn't expecting. I have an idea. It's dangerous, but it has a much better chance of succeeding than what we're doing now."

Briefly, he explained his thinking. No one would expect them to double back. It might throw off their pursuit long enough for them to reach the First Response barracks. First Response was highly trained and very capable, but it was also small. Most of its soldiers would have been sent to the gates. Only a handful would have been held back as reserves. The barracks would be mostly empty.

"And that's where they keep their airships," he finished.

"You think we can steal one?" Miriya asked.

"It's our best chance."

"What if they've taken them all?" Darconnen said, quiet until now. "Then we really will be trapped."

Paxon shook his head. "They always keep airships in reserve. They wouldn't risk losing them all."

"All right," Isaturin said. "If Paxon thinks this is our best chance, then this is what we'll do." He turned to the Highlander. "Lead us, Paxon. But let's hurry."

They made their way back through the city toward its center. First Response had been relocated to a more central position since its destruction in the demon assault more than a century ago. Paxon had visited the camp once or twice, anxious to learn more of its history and meet some of its leaders. He knew a few of them. Some were friends. He hoped he wouldn't encounter them now.

The return trip was much slower than the Highlander would have liked. The wind had increased, and it had become necessary for them to shield their eyes. And the sweep by the Federation soldiers was pushing everyone in the streets away from the city center. The Druids had to struggle against the crowds trying to get clear. Everyone around them seemed vaguely panicked, even without knowing exactly why. No one, after all, had told them what was going on. In situations like these, no one ever did. The search for the Druids was thorough and relentless, but the ignorance of the citizenry was not helping. Also, there were a lot of streets and buildings to be searched. That would require time and men, and the prevailing opinion would be that the Druids were already on their way out of the city. Those hunting them would not expend their efforts looking for them the way they had come.

At least, that's what Paxon hoped.

He kept everyone moving, but there was no need to try to rush. With the crowds pressing up against them and the wind blowing sharply, it was best to stay close to the walls and use back streets and alleyways when possible. Shouts and cries rose ahead of them. The search was advancing in their direction. The Highlander took his charges down a narrow passageway into a confluence of alleys and streets converging on a mostly empty square. They crossed to one of the narrower alleys and turned into it. The sounds faded a bit behind them, but Paxon could feel the sweat building inside his clothing.

He chose another couple of side streets and passageways. This area of the city was familiar to him from previous visits, and everyone was keeping pace, even old Consloe. A few minutes later they emerged at the top of a broad set of steps leading down toward the compound they had just escaped.

"Over there." Paxon pointed.

To their left sat the barracks of First Response. As Paxon had surmised, there were only a few soldiers visible. The gates leading in stood open, and the garrison was mostly emptied out. Motioning to get the attention of the others, he pointed again.

Atop an elevated platform connected to the buildings of the compound sat two fast cruisers and a handful of flits. Either of the larger airships was capable of carrying up to a dozen passengers and crew.

Paxon looked around. Standing where they were, they were mostly hidden from the soldiers below. But once they started down the platform steps, they would be seen immediately. Better if only a couple of them went down initially. When it was safer to do so, the others could follow.

He turned to Isaturin. "Miriya and I will clear a path. As soon as the guards at the gate are disabled, the rest of you come down. Don't hesitate. We have to get into one of those cruisers and off the ground before anyone sounds the alarm. We have to be quick."

The Ard Rhys nodded. "But let's be careful, as well."

Below, the grounds were empty of everyone but the guards at the First Response gates and a solitary soldier hauling material off a cart and into a storage building. Outside the barracks' walls, there was no one at all; the streets were empty. With Miriya next to him, Paxon descended the steps.

He began talking conversationally. "Just pretend we're old friends. Don't pay any attention to the guards. Just look at me and talk about anything."

"I know what to do," she said.

They took their time, doing what Paxon had suggested, ignoring the soldiers while they talked to each other, acting as if nothing much was happening, hoping they would look like they belonged.

They reached the bottom of the steps and were almost to the opening of the compound when one of the guards ordered them to stop and asked for identification.

"Now?" Miriya asked him softly.

Paxon shook his head. "Wait."

The speaker left his post and came toward them, leaving the second soldier standing at the gates, ready to summon help if it was needed.

"I'll disable this one, you disable the other," Paxon whispered.

Miriya said nothing. She didn't even nod. She looked away as if bored.

Paxon waited until the guard was right on top of them, aware of the flash rip pointed at his midsection. His sword was sheathed. Bringing it out now would give them away. So he stood there, gesturing toward his pocket, aware that he was completely defenseless if the guard used the flash rip on him.

"Who are you?" the man asked. "You don't belong here—either of you. What's your business?"

"Supply inventory," Paxon answered. "Can I show you my orders? They're in my pocket."

"Careful now," the other warned. "Do it slowly."

Miriya had taken a few casual steps away from Paxon while the guard was approaching, giving her some additional space and a better viewpoint of the guard at the gates.

"Who are those men atop the wall?" she said suddenly, the alarm in her voice apparent.

The guard looked at once, unable to help himself, and Paxon stepped forward and dropped him with a blow to the temple. By then Miriya had used gestures and words to summon her magic and disable the remaining guard. The way into the compound stood open.

Then everything went wrong at once.

As Paxon had instructed, the remaining Druids and Trolls came hurrying down the steps, but they failed to slow on reaching the flats. Instead, they simply changed direction as if of a single mind, and before the Highlander could prevent it they swept right through the open gates. Perhaps they thought that was what he intended. Perhaps they thought it was the safest choice.

They were wrong.

"No!" he shouted after them. "Stop!"

He heard the yells and cries start up even before they finished clearing the gates, saw the deadly flashes of Druid magic and Federation weapons, smelled burning flesh. He felt his insides tighten as he realized there must have been more soldiers inside the compound than he anticipated, and the sudden appearance of the Druids and Trolls, even without their black-and-silver uniforms, had triggered a deadly response.

Miriya was screaming at him. "Get in there! Help them!"

He charged ahead, pulling his sword from its sheath, ready to repel whatever attack was launched against him. Still, the first explosion caught him by surprise and, even with the sword's protection, knocked him off his feet. Miriya, who was right behind him, responded at once to the attack, launching a counterstrike at the soldier with the big shoulder-mounted flash rip, destroying his weapon and sending him sprawling.

Some of the others in their group were fighting back, as well. Isaturin, Oridian, and even old Consloe, hiding behind stacks of supplies and materials, were tossing off shards of magic designed to disable or numb. The Trolls were using crossbows, but they lacked anything more efficient without engaging in close contact. Two of them were injured. Darconnen Drue was down, too, his entire upper torso and head burned black.

A handful of Federation soldiers had taken up position against the barracks wall behind an overturned wagon, blocking the way inside the building and to the stairs leading up to the landing platform. They were armed with flash rips and stun rifles, effective from any distance you could see a target. Both sides were dug in. For the moment, the battle was a standoff.

It wouldn't stay that way for long, however. Time was running out, and Federation reinforcements would arrive soon. Paxon took a deep breath, leapt to his feet, and sprinted toward the Federation position, crouched forward, his sword held out like a shield, deflecting the stun bolts and flash rip fire that was directed toward him. Miriya followed him in from one side, her Druid magic a white-hot oval spitting flaming darts.

To their credit, the Federation soldiers held their ground a lot longer than Paxon would have. But when it became evident that their weapons were useless, they broke cover and ran for the safety of the building. Isaturin, however, had anticipated that. When they attempted to get inside, they found an invisible shield blocking their way.

Seconds later they were on the ground with their arms and legs spread wide and their weapons discarded. Paxon used their belts to bind their hands, hauled them to a storage room, and locked them up. In his absence, Miriya and Karlin determined what he already knew. Darconnen was dead. Isaturin insisted he be carried up the stairs and taken with them in the cruiser. Paxon didn't bother to argue.

In a knot, Druids ringed by Trolls climbed to the landing platform and boarded the nearest cruiser. Unhooding its parse tubes and powering up its diapson crystals, Paxon, the most accomplished pilot among them, took the controls. Within minutes, they were lifting off and flying northeast toward the city wall. There was no point in any attempt at further deception. Once the Federation knew they had stolen an airship and were flying it out of the city, they would give chase.

As their cruiser passed over the outer wall and headed for the safety of home, Paxon knew there was only one question that mattered now.

How long would it be before they were discovered?

He was afraid he already knew the answer.

6

FTER REGAINING CONSCIOUSNESS AND FINDING
Chrysallin gone, Leofur made a quick sweep of the area,
searching for some sign of what had happened, but she
found nothing. Growing increasingly desperate, she widened her
search, choosing openings in the heavy forest through which someone
might logically choose to pass. She looked for anything that seemed
out of place or suggested a disturbance. Again, she found nothing.

It didn't help that she lacked even the most basic tracking skills.
She was a city girl and had little experience with remote wilderness.
She had never been trained to search for sign or note the ways in
which native vegetation might have been disturbed. She flew airships
and engaged in trading and salvage recovery, and she saw most of the
world from above.

At last, she gave up. Time was slipping away, and she did not believe she was going to find anything useful no matter how long she
stayed there or how hard she searched. She had no idea who had
taken her friend. Unless, of course, it was her father. Arcannen would
certainly like to get his hands on Chrysallin, if only to use her against
Paxon. He had tried this twice before, and both times Chrys had escaped him. But that wouldn't necessarily stop him from trying again.
Before, Arcannen had planned to turn Chrys into a weapon to be

used against the Ard Rhys, and for that he had engaged the services of the witch Mischa. Since Mischa was dead, he would not be able to go down that road again. So what else could he have in mind?

Leofur returned swiftly to Paranor, entering the Druid's Keep at a run. She had been thinking all the way back about whom she should turn to for help. It would have been Paxon or Isaturin had either been there, but they were both in Arishaig. She considered Arnoxl, her instructor, and Zabb Ruh, who was Chrysallin's friend, but then decided against both. What she required was a tracker with the skills necessary to help her find Chrys.

She decided to go to Oost Mondara.

There were good reasons for this choice. Mondara had been Paxon's weapons instructor and mentor during his early days at Paranor, and they had remained friends. While Mondara would never say it to his face, he had told Leofur in confidence, more than once, that the Highlander was the best student he'd ever had. He was close to Paxon and Chrys both, and would want to help.

He was not, unfortunately, a tracker, but he had been at Paranor for many years, and Leofur was pretty sure that if anyone knew who possessed those skills, Oost did.

If he didn't, she was in serious trouble.

Once through the gates of both the inner and outer walls, she raced straight to the practice field to find him. When she discovered the field deserted, she continued into the armory and found him there, busy crafting new weapons.

He looked up at once as she entered and saw the distress and urgency reflected on her face. He got up from the bench on which he had been sitting, set down his work, and went to her.

"What's wrong, girl?"

She refused to let herself look away; the blame for what had happened was hers and she would not shrink from it. "I lost Chrysallin while we were on a walk outside the Keep. Someone knocked me out and took her. It happened so fast I didn't have time to stop it."

"She's gone? Are you sure?"

"I'm sure. I sensed someone following us, watching from the trees as we were headed back. I heard a swishing sound, then something hit me on the head. I lost consciousness. When I woke and looked for Chrysallin, I couldn't find her."

She exhaled sharply. "I didn't know who else to come to with Paxon and Isaturin both gone. I need a tracker who can read sign and make the educated guesses that I can't. I don't have the skills. I hoped you would know of someone who does."

Oost studied her a moment. "You think it might have been your father again? He seems to have his mind set on Paxon's sister."

"I don't know. That was my first thought, but I have to find her before I can be sure. This is the worst possible thing that could have happened! Paxon left her in my care, and I failed him. I have to get her back! Please, can you help me?"

"I don't know," he said quietly. "Shades. You are certain of this? You couldn't have just . . ."

"Couldn't have just what? Imagined it? Made it up? I need your help, Oost! Don't treat me like this."

"I'm sorry. But the help I might give you, the sort of thing this might require . . ." He shook his head. "I have to think about this."

"There isn't time for that!" she snapped angrily, frustrated by the thought of further delay. "What if Arcannen has taken Chrysallin?"

He sighed deeply. "All right. There is a man. *If* he would agree . . ."

"Why wouldn't he agree?" She was panicked now, her desperation beginning to win out over her determination to stay calm. "I will persuade him, if that's what it takes."

"No, it isn't that. The problem is that he isn't like other men. He isn't like . . . anyone."

She seized his shoulders and dug her fingers in. "I don't care what he is, or who he isn't like. Can he track? Can he read sign?"

"Better than anyone alive."

"Then take me to him. Please."

He studied her for long moments before nodding. "All right, but don't get your hopes up. Wait until you meet him. Listen to what he has to say." He broke away from her, then walked over to retrieve his Druid cloak and threw it over his shoulders. "Come with me."

Without waiting for her response, he went out the door of the armory. She caught up to him halfway across the practice field. The day had turned gray in the last hour, clouds moving in, the weather shifting to something darker and less promising. If it rained, they might lose any chance they had of tracking Chrysallin. Her sense of urgency quickened.

"I have to find her, Oost," she said, matching his pace. "I have to bring her back. It would destroy Paxon if he lost her now."

Oost hesitated before saying anything. "This man I'm taking you to see? He's dangerous." His response trailed off, as if he didn't quite know where to take it. "Unpredictable."

"But you said he's a tracker?"

"He's all of that, but his methods are unusual. *He's* unusual. As I said, he may not agree to do this. All I can promise is that he might agree to listen, so maybe . . ."

Again, he trailed off. She gave him a moment. "Why wouldn't he agree, if he's friends with you? Isn't that enough?"

"No. Besides, I didn't say we were friends. Only that I know him well enough to speak with him about this. Convincing him is more complicated than you know. There are demands you will be making of him that you don't yet realize. And not just of him. This will require something from you, as well. It will be a shared experience, if he agrees. You both will have to commit to what's needed, and that's not a thing to be taken lightly."

She had no idea what he was talking about, but she let it alone. He would tell her when he was ready.

They passed from the practice field through a series of courtyards that connected the buildings of the Keep and the inner wall. Parts of the wall also completed various towers that were integral to Paranor's structure. Paranor was a complex place, when you considered its makeup. It was constructed in ways not immediately apparent on the surface. It reminded her of the Druids themselves. Nothing was entirely as it seemed.

"I'll do whatever is needed," she said quietly.

"Will you?" Oost Mondara glanced over. "Don't be too hasty until you've heard more. In any case, whatever happens depends first and foremost on him."

"Who is he? What's his name?"

"His name is Imric Cort. Today, anyway. Tomorrow . . . maybe something else."

He left it at that—an enigmatic response that begged an explanation. But he was not ready to give it, and Leofur knew better than to insist. They continued on in silence, working their way through the courtyards to the north end of the Keep and then through the gates of the inner wall toward the stables and animal pens.

They were close enough to smell feed, straw, and manure when he pulled up short and turned to face her. "If you have second thoughts, now is the time to express them."

She stared at him in frustration. "I don't know enough to have second thoughts! Tell me something about this man. Let me in on a few of the secrets you are keeping."

The shrewd eyes studied her carefully. "All right. Imric Cort was a tracker once. As I said, he is maybe the best in the world. He could find a trail where no one else could even tell there was one. His instincts were those of an animal, a predator seeking prey. His senses were that much sharper than our own. But he had problems he could not overcome. Could not live with, in fact. He suffers from a rare condition, and he came to Paranor so the Druids could help him. Accepting our help meant he had to give up his life as a tracker and turn to something else. Now he cares for the animals."

"What rare condition?" she asked.

"One he can never entirely overcome, only manage. He is a shape-shifter."

Leofur frowned. "I thought they all died out. I thought they didn't exist anymore."

"They don't—save perhaps for Imric."

"What sort of help was he seeking?"

"He wanted to end his shape-shifter life and be a man. He wanted to unburden himself of what the shifting was doing to him. If you can be anything—as a shape-shifter can—you have no self, no permanent identity. You are the thing you become each time you change. This affects not just your physical being, but your personality, as well. The toll it was taking on him was destroying him. He was losing himself, fragmenting, becoming nothing."

She shook her head. "Can that really happen? I would think the ability to become anything you want would be freeing, a wonderful gift."

The Dwarf's rough features deepened with lines of sadness. "What seems to be isn't always the case—and perhaps it never is when it comes to the human condition. And he *is* human. Mostly—and more so now that we have worked with him. But going back to his life as a tracker risks all that, mostly because of the unusual way he goes about it. He has every reason to tell us no."

"Then perhaps we shouldn't ask him." Leofur brushed back strands of her honey-colored hair from her face. "If it's that dangerous for him, we should look somewhere else."

Oost sighed. "We are not an order to which trackers are normally drawn. There is no one else here who can do what is needed. To find someone else, we would have to travel to Varfleet or Tyrsis. Maybe even farther. But we don't have time for that. You were right about one thing. We can't let Paxon return to find his sister missing. So it would be negligent of us not to at least ask the closest source."

"Yet you seem doubtful about persuading this man."

"I am. Very. But it will be his choice to make. And one thing more, Leofur. He will want you to go with him, which I know you will agree to. But it is for reasons that are not immediately obvious. He will require something of you. Something personal. You may find it offensive, or perhaps impossible to agree to. You must make your own choice in this matter. I will leave it to him to explain if he agrees to help. You should decide this matter together. You will understand why once he's told you what's required. Come."

They continued on to the stables and pens, the Dwarf leading Leofur into the largest of the storage barns, where the grains, corn, and straw were stored in bales and bins. The structure was huge, its contents imported by airship from the countryside farms that flourished on the far-west side of the Dragon's Teeth bordering the grass-lands of the Streleheim.

Leofur looked around as they entered, intrigued by the size and complexity of the building. A network of huge crossbeams supported a second-story roof some forty feet up. She could see pieces of it through openings in the flooring of the second story that served to facilitate moving stores and supplies. Ropes with hooks hung down through the gaps, fastened in place at various points and attached to winches and long booms whose range could span the whole of the interior when loading or unloading was required.

Off to one side, the horses were stabled—big strong beasts that the Druids used to pull carriages and carts and sometimes to ride. In pens beyond, the sounds of other farm animals rose—cows, pigs, chickens, and sheep. Their pungent smells filled the air, a mingling of scents familiar to her from her youth.

Before she was brought into Dark House.

Before her childhood ended.

"Need something, Oost Mondara?" a voice said from behind her.

She turned. One of the most striking men she had ever seen was standing there—and she had seen many striking men in her day. He was tall and very lean, though stooped just a bit through his broad shoulders. A shock of black hair, wild and unkempt, became a fringe of beard that outlined the curve of his strong jaw. His hands seemed too big for the rest of him, and his eyes were a strange amber color that shone with an odd intensity.

Yet for all of that, there was a world-weariness about him that caused her to wonder what sort of life he had led, and what form of madness he had survived.

There was something more about him, too. Something that momentarily escaped her.

"Imric." Oost Mondara greeted the man solemnly. "This is Leofur Rai. She is Paxon Leah's life partner and my friend."

The man gave her a brief, dismissive nod, then turned back to Oost. "The answer is no."

"I haven't asked for anything yet," the Dwarf pointed out. "You are a little ahead of yourself, aren't you?"

"You reek of need," Imric said. "I read you the way I read sign—or did once. Your intentions are immediately obvious. If there is deception of any sort involved, leave now. Otherwise, get on with it. I have things to do."

"I'm sure you do, but time is the enemy here." The Dwarf sounded angry. "Can we sit?"

Anger, Leofur thought suddenly. *That's what's coming off this man, this Imric Cort. That's what I'm sensing.*

He took them into an empty stall with a grouping of hay bales and sat them down. "Nothing special, but you should be able to get on well enough for the short time you are here."

"You seem certain our stay will be brief," Leofur said, holding his gaze as she spoke. "Are we that much of an annoyance?"

He paused, then leaned forward on his bale. "I came here because I was ill. I knew if I were to stay on—which I wanted to, badly—I would have to find myself a job. This one is exactly right for me. I know animals. I understand them. I like being around them. And there's a reason I don't like spending time with people. Now, what do you want?"

"Better tell him, Leofur," Oost muttered. "He's already losing interest."

"I have a favor to ask of you," she declared. "A rather large one."

She proceeded to tell him what had happened while she was walking with Chrysallin, filling in the details of their background and her relationship with Paxon. She explained the nature of the danger to Chrys should the kidnapper turn out to be her father. She explained the need for haste and the problem if she failed to act quickly. He listened without comment, his gaze fixed on her in a rather unnerving way. She found herself growing hot under that gaze, made uncomfortable and irritated by both its intensity and its heat.

When she was finished, he shook his head. "No," he said.

"No?" she echoed when he left it there. "You have nothing else to say? You will not even consider it?"

Imric look irritated. "How much did Oost explain to you about me? Do you know how much it takes for me to track someone these days? Did he tell you anything of what it would require from you?"

She shook her head. "Not much. He said you would explain."

"Left it all to me, did you, Oost Mondara? How very Druidic. You bring this girl here with her expectations and just throw her at me with no warning about what might happen to her?"

"I thought it better coming from you. I thought you should tell her, and then perhaps you should talk about it together. It is a shared experience, after all."

Imric rose. "Get out of here. Both of you. You are children playing with fire—and you, Dwarf, are worse than that! You are a coward for leading her on. Get out!"

But Leofur, though rising with him, held her ground. "I won't. I can't. This is too important for me to just walk away. It is important enough, Imric, that no matter the risk involved, no matter the danger facing me, I have to see it through. So let's not mince words, and let's not pretend that your righteous anger is enough to send me packing. It isn't. I don't care what I have to give up. I don't care what it does to me. Better I die than Chrys. So just tell me. What is it that makes this business anathema? You are a tracker, aren't you? Why won't you track?"

He hesitated then, giving her a long, considering look. "Even to speak about it is painful to me. Even that."

"Your silence is painful to *me.* Your refusal to tell me anything is unbearable. Please, give me relief. Tell me at least a little of what troubles you. Let me try to understand. I would hear you out, I would give your words weight if you would speak them. Perhaps you are right. Why not find out?"

Imric Cort looked over at Oost Mondara. "I would imagine you had difficulty saying no to her, as well? She seems a very determined sort. I suppose if Arcannen Rai were my father, I would be the same."

He turned back to her. "All right. I can see this means a great deal to you, so I will tell you why you must let it go—at least so far as I am concerned. And don't blame me for the choice it leaves you with when I am done."

He sat down again on the hay bale, waited for her to do the same, then leaned forward. "Now listen well."

7

He discovers the truth about himself when he is six years old. One min-ute he is playing in his front yard the way he plays almost every day, pretending at being this or that, making up stories in his head and act-ing them out, and the next he is writhing and twisting, as if a beast contained within a skin too small, a creature desperate for a release that is impossible to achieve. It feels that perhaps he will break out of himself like a chick from its shell, cracking it apart and emerging into the world newly born. But what he finds is that it is his body itself that is changing—reassembling, re-forming—until he is no longer a boy but something vaguely wolfish. He has become the creature he was imagin-ing only a moment earlier. He has somehow brought that creature to life.

He is all alone when this happens, so he doesn't have to worry about being seen. He stands perfectly still and tries to process the reason for what has happened. Why would he be able to become something he was only pretending to be? How could he transform so suddenly and so completely?

Because this is what he has done. He is no longer a boy. No longer even human. He is another species entirely. Coarse black hair covers him everywhere. His body is strong and lithe; he experiences the primal instincts he imagined his creation would possess. His senses are so sharp he can barely register their limits. He can smell a dead mouse hundreds of yards off. He can see the hawk that dropped its carcass winging away a mile distant, scared off by the fox that is now moving in to claim the mouse. He can feel shifts in the air currents and breathe the scents they bear in their invisible hands.

Panic sets in, terror so thorough he does not think he can bear it. What will he tell his parents? How will he explain to them what has happened? How can he, when he doesn't know himself? They will not recognize him. They will drive him from his home without knowing who he is, without even trying to find out.

He starts to scream, then stops himself. In the split second before he opens his mouth, he senses his voice will not be a human's but an animal's. Words will not emerge, but growls and wolfish cries. His mother will come running. She will imagine the worst. She will be frantic and then enraged. At him.

He tests his voice in what he imagines is a bare whisper, and a low rumble emerges from his throat. He is right. He cannot go to her.

Oddly, this realization seems to calm him. He knows better in the few seconds it takes to discover his condition what he must do. He became the thing he is by pretending. He can become himself again in the same way. He must think himself back into being, re-create the boy he was five minutes ago, give new life to who and what he was. It worked before. Shouldn't it work again?

So he closes his eyes and reimagines himself.

When he opens them again, he is restored.

Physically, but not emotionally. That particular damage cannot be repaired so swiftly. Time will be needed.

He doesn't realize yet how much.

"I did not tell my mother or my father what happened that day. I did not tell them until much later and then only because it became necessary to do so. Instead, I worked at mastering this strange ability to change shapes. I quickly discovered I could be almost anything I wanted. All I had to do was imagine myself changing, and it would happen. It was a grand game for a six-year-old to play. In the beginning."

Imric Cort paused, measuring Leofur's stare. His eyes had a distant look to them, their depths reflecting memories that were tinged with regret. "But the game had rules I didn't understand. It was one thing to make myself another creature. It was something else again to learn to live with it. I didn't realize it at first, but it was stealing something from me. It was an insidious sort of theft, the kind where you don't even know it is happening until it becomes something so terrifying you think you have willingly embraced a special kind of slavery."

"You began to like it too much?" she guessed.

"You are quick, girl. But it was more than that. I didn't just like it. I loved it. I became obsessed with it. With this ability, I could make myself become anything I desired. I could go anywhere I chose just by selecting the right form. Increasingly, I began to crave the changing. I was always looking to try something else. I was still a boy, remember. I was excited and reckless with my newfound power, and I lacked the perspective to be wary of it. It wasn't enough just to change. I began to want to embed myself in adventures born out of my imagination. I began to create stories in which each new form had a principal role. I began to look for reasons to change so I could do the things I had never been able to do before.

"Eventually, I began to spy on others, taking forms they would not notice or find invasive. Animals, birds, insects. I became a part of their lives, just for the thrill of engaging in forbidden behavior, watching and listening so I could discover their secrets and learn what they were really like."

He paused. "It went well enough until I chose to spy on my parents."

It is all chance that it happens when it does; there is no planning involved when he decides to secretly observe them. He has never done this before, never even considered it. But with his growing success in adopting new forms for his clandestine intrusions, he feels emboldened enough to try. He will have to be very careful, he knows. He will have to be extremely cautious. If he is caught, he will be in terrible trouble. Yet the lure of listening in on whatever they might say in his supposed absence, the prospect of hearing something deliciously forbidden, is too strong to ignore. His parents are in many ways a mystery to him; he would like to change this.

So one night, after they have gone to bed and believe him asleep, he changes forms and becomes a wraith, as insubstantial as the air he breathes. He has only just learned how to do this. His skill has advanced, and he has become adept at changing in ways that at first would have been beyond him. He is invisible as he leaves his room and goes outside, pressing himself against the walls of their home, creeping along and leaving no sign of his passage, both hesitant and eager. He finds his way to their bedroom window, which is always open, and he crouches there. When at last he stands, knowing they cannot see him, he looks inside and watches them lying in bed, talking. He has heard them do this before, heard them through the walls that separate their bedrooms, their voices low and indistinct. They talk every night before sleep; it is their special, private time. He is certain that some of what they talk about will include him.

By now, he is comfortable with every form of invasion he can imagine. This secret observance of his parents is just his most recent experiment. It is more than a year since he discovered his ability to change, and this additional year has given him a fresh perspective on life. He understands the world of adults better. He sees more clearly the ways in which children are manipulated and controlled. He is already chafing to be free of these restraints, in large part because of the freedom he has found in changing shapes. He thinks what he will hear tonight might give him insights into how better to achieve this. He thinks it will help him avoid the rules and regulations placed upon him by his parents. He thinks it will enlighten him as to how his parents see him.

He is mistaken.

What he hears is a discussion about crops and weather and the new neighbors who have just finished building a home near them and other mundane and uninteresting bits of news. Nothing he hears is the least bit salacious or revealing, and eventually he creeps back along the side of the house to his room and to bed.

For various nights over the next month, he engages in further spying, always at night, and always in the same way. Each effort is wasted.

He learns nothing. He comes to believe he should stop. His parents do not seem the type to share confidences. Their talk is typical adult talk and holds no interest for him.

Until, one night, that changes. He is prepared for another failure, another conversation that will disappoint him. But this night is different. This night the conversation is most especially about him. It does not begin that way; there is small talk at first, none of it interesting, and he thinks again that perhaps he has been mistaken about the delicious secrets he will learn.

Then his father says suddenly, "I sense something is different about Imric of late."

His mother looks stricken. "I told you there was nothing. I have watched him closely and have seen no signs that would indicate otherwise."

"We had an agreement."

"Why speak of it? There is no reason to think we need to be concerned."

"He is gone all the time. He plays away from the house. He is secretive and restless."

"He is a boy, growing up, learning about life, experimenting with his world. Of course he is like that. All boys are."

His father shakes his head. "I think it is something more. I need to test him. If the blood is in him, you know what must happen."

"Stop it!" she snaps. "Don't speak like that. He is our child!"

"He is your child, but perhaps not mine."

There is cold fury reflected on his mother's face. "Don't try to make this something it isn't. I told you, I would know. I would tell you if it was there."

"I will still test him. If I find your shifter blood in him, I will do what I promised I would. We can make another child. Or accept that we are meant to have none."

His mother gives his father a dark and dangerous look. "Beware, Jonat. Do not travel too far down this road."

But his father lies back within the bedcovers, rolls over facing away from her, and goes to sleep.

His mother remains sitting up. But she does not look at him; she stares into space. The expression on her face is dark and threatening. Even in the dim light of the single lamp set off to one side, he can see this. He has never seen his mother look this way.

It makes him afraid.

He wishes he hadn't come.

"After taking time to reflect on what I'd heard, I began to understand better what was being kept from me. My mother shared my ability; my father clearly didn't. They had formed a pact—though I did not know the circumstances—that if her ability ever showed itself in me, I was to be . . ." He paused. "I cannot even now say the word. But you know it."

Leofur nodded. "Did you talk to your mother of this?"

"I went first to boys in the village with whom I played sometimes and asked them about people who could change shapes. I used the pretext of wanting to know if such a thing was even possible or only a rumor. One of them seemed to know. He said these people were called shape-shifters, and they did indeed exist. But because they could be anything and you might never know if they were real or pretending, they were hated and feared in many parts of the world. I asked if he had ever seen one, knowing he had seen my mother, but all of them said no."

He took a deep breath and exhaled. "So then I went to my mother and told her the truth. I confessed my discovery. I told her I did not understand its nature and was frightened by it. I told her, too, that it was clearly a part of me, and it was not something I could ignore. The lure of its use was too strong. I said nothing about overhearing their conversations. I said nothing about what my father had planned for me."

"Was it then you came here?" Leofur asked. "To the Druids?"

He shook his head. "That happened much later. I wish now I hadn't waited; things might have turned out differently. But my mother did not suggest it. She simply told me never to tell my father and never to let anyone see me changing shapes. 'If you must do it,' she said, 'do it in private and far away from everyone. No one must ever see you. If they do, I cannot be sure I can protect you. Even from your father.' She paused then—I still remember that pause. 'Maybe especially from your father,' she added."

"Your father would really have killed you, if he knew?"

"My mother thought so. Yet she loved him anyway. He was handsome and charming. He found her beautiful and smart, and he once loved her as much as she did him. They did not marry; they simply moved in together. They had lived alone, their parents gone, their families scattered. They were both looking for a fresh start. They pledged to be life partners in the way so many do. I think their feelings were genuine and strong back then. All went well for them until the night my mother admitted the truth about her identity.

"After she confessed—an act I have never been able to understand— she sensed an immediate change in him. He said he didn't believe her. He said she was making it up. But she told him it was so, that she had been born this way and seldom used her skills in any case. She was not compelled to do so in the way I was when I discovered my talent. She was content to be who she was and found the changing disquieting. But she felt he should know, so she told him. She hoped he would try to understand and accept her admission as proof of her love for him. It was a mistake."

He looked away, as if unable to face Leofur or Oost Mondara with the rest of it. "He was never the same man again. He never came back to her emotionally. He stayed with her, was kind to her and cared for her, but he told her they would never speak of it again. He told her he never wanted to see her undergo a change—not for any reason. And he made her promise that if they had a child and it was discovered to possess her blood and could change as she could, she would kill it.

"My mother agreed to all but the last. She said they would simply not have children, so the issue would never arise. They would live out their lives as a childless couple. This commitment sufficed for a time, but then she became pregnant with me. My father told her again what must happen if I was like her. He made her promise to tell him if she saw anything. He watched us both closely."

"Why didn't your mother leave him?" Leofur asked. "She could have, couldn't she? Why did she stay?"

He thought about it a moment. "She never spoke of it, but she did say once that she couldn't imagine life without him. I don't think the idea of leaving him ever crossed her mind; he was too important to her. More important, perhaps, than I was. So she stayed, caring for him, watching out for me, hoping she could keep things in balance."

A long silence followed. Imric seemed at a loss for words. Leofur waited patiently for him to continue, but when he didn't and it appeared he might not, she said, "Where does all this leave us? How does this tale impact what I have asked of you? How does it explain why you seem so reticent to help?"

The other's eyes shifted to meet hers again, and he grimaced. "Maybe it doesn't." He sighed. "It might be better if I just tell you how this story ends. I think at this point, the only thing you need to understand is exactly what could happen if I help you."

She sensed a tightening of his resolve, and she knew that what he was going to tell her would not be pleasant. She heard genuine pain in his voice, tremendous sadness and regret. For whatever reason, this was going to be extremely difficult for him.

"You don't have to explain anything you don't want to," Leofur said suddenly. "I only need to know one thing. Will you help me regardless of the risk to either of us?"

He looked at her as he might a curiosity. The lean, sharp features were bladed as hard as iron. "It would help if you understood why that question is not easily answered."

He straightened slightly, squaring up to her. "My father found out about me. About what I was. I don't know how; I never did learn the truth of it. But he did. He confronted my mother. I wasn't there when it happened. I expect she tried to calm him, to make him understand. But he was beyond rational behavior by then, crazed by what he must have perceived as an unforgivable act of betrayal. He reacted instinctively, driven by fear and hatred and his own personal demons. He killed her. She must not have been expecting it. She could have prevented it otherwise; she could have stopped him. But she died there in our home, not far from the front door. I think he wanted me to find her when I came in. He got his wish."

He took a deep, steadying breath. There were tears in his eyes. "He told me that it was my fault. That I had caused this to happen. She had to die because her blood was bad. Mine, as well. *Shape-shifters,* he spit at me. *Heathen spirits. Beasts.* We were all the same, abominations to nature. My mother was gone; I would follow. It was his duty to see to it.

"Those were the last words he ever spoke. He came at me with a knife. He was much bigger than I was, but I was prepared. I could change instantly by now. In my rage at what he had done, in my hatred of his defiance, I became something so terrible he just crumpled up in front of me, sobbing. But it wasn't enough. I seized him and I killed him like the animal I was. I shredded him until nothing recognizable remained."

He laughed softly, and the sound was jarring—a response so unexpected it unnerved Leofur. But his laugh was short and bitter and tinged with regret and sadness, and when it finally died out it did so as a soft wail of anguish.

"I ran then. A coward's way out, but I was nine years old and I didn't have the courage to do anything else. I think everyone in that village assumed I was carried off and torn to pieces like my father. I ran, and I never looked back. Afterward, for years, I lived a life no sane man would live. I don't know how I survived. Eventually I realized how bad things had become, so I found my way here, to the Druids, seeking help from their magic and their skills at healing. Fortunately, they heeded my pleas. They cured me, giving me a means to cope with what I had become. The cure was already a part of who I was, and now, unexpectedly, it became my lifeline to sanity."

He stopped again, and she said, "I don't understand. What sort of lifeline are we talking about?"

"A lifeline that will connect us, girl, if I agree to help you. A lifeline meant to keep us both safe by providing me with a tether. You will be in danger from the moment I agree to help you and you agree to the conditions involved in accepting my help."

He rose. "I don't think we need to talk about it further until I have a look at the place where your friend was taken."

"Does this mean you are thinking about helping me after all?"

He shook his head in an ambivalent way. "It means I am taking one small step toward deciding, by agreeing to see if I can find anything. Be happy, for the moment, with that. Now, do you want to show me where it happened?"

She did, of course. A sudden rush of hope bloomed within her. False or not, she would have to see.

Seconds later they were out the door, the shape-shifter and she—an odd pairing about to become even odder.

Oost Mondara remained behind, watching them go, wondering what he had done.

8

THE CONVERSATION RESUMED ONCE LEOFUR AND
Imric were outside the gates and moving toward the
clearing where Chrysallin Leah had disappeared.

"You still haven't told me why agreeing to help me places both of
us in such danger," she said finally.

His reply was a noncommittal grunt, so they walked from the
walls of the Keep toward their destination in silence. Leofur cast furtive glances in Imric's direction, hoping to find something revealing
in his look. But each time she risked glancing in his direction, he was
already looking back. His instincts were far superior to hers, it seemed.
Whatever advantage he enjoyed over normal men and women as a
shape-shifter must be remarkable. He carried himself easily, but there
was a weariness to his gait that reflected what she had observed in his
features when they had first been introduced.

As if life had beaten him down and left him less than complete.

As if the freedom he had once found so enthralling had been cur-
tailed so completely that he had been left only a part of what he had
been, and that part all but dead.

She was speculating on this point, but speculation was almost all
she had to work with. He had lost his parents in a terrible fashion
when he was very young, and that had clearly shocked and hurt him

deeply. The nature of their death was terrible enough. The fact that he had been told by his father that he was the cause of his mother's death would have left anyone stricken. And then to have killed his father in response? Impossible to imagine what that had done to him. Whatever had happened in the aftermath—in the years that had passed before he came to the Druids—had apparently not helped matters. Rather, it had led him down a path where he had felt so debilitated and perhaps so close to embracing his own death that he had taken what must have seemed like the only road left. If anyone could help him, it would indeed have been the Druids.

But that they had chosen to do so was interesting. Normally, they did not take in either supplicants or the emotionally damaged. Theirs was an order committed to gathering and preserving magic, not to healing.

Yet they had taken in Chrysallin Leah, hadn't they? They had taken her in because she possessed magic of such power, it seemed only logical that they should do what they could to keep her safe. So perhaps the Druids had felt the same way about Imric Cort. She didn't know exactly what his magic could do. She couldn't know the true extent of its power. It might be that it was greater than she imagined, and the Druids had realized this.

"How close are we to where you lost her?" he asked.

"Just ahead, through that screen of spruce." She risked another look and found his face empty.

"We'll wait on further explanations until I've had a look. You'll get the answers you need if I find it relevant enough to give them."

She glared at him. So self-important! Did he think he was the beginning and end of any effort to find and rescue Chrys? Well, he was in for a rude surprise. If he decided this wasn't *relevant enough,* she would find someone else to do what was needed. And if she couldn't find anyone else, she would go alone. She was resourceful; she would find a way.

She fumed in silence the rest of the journey. When they reached the clearing, she indicated with a sweep of her arm and a stony silence that this was where it had happened. He gave her a small grin and immediately began a search of the area. He did so in a seemingly haphazard fashion, every so often dropping to his knees to examine the ground or the vegetation. Several times he actually sniffed the air. He moved quickly, his gestures swift and sure—an indication that he had developed a process and was confident in its use.

His efforts consumed considerable time, but she was more patient with him now that she had gotten past his outright refusal to help. He might still turn her down, but at least this search indicated he was giving the matter some thought. She watched him closely as he worked, fascinated by the way in which he resembled a predatory animal. There was a sinuous grace to his movements, and in spite of her earlier irritation with him she found his fluidity and suppleness oddly attractive. She could envision him as a hunter.

Except he didn't know what he was hunting here, did he? So he must be searching for anything out of the ordinary, anything unfamiliar. How could anyone do that? How could you separate smells and tastes and physical indicators of an absent presence that were invisible to normal people? What must that be like?

She found herself wanting to know, wanting to find a way to understand how it felt.

He came out of his crouch suddenly and turned to face her. "They took your friend from the air," he said. "They must have used a sling weapon of some sort to render you unconscious, then snatched her from overhead and carried her off."

She stared at him in disbelief. "You can tell all that?"

"I can tell more than that, but I wanted to give you the general picture first." He grinned, and this time she found it infectious. "You can't always tell what's so by what you see. Sometimes it's more about what you don't see. Here, it's very obvious. Your footprints are present, but no others. There are no signs of a disturbance to the site. No wagon wheels, no hoofprints, no footprints, no marks of any sort. You eliminate what the signs don't show, and what's left gives you your answer."

"You said there was more?"

He nodded, sitting down in the grass, inviting her to join him.

They faced each other, eyes locked. "There are branches broken in the higher elevations of the surrounding trees. This suggests whoever took your friend wasn't flying anything particularly sophisticated or maneuverable. They were probably using an older vessel, one that has seen some use but is reliable. It would be wind-powered in order to escape detection. A diapson-crystal-powered vessel might have been heard, so they would have glided in. The branches also suggest that the pilot and crew of the vessel weren't all that skillful. They were experienced at stalking, but not so much at flying. They must have felt the need to hurry when they had your friend, so they rushed things. Also, they likely came from the south."

"How can you tell that?"

"The wind direction. It's been blowing northward for days. They would have taken note of that and made a conscious decision to take advantage of the wind. They must have been shadowing you previously, mapping your routes, charting your schedule, tracking the wind's direction. They made a careful study of your habits before acting."

Leofur felt a chill. So whoever took Chrys had planned it out in advance. They had watched from cover, taking note of everything the two of them did. It felt strange and invasive, knowing this. It made her angry.

"We have to go after them," she declared. Then she paused. "But how are we going to do that? Surely you can't track them through the air?"

"I think you're getting ahead of yourself," he said quietly. "I don't believe I've agreed to do this yet. Or even to consider it further. And you haven't heard anything about the possible consequences if I do."

Leofur had lost her patience. She brushed her hair from her face angrily. "You've danced around this matter long enough, Imric. Either you help me or you don't. You have all the information you need. What else is there to know? You've listened to my plea. You've examined the site. You've determined what happened. What more do you want? Are you afraid? Is that it? Tell me!"

He regarded her wordlessly for a long moment. "Aren't you afraid?"

"No!" she snapped.

"The daughter of Arcannen Rai," he mused. His words were slow and drawn out, a musing tone to his voice. "The child of the most famous sorcerer in the Four Lands. Yes, I think that perhaps you really aren't afraid. All the fear would have been driven out of you long ago. You'd have to have found great reserves of courage to get through your childhood."

That stopped her. She hesitated before answering. "More than you could possibly imagine. Although," she added, "perhaps no more than yourself. Your own childhood and adolescence must have demanded courage, as well. Why aren't you afraid?"

"I didn't say I wasn't. As a matter of fact, I am—but not for the reasons you think. I know things about this matter that you don't, and I am weighing them against the nature of your quest and my interest in you personally."

"Your . . . interest? What does that mean?"

"I am a member of the Druid household at their sufferance. I am not close to any of them, even Oost. They tolerate me, but not much more. There is a story, but I shall spare you from listening to it now. What matters is this. I live with men of power, but ones who have never known personal hardship. They did not grow up as you and I did. They did not suffer from the afflictions we did. You remind me in many ways of myself. Living with a father whose very presence was anathema. Living in fear of what he might do to you. Living with the knowledge that your life could go wrong with a snap of his fingers. Tell me, do you truly not possess any sort of magic?"

She shook her head. "Not that I have ever been aware of. Mine would not be inherited, in any case. It would be learned. But I purposefully distanced myself from allowing that to happen—much to my father's dismay and regret. He would have made me over into his image, but I am not him. I am nothing like him."

"You see? You complement me perfectly. You are entirely suitable for what must happen if we are to successfully complete this quest. There must be a balance—myself, with my shape-shifter magic, and you, with your self-reliance and your strong determination never to be anything or anyone but who you are now."

"Why is this important? I don't understand."

"Shhh, I am considering. Give me the silence and forbearance to do so."

So she quit talking and even quit looking at him. She stared instead into the greenery of the forest, into the maze of tree trunks, into the tangles of scrub and grasses. She lost herself in the sounds of the creatures that scurried through and flew over them. It was a music she had come to love since leaving Wayford. It chafed sometimes to be at Paranor, but more often than not the surrounding forest calmed her. She was at peace in its midst. She felt safe in its shelter.

She breathed the mountain air blowing down off the heights, took in the mix of scents, sweet and sharp, soft and rough. Time slowed. She thought of Paxon and how much she missed him. She imagined his return, wished she could be there for it, and was troubled she might not be. Any search for Chrysallin diminished the possibility. For whatever happened here, she must find her friend. She must do so for Paxon—and for herself, as well. Anything less would mark her for life.

"I like you," Imric said softly, interrupting her musings. "You lack experience in tracking, but you make up for it with your moral center. I see this in you. I see it the way animals do. They know when another creature is to be trusted or not. I need to be able to trust you, and I think I can. I am willing to risk it."

"You will go?" she asked, shocked in spite of herself. Excitement coursed through her. She could barely believe what she was hearing.

"I will go if you want me. But you may have second thoughts in spite of your insistence once you hear what it means for you should I agree to this. So listen well before you decide."

When he arrives at Paranor, he is barely hanging on to his sanity. He has been shape-changing so often, and for so long, that he no longer knows exactly who he is. His identity has blurred because he lives in his own skin so little of the time. He is still trying to escape his memories— his mother's body lying just inside the door of their home, his father telling him he was to blame, his own bloodlust as he tore his father to pieces in a blind rage, his flight from everything and everyone he had ever known. He is still trying to make sense of what has happened in his life, which is a whirling kaleidoscope of wild and reckless behavior intended to shed everything of his past through any means possible. He lives on the edge of despair and permanent damage. His mind is already balanced precariously, and his body is catching up. He drinks and fights and pleasures himself in every way imaginable. He becomes everything he knows or can envision and visits those creations on others just to hear them scream and see them run.

But when he wakes one morning with a woman he doesn't know in a place he can't recall and finds he cannot manage to remember who he actually is, even long enough to change back into himself, he flees into the woods and considers how far lost he is and how welcome death would be.

Instead of acting on that impulse, he sets out for Paranor, determined to find help. The Druids, after all, understand magic better than anyone. They study it, collect it, warehouse artifacts and talismans, visit places where magic shows itself in unexpected and often unpleasant ways, and in general record everything they learn.

Will they not have a way to help him?

Aphenglow Elessedil herself comes to speak with him in the outer courtyard, responding to a summons from the Troll guards. She sits with him in her gardens to hear his story. She is kind and patient and encouraging, and she does not judge or criticize. She does not offer advice, either. She just listens.

When he is finished, she agrees to let him stay the night while she considers his problem. If there is a way they can help him by using magic, they will. If not, he will have to leave and look elsewhere. Will he accept that condition in exchange for a night's lodging, a meal, and a chance to change his life?

He cannot make himself respond. He breaks down in front of her and weeps.

Because she is thorough and Paranor's records, though extensive, say little about shape-shifters and their magic, she lets him stay longer while she burrows into the Druid Histories, searching for information *that will reveal what is needed. She does not see him during that time; her involvement in her task is total. On the third day, she has her answer and while they sit together again in her gardens, secluded and alone, she tells him what it is.*

His problem, she explains, originates with his mix of human and shape-shifter blood. Being the offspring of a human father and a shape-shifter mother makes growing up much more difficult. Not telling him the truth of his heritage was a mistake. It would have helped if he had known even a little of what to expect. The gift of being able to change is offset by the danger of doing so too frequently and too casually—something he has found out for himself. There are instances when it has had no adverse effect on the offspring of such different species, but just as many when it has. There was, at one time, a shape-shifter who was integrally involved with the brother of a future Ard Rhys, and much of what is known about shape-shifters was recorded as a result.

In your case, she adds, you pushed yourself beyond your limits. You failed to act responsibly; you behaved recklessly and with complete disregard for your own health. The wisest thing for you to do now is to stop changing entirely. Accept yourself as you are and leave it at that. And if you think you cannot do this, you need to develop a way to protect yourself against the possible adverse effects of continuing to change. You need a safety line that will pull you back to shore when you have swum too far out into the current of your shifter compulsions.

He is listening without fully understanding what she is suggesting. Quitting is simple enough in the abstract, but almost impossible to envision as a reality. He is a shape-shifter. It defines him. It is what he does. It is as natural as breathing and every bit as necessary. Yet she is saying he should stop. In the alternative, she is saying he should . . . what?

In that moment, for the first time, he feels a hint of fear.

Imric paused in his explanation, his distress obvious. "She told me that I required a tether, a magically induced safety line to which I could be attached. When the urge to change became too strong, when it dominated my rational thinking and demanded that it be indulged— when my self-control slipped beyond my grasp—the safety line would be there to pull me back. It would, initially, remind me of the danger in which I was placing myself—willingly or not—so that I could take whatever steps were necessary to stop what I was doing. If that failed and I was unable to help myself, the tether would do the job for me."

Leofur nodded. "A safety line," she repeated. "And you require that here, in order to search for Chrys?"

"I do. It will be necessary if I am to undertake this hunt because I must be able to shape-shift into whatever is needed to track your friend successfully."

"Because you will need their instincts and senses to find what you seek? Because theirs are stronger than yours?"

"Much stronger."

"But this safety line? What would it be attached to?"

"It would be attached to you."

She stared, trying to grasp what he was saying. "To me?"

"Always to another person, to a human—preferably to one with courage and determination. Someone who is not subject to the same compulsions as I am; someone who does not suffer from the same condition. Someone I can depend upon to help me if things go wrong."

"And you think that would be me?"

"I do. I will be betting my life on it, in fact." He hesitated. "And so will you."

She frowned, confused anew. "You hinted at that before. What do you mean?"

"The magic that infuses the tether requires a living being on each end to achieve the balance I spoke about earlier. The tether is invisible, but it is formed of the emotions and memories of those that it joins. By tethering, you and I will become one. We will be bound together in ways too numerous to count if you decide to do this. You will share my thoughts and I yours. You will share my emotional state and I yours. We will be able to communicate with each other from long distances. When I allow it, you will even be able to see through my eyes. This continues as long as the tether is in place."

"Let me understand this. For as long as we are searching for Chrysallin, we will be *living inside* each other's heads?" she asked, trying to picture what that would mean.

"Not for the entire time. Only when we mutually agree to it. And either of us can sever it by choice. Mostly, it will happen when I am changed into another creature. You must have access to me then so that you can help me should my addiction begin to pull me away. The time we are joined would be limited, however. There is only so much anyone can stand of being exposed to another's thoughts and emotions."

She exhaled sharply. "I would think so. But why is it so dangerous?"

"Because you risk yourself by being tied to someone as unpredictable as I am. If I prove too strong for you, your own sanity might be compromised. You might be pulled away with me, dragged inside my consciousness and lost to your own. It has happened once already. It is why I no longer shape-shift, even though the urge to do so is almost too much to bear."

She could envision this happening. She could imagine herself made as bleak and wild as he was when he first came to Paranor—lost to himself, his sanity gone, a suicidal mess. Yet he thought she could handle it. He must have great confidence in her, if he truly believed that. She was not at all sure she did. She wondered if she should even consider it. Yet if she wanted his help, if she was serious about risking her own life to help get Chrysallin Leah back, what choice did she have?

"You are beginning to understand what I've been telling you," he said quietly. His lean features were pinched and drawn, and there was sadness in his eyes as he looked at her. "It is one thing to say you will do anything for your friend, but another entirely to actually do what is needed. You should think carefully about this. If you choose to abandon this plan, to not put yourself at risk, I will be the last one to pass judgment. I would expect that Paxon Leah would feel as I do, the fate of his sister notwithstanding."

He was wrong about this, of course. He did not understand what

Paxon had already been through to free Chrysallin from the machi-
nations of Arcannen. He had almost lost her twice, and the effect on
him had been devastating. There was no reason to think that this
time would be any different. And he might say he did not blame Leofur; he might, indeed, believe it to be the truth. But the fact of it happening would always be there. It would change their relationship in
ways that could not be repaired.

"You did this before with another person and it killed them?" she
asked suddenly, remembering.

"Not long after I first came to Paranor." He clasped his hands in
front of him, as if to hold on to something firm while he spoke. "It
was supposed to be an experiment. A member of the Druid order
volunteered to serve as my tether. The connection between us was
made, the safety line formed, and we were joined. I began to experiment with shifting into other forms. It went well enough at first. I did
not rush things; I took my time and kept my focus steady. Aphenglow
herself monitored what was happening, prepared to act if the need
should arise. When no problems surfaced, she gave us permission to
continue the experiment alone."

"Yet something went wrong."

"Something always goes wrong." His voice turned bitter, almost to
a growl. "I was content within myself, but I sensed an uneasiness in
my partner. He was not responding in a way that suggested he had
sufficient confidence in himself. I could feel his uncertainty, sense his
hesitation at the other end of the tether. I even talked to him about it
at one point, but he quickly dismissed my concerns. He was a good
man, but his inability to recognize his own weakness was a flaw. It
cost him his life. I can still feel him slipping away from me, dying on
his feet as he fought to stop me from changing. Because he lacked the
strength and the will to do so."

"Yet you survived."

"I think of this every single day of my life. I was responsible for
what happened to him. I took his life because I could not control my
powers. Since then, I have stopped shape-shifting entirely. I have
tended my animals and provided my services to the Druid order. I

stay at Paranor because I begged them not to turn me out, and they saw the need for keeping me close. They understood what might happen otherwise. But no one would tether to me again after that. I had no choice but to stop my shape-shifting."

He looked at her anew. "Which is where we stand now, you and I. This is where you tell me I am asking too much, and I agree. We part friends, and we go our separate ways."

She nodded, thinking about all he had said. He was trying to discourage her. He was deliberately telling her to back away while she could. Yet he had agreed to consider her request, and he had told her things he needn't have told her in the process. There was at least a small part of him that wanted her to agree.

"What makes you believe the tethering would work this time?" she asked. "Why do you think it would be different with me?"

He looked away quickly, then back again. "The Druid who served as my tether was provided to me; I was not given a choice. This time, I am. You are stronger. There may be uncertainty, but not when you are placed in a position of risk or danger. I think you would be a match for me. Enough so that I am persuaded to make the offer."

"But you wouldn't have if you thought me weaker than I am? If you found my response to your tale evidence of this weakness?"

He smiled, and for a moment he was almost handsome. "I find you stronger in every conceivable way. If I did not, you are right—I would not have made the offer at all."

They sat quietly for a time, studying each other. Leofur liked it that he had judged her capable enough to undertake the tethering. She liked it that he believed in her.

"But why do *you* want this? Why risk putting yourself right back in a deadly situation?" The words were spoken in a rush, before she could think better of them. "What I'm asking is, why would you take this chance when you needn't?"

His smile returned, sadder this time, more tentative. "Isn't it evident? I'm not happy, and I haven't been for a long time. I miss the changing. I miss shape-shifting the way you would miss food if it were withheld from you. I need to undergo the process in order to feel alive. I haven't done it before because there wasn't a way to do so safely. But now here you are, giving me the opportunity."

He took a deep breath and exhaled sharply. "I will admit it. I want this. Badly. I crave it."

"But you can't be sure about me."

"What can we be sure of in this life, Leofur, that really means anything? I would take this chance if you would give it to me. But only if you wish it for yourself."

She had already considered the reasons she should and shouldn't agree. When Oost Mondara had first brought them together, she thought that nothing could dissuade her from taking advantage of Imric's skills. But listening to him talk about what would be involved was chilling. To have another person living inside your mind and you living in his—even if not literally—was daunting. It might be no more than shared memories, visions, and thoughts, but even that might be too intimate. Everyone had secrets to hide. And everyone needed a place inside to call one's own.

Even so, she told him what she had intended to tell him all along.

"I do wish it. I will agree to be tethered to you."

They walked back to the Keep in silence, and it wasn't until they were almost to the gates that Imric spoke again.

"We will leave at sunrise. Oost will provide us with a two-man flit. We'll need an airship to cover ground quickly if we're to catch up with your friend's captors."

Leofur glanced over. "I would like you to stop calling her *my friend* and call her by her name. Chrysallin."

He nodded. "As you wish."

"How can we track anyone from the air unless we see them?"

"I'll show you."

"When do we make this tether?"

"When we set out. When I make the first change. But we'll test it first, in the morning, to make certain it can be done. You must discover for yourself what it feels like before we can be sure it will work."

"Why don't we leave now? Why wait?"

He gave her a look. "I realize you are eager, but there are preparations to be made. We need an airship readied and provisioned. We need a good night's sleep. We need to begin our search in daylight. The tethering may prove difficult for you. Tomorrow will be soon enough."

Tomorrow. It could not get here quickly enough. She would eat dinner, pack clothes and necessities and weapons, and sleep. She tried to imagine what tomorrow would be like and failed utterly. She knew it would not be as she envisioned it, so it was better not to settle on any expectations. What she could do now for herself that would help best was to stay calm.

When they entered the gates, Oost Mondara was waiting. "Leofur, I would speak with you a moment."

Imric Cort walked off without a word or a backward glance, his rangy form disappearing into the evening shadows. Leofur watched him go before turning to Oost.

"Did you agree to go?" he asked.

She nodded. "I did."

His blocky form shifted uncomfortably as he looked away. "Perhaps you will change your mind when I tell you that we received a message from one of our contacts in Arishaig. An arrow shrike flew in with it an hour ago. There's been an incident. This morning all the members of the Federation delegation, including the Prime Minister, were killed. While it is unclear how this happened, the rumor is that the Druids are to blame. Paxon and the others have fled the city. The Federation is hunting for them now."

"This is my father's doing!"

"Perhaps. There is no way of knowing yet. And I didn't tell you this because I want you to change your mind about Imric, but I wouldn't feel right letting you go without knowing what's happened."

She took his hand and squeezed it. "Thank you. I would not want that, either." She stepped away, giving him a quick smile. "I have to rest before dinner. I feel a little tired."

What she felt was frightened and confused. And conflicted. Having Paxon in danger put an unexpected wrinkle in her plans. In other circumstances, she would have gone after him. She would seek him out and do what she could to help him.

But how realistic was it to expect to find him, even if she backed out on her commitment to Imric?

And to Chrys?

She didn't know the answer. She didn't think now she ever would.

9

PAXON FLEW HIS BELEAGUERED BAND OF DRUIDS and their Troll protectors northeast, trusting to misdirection rather than speed to help them make their escape. Any pursuit coming out of Arishaig would expect them to fly in a direct line for Paranor, taking the shortest distance and relying on their head start. But the Highlander believed it unwise to trust such an obvious option—especially when the big cruisers and fast racers of the Federation almost certainly could catch them long before they reached their destination. Since night was approaching, maybe it was better to settle on a route that wouldn't be immediately obvious. This night there was a new moon. Light would be at a premium, and hunters would have trouble finding them in the darkness.

More to the point, perhaps, there was a storm coming in from the northwest. As Paxon saw it, this could be both a blessing and a curse. If it turned south rather than east as it drew nearer, they might be able to outrun it while hoping it impeded anyone following them. But if not, Paxon would have a hard night of flying ahead of him—and reason to worry whether they could even stay aloft.

It was a tight fit in the cockpit of the cruiser. Even with the canvas canopy pulled open, the space was small and cramped, and the back seats were little more than benches. Part of the problem was the body of Darconnen Drue and the two injured Troll guards tucked into the back of the passenger's area, taking up valuable space. On a positive note, there were no other injuries. Everyone was settled in, making space where they could, biding their time, talking to one another softly, and trying to be patient while they waited for the flight to be over.

Paxon knew what they were up against. It would take all that night and the next day to reach home. And that was only if there were no problems with the weather or with pursuers. Even if they reached Paranor safely, they could expect a visit from the Federation, undoubtedly in the form of warships and soldiers. He wasn't sure what Isaturin could say to convince the Federation government that the Druids were not involved in what had happened to the Southland delegation. Their killer was obviously a thing conceived of magic, and it had seemed to disappear by passing through Karlin Ryl. Everything suggested the Druids were responsible for what had happened.

Except for one thing.

There was no obvious reason for the Druids to want the negotiations with the Southlanders to fall apart.

Other questions surfaced as he thought about it further. When Isaturin appeared at his elbow an hour into their flight, he decided to voice them.

"Tired?" the Ard Rhys asked, his tone revealing his own weariness.

"A bit. But not too tired to keep us flying safely."

"No, you wouldn't be." Isaturin glanced over his shoulder at the others. "What a strange day."

Paxon gave him a look. "You recognized that thing back there in the Assembly. You called it by name."

Isaturin nodded. "A Sleath. A kind of demon. A thing of immense power. I've never encountered one, but I recognized it for what it was."

"It was conjured, then? Deliberately set on us?"

"It wouldn't have appeared otherwise. Some dark magic is at work—a very powerful magic. Only a sorcerer of great skill could bring a Sleath to life."

"Do we have the means to stand against this thing, if it should appear again? We didn't seem to back there."

Isaturin looked grimly determined. "We were unprepared. If there is a next time, we'll be ready."

Ahead and off to the northwest, the skies were darkening. The storm was drawing closer, masses of black clouds building on the horizon. The light had gone out of the sky, and the land beneath was cloaked in shadows. Lightning forked in wicked tongues through the inky dark—brilliant flashes followed by booming peals of thunder that shook the air. In spite of Paxon's hopes, the storm did not appear to be turning away from them.

"It's going to hit us, isn't it?" Isaturin asked quietly.

"Likely, if it stays on its present course. About thirty minutes from now, it should reach us."

"Should we set down?"

"We could. But if we do, we give up our advantage of having a head start. The big Federation vessels won't be slowed by a storm. They'll plow right on through. They might not know where we are, but Fero Darz will know how to search for us."

"On the ground, he might not see us."

"On the ground, we are sitting ducks."

"So we keep flying, then?"

"Until the storm becomes too bad. I don't like it, but our lives might depend on it. What will you say to the Federation when they catch up to us, be it out here somewhere or at Paranor? What will you say to them to convince them we aren't responsible for what happened?"

Isaturin shook his head. "I don't know. I don't know for certain what happened myself."

"How did that thing—that Sleath—disappear like it did?" Paxon added. "Where did it go?"

The Ard Rhys shook his head, a troubled look on his face.

Paxon shifted his gaze back to where Karlin sat cradled in Miriya's arms, the two talking quietly. Karlin looked stricken, but otherwise seemed the same as always. Miriya caught him looking, and he shifted his gaze away again.

"I don't like that it deflected your Druid magic so easily. It shouldn't have been able to do that. I don't like that it didn't seem affected by my sword, either. What sort of power will it take to stop that thing? At some point, we might have to find out. I don't think we've seen the last of it. Do you?"

Isaturin shrugged. "Let me think on it. There must be something that can stop it, something that can get past its defenses. We just need to be ready when it's time."

Sounds good, Paxon thought. *In theory.*

Winds struck the vessel crosswise moments later, further evidence of the storm's approach. Their ferocity was enough to elicit a few gasps from the passengers and a hint of the power that was coming for them.

"Have everyone fasten themselves in place with safety lines. They can find them in one of the storage bins." Paxon gave Isaturin a look. "We'll ride it out for as long as we can, but I don't think we're going to get through it."

The Ard Rhys didn't argue. He simply moved back to see that Paxon's orders were carried out. The Highlander adjusted their vessel's direction to bring them a little more directly into the wind. Too much sideways exposure in a storm could tear the masts and sails right off. He powered up the thrusters in a last-ditch effort to get clear, even knowing they couldn't. He glanced into the still-clear skies behind him for any sign of pursuit, but saw nothing. At least they had that to be grateful for.

It wasn't much, and after another ten minutes it didn't matter. The storm arrived—a whirlwind of rain and wind and darkness, engulfing them as a great beast might, striking them with mighty blows, each of which threatened to break the airship apart. There was no getting through it now, so Paxon turned the bow of the ship into the wind and tried to ride it out. In seconds they were rain-drenched and huddled down on the ship's decking in an effort to find protection. All save the Highlander, who had lashed himself to the wheel and remained upright so he could keep his bearings as he worked the controls.

It soon became apparent that his efforts would yield little.

The rain was blinding, and visibility dropped to zero. Had there been any mountains close by, they would have been in serious danger of being dashed to pieces. Fortunately, they were still far enough out on the grasslands below Leah that there was no real risk of striking anything if they could manage to stay airborne. Their greatest danger was the distinct possibility that the winds would send them tumbling out of the sky altogether.

"Take down the sheaths!" Paxon screamed at those behind him, but his words were lost in the howl of the wind.

After much waving of hands, he managed to attract the attention of Netheren, the Troll captain, who released his safety line and fought his way over to the pilot box. His voice rendered useless, Paxon managed to indicate by gestures that he wanted the Troll to take the wheel and hold the vessel steady. That done, he set about hauling down the light sheaths by himself. It took a tremendous effort, with the storm threatening to rip the sheaths out of his hands. He had to pull the heavy sail material close to his body as he gathered it in, careful not to let the wind grab it. The strain on his arms was excruciating, and by the time he had finished he was exhausted.

But there was neither time nor opportunity for him to rest. He stumbled back to the pilot box, sent Netheren back to his seat, and took control of the vessel once more.

Only seconds after that the funnel cloud struck.

A huge whirlwind that stretched for miles on either side, it was on top of them before he knew it was there. Buried in the center of the storm, it simply materialized out of the darkness. The dust, debris, and chunks of ice already caught in its invisible claws revealed its presence as it spun into view and came for them.

"Get down!" Paxon screamed at the others, the roar of the wind once again obscuring his words.

If he had been heard, it might have made a difference. Netheren had returned to his seat but failed to resecure his safety line. When the whirlwind struck the airship, it carried him away. Hands reached for him belatedly, grasping at air, too slow even to catch hold of his clothing. Like a scrap of loose paper, he was yanked into the maelstrom and gone.

Paxon didn't see it happen. His attention was fixed on flying their craft, trying to slip along the edges of the funnel cloud to its lee side where he might be able to use the thrusters to break its hold. The whirlwind was threatening to pull them in completely, but Paxon kept them at its edge, working the thrusters in small bursts. The ice and debris already in its grasp whipped past them, dangerous projectiles that could render anyone unconscious or dead if they were struck. The Highlander could do nothing to protect himself while he remained upright at the controls; he had to be content with hunching down and hoping for the best.

Shades protect me, he prayed.

The scope of the storm was immense, too large to measure accurately from so close in. Paxon lost his sense of direction once the airship was caught up in the funnel's broad sweep, and now he was reduced to fighting to break free and get them down. But where was back and where was forward at this point? He could no longer tell either the storm's direction or his own.

Then he saw a marginal lightening of the darkness and, heeling over hard, the bow of his vessel angling away, he gave full power to the thrusters. The airship lurched and bucked, but it broke the funnel cloud's grip and shot away with a long shudder that could be felt through every last timber.

It also shattered the rudders, tore off the rear-port parse tubes, and brought down the main mast.

Still, Paxon managed to keep the vessel flying, holding it steady while fighting to get clear of the storm. But then the power failed. For no discernible reason, everything stopped—the diapson crystals gone dark, all thrust terminated as if exhausted.

Instantly the ship went into a spin. Clear of the funnel but still caught in the tailing winds of the storm, it began spiraling downward. Paxon tried to regain control, but it was no use. With the power gone, there was no way to keep the ship steady. They were going to crash, whatever he did. He yelled a warning to the others, not sure if they heard him or not, but unable to do more. Any form of controlled flying was impossible. If he could get them down in one piece, he would have done as much as was humanly possible.

He wished suddenly he had been able to leave the sails up. He wished he had more time. He wished, in hindsight, he had chosen a different method of escape.

He crouched in the pilot box, the sound of the wind a shriek, its force like a giant hand pressing them down. Out of the corner of his eye he caught a glimpse of the ground rushing up to meet them.

Miles to the south, well out of the path of the storm engulfing the Druids and their ill-fated craft, Fero Darz was speaking with his new second. Pas Allett had been elevated to the position, given that its former holder lay in pieces following his ill-advised attack on the creature that had then proceeded to annihilate all of the Federation ministers and their guards. Darz knew he had been lucky to survive, but it's the lucky survivor that all too often bears both guilt and blame for the deaths of those he might have saved. It was so here. What had saved his skin for the moment was the fact that he was the only one left alive who could identify the creature. A hurried meeting of those senior ministers fortunate enough not to have been included in the negotiating delegation had determined that Darz should be left in place as Commander of the Ministerial Watch for at least as long as it took to clean up his mess, thus giving him a small chance to redeem himself sufficiently to avoid being executed for dereliction of duty.

Fero Darz was not a newcomer to the politics of the Coalition Council, and he understood how things worked in these situations. The only real surprise was that he was being given a chance to act on what he knew about Paxon Leah and the Druids. Or believed he knew, in any case.

Of one thing, he was certain. While Paxon Leah had been clever enough to circle back and commandeer that cruiser, he had missed a crucial detail. For there were things that even the clever Paxon Leah did not know about Federation technology, and one of them was that, in the past year, their scientists had developed a way to use diapson crystals to track one another. It had something to do with using pieces of a single crystal, the smallest of which were embedded in the airships while the largest was held back and placed in a power source that could detect the location of any airship. There couldn't be too many vessels flying north just now, so it would be easy enough to determine the direction and distance of the one Paxon was using.

Which Darz had already done, once his pursuit vessel was well away from the city.

"We are absolutely certain the Druids got out of the city?" he asked Allett for what must have been the tenth time.

The other nodded. "Paxon Leah was positively identified by the guards from whom he stole the cruiser. The Druids were seen at the walls, as well, flying out of the city and into the grasslands. It was them, all right."

Darz glanced down at the strange box with its lights, watching them glow and listening to the pinging sound the box emitted.

"Commander, we're heading into a storm," his second said suddenly.

Darz glanced up. He hadn't been paying much attention until now, but the darkness to the northwest had moved closer and was spreading out in a wide swath directly in front of him. They had perhaps another thirty minutes before they would be in it.

"Have the captain set down immediately," he said.

"Commander, if we do that . . ."

"If we do that, Pas, we might live to see another day. We need to stay out of that mess if we're to continue the hunt. The Druids aren't going anywhere. They have to fly through that if they're going north, and they won't risk it. And even if they do, our signal will pick them up again once the storm has passed." Darz allowed himself a small smile as he peered out into the gathering dark. "Now get going. I want us on the ground."

Allett, who had been called up with little notice, hadn't been told everything. There hadn't been time, and there wasn't any need. It was enough that Darz knew, enough that he could anticipate what would happen sometime during the next hour or so.

The storm, of course, was a bonus, but it was a crucial deficiency in the aircraft Paxon had stolen that would undo him. He might think himself well away, able to outdistance and outfly his pursuit, but he was sadly mistaken.

That airship had been left sitting on the landing pad for a reason. All of the diapson crystals were nearly drained of their power. It had less than three hours of flight time remaining, and there were no replacement crystals on board.

He took a moment to imagine the shock when Paxon and his Druid charges discovered they could no longer fly. He wished he could be there to see their faces.

10

Sunshine, like liquid gold, pours out of a cloudless sky, bathing Paxon's face in warmth and brightness. He sits on a hillside with Leofur beside him, his shoulder touching hers, looking out over the countryside. He cannot seem to decide where he is, but he knows it doesn't matter. Being with Leofur is what is important, and he feels her nearness the way he feels his skin—closely wrapped about him, holding him together.

They do not speak—have not spoken, he believes, in some time now. It is enough that they are close, bonded by their silence as surely as by their love and trust. There is a newly forged connection between them, a vow they have taken that will keep them together for the rest of their lives. It is their promise to engage in a life partnership, each pledging loyalty and commitment to the other, each agreeing to be true.

"You understand the nature of what you are promising me?" she asks quietly, the first words she has spoken since they took this vow.

"I think so," he answers.

"You are telling me you will always be there for me. No matter how far away you go, you will always come back to me. You will never leave me, no matter what."

He nods. "I promise that."

"It will not always be easy," she continues. "You will forever be at risk as the High Druid's Blade. You will always be facing dangers that could prevent your return."

"I will not let them," he says.

He bends to her and kisses her gently. Then he kisses her again, harder. She wraps her arms around him and pulls him to her. "Never leave me, Paxon. Or if you must, always come back to me," she whispers.

But even as she speaks the words, she is fading away. He can feel her slipping from his grasp. Around them, the day is darkening and the air is growing damp. There is a storm coming. It is out there on the horizon, but it is inside him, too. It is everywhere.

"Paxon," she cries, and he feels her disappear entirely.

He is alone, and rain pelts his face.

"Paxon!" A familiar voice called to him, and hands gripped his shoulders, squeezing hard. "Can you hear me?"

Miriya was leaning down, looking into his eyes. He was lying in the wreckage of the airship, shattered timbers and spars and bits of canvas surrounding him. Rain fell in streams, and the sky was filled with dark clouds that surged past in violent gusts as the wind howled and spit.

Miriya bent close. "Don't try to move just yet. Lie there and let Karlin have a look at you."

Karlin Ryl moved into view, her ethereal face pale and drawn, her large dark eyes fixed on him. Her hands moved up and down his legs and arms and then across his body. She paused in her examination now and again, as if waiting to see if he would respond to her touch. It took her only a few minutes, but it seemed much longer to Paxon.

When she was done, she said nothing but only rose and walked away.

Paxon pulled himself to his feet, the last of his vision of Leofur fading as the pain in his muscles and joints ratcheted through his body. He might not have broken anything, but it felt as if he had. He stood upright, testing his limbs gingerly. Rain continued to pour down and the wind whipped about him, rising to a shriek that threatened to cut off whatever Miriya was trying to say.

She leaned closer. "What do we do? The airship is finished, and I can't even determine the compass points in this soup!"

The Highlander glanced about, seeing immediately what the other meant. A deep mist swirled all about them, shifting with such frequency that it was impossible to tell if the storm was advancing or retreating. He could barely see a dozen feet in any direction. Any attempt to move about at this point would be foolhardy.

"We have to find shelter!" he shouted back. "We have to take cover until this blows over!"

She nodded in response. Then someone called out to him from the edge of the swirling blackness.

It took him a moment to realize that it was Isaturin, crouched next to a stand of boulders and scrub beyond the remains of the airship. As he started to respond, he caught sight of a twisted, broken body that lay off to one side amid the wreckage. He moved closer. It was Cresson Oridian, a jagged piece of broken spar thrust all the way through his chest. There was blood everywhere. His eyes were open and staring, as if he had seen something surprising just at the last minute but would not now ever be able to reveal it.

Paxon climbed to his feet and made his way over to the Ard Rhys. "I found him like that after the crash," the other shouted in his ear, overriding the howl of the wind. "Look over here!"

He pointed into the rocks. A natural opening was visible, not entirely free of rain, but otherwise sufficient to shelter all of them. Paxon nodded wordlessly and within minutes he had their little group safely inside. Miraculously, only Oridian had perished. Even old Consloe did not seem any the worse for wear. Together they hunkered down amid the rocks and tried not to think about being wet and cold.

Paxon took a silent head count. Of the Druids, there was Isaturin, Miriya, Karlin, and Consloe. Only three of the Trolls guards remained, now that Netheren was gone, and two of those were wounded. So eight in all, counting himself. A much smaller party to try to get back to Paranor safely, but smaller, too, if it came to a fight. Which, he imagined, it would, sooner or later. How could it not?

Without the airship to provide transportation, they would have to make their way north across the grasslands on foot. If they were lucky, they could reach the forests of the Duln and possibly find help from the residents of one of the small forest communities. But he couldn't count on that; these villages were poor and frequently lacked airships of any sort. They would have horses and wagons, and that would be it.

Huddled with the others, he sat waiting for the storm to abate, wondering how things could have gone so terribly wrong.

Miles to the south, Fero Darz was eating dinner inside the Federation fast cruiser he had appropriated for hunting down the fleeing Druids. Outside, the storm was raging, but it was much less severe on its southern edge than where Paxon and his sodden entourage were waiting it out. Darz had put down in plenty of time to search out a sheltered area, so while the storm howled and the winds moaned, the inside of the cruiser was mostly calm.

They had picked up the signal from the stolen Federation airship almost immediately after departing Arishaig, so tracking the Druids had been relatively simple. Darz had expected Paxon to fly directly north, which was pretty much what he had done. The only wrinkle was a noticeable deviation to the east, but he believed this to be an effort to shake off pursuit long enough for Paxon and company to reach the far shore of the Rainbow Lake. After that, it was only a few more hours to the Dragon's Teeth, and there were plenty of hiding places along the way.

He finished his meal, but then sat sipping his ale and thinking. Even having witnessed the carnage caused by the creature that had then disappeared, even having already decided that the Druids had brought this creature to life and set it on the Federation ministers and soldiers in order to kill them all, and even knowing that flight is almost always proof of guilt, he was having second thoughts. Several things about this incident troubled him, and he could not quite make himself dismiss them.

First of all, Paxon had asked well before anything had happened if their security was sufficient. He had seemed genuinely worried, and if he had known what was coming, why would he have asked that question? Why do anything to alert Darz to the possibility that something might be amiss? He kept thinking that it might have been that very question that created enough doubts to start him looking around and eventually finding the missing man and the unguarded door.

In addition to this, there was his assessment of Paxon Leah. He had never believed him in the least duplicitous and did not believe him so now. He had always found him forthright and trustworthy. To accept that he was part of such a treacherous act was almost impossible. The Highlander might not have known, but wouldn't that have been a dangerous secret to keep from the man charged with protecting the Ard Rhys and his Druids? Besides, hadn't he attempted to stop the creature himself, his fabled sword ablaze with magic?

Finally, there was the problem of motive—or the absence thereof. What possible reason could the Druids have for arranging a meeting to achieve common ground only to sabotage it? What could they hope to gain by killing the old Prime Minister and those closest to him when those men and women were perhaps the only allies within the Federation that the Druids could hope to find? There just didn't seem to be any point in all of this, any reason for the Druids to do what they had done.

He had been pondering these contradictions since they had set out from Arishaig in pursuit of the Druids. Once they were airborne, there had been plenty of time to think things over, and Fero Darz prided himself on being thorough and fair. Something about all this just didn't feel right, and he was wondering how he was going to handle things if it came to a direct confrontation with Paxon and the Druids. He had enough men and weapons to overcome them, even if they resisted. Their magic was formidable, but no more so than the weapons his Federation soldiers possessed. But if he was wrong about what had happened, he didn't want to find out about it after the Druids and the Federation soldiers both lay dead. It was bad enough the way things stood. He didn't want to compound one tragedy by instigating another.

He was brooding over this when his second appeared, bending down to set the tracking base next to him. "It's stopped working," Allett said without preliminaries.

Darz looked up at him. "How could that happen?"

"There's only one way. The diapson crystal shard embedded in the craft was shattered. Either it was discovered and destroyed, or the airship crashed."

Darz held his gaze. "You're sure about this?"

"Absolutely."

"The most likely possibility is that the vessel crashed, isn't it?"

"More likely than the shard being located when no one knew it was there in the first place."

"So maybe the storm took her down, and now the Druids are afoot—if they're even still alive. A crash strong enough to destroy the crystal might have killed them all."

"It's possible. Nothing left but bones and boards." Pas seemed pleased with his command of imagery.

"But we don't want to take that chance, do we?" Darz responded pointedly.

His second turned serious at once. "No, Commander. We do have an idea of how far away from us they were when the signal stopped. We can probably track them once the storm is over."

Fero Darz nodded. "Then you should monitor the storm and report back the moment it slackens enough for us to lift off again, shouldn't you?"

"Yes, Commander." His second saluted sharply and hurried away.

Darz shook his head in disgust. *Idiot.*

Darz slept after that, needing to rest now in case he couldn't do so later. The rain drumming on the airship hull was lulling, and his sleep was deep and undisturbed.

Until Pas Allett shook him awake, bringing him back into the real world and all its attendant misery. "Commander, it is morning and the rain is letting up. We are ready to get under way."

Wordlessly, Darz rose and went topside to look around. The sky was still gloomy and clouded over, spitting raindrops in small bursts, but the worst of the storm had moved east. The gale-force winds had diminished to a breeze, and visibility had returned to something approaching normal. He found the airship's captain and gave the order to lift off. His second clung to him slavishly, waiting to be given an order—a fresh annoyance that made him again regret losing Baliscom. But allowances were necessary, so he put his annoyance aside. He gave the man a few tasks to carry out and went forward to stand with the watch, searching the landscape ahead.

They had been able to pinpoint approximately the direction of and distance to the stolen airship from the last signal emitted by its diapson crystal shard. If they maintained course, they should be able to intersect it. But sharp eyes were necessary so as not to pass it by, and lookouts had been placed forward to port and starboard and aloft on the main mast. They flew at a steady pace, erring on the side of caution, but Darz was growing increasingly anxious as no sighting was called out.

When the call finally did come, they almost missed it anyway. The airship was buried amid a series of hillocks and clustered boulders off to one side, down in a depression where its shattered ruins could not be seen even when you were almost on top of them. It was the lookout on the mainmast that finally caught sight of the wreck and brought them around.

They swarmed off their vessel armed with heavy weapons, half expecting to find themselves under attack the moment they were on the ground. Even with the airship crashed and beyond repair—having sustained the sort of damage that made the possibility of survivors unlikely—the Federation soldiers were hesitant to expose themselves. Fero Darz was cautious, as well, if for a different reason. Paxon was smart and resourceful. If he and any of the others had survived, their first priority would be finding a new airship. Darz didn't fancy handing over his own through lack of attention. So he left the ship's captain and crew aboard with a contingent of guards, their orders to lift off instantly if they came under attack. The airship was not to fall into Druid hands. Besides, they could provide better support with their rail slings and flash rips from the air than they could by staying on the ground.

The search party spread out in small groups, front and rear guards working in teams, ready to provide assault and support fire should anything be lying in wait. But it became clear almost immediately that the area was deserted. After searching, they found a pair of graves and tracks leading off across the grasslands to the north. Darz called up one of his trackers to have a look. After studying the surrounding area, the man estimated there were seven or eight in the party, with at least two Trolls among them.

Darz nodded. He had them. The Druids were on foot in the middle of nowhere. They could not have set out more than an hour or two earlier. It would be a simple matter to track them from here. They would be brought to bay before the day was out.

Again, he experienced a twinge of regret. Doubt had wormed its way into his mind to the point that he could no longer dismiss it. He did not want this to end the way he was almost certain it would. Paxon and the Druids would not give themselves up. They would stand and fight. And if they all went down, any chance for a working relationship between the Druids and the Federation would go down with them.

But he was a soldier, and his duty was to carry out his orders.

"Allett," he called to his second. The other came running up. "Have the handler release the oketar from their cages and brought up from the hold. We're going hunting."

I I

SHORTLY AFTER SUNRISE, LEOFUR FOUND IMRIC CORT
waiting for her at the elevated landing platform just off the
north tower of the Keep, his gear stacked around him, his
face bathed in shadow and wreathed in dissatisfaction. She wasn't sure
what was troubling him, but it was clear he was unhappy. Carrying her
own backpack and weapons, including a chopped-down Arc-5 flash
rip that could stop a koden, she walked up to him and smiled.

"You don't look very happy. I thought you wanted this."

He nodded. "I do. I'm just not sure I want it for you."

"You seemed all right with it yesterday. What's changed your
mind?"

"Thinking about it some more. Considering what's at stake. Realizing I was giving more weight to my longing than to my conscience."
His bleak countenance tightened further. "I made sure I told you all
the things that you should be worried about, but I find myself wondering if I should have let it go even this far. Maybe I should have
stopped it sooner."

She faced him squarely. "It's a little late for that. Besides, I had as
much to do with it as you did. You committed to something I asked
you to commit to, so there's no point in second-guessing the matter
now. The agreement was freely made, and I don't want to revisit how
we got there."

"That's part of the problem. You are too eager. You seem capable enough. You seem committed. Everything I told you yesterday that I liked about you was true, and I stand behind it still. But the fact remains you just don't know what you're getting yourself into."

She dropped her gear, moving to within arm's length. "Then maybe you had better show me. I won't learn any more until you do."

He gave a deep sigh. "That's about what I expected you to say. All right. Let's begin by testing how things will be once the tether is in place. But not here, in front of anyone curious enough to wonder what we're doing. Let's go back to where we have to begin our search—to where Chrysallin Leah was snatched."

So they loaded their gear in the storage bins located at the rear of a little snub-nose—a hybridized version of the usual two-man flit, though somewhat wider and shorter, with both seats located forward rather than one behind the other. This configuration allowed for more effective searches in territory where you wanted one man's eyes on the controls and another's on the ground you were passing over. With this vessel, the nose narrowed down to allow just enough room for both the pilot and a passenger to sit as far forward as possible with clear views in three directions.

Leofur had seen these before but never flown one. Since she would be piloting the craft—Imric was untrained in the flying of airships—she took a few minutes to study the controls. She had been a good pilot before she met Paxon and had become a much better one since. He had taught her a great deal more about airships and flying than she had known previously, so it didn't require much time for her to take the measure of this new craft.

"Ready," she announced moments later, settling into her seat and waiting for Imric to do the same.

In minutes they were lifting off and flying out over Paranor's walls and into the woods beyond. The sun was just coming up, a silvery light on the eastern ridge of the Dragon's Teeth. West, the sky was still dark, the night's departure slow and reluctant.

"You seem so calm about this," Imric said as they passed beyond the Keep. His strange eyes were fixed on her.

"About flying or allowing myself to be tethered to you?"

He hesitated. "I meant flying, but now that you mention it . . ."

She laughed. "Calm on the outside, maybe. Good thing you can't see what's happening inside."

Though, of course, if all went well, he would be soon.

It took them only minutes to reach their destination. Leofur set the modified two-man down smoothly, negotiating the very real dangers of branches and trunks and the twisting shadows that suggested obstacles not really there, and switched off the controls.

"Now what?"

Imric climbed from the cockpit to the forest floor, and she followed. He stood looking around for a minute as if gaining his bearings, peering off into the trees, turning slightly from left to right as he did so. The woods were quiet save for birdsong, the dawn's new light pale and ephemeral.

He turned back to her. "What happens now is that we establish the tether. It requires a blood bonding and a few words of magic that I am empowered to speak. The Druids taught me to do this so I would always have a way to use my shape-shifting with some measure of control. For your purposes, you need only do what I tell you to. It's very simple, really. Once it is done, I will attempt a change and you will be able to see how it is with us tethered."

"Blood bonding?" she repeated.

"You have to let me cut your palm, then my own, and then we join hands for the speaking of the words. After that, it will be done."

She hesitated, suddenly aware of how much bigger and stronger he was than she. "How do we end it, if it doesn't work out?"

He shrugged. "The tethering requires two willing partners, so either can choose to end it. A simple thought, a verbal command, whatever seems best—that's enough to sever the ties. The danger comes from one or the other refusing to accept it."

"Is that what happened to the Druid who died? He hung on for too long?"

"She. Sarnya was a woman. I misled you about that. I don't know why. Perhaps because you are a woman, too." He looked embarrassed.

"Anyway, that was what happened to her. She believed she could save me. She was wrong. Or maybe she didn't care what it took. She refused to give up on me. She saved me at the cost of her own life."

"She was your lover," Leofur said suddenly, sensing it was true.

He shook his head at once. "No, she was infatuated with me. She was enamored with the possibilities of what I could become. I was more a project than a person to her. She was very analytical and very ambitious, and she overreached herself. I warned her, like I am warning you. Be careful."

Leofur permitted herself a small smile. "You are not a project to me. You are a man who represents the best hope I have for saving my friend. But I take your meaning. I will keep my head."

"Then there is nothing more to say. Hold out your hand."

She did so without hesitating, offering her left so she could keep her right—her fighting hand—undamaged. He took it gently, turned it palm-up, and produced a long knife from a sheath at his waist. Without asking, without preliminaries, he ran that blade across her skin and drew blood. Then he did the same with his own hand, and joined the two in a tight grip. She could feel the mix of pain and blood mingling as he did so, almost as if both his and hers were the same. Then he began to speak, the words unfamiliar to her, the cadence not quite a chant or song, more a prayer or pleading. She watched his face, saw his eyes close, and when he finished felt a sort of warmth spread through her body, originating in and emanating from him.

For a moment, she closed her own eyes, compelled to do so by an urging she did not understand, and in the ensuing comfort of darkness she felt herself being drawn to him, into him and through him, so that bits and pieces of who he was became suddenly revealed. His fear for her surfaced in a black cloud. His sharp, almost poignant need to use his shape-shifting abilities whispered softly. His feral nature, submerged until now within his human body, stirred and woke with hungry anticipation. But likewise, an innate kindness toward and kindred feeling for creatures great and small blossomed, as did his love of fruit, strong ale, and breads, and his deep commitment to promises made and responsibilities assumed. All were unexpectedly revealed to her.

Then her eyes opened, and he was staring at her. "Did you feel it?" he asked. She nodded wordlessly. He nodded back. "Then it's done."

He released her hand and gave her a strip of cloth to bind her wound. She tried to determine how much had changed within her, but there was nothing tangible to hold on to. The momentary feelings she had latched on to before were absent now. She was back to being herself with no recognizable indicators of anything out of the ordinary beyond the pain in her hand.

"I don't seem to—"

"You won't feel anything right away," he interrupted her quickly. "Not ever, really, unless I make a change and willfully link myself to you afterward. It is a melding that requires offer and consent. I cannot explain it, but you will recognize it when it happens."

"Which will be when?"

"Shortly. I will make a change now, and you will experience for the first time what it means to be tethered. Are you ready?"

She felt irritated by the question. "Of course."

It happened much faster than she had anticipated. Without giving her a chance to object, he stripped off his clothing and stood naked. Then he stepped away from her a few paces, closed his eyes, and a visible shudder ran through his body. He seemed to disappear into himself in those few moments, as if his conscious self was suddenly buried too far down to reach.

Then his body began to change, the man becoming a large bird— a creature with wings that spanned six or eight feet with eyes as sharp and black as obsidian and claws as wicked as hooked knives. One moment he was there, a whole man, and the next he was a nightmare rendering of a war shrike.

She took a quick breath in spite of herself. The change was breathtaking, but frightening, as well. She could feel the sensations that poured through him, the ruthless aggression of the war shrike lurking right behind his thoughts, almost overpowering them. Then, within her mind, he spoke to her.

That was much easier than I thought it would be. Are you hearing me?

She nodded. How clear his voice was! How savage the beast!

This is how it will be for us each time. You will hear me in your mind only. Now try speaking to me the same way.

She took a deep breath, composing herself, focusing on Imric and not the shrike. *That was astonishing!*

It is who I am. And good, we can communicate. Now stand where you are and look off into the distance. Not at anything in particular, just into space. In a few minutes you should be able to see what I am seeing. You will still be aware of what's happening around you, but you have to keep your attention focused mostly on me if we are to share visions. Ready?

The sharp bird eyes stared at her, their fierceness battering at the edges of her mind. She nodded.

The war shrike lifted off, soaring above the trees and disappearing into the sky. She watched for a minute, then shifted her gaze to a point ten feet in front of her, looking at nothing in particular.

Seconds later she was somewhere else entirely, looking down from above the forests surrounding Paranor. She gasped in amazement. She was flying! In the distance, she could see the Keep, its walls and gates, battlements and towers. The newly risen sun was just beginning to light the shadowy corners of the Druid haven, spreading out across the canopy of the forests below it, brightening the woodland greens with golden light. Smaller birds flew through the limbs and down into the interior, their songs lifting skyward. Far away, just at the ridge of the Dragon's Teeth south, an airship was making its way west. A transport. Slow and ponderous, but clearly delineated.

She was seeing all this, but what mattered, what took her breath away, was how it made her feel. She was in the air, the same as he. She was a bird on the wing, just as he. She was experiencing, as he did, the thrill of being airborne, the joy of viewing what seemed to be an entire world and the immense and wondrous freedom of flight. It made her want to shout with pleasure. It filled her with such happiness she could barely stand it.

In that moment, she understood fully why he was so desperate to go back to doing what he had been born to do. How could he not be? She realized how difficult it must have been to give it all up. She saw clearly what he had been missing—both visually and emotionally. Her heart went out to him, and a new and unexpected respect for what he had abandoned blossomed.

Are you seeing this? Is it clear to you?

Yes! Oh, Imric! How wonderful!

A long pause. *Right now, at this moment, yes. But there is another side. Be warned anew. Stay objective.*

I don't know if I can.

I will help you. I will provide you with a small demonstration of the other side of these powers. Hold on.

He circled for a few minutes, sweeping across the treetops, looking down into the shadows and brightness, scanning for movement. His bird sight was clear and sharp, so much better than she had imagined sight could ever be. From hundreds of feet in the air she could see leaves on the forest floor. She could see twigs and stands of grasses and tiny holes.

At the entrance to one of those holes, she saw movement.

The war shrike's instincts surged to the forefront as it went into a dive, taking her with it, plummeting through gaps between the limbs, bursting through rays of brightness and bands of dark, a single-minded predator in search of prey. There seemed to be nothing left of Imric at all. She held her breath for the few seconds it took the shrike to reach the tiny rodent, snatch it up, and carry it away, squealing and wriggling helplessly.

In the tallest treetops, the shrike landed and began to eat the rodent while it was still alive. She felt the claws and beak tearing into it with savage joy. She felt the life go out of it. It died screaming.

The war shrike had been merciless. *Imric* had been merciless. They were the same; there was no difference between them once the change was made, his humanity submerged within the creature he had become. He was fully possessed by a war shrike's instincts and behaviors.

She understood his warning better now. She had experienced the entire killing and devouring through her senses, and there was a part of her that would never forget it. She could barely keep her sight affixed to his. But she managed, wanting to make certain she understood fully what it meant to make the change. She would not let herself look away.

Do you understand what it can be like to be tethered to me? His words swam out of the war shrike's mind, seeming disembodied. *Can you taste the blood and flesh in your mouth?*

Somehow, without actually being able to do so, she could. It was a deeply unpleasant bitterness on her tongue, but it was there. She tried to dismiss it, but she could not. Not quite.

I see what you mean.

Another pause. *Not yet, you don't. But you will.*

She had no doubt. She did not respond this time but simply stood there and waited for him to fly back to her. It took him almost no time at all. When she decided finally to experiment further, to glance away into the trees, fixing on a specific spruce to break the contact, her own vision quickly returned, supplanting his. Moments later, the war shrike descended through the heavy branches of the forest and landed off to one side of the clearing. It sat there for a moment, very still, its eyes fixed on her. Then, abruptly, it changed back again into Imric, still naked as his body lengthened and re-formed.

Eyes downcast, he walked over to his clothing and began to dress.

"It went well for you?" he asked her.

"Well enough. And you?"

He frowned. "As well as could be expected. It felt odd at first. And a little scary." He paused. "But good, too."

She tried not to look at him, but curiosity won out. She was desperate to know more, to understand everything. She thought she might see something different in his physique, something in the composition or form of his human body that was unfamiliar and would provide a clue to his shape-shifter nature. But aside from a few scars and one odd birthmark, there was nothing. She looked away as he finished, and if he had seen her examining him he gave no sign of it.

"So now you have a small experience with how it works," he said.

"Not as much as you would like, I'm guessing."

"No, but the rest will take time. And some of what you need to know will be better learned through personal experience. That was where I failed Sarnya. That was how I lost her. Whatever happens, I don't intend to lose you. So remember this. If I start to shape-shift too quickly or too eagerly, if the lure of shifting overpowers me and I lose all control, you have to act at once to stop that from happening. If you feel it coming on me or sense any failure in my self-possession, you have to bring me back to myself right away. You can do this by reaching out to me with your mind and with your heart. A physical rescue isn't all that's required. It must be emotional, too. It must be accomplished through an objective and impartial commitment to my well-being. You must not let yourself be caught up in the wildness that will have ensnared me. This is what happened to Sarnya."

He took a breath. "We share our feelings when we are tethered, remember. What is needed is for me to feel the intensity and strength of your will to bring me back, and I will respond. But you must be quick, and you must be determined."

"Is this even possible?" she asked. "If you are in the grip of your own wildness, out of control and caught up in this addiction to changing, what chance will I have to stop you?"

"A better chance than you think. I am tethered to you, remember. I am joined to you in a way to makes us a part of each other. We are, to a very great extent, one person. It will be like having my conscience whispering to me, telling me to come back to myself, to regain control. That is sufficient to break through to me. If it comes quickly enough, I will be all right."

Again he paused. "If not, you must break the tether. Immediately, if you sense I am not responding. In spite of the fact that you will find yourself reluctant to do so, you must let go. If you fail to do this and if in the throes of my shifting I am unable to release you, I will drag you so deeply into what I have become that you will be consumed. As Sarnya was."

She could see how it might have happened. She could visualize the moment when Sarnya realized he was at risk. She could imagine how her determination to save him overcame her good sense and drew her so far in she could not get back.

"I may be stronger than Sarnya," she said.

His face clouded with frustration. "I don't think you appreciate the danger. If you wait too long to break free, you won't be able to. Not because you can't, but because you won't want to. You will fall into the same trap as me. You will become obsessed by the feelings the shifting generates. You will want more, the same as me. All your promises to yourself and to me will vanish. The shifting is that addictive. You will want more and more, and you will end up like Sarnya did."

He made it sound far more ominous than she had believed it to be; the urgency and concern in his voice was evident. The shape-shifting, it appeared, could become a drug you had to have. Or if you were not a shifter yourself, one you had to experience. No matter the risk, no matter your good intentions, you needed it. She tried to imagine what that would feel like, and failed.

"So Sarnya was destroyed because she was not a shape-shifter. And you survived because you were?"

He nodded. "She lacked the protections that were mine from birth. I can recover on my own, given time. The danger is in what I do while I am caught up in the addiction. I am not able to help myself. I become the things I change into, and those about me are placed at risk. I can do terrible things and not be able to stop myself. One day, Aphenglow Elessedil told me, I might become lost entirely and descend into madness. I understood this. It was my fear of this possibility that brought me to the Druids. It was what I sensed was consuming me, drawing steadily closer with the increasing recklessness of my behavior. We had to stop it now, she told me, if I was to survive. I agreed. I knew she was right. Thus, the tether."

"But it didn't work."

"Not with Sarnya. So I took a vow of abstinence—a complete withdrawal to protect against the inevitable. No more shape-shifting. No more tethering. But it was a terrible price to pay. I was dying by inches as a result. I was longing for a return to my former self, to what I was born to be. I might as well have gone blind or stopped eating as given up shifting. I missed it every day. There was no succor to be found, no respite from the terrible emptiness, the deep sense of loss. I had no way to assuage that pain. When you came to me with your plea . . ."

He trailed off, gave her a smile. "It didn't work with Sarnya, but that doesn't mean it cannot work at all. She was the wrong person for me to tether to. You are a much better match. I have sensed it from the beginning, and every moment we spend together—especially after your reaction to my first shifting—tells me it will succeed. You are the right counterpart to my shape-shifter self. You are grounded in a way I am not. You know who you are; you found yourself a long time back, probably while you were still growing up. You had to, given the nature of your father. I require that steadiness. My weakness has always been in the lure of the shifting. I think maybe you can resist that lure. You will be able to hold me fast. In turn, I will find your friend Chrysallin, and help you return her to her brother."

"But what will happen if you do? What happens to you when this is over and you no longer have me for a tether?" She stared at him, already recognizing the truth of what it would mean for him. "You will no longer be able to change. Perhaps ever again."

"Perhaps. Perhaps not." He shrugged. "I am resigned to taking that risk if only to experience the changing once more before I die. Today confirmed the wisdom of my choice. I will trade those tomorrows for what time I can get if it means I am given back even a small taste of my freedom."

He smiled at the look on her face. "But don't let's get ahead of ourselves, girl. I knew what this meant when I agreed to help you. Just as you know now what it means to be tethered. Given that, does either of us think we should abandon the plan and go our separate ways?"

A part of her did. But it was a tiny part, and the greater part accepted that their individual needs outweighed the risk. He would have his shape-shifting back, at least for a time. She would retrieve Chrysallin and return her to Paxon. You were guaranteed so little in this life, and so sometimes you took what was offered even though you knew it might end badly. Imric had made that choice. She believed she must, too.

"If you are still willing, so am I," she said.

"Then the matter is settled. We'll leave at once. We'll fly south and have a look about the countryside. We need to find that camp I spoke of yesterday and uncover whatever traces remain of those who occupied it. After that, we will see."

She nodded wordlessly in agreement, but even as she did so she couldn't help wondering what she was getting herself into.

12

LEOFUR AND IMRIC BOARDED THE TWO-MAN AND lifted into the sky, the sun fully risen by now, a bright wash of gold in a cloudless sky. They flew south for several hours until they reached the stark, jagged wall of the Dragon's Teeth, and then turned east, parallel to its soaring heights. Imric offered no explanation as to why he was making this choice, and Leofur didn't ask for one. She had to assume he knew what he was doing or any chance she had of finding Chrysallin was gone. She concentrated instead on keeping the two-man as close to the treetops as she could, giving her silent companion every opportunity to find what he was looking for. They traveled slowly so as not to miss anything, and their tedious progress was made even more so by his refusal to talk to her. The few attempts she made to engage him were ignored. He seemed almost oblivious to her.

Or, she hoped, he was dedicating all his efforts to tracking Chrysallin and did not wish anything to distract him.

She let her thoughts drift elsewhere to help pass the time. She replayed in her mind the circumstances of her parting from Paxon just before he left for Arishaig. They had stood together in a secluded hallway no more than twenty feet from where he would mount the landing platform and set out. They had held each other close, whispering as if afraid to break the surrounding silence.

"Please be careful," she told him. "Remember, you are of no use to the Druids if you are not."

"I know," he responded. "I am always careful."

"I need to say it anyway."

"And I need to hear it. Will you be all right without me?"

"I am without you most of the time anyway, Paxon. Even when you are here, you are always engaged in your work." She sighed. "I miss you so badly sometimes. And more so because I feel as if I have no real purpose in your life."

"That could never be true. I love you. You know that."

She nodded wordlessly. "But what does that mean to you? Being in love, to me, means having time to share together, and we have so little. I want you to *need* to be with me. I want us to be close in all the ways that matter."

He was silent then, thinking. She moved into him and wrapped her arms around his body. "I don't want to be alone. I want to be with you."

"When I come back," he said, his lips against her ear, "we will find new ways to be close. We will rededicate ourselves. I will stop working so hard and be with you more. I promise. Will that help?"

She accepted his kiss and his whispered words of love, and gave both back. Yet she remained afraid for his safety, and she wondered now, thinking back on those last moments, if she shouldn't be afraid for her own.

It was nearing midafternoon, the sun slipping steadily toward the western rim of the Dragon's Teeth, twilight no more than a couple of hours away, when after hours of saying nothing Imric stiffened suddenly and exclaimed, "There!"

He was pointing into a stand of scrubby pines in which huge boulders jutted from the earth like bones trying to break free of their grave, all spiky and sharp-edged. Amid the jumble, she saw what appeared to be a small wind-sail skiff, tipped on its side, its canvas down and its hull cracked wide.

She brought the two-man down in the closest open space she could find, which turned out to be several hundred yards away from the wreck. Alighting, they walked toward it. The terrain was rough and heavily overgrown—gullies and hillocks and rocky protrusions were covered with layers of scrub and brambles. It took them a long time and more than a little effort to reach their destination, and by then Leofur was bruised and scratched in a dozen places.

They stopped before they reached the skiff, and Imric placed a restraining hand on her shoulder. "Wait. Something isn't right."

They stood together while he studied the wreck and then did a short visual survey of their surroundings. She waited patiently, wondering what he saw that she didn't. Or perhaps it was something he sensed. Were his instincts that much sharper than her own? Did shape-shifters have innate abilities greater than those possessed by humans? She thought they probably did—after all, he had already hinted at it—so she let him take the lead.

He stepped away. "I want to get a better look, but I need to change forms. Wait here for me. Do not move until I tell you to."

Without bothering to remove his clothes, he began to shrink. In seconds, he had changed into a species of ferret or weasel, although not one she recognized. Long and sinuous and silvery, it slithered out from beneath the pile of clothing and disappeared into the brush. She waited a moment, then fixed on a point in space and linked to him.

She was immediately at ground level, tracking close to the earth through leaves and grasses and scrub, the trees so far above her they seemed lost in the clouds. The ferret crept forward, head snapping from side to side, its view changing so quickly she was left dizzy. She tried to keep up with its rapidly changing views and could not.

I can't do this, Imric. My eyes, or maybe my mind, won't focus quickly enough.

Never mind. Break the link. I will connect to you again when there is something to see.

She shifted her gaze to a tree, and her own sight returned. She tried to catch a glimpse of him, but the terrain was so jumbled she could not make out anything. So she waited, searching the landscape about her, listening for any foreign sounds, one hand on the flash rip at her waist.

Leofur.

She focused her eyes on the emptiness directly in front of her to link with him again. *I'm here.*

Tracks, leading east from the skiff. Several men, one woman. A day old, maybe a little more. I'm coming back to you.

So he had found a trail. How had he managed it? What traces had brought him here when there was nothing by which to read sign save air? She was still pondering the matter when the skiff exploded. One minute everything was calm and silent, and the next the earth erupted in flames and smoke. Rocks and clods of earth went flying everywhere, and the remains of the skiff hurtled skyward in a fiery ball. She dropped to her knees, covering her head protectively as debris rained all about her.

In the aftermath, she tried to link to him. *Imric!*

Nothing. She couldn't make the link work, couldn't see anything through his eyes. She looked around frantically, then tried again. His vision joined hers this time, a blurry smear that was feeble and unclear.

Where are you?

Still nothing. She fought to make sense of the smeared images, of the brief images of ruined terrain she had seen through his eyes. But there was nothing distinctive to latch on to; he could have been anywhere. She tried to sense if he was hurt or not, but his thoughts were opaque and his emotions locked down. What had happened? Had he caused the explosion?

She climbed back to her feet and began to move—in spite of his warning to stay where she was. She had to. He might be hurt, perhaps seriously. He might be unable to come to her. So she would have to go to him. She would search for him as best she could. Maybe at some point he would reach out to her again. He didn't seem unconscious, so maybe he was just stunned. She pushed her way through the heavy undergrowth, hunting for him, searching everywhere as she went, trying to catch sight of his silvery ferret coat against the dark greens and browns of the forest floor.

By the time she found him, she was already halfway around the island of pines and rocks she had been skirting, having kept a wary distance from the debris even though she did not think there would be another explosion. He had returned to his human form and was lying sprawled on the ground amid clumps of saw grass and wild-flowers. She knelt beside him and felt for a pulse. He stirred as she did so and gave a low moan. There were blood tracks and raw patches at various places on his body where the skin had been burned away, but no obvious bone breaks or deep wounds.

His eyes opened. "I told you . . ."

"Stop," she interrupted quickly. "Don't say it. I was worried your injuries were serious. Are you all right?"

He sat up, held his head in his hands. "Mostly. The greatest injury is to my pride. In the old days, I would never have let this happen."

"What *did* happen, exactly?"

"A wire so thin I didn't see it until it was too late. It appears our quarry is reasonably sophisticated about laying traps and setting ex-plosive charges. I hadn't thought any wires would extend so far out, but I was wrong. You're not injured, are you?"

"No. Are you sure about yourself?"

He nodded, his lips compressing against a wash of pain. He combed back his lank, dark hair with his fingers. "Help me up."

She put an arm around his waist and got him to his feet. He was much heavier than he looked, his rangy frame muscular and taut. She held him in place, giving him time to regain his balance and shake off his lingering dizziness.

"I didn't mean to be naked so much of the time," he muttered, al-most to himself.

She laughed. "It's nothing I haven't seen before. But if you'd stayed a ferret, I could have carried you."

"I can't stay in any form but my own once I lose consciousness." He limped ahead of her. "Let's find my clothes."

They made their way back to where they had started, and as he was dressing he said, "I think the airship must have come down un-expectedly or it would have continued on to wherever it was going in the first place. Maybe the winds played them false. Maybe the power drained from their diapsons, or this flier didn't know his stuff. But he didn't intend to come down here, I'm pretty sure."

"How did you even know to look for him here?" she asked, still curious.

He glanced at her. "Oh, you mean what sort of special instincts do I possess that allow me to divine where people are going? None, in this instance. This was mostly common sense. Leaving Paranor through the Dragon's Teeth by the most direct route, unless you are going north, means going through the Kennon Pass. Winds are tricky at higher altitudes otherwise, if you try to fly out. And given that our pilot lacks those skills, he'd go through the Kennon. I just decided to search in that direction, thinking it was likely he would put his camp against the base of the cliffs in a sheltered space. I still think so. I don't know where that camp is exactly, but those tracks will lead us to it. He and his friends are afoot, so that's where he'll head. He doesn't think we can follow him. He probably thinks we're dead if he heard the explosion."

"So you were playing a hunch?"

"You don't think hunches are a good idea?"

"Kind of chancy when there is a whole country to disappear into. What if you were wrong?"

"How about this, then? Our kidnapper's path through the tree-tops, where he scraped several dozen branches trying to get out, revealed his airship's course pretty clearly. You have to assume he wasn't trying to lead us astray at that point, but that is an assumption I am willing to make."

She nodded doubtfully. "But how can you be sure about any of this since he crashed? Can you track his footprints?"

He shrugged. "We're about to find out."

They continued on to the airship with little conversation. Imric asked again if she was all right, apparently worried that she had somehow been injured and was keeping it to herself. Perhaps, she thought, because that was what he would do. His life of secrecy had shaped his character, and what he knew to be true about himself he probably saw frequently in others, whether it was there or not. He stumbled a bit as they went, and she could tell he was still not completely himself. But he seemed to get stronger, and by the time they had reached the two-man he was fully recovered.

"All right, then," he said, turning to face her. "Another change is required, which means we will have to tether again. I'm not sure exactly what's happened, and I won't know until we catch up with whoever made the two sets of footprints. I have to track them on the ground, and you have to follow me in the airship. We can't afford to leave it behind; we will almost certainly need it again before this is over."

"Do you think we can catch up to Chrysallin today? How far ahead is she?"

He shook his head. "I can't be sure it's Chrysallin we're tracking. Although," he added hastily, "I can't imagine it isn't. More to the point, I don't know the nature or identity of those who took her. At least one of them is pretty clever with explosives and traps, so I have to be prepared for the worst. I'm choosing a form that allows for that."

"What form will you take?"

"That's what I want to talk to you about. I need something that possesses both tracking and defensive skills—a big, strong creature that can run and evade, one with stamina and heart. A predator, in other words. I will change into a Parsk wolf."

She recognized the name. These were big, powerful animals from the deep Eastland, fierce enough to stand against a koden. They were named for the region that had birthed them, the Parsk Valley, deep inside the Rock Spur north of the High Bens. She had never seen one, but she had heard stories about how dangerous they were.

"You know of them?" he asked, seeing the look on her face. "Well, then, you understand the need. There is no better combination of tracker and fighter, no creature more suited to what we require than a Parsk wolf. But Parsk wolves are unpredictable creatures, and I have to be wary about losing control once I change. Its temperament and emotional instability may be too much for me. So you will need to keep close watch and bring me back at once if you sense anything at all going wrong."

"Not to question your judgment, but what if you're wrong about this? What if it turns out you can't control yourself once you change? What if I'm not strong enough to save you?"

He cocked an eyebrow. "But you are. I wouldn't be doing this otherwise. So now that you know what's going to happen, let's get on with it. We have to cover as much ground as possible before it gets dark."

Without waiting for her response, he stripped off his clothes once more and stowed them in the pilot box. Then he stepped away. "Climb back into the two-man and lift off. Once you're away, I'll make the change. No sense in taking chances."

"Imric, no, don't . . ."

But he waved her off, his features stiff and forbidding, his posture a clear indication that he was not interested in hearing further objections. She retreated to the airship, climbed into the pilot box, engaged the controls, and powered up the parse tubes.

Seconds later she was airborne, hovering thirty feet above him, watching warily as he prepared himself. He was standing there in the sunlight, scratched and bruised but somehow looking heroic. His willingness to put himself in peril was admirable if not necessarily wise. He clearly understood that this change carried special risk. To achieve what was needed to find Chrysallin, he was willing to gamble.

Or perhaps, she thought suddenly, he was actually eager for it. Without understanding why, she knew even as she completed the thought that she was right.

This shape-shifting experience was entirely different from the last. Before, it had been a more gradual, unhurried evolution as he changed from human to animal. Now it was more like an explosive reimagining. The muscles of his body rippled with an expansion of raw power, extrusions and disconnections ripping at him, bones and flesh and blood all re-forming in a whirlwind of pulsing fury. The Parsk wolf came alive in mere seconds. It surfaced with a vengeance as if desperate for life, as if escaping a cage.

Leofur, linked by the tether, was at the center of the change. She was infused with a strong sense of the Parsk wolf's predatory nature and savage instincts. She could feel its hunger, its urge to hunt, its willingness to kill. Its lean, muscular shape was a more proper fit for Imric's human form than the ferret's had been. Its formidable nature made it a suitable match for Imric's own. She sensed the comfort he experienced in this body. She sensed that this was a creature he knew intimately, one with which he instinctively bonded.

In every way that mattered, he *was* the Parsk wolf.

He was down on all fours now, the wolf form complete. His broad, shaggy head swung from side to side, gimlet eyes searching. He circled in a crouch, sniffed the ground, then began loping back along the path Imric had taken earlier to where the tracks of the crashed airship's occupants began. Watching him with a mix of excitement and horror, disturbed by his size and look and clear desire to hunt, Leofur followed. Engaging the airship thrusters, she cruised along behind him, staying safely overhead.

When they reached the tracks, the Parsk wolf began sniffing around, moving from place to place, its huge grizzled head lowered so close to the ground that at times its nose was pressed right up against the earth it searched. Leofur's own senses were filled with what the wolf was finding—smells that were raw and dark. Its eager response felt threatening, exuding menace and a potential for explosiveness, the promise of unleashing its raw, destructive power only a heartbeat away. Leofur was already sorry she had agreed to this. She understood the danger Imric was facing, and was convinced he should have chosen a less lethal form.

Still, it was too late for second-guessing. The wolf had picked up the trail and was trotting ahead through the brush and trees at a steady pace, all grace and power and dark intent.

Stay with me. Keep me in sight. The lure of this form is very strong, and I am hungry for the feel of it.

Shades! He was already succumbing.

Imric, stop there! This is too much for you! Change back! Find another form!

Her plea went unanswered. She tried again, and his vision cut away from her, the link broken. She tracked him as best she could, all the while trying to reestablish visual contact and never finding him ready to allow for it. She lost him eventually, found him again in a flash of black-and-gray fur for a matter of seconds, and then he disappeared for good.

She flew on, doing her best to hold her course, to keep to where she thought he had gone, but blind for all intents and purposes to his progress. She could not shed the sinking feeling in her stomach, wondering if she had seen the last of him. This whole plan had been flawed from the start, weighted too much in his favor and too little in hers. He had used her. How, she was uncertain, but the feeling was there. The afternoon slipped into evening, the twilight a deep, rich purple as the sun slid below the horizon and darkness settled in.

By midnight, the sky was filled with stars, the forest below and the mountains to her left mere shadows in the darkness. She had just arrived at the deep, broad cut of the Kennon Pass when, from out of its dark reaches, disembodied and terrible, she heard his voice once more.

I have them.

13

IT WAS STILL AND MISTY WHEN MIRIYA SHOOK PAXON awake. He was deep in sleep, exhausted from the events of the previous day, his slumber a protective cocoon in which he had wrapped himself and from which he did not wish to emerge.

"Paxon, get up!" she hissed at him, the urgency in her voice apparent.

He opened his eyes and found her face only inches from his. "What is it?"

"We have to go. The storm is almost past and the rain is letting up. I know it's still dark, but I don't think we ought to linger."

He nodded. She was right of course. Miriya's instinct for self-protection was always front and center. She wouldn't have survived all the struggles she'd been through if it weren't. There would be Federation warships searching for them. Even if the storm had forced all nearby aircraft down earlier, they would be up flying again soon. If the Druids wanted to put some distance between themselves and their pursuers, and perhaps do a little something to throw them off their trail, now was the time to do it.

He climbed to his feet woodenly. "Did you sleep? What time is it?"

She gave him a look. "How would I know the time? And no, I did not sleep."

He thought she would offer something more, but then she turned away quickly. "I have to wake the others. Get yourself up, then get everyone organized. Tell them to pack what they need, but nothing more. We have a long way to go to reach any sort of shelter and the lighter the pack, the better. Don't drag your feet."

He smiled, thinking she had decided to take charge whether she realized it or not. He didn't mind. She was a Druid; he was there to serve her. She should take charge. He was already unhappy that Isaturin hadn't done so. But Miriya was a much stronger personality than the Ard Rhys, so it didn't surprise him that she was finally asserting herself.

"How long have you been awake?" he asked her.

Miriya shrugged. "I don't think I slept. I couldn't. I can't stop thinking about what happened back in Arishaig."

"Not much we can do about it now. We have to worry about finding a way back to Paranor."

"Yes, but that doesn't stop me from thinking about what's waiting for us. You realize, don't you, that whatever happens, the Federation is going to attack Paranor?"

Paxon stared at her. "You think it's that certain? That they have already decided?"

"Don't you? Those ministers and army commanders who are left, who were not killed at the conference, are among the worst of our Federation enemies. They will come after us. They will claim they want justice, but what they will really be seeking is to put an end to the Druids once and for all."

Paxon moved close and lowered his voice. "You think this is Arcannen's work, don't you?"

"Of course. This bears his mark. He conceived of it, and he carried it out. I don't know how he managed it, but he is responsible. Now go wake the others."

Paxon left her there, brushing off stray leaves and twigs that had blown in with the storm and cinching his sword across his back as he went. The big Trolls grumbled as they rolled out of their blankets, sodden and bedraggled and looking much more dangerous than usual. Dangerous enough, in fact, that Paxon suspected that if any of them were confronted with a fight, they would welcome it.

In short order everyone was packed and ready, and they were setting out into the darkness. The cruiser had not been provisioned when they stole it, and there was no water and only a little food. They were forced to leave their dead behind. Without an airship, they had no realistic choice. Carrying them afoot would have been impossible. They covered the bodies in shallow graves, knowing they were abandoning them along with their promise to bear them home, and wondering as they did so how long it would be before any of them were left behind, too.

"Are we heading north?" he asked Miriya, standing close so no one else could hear. "Can you tell?"

She shook her head. "I can't tell anything in this darkness. No moon, no stars, no sky, no landmarks, almost no visibility. Instinct tells me this is north, but who knows? I thought maybe you could tell me. I thought maybe you might have some idea."

He looked away. "Not as yet, I don't."

They were walking point. Behind them came Isaturin, Karlin Ryl, and old Consloe, and behind them the three remaining Trolls. The ground on which they walked was sodden and pocked with puddles and mud holes, some of them quite deep. Paxon worked hard to keep the little company on what solid or near-solid ground was available, but the effort slowed them considerably and limited their progress. He was furious with himself for losing the airship. He should have set down earlier. He should have ridden it out on the ground. He should have been smarter.

Well, that's what you did when things went wrong. You thought about what you would do if you had that second chance you would never get.

Miriya, who had moved away a step or two while they walked, moved back again. "I don't like how Karlin is acting," she whispered.

Paxon forced himself to keep from looking around. "What's wrong?"

"I'm not sure. She's not talking, for one thing. She nods and shrugs and listens to me, but she doesn't talk. That's never happened before. It's almost as if she can't. And she's . . ." Miriya hesitated. "She's not very affectionate. She doesn't seem to want to be . . . touched."

She shook her head in reproof and exhaled sharply. "Let me try that again. It doesn't sound right when I put it that way. It's like, if I put a hand on her or try to hug her, she shies away. All I want to do is reassure her that everything's fine, but she won't allow it."

"Maybe she's still bothered by what happened in Arishaig. The Sleath got right up against her when it disintegrated. Maybe it infected her in some way. Maybe it damaged her."

"I've been thinking the same. I even asked her about it. She wouldn't answer me. Just shook her head and stopped looking at me. It's almost like she's ashamed or maybe frightened to say anything. I hate it, Paxon. I feel like I'm losing her, like she's going away and I'm not doing anything about it."

"You want me to try talking to her?"

"It couldn't hurt. Maybe you will see something I don't."

"I'll give it a try. Later, when we stop to rest."

Later was a long time in coming. The trek was endless, even after the darkness faded and the sunlight returned—a pale, diffuse glow through layers of still-dark clouds. The brightness was enough to better illuminate the path ahead, but still did not give them any real idea of what waited in the distance. The one thing it did confirm was that they were indeed walking north, if slightly east in the process. At one point in their march there was enough of a clearing to the west to reveal a series of broad escarpments of varying sizes. Paxon stared at them, trying to make sense of what he was seeing.

"That's the Prekkendorran!" Miriya declared, coming back to where Paxon was now walking with Isaturin. "We're way south and east of where we should be. That storm must have blown us off course and back the way we came! Shades, Paxon! We've got miles to go to reach the Duln. Or anything else but this scrub country."

She was clearly incensed, and truth be told he wasn't particularly happy, either. He had assumed they had gotten well north of the Heights and needed only to push on a short distance to reach the forests of the upper Southland. But given what he was seeing, they weren't even very far from the city of Dechtera, which meant that Federation air and ground forces could reach them easily.

We are going to need a miracle to escape now, he thought.

They pushed on, the trek becoming a slog. Old Consloe was failing, his limited strength close to exhausted. One of the Trolls stepped up to help support him, but it was clear the entire company was going to have to move at a slower pace if they were to stay together. The terrain about them failed to improve, remaining sodden and uneven. Water was pooled everywhere, the ground too saturated to absorb it. At least the air was dry, the rain ended, and the winds diminished. But now the temperature had dropped, and their damp clothing was chill and slick against their bodies. Worse, to the west, a fresh storm was building.

When they stopped next to rest, Paxon moved over to sit beside Karlin. He smiled at her, nodded a greeting. No response. She barely looked at him.

"How are you holding up?" he asked.

Nothing.

"We're worried for you. Miriya is worried. You look as if maybe you're having a problem. Is there something we can do? Can we talk about it?"

Her lips compressed in a tight line and she looked away. Her dark, slender features seemed pinched and her pallor was unhealthy. She was small to begin with, but now she looked so diminished she might have been drained of life. Her eyes were luminous and haunted.

Something was clearly wrong.

He gave her a moment more. "Thank you for helping me with my injuries after the crash. You have healing skills as well as the sight. I didn't know that. Who did you study with?"

She gave him a long, slow look, then rose and moved away. All without speaking a word.

He waited until the members of the company were on their feet and moving off again before he caught Miriya's eye. She moved over at once to walk next to him. "What did you find out?" she asked, keeping her voice low.

"Nothing more than you did. She won't talk. Not a word. She

barely paid attention to me. When I tried to press her, she just got up and walked away."

Miriya hissed softly and her jaw tightened. The frustration and anger in her eyes were palpable. "I don't understand it! She's just not like this. Not ever!"

He gave it a moment, and then said, "Allow her a little time. Maybe she's working through something. Maybe that encounter with the Sleath caused problems we don't know about. Just be patient."

Miriya looked at him and snorted. "You be patient, if you can. I can't. I'm in love with her. I need to do something!"

Then she dropped back and did not speak with him again. It was getting to be a habit with this company. He let her go without saying anything more, staying where he was at the head of the line, leading the way into the gray sameness ahead.

Earlier, he had worried about hiding their tracks, even knowing how impossible it would be to achieve with a group this large. But now he decided that the rains would do the job as well as they could. Not by obscuring their prints, but by leaving the ground so thoroughly saturated that fresh depressions were filled almost as quickly as they appeared. When he looked back—which he did several times, just to make sure—there was no sign of their passage. If the Federation was going to track them out here, as far off course as they were, completely away from where they intended to be, they were going to have to be lucky as well as good.

The hours slipped by. Twilight settled in. Paxon glanced at the sky. Another hour of light, and it would be pitch-black. They had to find shelter quickly, a dry place that would conceal them, but it was going to be hard to do that. There wasn't anywhere to hide in this flat scrubland, even where the rocks jutted from the earth in ragged clusters or deep gullies opened down into hidden depressions.

Isaturin moved up beside him. "We have to stop and rest for the night. Everyone is exhausted."

Before Paxon could respond, Miriya called to him from behind. "Paxon, come here! Now!"

The urgency in her voice was apparent. He glanced over his shoulder and found the warrior Druid standing helplessly next to Karlin Ryl, who had stopped dead in her tracks and was staring into space, muttering softly. He hurried back to them and leaned close to the seer to hear what she was saying.

". . . coming. Too many! Animals and men. Coming now . . . Flee them . . . Flee! They are . . . too many . . ."

He kept listening, but she just repeated the same words over and over. She seemed to be in a kind of trance, the sort of far-sight look that suggested she was in the midst of one of her visions. He stepped back, and at once she stopped speaking. He hesitated for a moment in case she resumed, but she didn't say another word or even look at them.

"What's wrong with her?" he asked Miriya.

"I don't know. She's had a vision, though. She thinks we are being hunted, and it appears that whoever it is, they've found us. If she's right, we don't have long before they catch up. We have to do something to stop them before that happens."

He glanced at the others. "I can't do this alone. Isn't there a magic of some sort that would slow them down? Or at least slow their hunting animals? If it's the Federation, they're probably using oketar."

For a long moment everyone was silent, each member of the party seemingly waiting for someone else to speak.

Then Isaturin, his voice soft but steely, said, "I think we will have to resort to smoke and mirrors."

A mile back, Fero Darz walked with the oketar and their trainer, after abandoning his bow watch aboard the Federation cruiser when the animals suddenly and unexpectedly became excited.

This was after almost a day of desultory sniffing and scurrying back and forth with no clear indication that they had found anything more interesting than an animal burrow. Standing at the bow of the airship and observing their apparent lack of progress, he had almost decided to abandon the effort in favor of a broad sweep across the terrain ahead, hoping to sight their quarry. But once the oketar started growling and snapping at the air, he had ordered the airship to descend immediately so that he could lower the rope ladder and hop down to join the hunt. Whatever was going to happen next, he wanted to be in the thick of it. He was never good at letting others do while he watched, and although he respected the trainer and his animals, he did not want to rely on them unless he was supervising. Better that he be right there when they found something. Better that he be able to decide on the spot what needed doing when they got close enough to act.

Now, seeing the oketar become increasingly eager, Darz was certain the end of the hunt was at hand. He had left word with the captain of the airship and Pas Allett that they were to wait for his signal before doing anything from aboard the ship, and under no circumstances were they to kill any of the Druids or their Blade unless it proved impossible to take them alive. They were to remember that these men and women were the only ones who could shed light on the reason behind the attack on the Federation ministers, or reveal the identities of those behind it.

He had faith that those under his command would carry out his orders—mostly because he had let them know, in no uncertain terms, what would happen if they disobeyed.

Darz was not a violent or intemperate man. In other circumstances, he would not have made threats like these. But there was a great deal at stake here, and he could not afford to have his soldiers ignore his orders. He certainly could not afford mistakes, or any form of spontaneous rogue behavior. He was still struggling with the idea that Paxon and the Druids were not to blame for what had happened and were as much victims as the Federation. Without knowing exactly who was responsible and why, he could not dismiss the possibility. And if things went wrong here, he wasn't sure he would ever be able to sort out the truth. He did not care to speculate on where that would leave him, or where it would leave the heretofore relatively peaceful relationship between the Federation and the Druids.

So while he was committed to performing his duty, he was also determined to discover the truth in the process.

He moved up to where the handler was calling his animals back so he could leash them. Already, they were beginning to stray, and no one wanted them to rush into something they were not able to handle. While tough and experienced, they were not fighting animals; they were just highly trained trackers. He did not want to lose them through precipitous action.

"What do they have?" Darz asked, coming close.

"A trail of some sort," came the answer. The handler did not bother to turn away from his task, snapping the links to his leashes on their neck collars. "They've had a whiff of their quarry all afternoon, but only now have they gotten a real taste. Whatever they've found, it's human and there's more than one. So I'd say we've got the ones we're searching for."

He snapped the last of the leashes in place. All three animals were straining against their restraints. "Come, Commander. We've got to hurry!"

They surged forward, the handler practically dragged by the oketar, Darz right on his heels. The terrain continued in an uneven carpet of brush and rocks riven with gullies and deep ravines. Behind them, the airship tracked slowly, staying in sight.

Ahead . . .

Darz stared. A heavy fog bank had appeared, thick with white layers, impenetrable. It hadn't been there a moment ago. Or had he simply failed to notice it? Instinctively, he slowed. But the oketar and their handler were pressing ahead eagerly, ignoring the fog, staying on the trail of those they were hunting.

Darz started to shout a warning, then stopped. He was being needlessly overprotective, he thought. He watched the mist swirl sluggishly, expanding and contracting. Was that even possible? It was almost as if it were a living, breathing thing. They were almost on top of it now, and he couldn't see anything beyond its leading edge.

"Do you see . . . ," he began.

But the oketar and their handler had disappeared and were gone.

Without hesitating, he followed. What else could he do? As soon as he was inside the fog, he couldn't see the airship. He felt like he had been swallowed whole.

Then he heard the oketar whimper like whipped pups. A moment later, there was silence. He called the handler's name. Nothing from him, either. He blundered ahead, weapon swinging left and right, ready for anything. This was a mistake. They had walked into a trap.

A moment later his leading foot bumped into the body of an oketar.

"Shades!" he hissed softly, taking a step back.

Now he could see all three of the animals, sprawled on the ground, unmoving. Their handler lay off to one side, equally still.

"Hello, Fero," said a voice from behind him.

A second later, everything went black.

14

I have them!

Imric Cort's words echoed through the dark recesses of Leofur's mind, a clear indication of his mood, a warning of what almost certainly was about to happen.

No, Imric! Stay where you are! Wait for me to reach you!

My hunger is strong. Human flesh. I need to taste it. Talk to me. Tell me to stop!

She felt the sharp edge of his desperation pressing against her heart. She felt his killing instincts taking hold, his need to hunt consuming him.

This isn't what you want! Shift back to your real form. Make the change! Do not remain a Parsk wolf.

There was a long pause, his silence complete and seemingly endless. She waited, her desperation cutting deep, leaving her hopes for him in tatters.

Imric, listen to me!

I am afraid.

Don't be. I am coming. I am almost there! Strengthen the link between us until I reach you. I am at the entrance to the pass.

Changing robs me of my power. I will be vulnerable. I will be exposed. They will hurt me. They will see.

Stay hidden! Wait for me!

I must end it now. While I can. I must finish them. A few seconds is all it will take . . .

Imric, no! Don't!

But the link was broken, and he was gone.

"Imric!" she screamed aloud.

She couldn't seem to do anything properly where he was concerned. All his talk about how she was the right one, all his promises that she could bring him back when he needed it, that she possessed sufficient strength, yet this was the second time she had tried and failed to call him back. She might as well have been trying to leash the wind.

She turned her attention to the controls again, moving the thruster forward, sweeping into the Kennon Pass almost recklessly, all thought of caution abandoned. She had to reach him, had to try to stop him. Ahead, the canyon was a black wall, the sky so overcast that no light from moon or stars brightened the earth below. Her eyes were sharp, however, and well adjusted to the darkness by now, so she found her way easily to where the first flicker of firelight winked brightly in the distance. Their camp. But was anyone still alive?

She skimmed the valley floor, hooding the diapson crystals to diminish their power, searching for a place to land. She found one quickly enough. The floor of the Kennon was broad and open, allowing her to land almost anywhere she chose. She moved as close as she dared to the firelight without giving herself away, then brought the little craft down.

In seconds she had it secured and was out of the cockpit and hurrying forward, eyes straining and ears pricked. To her surprise, she could hear voices, so maybe everything was all right. She could smell cooking. She eased her pace, shifting into a crouch as she got close enough to see figures moving about and hear the words they spoke. Men. A handful of speakers, their dialect identifying them as Southlanders, perhaps from the eastern seaboard. They seemed entirely at ease, unworried and confident of their safety. They would not be so if they knew what was out there stalking them.

Imric? She said his name in her mind, into the blackness, trying to tether to him.

No response.

She looked toward the campfire. What should she do? Wait on him? That wasn't her way. She would do what needed doing without him. She was armed and she had the advantage of surprise. A few minutes' time and she would have what she wanted. He could catch up to her later.

Cradling the Arc-5, she walked directly toward the firelight and the men who were lit by it. She counted three, then spied a fourth off to one side. They were average looking, clearly hunters. Their rough, weathered faces indicated a life led outdoors. All were carrying long knives and two a couple of weapons she had never seen before. One weapon was a flat piece of wood bent at right angles and shaved to a narrow edge from inner curve to outer. The other consisted of a series of leather-wrapped balls attached to short cords. Both were cinched at the waist. She saw no weapons like her own. She clearly held the advantage.

"Evening," she said, stepping out of the darkness, her flash rip pointed their way.

Heads turned, surprise reflected on the men's bluff faces. A hint of fear showed in their eyes. "Who are you?" one asked. "What do you want?"

"I want my friend back. You took her from outside Paranor's walls. I was there. Where is she?"

Looks were exchanged. "We don't know what you're talking about," one finally said.

Almost casually, Leofur swung the barrel of her weapon toward the speaker and pulled the trigger. The explosive charge passed between his legs, close enough to set the fabric of his pants on fire before exploding into a fireball behind him. The man screamed in shock and anger and began beating at his pants where the cloth was burning.

Everyone else dropped back a step, aware that her weapon was now trained on them, its black barrel swinging from one man to the next as if searching for a suitable target.

"Let's assume I'm not stupid," she snapped. "Let's assume, instead, that I'm just really angry. Now where is my friend?"

"She's gone," another man said quickly. His sunburned features reflected menace and challenge.

"Gone where?"

"We don't know."

She lifted the barrel of the flash rip until it was pointing at his midsection. "I didn't hear you."

"Melis took her."

"Who is Melis?"

"You haven't heard of her? She hired us to snatch the girl. She told us to bring her here and wait until she came to fetch her. That's what we did. She's come and gone. Took the girl with her."

Another said, "How did you find us? We left no trail at all. How did you track our airship?"

Leofur wanted to tell them it was because they were stupid, but decided that would be getting off point. "You're lying. You couldn't have taken my friend so easily. She has the use of magic. She would have tossed you away like old scrap."

"Melis told us to be sure she was unconscious before we tried anything, then to gag her and keep her gagged so she couldn't make a sound," said the first speaker. "Said the magic was in her voice, and if she couldn't use her voice she was harmless."

"Where do I find this Melis? Where did she take my friend?"

Everyone went silent. "We don't know," the first speaker said.

Leofur nodded. "Your friend said that earlier, and you saw what happened to him. Do you want the same thing to happen to you? Maybe I should aim a little higher this time, say about there?" She pointed the flash rip at his crotch.

"You won't shoot," the speaker said, "and it wouldn't matter if you did. We can't tell you. She would know if we did. She would come after us."

"You should be worried about me, not Melis." Leofur moved a few steps closer and gestured with her weapon. "Better tell me what you know before you find out what that means."

Suddenly the fourth man, who was still standing well off to one side at the periphery of her vision, rushed her. She had moved too close to the other three. She swung the flash rip about, but another man charged in from the front and was on top of her before she could use it. She went down beneath him, thrashing and clawing. They stripped her weapon from her and tossed it aside. As she fought to get free, the rest of the men closed in.

"Not so tough now, are you?" the man on top of her said, hauling her to her feet and backhanding her hard across the face.

"What should we do with her?" another asked.

"Let's have some fun!" exclaimed a third eagerly.

But in the next instant a huge shadow appeared out of the darkness, an eight-legged horror the size of a carriage, a nightmare of clicking mandibles and glistening eyes. It scurried toward them and knocked them aside like toys before they could react. It pinned them to the ground and hovered over them hungrily. Even Leofur was terrified for a moment—an instinctive reaction to this monstrous apparition—before she reclaimed her wits sufficiently to realize who it was. She scrambled away from the screaming, squirming men and recovered her weapon.

Let them up, she said to Imric.

The spider backed away, but not far enough to suggest that any of them should make a run for it. Even so, Leofur said, "Stay down and answer my questions. Answer them in full and maybe you will still be alive when we're finished."

One man had buried his face in his hands. Another was weeping. "What is that thing?" asked the bravest of the four.

"A pet," she offered. "Now tell me where Melis is. Where did she take my friend?"

"All right." A quick, anxious gesture. "Just keep that thing off us. Melis lives in the Murk Sink, in the Wilderun."

"Where, exactly?"

"How would we know? She never invited us over for tea! Somewhere below Grimpen Ward, I think. It's all swamp. You won't be able to reach your friend down there."

She remembered it now, although she had only flown over and not gone down into it. A dismal, forested stretch of backwater and tangled roots that stretched for miles. She couldn't quite imagine how anything could live in it, but then she had no idea what Melis was like.

"So Melis must have been watching for weeks. To know where to send you and how to overcome my friend, she must have spent days watching. Is that what she told you?"

The man nodded. "Said she knew all about both of you. Said you never suspected she was there, so we could snatch your friend away once you were . . ." He trailed off.

"Out of the way, so I wouldn't interfere," she finished. "All done from the air, somewhere she knew we wouldn't be looking. But what does Melis want with my friend?"

"She didn't say. And I didn't think it a good idea to ask. Melis is a lot more dangerous than you think. You'll find out if you go after her. You and your pet."

Although he didn't sound convinced, casting a worried look over at the hovering spider. Leofur shrugged. "We'll see. Where's home for you four?"

The man shrugged. "Varfleet, mostly."

"Varfleet. You're on foot, right? I'll let you go if you promise to start walking and not stop until you reach the Mermidon. From there, get back to Varfleet any way you can manage. Or go anywhere, for that matter, so long as it doesn't involve going to Melis and telling her what's just happened. Because—now pay attention—if you've lied to me or you disobey me and go looking for her, I will come right back here with my pet and start tracking you. I will track you until I find you."

The man held up both hands in a warding gesture. "All right, no need to threaten. We've had enough of this business anyway."

"Just so you understand. Remember how easy it was to find you this time? My pet can find you anywhere. Look at him. Do you believe me?"

All of them nodded except for the one who wouldn't look up. He just whimpered a bit.

"Get out of here," she said, gesturing dismissively.

All four scrambled up, grabbed their few possessions, and bolted into the darkness of the pass leading south toward the river. Not one bothered to cast even a single look back.

She waited until they were well out of sight and the night had gone still again. *Cowards,* she thought. *Liars, too.*

"Okay," she said to Imric. "It's over for now. You can change back again."

Instantly he returned to his human self. She didn't bother watching. She didn't want to see what it looked like when he did so.

When he was fully re-formed, they stood together in the darkness staring off in the direction of the fleeing men. She glanced over at him. "I thought I had lost you when you didn't answer me."

His smile was surprisingly shy. "No, the opposite, in fact. You found me at just the right moment. Your voice kept me from acting on my animal urges. It stopped me from going on the attack and killing them all. I would have done so otherwise."

Imagining it sent a shiver racing down her neck. "It didn't feel like I did anything." She let a hint of her anger show in her voice. "You seemed to ignore me when I pleaded with you. You kept talking about your hunger."

"It was the wolf. The Parsk wolf is a very powerful creature once you become it. I knew this. I knew the risk when I made the change. The wolf was dominant. It kept me from saying more. But I stayed focused on not letting it take me over entirely. I did what was needed. Still, it required your help."

"I wish you would explain these things better before they happen. It's awfully hard to know what's going on."

"But now you see, don't you? Everything worked out. I was able to keep the Parsk wolf form and not succumb to its instinctual needs."

So she had been wrong about what had happened to him, she thought. He had managed, with her help, to control himself when it was needed. She must remember not to judge him too quickly in the future, to remember how difficult the shape-shifting could be sometimes. And he must remember she was still learning what to expect.

"That was foolish of you to go after them alone," he said finally.

"I thought I had no choice."

"Foolish, nevertheless."

"Why didn't you answer me when I called you?"

"You caught me mid-change. Things are always muddled when that happens. Your words were garbled. I came as quickly as I could."

"It was quick enough, I guess." She looked at him. "Do you think my warning was sufficient? Will they try to warn this Melis?"

"I doubt it. Look at how they talked about her. They're terrified of her." Imric paused. "What's going on here, Leofur? With your friend. What's this all about?"

"I don't know. I've never heard of Melis. As far as I know, Chrysallin has never been to the Murk Sink. Or even to that part of the Westland."

She wondered again if whatever was happening might have something to do with her father, but if he was waiting for them in Murk Sink, she would find out soon enough.

"How was my timing back there?" Imric asked as they walked back toward the two-man. "Even though you didn't actually call for me and clearly didn't need my help . . ."

"All right. I admit it. I was foolish." She grimaced. "I was careless. Thank you for coming so quickly."

"You're welcome." He smiled. "I appreciate you saying so."

"Well, I owe you for that."

"You owe me nothing. You brought me back from the brink of losing control. If you hadn't, I would have torn into those men and we would never have found out anything. I wanted that very badly. I could taste their blood; I was hungry for their flesh." He glanced over. "I'm sorry. I know this makes you uncomfortable, but I think you need to understand what it's like when you change forms. When you become another creature, you become more than its shell. You become the whole animal. You become infused with its life. You don't get to pick and choose which parts you will adopt. You have to embrace the whole, and do what you can to keep it from overpowering you. That's not always an easy task."

She understood. She saw how hard this must be, a foreign creature's habits and needs and urges and behavior pushing for dominance against the human part you somehow had to cling to. She remembered feeling the fury of both the war shrike and the Parsk wolf battering against the tether. How different this was from her father's ability to take another form! Arcannen could use his magic to create the *appearance* of being another without actually taking on any of the emotional or behavioral aspects.

All something Imric Cort could never manage.

"I stand by what I said when we set out," he continued, not looking at her. "You have a strong sense of self, a certainty of identity that I have never had. For me, becoming other creatures has always been normal, and that makes it just that much harder to come back to my birth form. You don't have that struggle. You know exactly who you are."

Do I? she wondered. *It doesn't feel that way. It feels like I am drifting, searching for identity and purpose both.*

"I'm doing my best to learn about shape-shifting," she told him, "but it is a difficult education, and I'm not as comfortable with it as you seem to think. It will help me if you remember to tell me more about what to expect before you change. I can't learn by intuiting the results. And I can't keep educating myself through personal experience. Sooner or later, that's going to go badly for both of us."

They were at the airship now, and he found his clothes in the pilot box and began pulling them on again. "I'll try my best." He caught her looking at him. "I'll also try not to be naked so much of the time. I'm not the world's most beautiful specimen, after all."

She laughed. "Oh, you'll do well enough. Besides, I'm getting used to it."

He nodded without looking at her. But something in the way he did so and then turned his back on her further suggested he was troubled by her response.

A strange man, she thought. He hid so much about himself. Even the Druids seemed very much in the dark. She had never heard any of them even speak about him before Oost had mentioned him.

Paxon never spoke of him. It was as if Imric hadn't existed before she met him. It was difficult to know if his secluded life at Paranor was by virtue of his circumstances or by deliberate choice.

It made her wonder how much he was hiding.

It made her wonder if she would ever find out.

15

PAXON LEAH TOOK FERO DARZ BY THE SHOULDERS and pulled him away from the bodies of the oketar and their handler and through the magic-induced mists created by the Druids. None of them was dead or even injured; they were simply unconscious. In the neighborhood of another twenty minutes, they would all be up and functioning.

The oketar, of course, would sense that being in the mist was the cause of their problem and that staying one second longer was a very bad idea. They would bolt back toward the airship instantly, and their handler would have no choice but to follow.

Fero Darz was a different matter. No one had planned on his appearance, thinking him still back on board the approaching airship. But now that he was here, Paxon decided to find a use for him. If Fero failed to return, his entire command would have to decide whether to come looking for him in a place where men and animals disappeared. Their enthusiasm would not be high, and their assigned purpose would suddenly be thrown into doubt. Who was authorized to give orders at this point? What was the best course of action? Further searching for the Druids would likely seem ill advised—especially when it was discovered that flying over the wall of mist or skirting its edges was impossible, or would be for a while, at least. Leaving Darz would be painful, but wasn't it smarter to fly back to the command post at Dechtera for reinforcements?

That was what Paxon was hoping for. But at the very least, there would be discussion and dithering, all of which would give the Druids time to slip farther away while darkness continued to descend with the close of the day. If Paxon could get his little company a few miles off, he would have a chance of hiding them for another day.

It wasn't the ideal situation, but it was what he had to work with.

Besides, having Darz as his prisoner gave him not only bargaining power but also a chance to talk to the other about what he believed had really happened in Arishaig.

He pulled Darz all the way clear of the mist and onto open ground where the Druids were putting the finishing touches on their magical handiwork. The mist would respond to those approaching, rising to impede their airship and spreading out to prevent any effort to skirt its edges. It would do this for at least the next hour before its energy failed and it faded away.

"Who have you got there?" Isaturin asked, walking over.

"Fero Darz," Paxon answered, permitting himself a small grin.

"Darz?" Miriya spat. "What's he doing here? What were you thinking, Paxon?"

Paxon could feel the anger radiating off her. He forced himself not to respond. "Well, I was thinking that at some point we're going to have to persuade the Federation that the Druids aren't responsible for the deaths of their ministers and soldiers back in Arishaig. The Commander of the Ministerial Watch, as the only one left alive who witnessed what happened, would be a good person to start with. This way, we have time to talk to him about it, maybe persuade him of our innocence. Also, without his leadership, maybe our pursuers won't be quite so quick to come after us. Cut off the head . . ."

"Let him alone," Isaturin said to Miriya. "Paxon is right." Signaling for one of the Trolls to pick up Darz and carry him, Isaturin added, "We need to go."

Paxon was already searching the terrain north and east for passage, trying to discover the route that would best hide their tracks from their pursuers. When he started walking, Miriya fell into step beside him.

"Don't mind me," she said quietly. "I'm just upset about Karlin."

"Not any better?"

"No. We need to get her to a healer and have her examined."

"We need to find someplace safe, first," Paxon said. "I just hope you're not mistaken about how the mist affects the oketar."

She gave him a look. "I've worked this particular magic before. The mist will stunt their sense of smell for twenty-four hours, maybe longer. They won't be able to track us until after that. Either the Federation will bring in different animals or hunt us without. But how far can we get in that time?"

Paxon shook his head. "Far enough, I hope, that they can't find us. But it's asking a lot."

They trudged on, the endlessly unchanging landscape giving the impression they were making no progress at all. The wall of mist disappeared behind them, and no pursuit showed itself. Paxon had chosen to angle to the northeast in an effort to disguise their direction. He still wasn't certain where they were in relation to the Duln, only that they were much farther east of the Prekkendorran than he had hoped, and miles from any real cover.

They were perhaps half an hour into their march when Paxon heard a familiar voice. "Would it be asking too much to have your Troll put me down?"

Fero Darz was awake.

Paxon glanced back, past the other members of the party. The Druid Guard carrying the Federation commander had come to a stop and was awaiting instructions. "Set him on his feet," Paxon said.

He walked back to Darz and faced him. "You are free to walk with us so long as you stay quiet and don't try to run off. Once you do that, you will be bound and gagged and carried again. Understood?"

The other man nodded. "What happened back there?"

"Come up front with me, and I'll tell you while we walk. But remember what I said."

They moved to the head of the company and Paxon again began

leading the way. "The Druids conjured a mist that rendered your handler and the oketar unconscious. Then you blundered in and went down, too. I decided to bring you with us. I wanted a chance to explain what I think happened back in the Assembly."

Darz gave him a disgruntled look. "I know what happened. I was there."

"You *think* you know. You only know what you saw, but that doesn't tell the whole story. Now that we have time to talk about it, maybe I can make you understand."

"You don't have that kind of time, Paxon. My men will be up and tracking you again before long. They probably already are."

"Well, they'll be doing it without the oketar. The mist took away their sense of smell, and they won't get it back for another day. You got something else that can sniff out our tracks?"

Darz gave him a look. "They'll track you from the air. We'll find you."

Paxon shook his head. "I don't think so. But for the sake of avoiding a lengthy and pointless argument while we wait to find out, let's review what happened back in the Assembly."

Darz rubbed his face and ran his fingers through his hair. He looked rumpled and decidedly lost. "All right. Make your point."

"My point is this. You can't seriously tell me you don't have doubts about whether we were behind what happened. I even warned you that your security precautions were a concern. I fought to stop that thing myself. So did Isaturin and Miriya. If you really did see what happened, you saw that, too."

He was angry by now, and he let it show. Darz was quiet for a time, clearly thinking things through. They continued to walk through the gully-riven terrain, skirting clusters of boulders and sinkholes. Paxon wondered if he should start thinking about shelter; there were already signs of a fresh storm rolling in.

"I'll admit to some doubts," Fero Darz said. "The evidence says this is your doing, but I can't come up with a good reason for why you would do it. There doesn't seem to be anything you would gain by killing off a delegation of peace negotiators—not when you're the ones seeking to put a peace agreement with the Federation in place. But I still have to answer to my superiors."

"I understand your position. But we need your help to convince the Federation. There's no good reason for the Druids to have killed off the Prime Minister when he was so close to Aphenglow Elessedil and is now working on an equally strong friendship with Isaturin. Why in the world would we want to disrupt that friendship by killing off our strongest Federation ally?"

Darz glanced over. "But you think you know someone who might have wanted exactly that?"

"Don't you?"

The other nodded. "Arcannen Rai. We haven't been able to track him down, and he knows we won't give up. Causing a war between the Druids and the Federation would suit his purposes just fine. Distract us from him, give us something bigger and potentially more far reaching to deal with."

"That's my thinking, too. Arcannen Rai. He hates both of us equally."

Ahead, the land was undergoing a change. The rain-carved flats were giving way to hills and ridges, the land beginning to slope upward toward what appeared to be the distant outline of huge mountains. Paxon had been watching this landscape materialize in a distracted sort of way, concentrating on his arguments with Darz. But now he took a closer look, realizing what he was seeing. So much for his thoughts of stopping.

"Isaturin," he called, bringing the company to a halt.

The Ard Rhys moved forward to join him, his face dark and impatient. "What is it?"

Paxon pointed. "Those are the Ravenshorn. That storm blew us all the way east of the Duln. I can't be sure, but from estimating the distance to those peaks, I'd say we are somewhere below the Battlemound, more east than west. What do you want to do?"

"What do *you* want to do?" Isaturin countered. "You're the one leading us home."

Paxon considered. Off to one side, Fero Darz shook his head in a gesture of disgust. Clearly, he thought Paxon and the Druids were in over their heads. Paxon took Isaturin's arm and steered him away from Darz and out of his hearing.

"I think we should continue east until we sight the forests of the Lower Anar. There's nothing much between here and there. Certainly no towns large enough to have airships. If we can reach the Anar, we can find concealment. Then we turn north until we reach Culhaven. We can ask help from the Dwarves once we get that far."

The Ard Rhys shook his head. "The others are very tired, Paxon. I don't know how much farther they can go without sleep. Do we really need to keep walking?"

"If we don't, we'll have to sleep out in the open. If we're spotted, we'll have to defend ourselves. What sort of shape are we in to do that? The mist wall won't work a second time. They'll be expecting it. I think we have to keep moving."

Isaturin took a moment to think about it, looking off in the direction of the Ravenshorn. "All right, but we rest when it gets light. No arguments."

Paxon nodded. "I wish there was another way. I wish we could *go* another way. But nothing else makes any sense at this point. If we want to get home again, we have to get off these flats."

Isaturin responded by giving him a curt nod and walking away. Paxon watched him, puzzled by his abruptness. Then Fero Darz walked back over.

"Maybe you should consider turning yourselves over to the Federation. I would speak on your behalf, if you did that. The Druids have enemies within the Coalition Council, but they have friends, as well."

"And most of them are dead, killed in the Assembly."

"Still, I would stand up for you. I would find a way to persuade the others."

Paxon smiled. "If they were all as reasonable as you, I would be more willing to agree. For now, though, I have to consider how things might go if they got their hands on us while they are still convinced we caused all those deaths in Arishaig." He shrugged. "I guess what we really need is proof that what we claim is true. We need Arcannen."

"I wish you luck." Darz did not bother to hide his skepticism. "But no one has been able to find him, have they? Including you. So I hope you have a plan for changing that."

Paxon ignored him and started walking once more. Because there was no one else with whom he felt comfortable walking, Darz stayed at his side. It was fully dark by now, with storm clouds gathering in the west. The wind was blowing crossways to those clouds, however, so it appeared as if the storm might pass behind them. Paxon tried to estimate how far it was to the still-invisible forests of the Anar. It was difficult to know, but he thought that if they kept walking through the night, they might get reasonably close by morning. He knew how tired the rest of his little company must be. He was practically dead on his feet himself.

"Why don't you think about what you're doing?" Fero Darz grumbled next to him. "Maybe consider a new approach."

"Stop talking," Paxon snapped. "If you haven't got something constructive to say, don't talk at all."

They walked in silence. Paxon kept a steady pace for the next hour, casting regular glances back at the storm. It did not appear to be gaining on them. If anything, it seemed to be moving south, as he had hoped it might. The night sky had cleared overhead, but with no moon, traversing the rough terrain was a challenge. He thought he could see the low, dark outline of a forest ahead, running north to south. Maybe things were going to work out, after all.

As the night continued, conversation died and everyone began concentrating on putting one foot in front of the other. Their group began to stretch out into a single line, one member following another, heads down and eyes forward. Old Consloe dropped back until he was almost no longer in view. At that point, Isaturin ordered the Trolls to take turns carrying him on their backs and the march resumed.

Midnight came and went.

Paxon's thoughts strayed to Leofur. He wondered what she was doing, if she had received the news of what had happened to him. If so, she must be frantic with worry. He remembered his promise to come back safe. He was doing the best he could, but he knew the odds were against him. Worse, he couldn't get word to her about where he was or what he was trying to do. He was cut off from her as surely as if he were locked away in a Federation prison.

And Chrysallin? She was the more fragile of the two. She was the one most likely to be emotionally unsettled by not knowing his fate. Would she come looking for him? Would Leofur? They would want to, both of them; he knew them well enough to be certain of that. They would not sit back patiently and wait for his return—not if they decided that maybe he wasn't coming. But would they act on those impulses or would common sense prevail?

Then he had another thought, one so dark he could barely stand to consider it. What if he was right about Arcannen Rai being responsible for what had happened in Arishaig? If Arcannen had orchestrated the killings in the Assembly, was it such a stretch to think he might also intend to harm both his daughter and Chrysallin, if only to gain revenge for being thwarted twice before? Settling scores was an integral part of his character. That had been apparent with Arbrox and the Red Slash in their last encounter. Arcannen would never forget or forgive those who crossed him, and it was very likely he was already balancing the scales if he was behind the attacks in Arishaig.

Which by now Paxon was pretty sure he was.

All the more reason to get home to Paranor to make sure his sister and his life partner were safe.

He trudged on, aware of the many worries pressing down on him. But all he could do was to keep walking and hope things would work out. It was a poor solution to a complicated situation, but sometimes you had to take things as you found them.

They were nearing the dark line of the eastern horizon, close enough that Paxon could almost define what he believed to be the canopy of the Anar, when Miriya gave a small cry. He wheeled back to see her holding Karlin Ryl in her arms; the other had gone limp and unresisting. With her head thrown back and her mouth open, she was making a series of strange sounds intermingled with scattered words.

He went back to them immediately, asking the others to step back as he knelt down close to her. He was aware of Miriya at his shoulder.

"Karlin's having a vision," she said quietly.

". . . inside me, squirming . . ." A strangling sound, a gurgling. ". . . can't get it out, seeing . . . oh seeing . . . terrible, all gone, all dead . . ."

She broke off abruptly, her breathing heavy and liquid sounding, as if she were drowning. The seer did not squirm or try to free herself from Miriya's arms, but just let herself be held as she stared up at the sky, eyes wide open, mouth slack.

"What do you see?" Paxon pressed. "Who's gone? Who is it that's dead?"

A head shake, violent and sharp, as if something had latched on to Karlin and she was trying to shake it off. The others of the company exchanged glances, doubt and sadness reflected on their faces. Even the Trolls managed to convey their distress. Only Fero Darz revealed nothing of his feelings, his face expressionless as he watched.

". . . airship down, smashed, all lost . . ." Karlin was speaking again, her words so soft only Paxon and Miriya could hear them. ". . . storm winds took her . . . tore her apart . . . threw her away . . . with all aboard." A gasp, a small shriek. "Killed! All of them killed!"

Us, Paxon thought. *She's talking about us. Our airship brought down by the funnel, smashed to pieces, some dead, and the rest of us . . . What? Soon to be dead? Is that what she is seeing? Our future? We will all be killed?*

He leaned close, his hand touching her face gently. "Karlin, listen to me. We aren't dead. We are all here, all who crashed and survived. Is there something else that threatens us? Are we in danger?"

Her head jerked forward and her eyes fixed on him. She saw him clearly; there was no doubting it. She held his gaze, though her eyes were wide and staring, and her face stricken. For a moment it looked as if she would not speak again, her mouth a tight line, her lips sealed. But then she leaned toward him, her head shaking slowly from side to side.

". . . no, Paxon! Not us. The . . . Federation airship . . . pursuing, out there . . ." She pointed back the way they had come, gesturing for emphasis. Her pale face was suddenly calm, her gaze no longer intense, but so sad he could barely stand to meet it. "The . . . storm took them all, Paxon. They are . . . all dead."

The Highlander glanced hurriedly over at Fero Darz. He could tell at once that the other had heard. There was defiance and anger reflected on his face as he spoke. There was denial in his voice.

"No, she's mistaken! Or crazy! That's impossible! A Federation cruiser and its entire crew? No, I don't believe her."

But Karlin Ryl did not shrink away or speak even one word of equivocation. "All dead. There is no longer . . . a pursuit. There is no one left. No one."

Then she turned to Paxon again, and her look changed once more, this time to one so stricken and rife with sadness that the Highlander flinched in spite of himself. She was trying to speak, and he leaned close to hear her words.

"Help me, Paxon," she whispered. "Please, help me!"

16

NIGHT CREPT WEST, GIVING WAY GRUDGINGLY with the first tinge of dawn's silvery light in the east, and as it did so a strange mist surfaced ahead of the fleeing Druids. It was a brume formed of cool air and warm earth, and it swirled and shifted like a living thing. To those approaching, it seemed ominous. Fero Darz, walking apart from the others and still stunned by the seer's revelations regarding the loss of his ship and crew, found it especially disconcerting—enough so that he could not take his eyes off it.

He was walking by rote—walking because to give up and sit down would have been akin to admitting the hopelessness of his situation, and that he would never do. He could not believe the seer was right, no matter how certain she sounded. He could not accept that his soldiers—many of them from the Ministerial Watch command—were all dead. Pas Allett, irritating as he was, gone? The captain and crew of his heavy cruiser? Even the oketar and their handler? It was too much to take in, and the part of his mind trained to accept the inevitable rebelled at the very idea of it.

At one point, he even wandered back over to the main group, his Druid Guard shadowing him all the way, and fell into step beside Paxon.

"Could she be mistaken?" he asked quietly, walking shoulder-to-shoulder with the other.

Paxon nodded. "She could."

When he said nothing more, Darz added, "But you don't think she is?"

"Only because she hasn't been wrong before. When she has a vision, that vision has always proven true. So, no, I don't think she is wrong."

An irrational part of Darz wanted to blame Paxon and his Druid friends. They were the ones that had caused this to happen. By fleeing Arishaig, they had brought Darz and his ship and crew in pursuit. If not for that, there would have been no accident, no crash, and no deaths. Perhaps they had even done something with their infernal magic to cause that storm to seek out the ship and men and destroy them. Paxon's behavior didn't seem to suggest any of this, but what if Paxon didn't know about it? As the High Druid's Blade, he might be their protector, but that didn't mean they told him everything. Especially in this case, where it was apparent he was close enough to Darz to give away something of the truth, even by accident . . .

At this point, Darz squeezed his eyes shut against his foolish musings and stopped speculating. There was no point. The accident was nothing more than that—an accident. He must let go of it; he must put it behind him. He was alive, and he must still attempt to do his duty as Commander of the Ministerial Watch.

Especially when he coupled his continued doubts about what had really happened in the Assembly with his need to determine the truth.

But this heavy brume that, in the soft first light of morning, presented a barrier to their passage north disturbed him. It had brought back unpleasant memories of the Druid-conjured haze that had ensnared the oketar and their handler and, ultimately, himself. They were walking straight toward it—with no hesitation, no delay. No one even seemed the least bit concerned.

He glanced over at Paxon. For a moment, he hesitated. "Is this a good idea?" he asked at last.

Paxon glanced over. "What do you mean?"

"I mean this heavy fog. I don't like the look of it."

"It's only mist." Paxon looked away. "We're done with fighting, Fero. We just want to go home. Do you want to talk some more about what happened in the Assembly? Have you had time to think about what I said?"

"Time enough. You may be telling the truth—as you know it. But I worry there is more to this than the Druids are telling you."

"That could be. But I still think Arcannen was behind this. Or someone very much like him."

Fero nodded, looking anxiously at the mist, peering into its sinuous net. "Look, Paxon. Is something in there? What is that?"

Paxon looked where the other was suddenly pointing. He saw it, too. "I don't know."

What Fero Darz had seen was a series of bulky figures. They were big, vaguely man-shaped forms. They weren't moving, but there were a lot of them. With the mist shifting as steadily as it did, it almost gave the impression that they were shifting with it. Darz peered closer, trying to separate the mist from the figures. For a second or two, he managed it.

They were moving. Their arms were lifting.

"Paxon," he said softly.

"I see it," the other said.

Paxon held up his arm to stop the rest of the ragged procession, thinking this was all they needed—another distraction, another potential risk. Those bulky objects didn't exactly look like men, and probably weren't. But what were they? He peered closer, then took a few more steps forward. What was moving were arm-like appendages that seemed to be gently waving. But there were more than two attached to each figure, so these were definitely not men.

"Stay here," he told the others, and moved ahead.

He did not go into the fog, only close enough to its edges to get a better look. They were a species of plant, he saw. They had broad, bark-encrusted trunks rooted in the earth and supple limbs that sprouted from their upper regions. At the top of each trunk sat a low cone-shaped protuberance with a rippled surface and thin strands of moss. Glancing left and right, he found them rooted across their path in a seemingly endless array.

There were thousands of them.

He turned and walked back to join the others, uncertain what to do.

"What are they?" Fero Darz demanded.

"I can't be sure. They appear to be large plants, but they're nothing like the plants I'm familiar with."

"Do they seem dangerous?" Isaturin asked.

Paxon shrugged. "Everything living in the Battlemound is dangerous."

"Can we go around them?"

"Maybe, but it would take time. I think we have to find a way through them. They're spread out in front of us as far as the eye can see, blocking our way, but there are gaps we might be able to navigate. We just have to be careful. I don't think it would be a good idea to come into contact with them."

"We should just burn a path through them," Miriya snapped. "Why bother going around?"

"Because," Paxon said, drawing out the word slowly, "we don't know what they are or what they can do. And I would hate to find out the hard way."

Miriya grumbled under her breath and moved away to stand with Karlin. The latter looked pale and distracted, a mix of resignation and confusion on her face. She didn't seem to be aware of what was happening around her. She seemed to have her thoughts on something else entirely.

"We'll continue on," Isaturin declared, "but let's be careful. Lead the way, Paxon."

The Highlander nodded and started ahead. At once Fero Darz was beside him, leaning in. "I think this is a bad idea. I think we should go another way."

"Well, you don't get to decide."

"I think you should reconsider your choice, at least."

"Isaturin is right. We are all exhausted. We need to get back to Paranor as quickly as possible—and by the shortest route possible."

"Assuming that's the safest route."

Paxon gave him a look. "We don't have a safest route. At least, not one we know about. We have choices, but who knows if any of them is safe or not? Please drop it."

Darz went silent for a moment, but Paxon could tell he was seething. "Give me a weapon."

There it was, what the Commander of the Ministerial Watch really wanted. "I don't think anyone is ready for that. If there's trouble, just stay clear of it."

They trudged ahead, entering the wall of mist and finding themselves enveloped in a thick gray blanket that immediately obscured all sense of direction. No landmarks stood out; no paths offered themselves. They were in a maze. Paxon had chosen an entry point where the bulky plants were more spread out so that passage through their massed trunks was easier, but he had to work hard at maintaining his sense of direction. Within minutes, everything beyond the mist and the plants disappeared.

Behind him, the others bunched together, a reaction to their feelings of disorientation and confusion. The mist was creating its own world—a tight, claustrophobic morass. It was disconcerting—and even Paxon, who had some experience with situations of this sort, found himself gripping his sword more tightly than usual. His eyes and ears were tightly focused on his surroundings, straining to see and hear anything that suggested danger. But there was only gloom and silence and gently waving plant limbs.

Beside him, Fero Darz walked stiffly, his face a mask of anger and mistrust, his mouth clamped into a tight line. Paxon would have given him a weapon if he thought the other could be trusted, but he couldn't be sure what Darz might do. And adding another element of risk to this already risky flight was foolish. Better to keep him safely away from weapons. Better to let him be angry than dangerous.

The trek dragged on, and nothing about them changed. More gloom, more mist, more plants, and no end in sight. Paxon had to hope they were going in the right direction and maintaining a straight line. He imagined they were well within the boundaries of the Battlemound Lowlands by now, and he had heard stories of the things that resided there. All sorts of creatures—plants and animals alike—that fed off unwary travelers. Dangerous predators that could overpower you in ways you weren't expecting before you could manage to act. It was a place to avoid, for sure.

If you could.

And if you couldn't, then at least you should do your best not to attract attention.

These were Paxon's last thoughts before everything exploded into violence.

It was hard to tell exactly what went wrong. He wasn't paying attention to what was happening behind him, his eyes scanning the way forward and taking note of the plants that waited within the soupy haze—counting their numbers, measuring the distances separating them, choosing a path. Isaturin told him later that old Consloe stumbled. The Troll who was carrying him had set him down at his insistence a short time earlier. Apparently shamed by the fact that everyone else was managing without help, the old Druid must have felt that he should be doing so, too. But his efforts quickly began to fail, and Isaturin noticed. Rather than ask another to step in when everyone else was also on the verge of exhaustion, he had gone to the old man's aid, but he was not quick enough. Old Consloe lost his footing before the Ard Rhys could reach him and went down.

Unfortunately his momentum carried him right into the base of one of the plants.

The old man was still struggling to regain his feet when the plant he had rolled up against grabbed him. Roots appeared from the earth, snake-like tendrils that writhed and twisted and swiftly wrapped themselves around his frail body. He cried out, then screamed as the roots tightened.

Isaturin conjured magic instantly, and directed a bolt of brilliant blue fire into the trunk of the offending plant, but that achieved nothing. The plant began to burn, its bark catching fire, but the roots continued to hold Consloe fast. Isaturin struck at it again, burning the roots closest to the old man. But even when they caught fire, the plant refused to let go.

It all happened in seconds.

Paxon raced to their aid, but Miriya got there first. Blade drawn, she extended her arms and her sharpened steel flashed bright and quick in the gloom. One of the roots fell away, but another swiftly took its place. Again, the warrior Druid struck. And again, and again. Each time a root was severed, more appeared. By now the roots were reaching for her, as well; several wrapped about her legs and pulled her down. Paxon arrived, and with the green snakes of the sword's magic racing up and down his blade like living creatures, he cut her free. Barely pausing, he grabbed her arms and pulled her clear. Other roots grappled for them. In no time, a circle of waving, grasping tentacles hemmed them in, separating them from the others.

Backs together, Paxon, Miriya, and Isaturin hacked at every root that came close. It was not enough. They were being overwhelmed. From outside the deadly circle, the Trolls and Fero Darz watched helplessly. Even Karlin Ryl stood motionless, a statue in the gloom.

Then Paxon turned at the sound of a strangled cry and caught a glimpse of old Consloe as he was pulled beneath the earth. He disappeared slowly—limbs, body, and head—screaming as he was consumed. None of his companions could reach him; the roots blocked their way. In seconds he was gone.

And we are next, Paxon thought, his strength beginning to wane.

Even before the thought was completed, however, Karlin Ryl suddenly cried out, her voice high and piercing, cutting through the sounds of battle, drawing everyone's attention. She stood with her arms outflung and her head thrown back. Even the roots seemed to hesitate in the wake of her terrible, painful wail. Abruptly, a familiar shape emerged from her body, separating itself from where it had hidden within, a lithe and powerful figure released into the night. Growing larger, taking on new size, it became a monstrous presence.

The Sleath.

Once it was free of Karlin, she collapsed instantly. Before she was even on the ground, the Sleath attacked. It did not go after the Trolls or Fero Darz, who stood almost on top of it. Instead, it tore into the plants. It did not shy from them when they tried to respond; it did not hesitate or slow. It created a path of destruction, leaving behind shredded trunks, twisted roots, and an ichor that seeped from within each dying plant, black in the gloom.

Paxon braced himself. The Sleath was coming toward them.

Wordlessly, Miriya and Isaturin moved next to him, standing shoulder-to-shoulder on either side. This didn't feel like a rescue; it felt like a fresh promise of death. They stood firm against it, nevertheless. But given the outcome of their last encounter with this demonkind, Paxon had no illusions about their chances of survival.

The Sleath, in the meantime, continued to bull its way toward them through a tangle of roots and plants. Nothing seemed able to stop it—certainly not the masses of vegetation. They snapped and whipped at the Sleath. They tried desperately to wrap themselves around it. They reached up for it from beneath the earth and out to it from behind the cover of other plants. Paxon found himself wondering if perhaps they were all one plant, joined underground where the binding could not be detected.

Whatever the case, nothing they did seemed to matter. The Sleath continued to tear them to pieces.

Then Paxon heard an urgent shout. Fero Darz was howling at him. The Commander of the Ministerial Watch had moved farther away from the Sleath and now stood off to one side. The Troll guards had joined him. The uninjured one carried Karlin Ryl over his broad shoulder, as he had carried Consloe before. The roots that encircled them only moments earlier had drawn back into the earth, perhaps gone to the aid of their fellows in the fight against the Sleath. A path through had opened, a corridor to safety. Darz gestured wildly for Paxon and the Druids to take advantage.

The Highlander swiftly made the choice for the others. He practically shoved Isaturin—who was standing statue-like next to him, seemingly mesmerized by the Sleath—toward the opening. Miriya was already moving, and together the three fled, the Highlander bringing up the rear, sword in hand, ready to turn and fight.

He did not need to worry. The Sleath had all it could do to ward off the roots. It was beginning to show signs of tiring, and the number of roots had not diminished. Although hundreds were destroyed, thousands more were waiting. The Sleath continued its advance, but the roots refused to give way, forcing it to struggle for every foot it gained. It was an impossible fight to win.

Paxon and his little company continued in a lateral direction across the open ground. The plants they passed seemed disinterested in them. Their roots did not surface to bar the way or reach out to snare them. Perhaps it was taking all their energy to wear down the Sleath. For, magic or no, the creature was faltering. Paxon, glancing back, could hardly believe it. It seemed even extreme magic of the sort that created the Sleath had its limits. Nothing was indestructible.

Too late, the Sleath seemed to realize the danger. It struggled to pull back, sensing it was in trouble, but too late. The roots had it, their sinuous lengths wrapped firmly about the Sleath until it could not move at all. Then it went down, the roots enfolding it, wrapping it as a spider might a fly in a cocoon of webbing. In seconds it seemed to lose substance. Its body shimmered, and for an instant Paxon believed it was attempting to meld with the plants as it had with Karlin. But the plants resisted and began a slow but inexorable dismemberment of the Sleath. It took awhile, the effort a ferocious exhibition of strength against strength until, finally, the Sleath succumbed. It came apart with a rending of flesh and a snapping of bones, and in seconds it was pulled into the earth.

By now the little company fleeing it had gotten well forward of the battle, weaving steadily through plants that remained disinterested. Paxon, who was back in the lead, chose their path, marking the open spaces and measuring the potential for danger. No one talked. No one saw the need. They simply pushed on through the endless mist.

They walked for a long time, waiting for the plants to rise out of the earth to stop them. But all was quiescent. It was as if they had gone dormant with the destruction of the Sleath. The morning was still, the world about them an empty, lifeless expanse. Eventually, the mist fell away and the sun burned high overhead.

Miriya dropped back to walk beside Karlin Ryl, taking her life partner's small hand in her own as she kept pace with the Troll who carried her. She spoke softly to her, but Paxon could hear anyway.

"Don't leave me," the warrior Druid begged softly. "Be strong. It won't be much longer now. Then we will be clear of these things. Please, Karl, don't die. I am here with you. I won't leave you."

She squeezed Karlin's hand, and reached over to stroke her hair where it fell across her face. The seer seemed lifeless, but Paxon heard Miriya say, "That's my girl. I feel you squeezing back. I feel you reaching out to me. I am here, love. I am always here."

Time passed. Miriya continued to murmur softly to Karlin. The plants thinned and finally disappeared, and the little company was out in the open once more, closer now to the forests of the Anar, which rose like a dark wall off to their right.

The company stopped, and the Troll carrying Karlin Ryl lowered her gently to the ground. Miriya knelt hurriedly next to her, still holding her hand, still murmuring softly. But Karlin was no longer responding, and a moment later Miriya released a wail of anguish that cut through the silence with a razor's sharpness.

Karlin Ryl was gone.

17

LEOFUR AND IMRIC TOOK TURNS SLEEPING UNTIL dawn, one always awake in case the men decided to return. When the sun was up, they climbed back into the two-man and set out for the Wilderun. The day was gray and sunless, the sky clouded over in the wake of the storms that had passed south of them, with the threat of more visible ahead. Leofur knew better than to try to fly a small craft through such heavy weather, but she was hoping that by staying north she would be able to skirt its edges. A little rain wouldn't matter, but heavy thunderstorms and high winds could take them down.

She sat at the controls, her eyes forward and her concentration focused on her flying. Even so, she found herself thinking of Paxon. She wondered where he was, wondered if he had escaped Arishaig. It was troubling that she didn't know anything more. She was worried for him, even knowing how experienced he was at dealing with dangerous situations. She had never known anyone as confident—with one exception. Her father shared that quality, even if he was the Highlander's opposite in every other way. Paxon was one of those people who would always land on his feet and never be at a loss for what to do in a challenging situation. It was as if it was bred into him. His resiliency was tested often, but he never faltered. The only time she had ever seen him unmoored was when he had come to her in

Wayford after his return from the Westland. Then, he was so adrift he could barely function. He had left the Druid order, his confidence in his purpose as the High Druid's Blade diminished. He had lost several Druids under his protection and twice been bested by her father.

Then, and only then, had he needed her help so badly he might not have survived without it. But that was an aberration. She had never seen even a hint of such weakness since.

Though perhaps she would see it again if she failed to find and return Chrysallin.

She wondered if Paxon's return to her before was in any way connected with his ongoing struggle with her father. It was an odd thought, but valid. Paxon was complex, driven both by personal demons and a need to accomplish something important. He had always believed he was meant to do great things. He wanted his life to have meaning—and not in a small, inconsequential way. It was possible that he measured his own successes against those of her father, and found himself wanting. After all, he had failed repeatedly to find a way to hold her father accountable for the deaths of his Druid friends. As a result, perhaps he felt his relationship with her was diminished in some way by his failure to gain closure with her father.

She wished she knew. She wished he would talk about it with her. She wished he would be more open when they were together. He was so protective of his feelings, so secretive about himself. And so often apart from her. As Druid protector, he was constantly being sent on assignment, and she was constantly being abandoned. If not for Chrysallin, she would have been lonely beyond words. She had no other real friends at Paranor. She had no real life.

Or purpose.

Or direction.

Or anything.

Given half a reason, she would consider leaving Paxon and going home.

The thought stunned her. It came all at once and unbidden, but there it was. She hated it and at the same time knew it was so.

She pushed it aside quickly.

"You look pretty intense," Imric said suddenly, and she glanced over to find him watching her. As if he could read her thoughts, or as if he was trying.

"Just thinking about Paxon. Wondering how he is."

He nodded, saying nothing for a moment. "What will we do when we get to the Wilderun? I don't have a trail to follow this time."

"Maybe we'll find you one. Someone in Grimpen Ward will know something about the Murk Sink and Melis. We just have to ask around."

"I'm not good at that sort of thing." He looked away self-consciously. "I'm better the less I have to interact with others."

"Then it's a good thing you have me along this time."

Just before they had departed earlier, she had given him a chance to go back to Paranor. After all, he had fulfilled his promise to her by tracking down Chrysallin's kidnappers and determining where her friend had been taken. She could not have done that on her own, but now she could reasonably expect to find both the Murk Sink and the witch without his help. She had no reason to expect him to continue on with her.

But he saw it differently. She might still have need of him, he pointed out. She didn't know what she would find once she arrived in the Wilderun. If she had to go into Murk Sink, she might have need of someone who could read sign and smell scent and otherwise find a trail hidden from ordinary eyes. Besides, he had added, this quest gave him something he had been missing for too long—a way to use his shape-shifting productively for the first time in years. It infused him with new life. She had done this with her strange request for his services. Would she deprive him of it at this point? Ostensibly she would be releasing him from her service, but actually she would be sending him back into a life of self-deprivation and renewed loss of purpose, wouldn't she?

She almost laughed at that. She knew he was asking to be included, that coming with her was more important than staying safe at home. It was clear that using his shape-shifting ability provided him with such pleasure that he could no longer imagine doing without it. Anchored to her through the tether, he had found a way to exorcise the demons of his suspect control over his abilities while indulging in the exquisite freedom they provided him.

That he was asking her to risk herself for him seemed fair since she was asking the same of him. Possibly she would be placing herself in situations where a loss of control could damage her permanently, but she found the challenge oddly attractive. She liked being depended on again, liked having a purpose beyond providing company for Paxon's sister.

So she had relented and said he could come, inwardly pleased that he wanted to, happy to have someone to share her quest. To some extent, she could admit, she was eager to continue to share in his shape-shifting, no matter the risk the tethering demanded. Even vicariously, it was wondrous. In being tethered to him, she was transported to a reality beyond anything she had ever experienced. It was terrifying and enthralling, intimidating and exciting, all at once. Having been a part of it, having seen how it worked and how it made her feel, she understood why it was so important to him. She was only a newly minted participant. But to be born with it? To have it be as much a part of you as breathing? She could understand why it was so addictive, so hard to give up. She did not see how he could ever have done so while at Paranor. She did not know how he could ever do so again.

"Well," he said, breaking into her musings, responding finally to her earlier comment, "I guess I'm here because I don't have anything better to do. Going back to Paranor's stables is unacceptable. I would not be happy knowing you were out here alone. I would be worrying that you needed me. I made a commitment to see this through, to stick with you until we found your friend, and that is what I will do. I want to see you and Chrysallin safely home."

"And the risk does not trouble you?"

"Does it trouble you?"

"Of course. But Chrysallin is my friend, and the sister of my life partner. That's different."

"Is it?"

She did not know what he meant by that, and she looked over again, studying his face. But he gave nothing away as he scanned the countryside below them, watching forests and grasslands passing beneath them as the two-man continued its steady pace westward.

They didn't talk again for a while. Leofur watched the new storm approach out of the Streleheim, drifting south toward the lower Borderlands. This fresh batch of clouds roiled and churned but seemed less threatening, and the winds that propelled them seemed less violent than the ones now fading east into the Southland. She knew they would be able to continue on if there was no unexpected shift in the weather. By nightfall, they would be all the way to the edge of the Westland. By tomorrow night, they would be down into the Wilderun, their search for the Murk Sink begun in earnest.

For now, she had time and space to let go of everything as she gave herself over to flying. It was always like this. She didn't know exactly how it affected Paxon; he never talked about it. But she supposed it was the same for him—musing amid the automatic tasks that flying required. She wasn't as experienced with airships as he was, but she was competent enough to be able to think about other things while engaged in the act. Everything came instinctively, all of the movements and choices and assessments required. She could rely on herself to let her thoughts drift and still keep them safe.

She could let herself be at peace.

"What was your life like when you were young?" she asked Imric as they sat together later, far out on the grasslands, eating their lunch of cold meat and cheese and ale. "Did you have friends?"

He shook his head, his bladed features somber, his eyes dark with memories. "Not close ones, no. My parents kept me apart from other children when I was very young. Perhaps they feared what I might become. What, in fact, I already was, though none of us knew it then. After I discovered my talent, I deliberately stayed away. I couldn't risk anyone finding out. I couldn't be certain of my control over the shifting. I was essentially alone after that."

"No lover? No woman to care for you?"

He laughed. "What woman could love someone like me? No, I had no one like that. I had female companions now and then, but only for a single night's pleasure. I knew what I was. I understood the risk I posed to anyone who got close to me—especially after I lost my parents." He hesitated. "Especially after I killed my father. It's hard to say those words, but they need saying. I haven't said them to anyone since after coming to Paranor. There's a certain release in doing so now."

"Why do you stay at Paranor? You seem able to control yourself well enough. Even without a tether, I sense you could manage it. Perhaps you could find a new life."

The strong features tightened, then turned incredibly sad, as if the very idea of what she was suggesting was cruel beyond accepting. She instantly wished she could take back the words. She reached out and put her hand on his arm. "I'm sorry. I spoke out of turn."

"You spoke from your heart," he corrected gently. "You want something good for me, and that's not to be regretted. But the truth is I cannot leave Paranor and go back out into the larger world. The danger of reverting to what I was before, when I could lose control so easily, remains. The temptation to let that happen is too great. I need the safety net the Druids provide me with. I need the solitude they offer. Yes, it is lonely, but I have been lonely all my life, so I am used to it. It's best for everyone."

He looked over, a smile on his lips. "I consider myself fortunate to have this time away, this chance to escape my ordinary life. I thank you for that, Leofur Rai. It means so much. You can't imagine how much."

Perhaps I can, she thought, smiling back. But she saw no reason to say so, and so left it there.

They flew through the remainder of the day and spent the night out on the open grasslands of the lower Streleheim, not far above the Tirfing. The ground was cool and damp, so they slept in the two-man, crammed into its tiny interior, wrapped in blankets and pressed up against each other as they sought enough space to stretch out. On rising, they ate breakfast and set out again. The storms had rolled past and the clouds had moved on. The temperature had fallen, as well, but the air was clear and the sky blue from horizon to horizon. They talked now and then, but mostly remained locked in their thoughts. The landscape changed with the approach of nightfall, the grasslands giving way to a mix of mountains and forests, the openness of the plains disappearing.

"Is this a good idea?" Imric asked her, as he recognized where they were going.

Ahead, the lights of Grimpen Ward had come into view, a scattering of isolated residences clustered around the central core of the town.

She knew what he was getting at; undoubtedly he had been here a time or two on his own before coming to Paranor. There was nothing good about Grimpen Ward—a town filled with people running from their old lives or engaging in various forms of indulgence. Pleasure houses, gambling dens, opportunities for doing things best left unsaid, chances for quick money and changes of fortune abounded.

"You don't think so?" she replied, cocking an eyebrow at him.

"This is a dangerous place. Especially for women." He didn't say what he was thinking, but she knew anyway—that she had already overestimated her abilities when she had let those men in the Kennon Pass get the best of her. That she was young and unready in spite of her bravado. That her determination to find and rescue Chrysallin had clouded her judgment. "I just wonder if it's necessary to come here to find out what we need to know about the witch."

Leofur smiled. "I used to come here all the time. I've traded and bargained with these people. Done deals and moved on. No one ever bothered me. Not after the first time someone tried it and word got around. And yes, coming here is necessary, Imric. I have contacts here who will help us—people who have helped me before. People who will tell me what I need to know."

People who will cut your throat for the price of a drink, she knew he was thinking, but again he kept quiet. This was her decision, and he was ceding her the right to make it. All he could do was to try to keep her safe. Leofur understood him well enough. She knew he admired the fact that she was bold and capable. But she could tell there was something else happening, too—something beyond what she had expected when they set out together. She was still figuring out exactly what that something was, but she knew it was important enough for him to believe it well worth his time.

They landed in a small airfield at the edge of the town, a space that was little more than a grassy field and lacked security and services—a place where you left your craft and took your chances. But the two-man was armed with warning systems and self-destruct mechanisms in case of attempted theft, and that was usually enough to deter thieves looking for an easy target. There were other vessels about, a few of them valuable, a few with guards aboard keeping watch, and Leofur anchored their ship close to these.

Once the two-man was secured, they set out for the lights of the village.

It was a short walk. The town consisted of buildings densely packed together, their walls either shared or close enough that you could touch both at the same time if you wished to squeeze between them. The streets were muddied and rutted from recent rains and spilled ale, the smell both rank and vaguely intoxicating. The doors and windows of the pleasure houses and gambling and drinking halls were thrown open to the night, their lights ablaze against the coming darkness. Shouts and laughter filled the air, and men and women roamed the streets in search of business and fun—though the two were often indistinguishable. More than a few of those who passed were either wildly inebriated or well on their way.

Imric watched everyone, ready to act if there should be need. He stayed close to Leofur—perhaps because she was deliberately manifesting a lack of concern with what was happening around her, which caused him obvious dismay. Again, she could read his thoughts. He thought her too casual about the dangers surrounding her, lacking any sense of caution for what she might come up against. But this, of course, was only her surface appearance; inside she was tightly wound and ready to act. He should have known as much. She had survived a lot in her life; she had learned to be wary. But if he recognized this, it apparently made him feel no less protective toward her. She found it strange but charming.

Once, she even wheeled back on him, telling him he was walking too close. Reluctantly, he backed off a step, but then he reclaimed the distance a little while later.

She slowed as they reached an alehouse with a large wooden sign that read BURNING MAN. Below, charmingly depicted in garish red and yellow, was what was clearly supposed to be an image that reflected the name. That it in any way did was something of a stretch.

She turned to Imric. "The man we've come to see is Talis Closteralt. He's the owner, and I've done business with him in the past. He's done considerable trapping and hunting throughout the Wilderun before opening this establishment. He will know of the Murk Sink and the witch. He may even know how to find her."

The shape-shifter nodded wordlessly. His brow furrowed, but she let it pass and forged ahead, pushing her way through a cluster of half-drunk men as she entered the building. She didn't bother to glance back to see if Imric was following. She didn't need to.

She worked her way through the patrons and serving girls to the long bar at the back of the room, spying Closteralt behind the counter. He was a slight wisp of a man, his hair thinning, his skin still brown from sun and weather even though he no longer worked outdoors. His sharp eyes flicked left and right as he moved from ale keg to patron and back again, always searching.

It took only moments for his gaze to light on her. She nodded a greeting and moved to the far end of the bar to wait.

When a fight broke out next to her, she could feel the tension in Imric as he moved in front of her, but she pulled him back, shaking her head. Fights happened in alehouses all the time. No one beyond those involved took it personally. In seconds a pair of very large men had moved over, separated the combatants, and thrown them through the door and into the street. Closteralt had nothing against fighting so long as it didn't happen in his place of business.

The barkeep was in front of her seconds later, his eyes shifting from her to Imric and back again. "A friend?"

"A partner," she corrected. "Can we talk somewhere less public?"

He took them behind the counter and through the kitchen to a small porch in the narrow alley behind. It was hardly private; there were windows opening onto the alley all around them, and the sounds of men and women enjoying themselves drifted down from more than a few.

She ignored all that and turned to him. "I have a favor to ask," she said. "I will pay you well if your answer has value."

The thin lips twisted, and the rest of his narrow face followed suit, like a rubber mask. "Anything I tell you will have value. You can depend on it. Payment, of course, is always appreciated."

"So is accuracy. I will need to know that what you tell me comes with a guarantee."

"For you, always. If I know something, I will tell you. If I don't, I will simply bid you farewell." He paused, giving her a smile. "It's good to have you back for a visit. Time spent with you, sweet Leofur, whether for business or ... pleasure ... has always been ... enjoyable."

The way he said it was so deliberately suggestive, she almost laughed. But then she saw his features change, the momentary smarminess wiped clean. A second later Imric had surged past her, snatching up Closteralt by the front of his shirt and yanking him close. The look on his face was terrifying. She couldn't decide what he intended to do, but it wasn't anything good.

"What's the trouble, big man?" Talis said, somehow managing to keep calm in spite of being lifted off the floor. "Don't like hearing about Leofur and me?"

Leofur grabbed Imric's arm and forced it down so that Closteralt was standing on his own two feet again. Carefully, she pried Imric's fingers loose from the other's shirt and moved him back.

"What's wrong with you?" she hissed. Then she turned to Closteralt, all business. "What gives you the right to talk about me like that? Do you think telling lies and making false claims is a good idea? Especially where I'm concerned? I think you'd better tell him it isn't true."

There was a long pause. "It isn't true," Closteralt said finally. He exhaled sharply, a sour look on his face. "Are you satisfied?"

"Not in the least. You shouldn't play games when you don't know the rules. It might get you hurt. My partner doesn't like thinking of me with other men. Especially men who make things up."

Closteralt held up his hands in a placating gesture. "I didn't mean anything by it. It was a joke! Of course it has always been business between you and me. Never anything else. But a man can dream, can't he?"

"Keep your dreams to yourself," she snapped. "Now, are you ready to hear me out or not?" She waited for him to nod. "That's better. Then let's get to it. The Murk Sink. Tell me what you know."

"What I know?" He laughed, the sound high-pitched and nervous. "I know to stay away! I know that those who travel there quite often don't come back again. Why would you ask me about this? You're not thinking of going there, are you?"

"Do you know of a witch who lives there?" she pressed, ignoring the question. "A witch called Melis?"

Now he looked genuinely frightened. He put a finger to his lips. "The walls have ears where she's concerned. Even to speak of her is dangerous!"

"Then do so softly," she whispered. She leaned close. "Tell me what you know."

The other blinked rapidly. "I know that she is far more dangerous than you and your friend could ever hope to be. I know that one word in her ear about anything I say would mean the end of me. So why don't we just leave it at that? In fact, why don't you just pack up and get out?"

It was a clear dismissal, but she ignored it. "What if I were to find her on my own, and one way or another let it slip that you were the one who told me how? How would you feel about that?"

His pinched features tightened. "You would, too, wouldn't you? Nasty little piece of . . ." Her look cut him short. "All right, then. Let's end this. Here's what I know . . . but you never heard a word of it from me. Melis is called the Murk Witch because she lives in the Sink. She only comes out once in a while. She has magic. I haven't seen her use it myself, but I've heard about it from some who have. Very bad stuff. Very dangerous."

"How do we find her?"

He shook his head. "Why would you want to do that? Bah, it doesn't matter! I can't tell you anyway; I don't know. But I know someone who does. It's dangerous to ask, though. Word has a way of getting back to those you don't want to hear. Is this really so important?"

She nodded slowly. "Give me a name."

"Olin. A boy, a young swamp rat, come out on dry land a few years back. He grew up in the Murk Sink, lived there with his family. They all died except for him. Fever, I was told. I don't know the whole story. But he knows the witch. Some say he lived with her after he lost his family. Some say they were lovers. Now he's just another drunk, barely out of his teens. Lives above the Weathervane, a little farther down the road. Maybe if you sober him up he will talk to you. Or maybe not."

"This is true, all of it?"

"All of it. Now pay me."

"After I speak with him. After it's confirmed."

"Do that, and you won't be coming back."

Leofur rose, and Imric immediately stood up with her. "I liked you better when you were buying weapons and information and knew how to keep your mouth shut," Leofur said. "I like you less now that you've decided you can make up stories about me." She brought out the flash rip. "In fact, I don't think I like you at all."

"Wait!" he gasped. "I never said anything about you to anyone until just now. I was just playing with you. I made a mistake! Please."

She gave him a long look, then nodded finally and slipped the weapon back under her cloak. "Then don't ever do it again. Don't use my name for any reason. Don't speak of me. Even if the witch doesn't hear, my father might."

Closteralt got up, lips compressed and eyes hard. He hesitated a moment, then went back inside the building.

Imric looked at her with approval after he was gone. "That was good. You handled that perfectly."

Fury filled her. "No, I didn't—no thanks to you! Now come. Let's find this boy."

18

ONCE THROUGH THE INTERIOR OF THE TAVERN and back out onto the street, Leofur hauled Imric down the roadway a few buildings farther, then pushed him into an alley and against a wall. "What did you think you were doing back there?" she demanded.

He looked confused. "What do you mean? When?"

"When you looked like you were making my personal life your business! That disrupted everything I'd planned. You came to my defense as if I were some callow girl in danger of assault! Why would you do that? What were you thinking?"

He straightened but did not flinch. "I didn't like him talking about you that way. I didn't like him period. How can you trust people like that?"

She was so mad she could have spit. Imric might have powerful gifts, but his ability to navigate certain social situations was sorely lacking. Couldn't he see what she had been doing? Couldn't he understand that letting Closteralt brag a bit about their relationship was harmless rhetoric and might even have resulted in getting them more information? But instead, he had bulled in and turned her negotiation with the other man adversarial. Could Imric really not understand that she knew how to handle herself in these situations?

But then, abruptly, she realized that he couldn't. He didn't understand any of it. Shut away at Paranor with no companions and no experience in the ways of men and women, he was woefully ignorant. He reacted the way a child would—coming to her defense, championing her virtue, standing up for her character. He saw himself as her protector in all things, and not just the physical.

She was suddenly ashamed, for she could see the hurt in his face and hear the pain in his explanation. It was as if she had kicked a puppy. She stepped back quickly, giving herself space and a moment's time in which to recover.

Her apology came slowly. "I overreacted. You couldn't have known what I was thinking. Forgive me."

He shook his head, not looking at her. "There is nothing to forgive. I should have done as you say. I should have stayed out of it. I keep thinking that you're vulnerable, but I have to remember how strong and capable you are. I wish I were better at remembering, but I don't know that I ever will be."

"Yes, you will," she said, reaching for his arm, linking it with her own, and tugging hard on it. "I'll make sure of it."

They began walking again, side by side, heads lowered as they put one foot in front of the other and tried to think of something to say. "You don't think he will betray us later?" Imric asked finally.

She shook her head. "It would come back to haunt him if he does. You heard what he said about the witch. And my father isn't much better."

"It's up to this boy, then, to tell us what we need to know?"

"It looks that way. We have to find him first, and then see if he actually has anything to tell us. And it would help if he were sober when we found him, too."

They were in luck. They found the Weathervane not far ahead, a shabby building badly in need of repair. It was another tavern, of course, a darkened and unwelcoming gathering place for those who most likely could afford no better. There were windows with the glass broken out, windows boarded over, and windows with the shutters closed against the outside world. A pair of doors opened to the interior, and within the bar and serving area—a dim and dingy space half the size of the Burning Man—smoke clung to the ceiling in a thick, airless fog.

Wasting no time, Leofur walked over to a worn-down serving girl standing at one end of the bar and pressed some credits into her hand. "Olin?"

The girl looked at the credits, then at Leofur and Imric. "You don't intend to hurt him, do you?" she asked.

Leofur couldn't believe it made any difference to this sad-faced girl, but she shook her head anyway. "We just want to talk to him."

The girl nodded hopefully. "Upstairs, second door on the left." She glanced around, as if someone might be watching. "But maybe you should knock first. He's not alone."

Leofur nodded and walked over to the stairway the girl had indicated, a very steep, narrow set of steps that made her wonder how anyone could make it up after more than one drink. But she supposed that the promise of even momentary passion gave you sufficient strength.

"Stay close," she whispered over her shoulder, wanting Imric to feel his protective presence was needed.

And maybe it was. Who knew what was up there?

They climbed to the second floor and found a darkened hallway only marginally wider than the stairs. At the second door, they stopped and Leofur knocked softly. "Olin?"

There was a rustling sound, footfalls, and the door opened a few inches. A face peered out. "I'm busy. Who are you?"

Not much of a boy, this one, she thought, in spite of what Closteralt claimed. A wasted youth with sallow skin, pinched features, an unkempt appearance, and furtive eyes. Oddly, he reminded her of Closteralt. She reached out and placed more of her credits into his hand. "We need to talk. It's important."

He looked at the credits, just as the serving girl had, and then at her. "Come back later. We can talk then."

He started to close the door, but she blocked it with her boot. "This can't wait. We'll talk now."

Olin peered at her suspiciously. "I don't know who you are. I've never seen you before."

"I'm not here to cause you trouble. All I want to do is talk."

"Others have said as much, but never meant it."

"Well, I'm not those others." She was growing impatient. "Do you see my friend, standing just behind me? If you don't want to see a whole lot more of him up close, you will open the door. Right now."

Olin hesitated, then stepped back and let her push the door open. He was half dressed. The woman in the bed was not. She took one look at Imric, wrapped herself in a blanket, then snatched up her clothes and went out the door in a rush.

The young man looked after her for a moment, then walked over and sat down on the edge of the bed, looking dejected. He picked up a glass of ale from the nightstand and drank deeply. "I won't see that money back. Or what it was supposed to buy. What do you want?"

He did not sound inebriated. He sounded perfectly sober, if a bit sullen. He did not seem alarmed or particularly angry. If anything, he seemed resigned. Even without knowing who they were or what they were doing there, he seemed unsurprised they had come.

"We want to know how to find the Murk Witch," Leofur replied, watching his eyes. "She has taken our friend, and we want her back."

The young man's stare was blank. "If she's got your friend, then your friend isn't coming back."

His words were stark, delivered in a flat tone—an implacable declaration that did not leave room for argument. Leofur went cold inside, but she pressed on anyway.

"She's coming back if we go get her. You've lived in the swamp. You've lived with the witch. You must know how to reach her."

Olin sighed, his features tightening. "I know nothing of the sort. Whoever told you otherwise is wrong. Melis means something to me, but that doesn't change the facts. I've already tried to find her. I've tried repeatedly. I know the Sink. I know every inch of it. But even that doesn't help. I've searched extensively, but I cannot find her, and I know now I never will. She is lost to me."

Leofur exchanged a quick glance with Imric. "Why were you trying to find her in the first place?" she asked.

Olin shrugged. "I love her. I've always loved her—from the moment she took me in and made me her creature. I knew what she was doing. I knew what she wanted from me. It didn't matter. She was so beautiful. She was kind and she cared about me. She was like no one I had ever met. I would have done anything for her."

"Yet you left her?" Leofur was trying to understand. "If you loved her, then why did you . . . ?"

His head snapped up. "No! I didn't leave her. I would never have left her! I was hers forever. She was the one who left *me*!"

"How did you come to be with her in the first place?" Imric asked suddenly. "Weren't you just a boy?"

Olin looked pained. "Just a boy. True enough, that's what I was. My family was dead, I was alone, I had nowhere to go, and she took me in. I don't know how she found me, but she did. She brought me to her home, and she raised me. She kept me until she grew tired of me, and then she cast me out."

"How did she 'cast you out,' Olin?" Leofur asked, sitting down on the bed next to him. "How did that happen?"

He didn't look at her. "She drugged me, carried me to the edge of the swamp, and left me. I thought I could find my way back to her easy enough. I knew the Sink well. It was my home, too. But I couldn't. I tried and tried. I nearly died trying, but I couldn't find a trace of her. So I found my way here instead."

"She grew tired of you?"

He shook his head. "I don't want to talk about it anymore. I'm tired of talking about it."

"Wait. Why do you say you were her creature? That seems an odd way to refer to yourself."

His face turned stony. "I did whatever she wanted me to do. Things I will never talk about with anyone. Things only a *creature* would do. I amused her. I made her smile." He made a dismissive gesture. "Now go away. I told you what you wanted to know. I can't help you. So leave me alone."

Leofur sighed. "We can't do that. You seem to be the only one who may be able to help us. If not now, maybe later. We need you to come with us, to go into the swamp and try one more time. This friend, she needs us to rescue her. No one else will, if we don't. So that's what we're going to do."

He looked at her now. "I already told you. I can't help."

"Maybe you only think you can't help. Maybe once we're back in the swamp, something will occur to you, something you haven't thought of before. It's worth a try."

"Not to me, it isn't." Bitter, disheartened. "I won't do it."

"So you don't want to find Melis again? Wouldn't you give up everything for another chance to be with her?"

That was Imric speaking, asking a question that Leofur had not thought to ask. She watched the young man hesitate before answering. "I told you . . ."

"That you've given up. We heard. But maybe you should reconsider. We're here now, and we don't believe in giving up. Besides, I'm the best tracker you've ever met. Maybe with us to help, you might find her this time."

"But why would she take me back after throwing me out? Why would she even think about it?"

"Because maybe she's like you. Maybe she knows she made a mistake and wishes she could take it back. Or maybe it's a test. But if you come to her and tell her how you feel, if you are standing there in front of her asking, how do you know what she will say? How can you ever be sure, if you don't give it a try?"

A part of Leofur felt as if they were leading the young man on. But Chrysallin's life was likely at stake, so she kept quiet as Imric continued to push against the boy's resolve.

"Stranger things have happened," the shape-shifter continued. "Couples meet, part, and come back together all the time. She loved you once. Why couldn't she love you again? You are different now. You are grown up. A man. Perhaps that will attract her anew. Perhaps she will see you with fresh eyes."

Olin shook his head emphatically. "You don't know how she thinks. You can't even begin to guess."

"But you can. Are you sure she wouldn't take you back? Are you so certain you are willing to forgo our help?"

The boy sat silently for a long time. Leofur and Imric waited him out. He seemed to be weighing his decision, turning it over in his mind, considering its merits and flaws.

"Let me think about it," he said at last.

"There's no time for that," Leofur said quickly.

"There's tonight, isn't there? You can't go into the swamp until it's daylight, in any case. No one enters the Murk Sink at night, and I have to think about this. Come back at sunrise."

"You'll be waiting for us?"

He nodded.

"You won't try to run?"

He looked at her incredulously. "Run where? There's nowhere left for me to run. And there's no reason. Either I go with you or I don't go anywhere."

The way he said it convinced her. He was staring at the dead end of his life, the rest of it unchanging, his interest in its outcome so muted that he no longer had hope for himself.

Unless he agreed to what they were asking.

They left him to it.

They walked back through the streets of Grimpen Ward to the small airfield and climbed into the cockpit to wait out the night. Neither wanted to stay in the town itself any longer than was necessary. There was a claustrophobic, unsafe feeling to the rooms and buildings, and to the crowds who roamed the streets and alleyways. They knew it would be like that all night if they stayed, and they felt that even in the cramped space of the two-man cockpit, at least they would be out in the open air with the sky spread out above them and the air fresh and clean.

They wrapped up in their blankets, arranged themselves as best they could, and lay back to look up at the sky. Stars were out, bright and reassuring overhead; it was a promise of good weather. The airfield was deserted save for the guards who stood watch over the larger aircraft nearby, but even those few had settled in and gone silent. The lights of Grimpen Ward were a dull yellow against the horizon where they shone above the intervening trees, but the sounds of the inhabitants were muted and distant.

It was as if the world had disappeared, taking all of its many people and creatures with it. It made Leofur feel at peace.

After a long silence, Imric spoke. "Olin might try to run from us."

She made a face. "He won't run. He said it himself. He has no-where to go and no desire to go there. He is lost and doesn't know how to find the way back." She looked over. "But you gave him a way to change that. Very clever of you. I think he will decide to go with us."

"Clever maybe, but not very honest. I don't think Melis will ever take him back. She doesn't appear to be someone who regrets the past. I think she will probably kill him if she gets her hands on him."

"But we won't let that happen, will we?"

He did not respond right away. He seemed to be thinking it over. "I look at it like this. If nothing changes in his life, he's already as good as dead." His words were soft and sad. "If he dies coming with us, he's no worse off."

"In your opinion."

"Not in yours?"

"I don't know. I don't like the idea of deciding such things for other people. It would be hard enough deciding for myself."

"Maybe this is something you couldn't decide for yourself. You might be too close to do so. Maybe you would welcome someone else making the decision."

She paused. "What are we talking about here? This isn't just about Olin and the witch, is it?" She made it a statement of fact, challenging him. "What else is it about?"

He was silent a lot longer this time. She had almost decided he wasn't going to respond at all when he suddenly sat up straight and looked down at her.

"Do you really want me to answer that question?"

Now it was her turn to hesitate. She sat up beside him and looked him in the eyes. "Don't you want to?"

"If you promise not to judge me. This is you asking, not me offer-ing. I need to know you won't let my answer change our relationship."

"How can I promise something like that without knowing what your answer is?"

He lay down again. "Then let it go. Maybe ask again another time when we've known each other longer."

She stared at him for a few moments, irritated and confused, but he had closed his eyes as if intending to go to sleep. She did want to know, of course. She wanted to know everything about him. The details he had shared about his life were sketchy at best, and the nature of his emotional makeup was a cypher. Sure, he was in turmoil. Sure, he had struggled long and hard to accept who and what he was. But how he felt deep down inside, where it counted, about his childhood experiences, his parents, his time at Paranor, and now his time with her, were largely a mystery.

Shades, but he is difficult to fathom! It's bad enough trying to read Paxon's moods and thoughts, but Imric is in a class of his own.

She pushed the matter aside and prepared to join him in sleep. The quiet had returned in the absence of conversation, and the blanket of stars in the dark sky was soothing.

"Leofur," Imric said suddenly.

"Yes?"

"Do you know why I acted the way I did with Closteralt? The real reason?" His words were so soft that she almost missed them entirely. "It was the tether."

She glanced over. He was looking directly at her. "The tether joins us. It links us while I am in my shape-shifter form. It allows you to see what I see, to share those experiences with me. And it does the same for me. It ties me to you so that I feel you there with me. If I lose control after shifting, I can count on you to call me back again. You can reach out to me and bring me home. To you. You are my home."

She was startled. "I don't consider myself your home."

"Not in the traditional sense. But emotionally. You provide me with a center. I have no real home or family. I haven't for years. Tethering provides that for me. The Druids decided that this would be the best way to protect me against my shifter impulses. The ties we have with people are always the strongest. Surely you must feel that with Paxon?"

She nodded. "Of course I do."

"With you and me, it is a different sort of emotional tie, one generated by mutual dependence. It creates a different kind of closeness. It relies on a sort of blind trust. It isn't gentle. It is strong and rough and sometimes terrifying. And it is instinctive. It is an almost innate response to choosing life over death, reason over madness. That's what is always at stake. Do you see?"

"I think so. But what about your response to Closteralt? How is what you're telling me relevant to that?"

"Almost everything that happens between us is influenced by the tether. Not just when we are linked, but afterward, as well. Closteralt's possessiveness generated an immediate response. I slipped into protective mode even without intending to, without consciously thinking about it. It was a reaction to a feeling of anger and concern and I don't know what else. I felt as if I had been struck a physical blow. I saw you being threatened. I was afraid you could be harmed. You are my home, my safety line. I could not stand by without acting."

He paused, sighed. "I didn't tell you everything about the tethering before. It was all I could do to tell you as much as I did. Besides, I thought you would reject me just from what I had revealed. I held back the things I believed could wait. This was one: The power of the tethering to bind us, the ways it could influence us. The nature of the dependence it would create and the possible consequences thereof. When it surfaces, it removes all choice. There is only time for reaction, and that reaction is instantaneous—a reflex akin to an eyeblink. You act because you must. In those moments, you are the tether's creature, and you do its bidding."

"But I don't feel that way about you!" Leofur blurted out before she could stop herself, realizing only after she had spoken what she had said. Hastily, she tried to backtrack. "Wait. I didn't mean . . ."

"Yes, you did," he interrupted quickly, his voice rough. "You spoke honestly. There can be no condemnation for that. And I understand. Your feelings are your own. We are different people. My response to the tether is necessarily different from yours. I don't presume anything about how you should feel. I am telling you this so you will understand how it affects me. I would never suggest it should be the same for you."

Well, it wasn't the same with her. Was it? She thought of earlier conversations when he had insisted she was a perfect complement to him—different, but in a way that strengthened him. It made her wonder. How alike were they? More so than she wanted to admit, perhaps. She knew she hadn't gotten a firm grasp on this yet; her understanding of their relationship was still vague and one-dimensional. How much of what it meant was she still missing?

She lay back again, looking up at the sky, letting the particulars of the conversation settle in, considering them one by one—and especially the last. How *did* the tether impact her? She wasn't entirely sure. It was hard to deny that it was a powerful experience. Or that it generated feelings in her she was still sorting out. She had been frightened for him when he had broken the link between them that first day while they were hunting the men who took Chrysallin. She had been furious and disappointed and a whole raft of other things. So she couldn't say the tether had not affected her at all.

Just not the same way as it affected him.

And she did think she would have responded differently to Closteralt than he had if their positions had been reversed. She did think that whatever the impact of her link to him, it was nowhere near as strong and volatile as his to her.

And good thing, too. One of them needed to stay calm in confrontational situations. One of them needed to provide stability if the tethering was to work as it was intended to.

At least one of them, although both would be better.

Otherwise . . .

Otherwise what?

She was unable to say. The answer to that question was still hidden.

19

EVERY DAY BEGAN EXACTLY THE SAME FOR CHRYS-allin Leah. She would wake up in her box, the wooden slats and the layers of mesh over the airholes preventing her from seeing anything clearly. It might be morning, or it might be afternoon. She'd managed to settle into a schedule that let her sleep at night and wake during the day. What good this did her, she couldn't say. Perhaps the consistency helped keep her sane.

Perhaps.

Every day she would wake inside the wooden crate, lying on the padding they had provided, her head on her pillow and her blanket wrapped around her. She would stretch her limbs in a space that was a little more than eight feet long (she had measured it herself), then she would give herself a moment to wake fully, lying very still and listening for sounds, even though there never were any. After she was awake, she would sit up and recite in her head the names of those she loved and missed and whom she was determined to return to.

It was a ritualistic list: Paxon, Leofur, her mother, her Druid friends, her Troll friends, her friends from the old days in Wayford, and always one or two she made up to allow for a little variation in the ritual.

When that was finished, she would lie back again and wait.

The waiting was the hardest. There was never any way to measure how long it would last. It varied so widely she had given up trying to find a pattern. Sometimes, it happened quickly. Sometimes, it took all day. But it always happened sooner or later. At some point, the little girl would come to her.

In the beginning, she used to try summoning this elfin creature. She would rap on the crate boards or even bang sharply on them. She would stamp her feet. But there was never a response to any of this. Only silence.

Chrysallin supposed she could have fallen victim to the kind of madness that had claimed her when Arcannen had abducted her and given her over to that other witch, the one who called herself Mischa. She could have given in to the urge to merge the two witches in her mind and imagine the situations were similar. But in truth, the situations were not similar, and neither were the witches involved. Not even a little.

For starters, she wasn't being drugged and subverted by potions and magic to be made over into some creature meant to serve. Arcannen, in fact, had not appeared even once. She was assured he was coming, of course. The little girl had seen to that, instructed to do so, she claimed, by the Murk Witch. Well, maybe. But then the little girl was insane, so you couldn't put too much stock in what she said.

The Murk Witch never showed herself, either—at least not so as to reveal what she actually looked like. Chrys supposed she would do so when Arcannen came as a final provocative gesture, another variation on the game. But perhaps it wouldn't be either the sorcerer or the witch who came for her. Perhaps it would be Leofur or her brother. Perhaps it would be her Druid protectors and their Troll guards. That someone who loved and cared about her was coming was never in doubt. She had been down this road before. In the end, someone always came for her. They would do so this time, as well.

She refused to believe anything else.

Firming up her resolve, just as she had done every day since the beginning of her captivity, she reaffirmed this certainty, as well.

She remembered almost nothing of her abduction. One minute

she was walking with Leofur, then both had sensed a presence and begun to move away. She remembered Leofur going down first, collapsed in a heap, unmoving. She remembered starting toward her, then everything had gone black. She thought she remembered receiving a blow to the head. She definitely remembered waking later with a headache.

She had been bound and gagged, unable to move or speak, or use her magic or free herself. She remembered a bitter taste in her mouth, and efforts to swallow it had failed. It had permeated and clotted her throat with an unpleasant layer of mucus.

She had not at that point understood what it meant.

She was blindfolded, as well, so she could not tell who had her or how many of them there were or where they might be taking her. They barely spoke, and when they did it was airship-speak—directions, control management, and navigational terms delivered mostly in one or two words. They were men, but that was all she could tell. Their voices gave nothing away of their origins. They gave nothing away of their numbers.

She waited for them to remove the blindfold and gag, but they never did. They must have known what might happen if they gave her even a single breath by which to summon her magic. They must have understood what she was. They would not have bothered with all the bindings otherwise.

They were flying, though. She could tell that much from the movement of the vessel in which she lay trussed. She tried to guess what sort of airship, but it was impossible to know without some small allowance for sight or movement. She was frustrated in every aspect by her kidnapping. She hated not knowing. Was Leofur all right? Had they brought her along, too?

Who was responsible for this?

Arcannen, she thought. Who else would dare such an intrusion into Druid country, practically in sight of Paranor's walls? They would be missing her already. They would have begun to search. They had the means to find her and they would act. She would be free again soon enough.

But to be in the sorcerer's hands? Yet again? Had he nothing else to do than keep coming after her? And to what end? She told herself that if it was Arcannen, at least she was ready for him this time. There would be no more mind bending, no more illusions and trickery. She had learned a thing or two since about how to use her magic, how to protect herself if she should come under attack. Once she got that gag off, things would be different.

So her thinking went. And then they had landed—a hard, jarring descent that threw her across the floor of the vessel. It was rough enough that she believed they might have crashed. And indeed they quickly hauled her out once they were down and, apparently recovered enough to do so, carted her away. This time she could tell a little more about them. There were at least three—two carrying her and another leading the way. Others joined them a little later, and there was a campfire and the smell of food cooking, though none was offered to her. Still no one spoke except in whispers, most of which were too soft for her to follow.

She was terribly hungry and thirsty by then, but no effort was made to allow her to eat or drink. She was left bound, gagged, and blindfolded throughout her time with them. She was wrapped in a blanket and left to her thoughts with no indication that anything would change.

Then she heard the airship. Its sounds were soft and distant, but she heard them clearly enough to identify what they were. It landed somewhere close by, the thrusters powering down. Hands reached for her, lifted her, and carried her off to meet it. She was placed inside. Further talk ensued, all of it too soft to make out. When the airship rose she was aboard and the men were gone, and her life was about to enter a new phase of miserable.

The witch had her.

The Murk Sink was her new home.

She ran through her memories one more time, trying to glean a fresh scrap of information about what had happened, but her memories were all scraped clean, and there was nothing more she could do to fill in the missing pieces until someone told her all the things she still didn't know.

A gentle rustling caught her attention, the soft sound of footsteps as they crossed the wooden floor of the cabin. She waited for the hateful voice.

"Good morning, Chrysallin," the little girl greeted her.

She gritted her teeth. *It begins anew,* she thought. She felt an unexpected rush of elation and relief—because this was all she had to look forward to—and it shamed her.

At least now she would be released from the cage so she could play the game. The bindings, gag, and blindfold had come off days ago, almost the minute she arrived. She was put in the cage, of course, but even so it allowed for some small freedom of movement. And almost every day she was taken out so she could move around the cabin, unrestricted save for the chain cuffed to her ankle.

Of course, there was the matter of the mysterious root she was forced to chew and ingest. Always the root. The little girl stood right there while she ate it, then examined Chrysallin's mouth afterward to make sure she had swallowed all of it. Hiding it never worked.

There was no avoiding the root.

Or its immediate and lasting effects on her voice. It was the same root forced into her mouth when the men had taken her at Paranor. It was the same bitter taste. She understood its purpose now. The little girl had told her.

"You have to take this, Chrysallin," she announced apologetically. "You must chew it and swallow it. The witch will know if you don't. She knows everything. She will hurt me if you disobey, and then she will hurt you. The root takes away your voice. That way you won't be able to speak. Your magic won't work. The wishsong relies on strength of voice, and you will have none. The effect is immediate and complete. So there will be no point in trying to cast spells. Do you understand what I am telling you?"

Chrys had understood, all right. But of course she had tried anyway, only to discover the little girl was right. Her voice—and therefore her control over any form of the wishsong magic—was gone. Her one weapon, her one chance of breaking free, had been taken away.

The locks on the door to her cage began to release, their sharp snicks a reminder of what her patience could yield. The bolts slid back and her cage door opened to the gray and murky swamp light.

And the beaming face of the little girl.

"Come out, come out! It's time to play!"

A bit stiff and feeling awkward and exposed, Chrysallin stooped and crawled out of her cage. The little girl leaned down and patted her head—like you might a pet let out for food and drink and play-time. Chrys wore one of the two white shifts she was allowed, the only clothes she was given—one to be worn while she washed the other. She was permitted no shoes. Not that she would have tried to run anywhere if she had them.

The little girl stood before her, half her size, small and frail and so unassuming it was ludicrous. But this was no one Chrys would ever think of trying to overpower. The freckled face, the blue eyes, the but-ton nose, and the endless smile were all for her benefit, meant to be reassuring. They were anything but. The little girl, after all, was al-ways pretending. She was always playing the game.

"Let's start you out with some good bread and milk," she an-nounced brightly after cuffing Chrysallin's ankle to the chain. She took her prisoner's hand and led her over to the little table where her meal was waiting. Together, they sat down and the little girl watched while Chrys ate her breakfast. Irritating, but there was nothing she could do about it. The little girl made all the choices.

Oddly, she did not have a name. Chrys had signaled, but the little girl only shook her head. "I belong to the witch," was all she would say. "She will not tell me my name. She likes me as I am."

Which was one way of putting it, but Chrys knew better.

"What shall we do today?" the little girl asked.

Chrys shook her head, giving no suggestion of an answer. This was the only show of defiance behind which she could take refuge—a small and rather insignificant act of protest. If she was not to be al-lowed the use of her voice, she would respond as little as possible. Of course, sometimes she had no choice. The little girl made certain of that.

"Why don't we sit over there at the window and watch for Mr.

Teeth?" the little girl suggested, clapping her hands. "He is so much fun when he jumps up and snatches the birds! Or some other foolish creature trying to swim the waters of the Sink. I just love watching Mr. Teeth! Wouldn't that be fun to do?"

Chrys shrugged.

"Oh, Chrysallin, I wish you wouldn't be like this. Don't be so unhappy. This isn't my fault. I would let you go if I could, you know that!"

The plea sounded so genuine, the words so sincere, that at first Chrys had believed them. Had wanted desperately to believe them. But that was before she figured out the truth. Before the nature of the game revealed itself. Now she knew not to believe anything.

On that first day after her arrival and upon her release from the cage, the little girl had explained her situation in detail. She had started with the warning that any attempt to use her magic would fail—worse, that it would cause her extreme pain. She must never try to speak. Also, she must take the root she would be given each day. She must chew it and swallow it in the little girl's presence. Her mouth would be examined afterward. This was regrettable, but the little girl was afraid of the witch, who had invested her with responsibility for seeing that Chrys obeyed and promised that any failure would cause her pain of a kind she had already experienced and never cared to experience again.

The chain about Chrys's leg was intended to keep her from going outside the cabin. She was never to do that. She was never even to try. If she did and somehow succeeded, Mr. Teeth or one of the other things that lived in the Murk Sink would eat her. Some of those things were very big—bigger even than Mr. Teeth. Some lived very close. They would not bother the witch or the cabin and those who lived in it. Wards prevented that from happening. But anything that went beyond their protective shield was fair game. Thus the chain and the warning as preventives.

She was allowed three meals a day and regular baths and changes of clothes. She was not mistreated so long as she obeyed the rules. She had the little girl for a companion, and they could play together and visit for several hours each day.

But this arrangement quickly went from bad to worse. After the first few days, the little girl would stay anywhere from several hours to all day. Until Chrysallin, having figured out what was going on, thought she would scream.

"The witch might come visit today," the little girl said as Chrys finished her breakfast. She smiled brightly. "She just might."

Or not. She said the same thing every day, and it never happened. Big joke. Build up expectation, then watch hope fade to nothing. Chrys nodded in response but didn't smile. There was no point in encouraging the little snit.

The girl frowned in disapproval, then took Chrys's hand firmly in her own and led her over to the bench in front of the window by the locked door where they could look out at the swamp. "Let's sit and watch," she whispered conspiratorially.

They sat together, looking into the mist. The cottage sat well back in a heavy stand of cypress, which sheltered and protected it, with enough gaps between the trees to allow them to look out over the huge, weed-choked lake and its grass-tufted islands. The Murk Sink was a sprawling wetlands dotted with pools of water (some miles wide), thick stands of mango and cypress, large clumps of swamp grasses, and hidden stretches of quicksand. For those unfamiliar with swamps, it should be said that no one in his or her right mind should ever wish to stumble into one. Perversely, only familiarity could save you. There were things living there that couldn't be found anywhere else except farther north in the Matted Brakes—things bigger than buildings and with teeth the size of arms and legs. The Murk Sink was perpetually shrouded in mist and clouds, colored in shades of washed-out gray and green, infused with chilling noises of dubious origin, and inhabited by dozens of creatures that could kill you without warning.

Chrysallin had been told all this by the little girl on that first day. She had been warned what running away would get her. She could simply look out the cottage windows to confirm that it was so. As for what she couldn't see, she had only to sit where she was sitting now and wait patiently for the visible proof to surface.

It did so quickly on this day. A large heron and its mate settled on a wide stretch of water perhaps a hundred feet away from the window through which she was looking, finding a log that provided them with a sure-footed resting place. They had just folded their wings and set about surveying their surroundings when the log dropped away beneath them and the waters parted in a surge of open jaws and blinding spray. They were gone in an instant, caught between those hideous jaws and dragged beneath the surface. After only seconds, the waters stilled and turned placid once more, the log that wasn't a log reappeared, and it was just as if nothing at all had happened.

The little girl clapped and squealed. "Did you see that? Wasn't that wonderful? Wasn't it exciting?"

She went on like that for a while longer, enthusiastic and voluble, using words like *crush* and *blood* and *teeth* and *ripped apart*. Chrysallin was used to it and simply ignored her, but it was hard pretending she didn't care. She hated the little girl. She wanted her dead. She wished she could manage it on her own, but she knew she couldn't. In the meantime, there was no reason to give this little monster even the slightest satisfaction.

This, after all, was how her days were spent. All of her days, thus far. All those yet to come, too, she imagined, until Arcannen finally came for her. The little girl required a playmate, and Chrys was the closest thing at hand. So the position fell to her by default, and there was nothing she could do but endure her forced participation.

She thought about being back in the sorcerer's hands, and though anything seemed preferable to spending even one more day with the little girl, the prospect was terrifying. She might feel better prepared to deal with Arcannen this time around, but she knew she was only kidding herself. It would be a nightmare, whatever his plans for her, and not knowing what he had planned for her only added to her fear.

Staying with the little girl, however hateful, was at least predictable. She knew what she could expect, so long as she obeyed the rules. It might be unpleasant, but it was a fixed routine with minimal danger, because she was being kept for Arcannen and no harm was to come to her.

So she did what she was told (not much choice there, anyway) and followed the rules and caused no trouble. If it wasn't for the pretense and the lies and the stupid, stupid game, it might even have been bearable. But the game was a nightmare. Everything the little girl did was in furtherance of the game. The game was everything to her. The game was life itself.

But that wasn't why the little girl was insane. The little girl was insane because she actually believed all the stuff she kept insisting was true, not the least of which was her relationship to the witch.

The little girl was neither a prisoner nor an unwilling servant.

The little girl *was* the witch.

20

SOMETIMES YOUR CHOICES ARE PREDETERMINED, NO matter how you might wish otherwise. It was certainly so for Paxon Leah and the remainder of his little company as night fell. They had walked for the rest of the day after burying Karlin Ryl. Miriya had argued for carrying her into the forests of the Anar, but both Paxon and Isaturin had insisted that none of them had the strength. All five were bone-weary, so they chose to bury her on the plains and go on as best they could. Miriya was inconsolable but accepted their decision. They dug a trench as deep as they could manage using blades and hands, then wrapped the young Druid seer in a blanket and laid her to rest.

Miriya did not speak to anyone after that, or even walk close to them. It was as if she were a stray following at the edges of a pack, her grief a burden so terrible she could not find a way to share it.

The presence of more plants in the distance forced them toward the Wolfsktaag Mountains, and this was a choice that Paxon, at least, was not happy about. There were worse things than man-eating plants in those mountains—things so huge and terrible that the stories recounted about them had become the stuff of legend. Almost no one had ever seen these creatures, and most of those who had were dead. But even in the family history of the Leahs the stories persisted, a part of the family's connection to the Ohmsfords and the Druids of

Paranor. Paxon knew them—and, whatever anyone else might think, he believed them.

But turning north would take them back into a fresh maze of plants, and no one could bear to think about that.

So they left the flats and went into the foothills with the setting sun and found shelter in a copse of fir where they could sleep safely enough to recover from their ordeal. Paxon couldn't remember the last time he had slept, but as nominal leader of this small band, it didn't feel right letting anyone else take first watch, so he took up his position. His weariness had drained him of the ability to dispel his sense of disorientation, and it took time to recover. Standing watch gave him that chance, and within the stand of fir, still well short of the Wolfsktaag Mountains, he felt safe enough to take advantage of it.

At midnight, he tapped one of the Trolls to take his place and went straight to sleep.

His sleep was untroubled, which surprised him. He would have thought he would experience nightmares of some sort, given what he had been through. But not once did he emerge even for a moment from his dark peace. When he woke, the sky east was just beginning to lighten with the sunrise. He glanced around and found everyone still asleep save for Miriya, who had taken the last watch and was looking straight at him from atop her perch on a fallen log perhaps twenty feet away. He rolled to a sitting position and nodded to her. She nodded back, but there was such despair in her eyes that he rose immediately and went to sit with her.

"Did you sleep at all?" he asked quietly, settling himself close.

She shook her head. "I couldn't. I might never again. I keep seeing that thing coming out of Karlin, seeing her collapse, a shell it used and then discarded. I keep seeing her face."

She shuddered and clasped her hands as if attempting to hold herself together. "I don't understand it, Paxon. Why didn't she tell me? Why didn't she say something about what was happening?"

"Maybe she didn't know. Maybe she didn't understand what was happening. She could have known something was wrong without knowing exactly what it was."

"But she asked us to help her! You heard her. She must have known something!"

"I don't think her asking for help means she knew what was wrong." He paused and exhaled toward the mountains. "But even if she did, there's nothing to say she could do anything about it. Having that thing inside her might have stolen her ability to act. It might have been controlling her."

They were silent for a moment, looking at each other, then looking away, as if the conversation was too uncomfortable to continue. Paxon thought about Karlin's horror at finding she was inhabited by another being—one she knew was evil and dangerous. What must that have been like? She had to have been incredibly strong to withstand it. He wouldn't judge her for it. He wasn't sure what he would have done if it had been him.

"Maybe she knew what would happen," Miriya said suddenly, talking to her feet. "Maybe she knew if it left her, she would die."

Paxon leaned close. "Yet she managed to ask for help and even managed to tell us when the Federation pursuit crashed. She exercised as much freedom of speech as she could. It took courage to do even that."

Miriya nodded wordlessly. Then she gave a strangled sob and began to cry. "I just want her back! I want this never to have happened! I hate it that she left me! I hate it!"

Now Paxon did put his arm around her, feeling her wince as he did so. But he held on anyway, his grip firm. "She didn't want to. She tried to prevent it, I think. She loved you. She might even have been trying to protect you."

Miriya looked at him. "That would be like her. She always worried about me, never herself. She was always trying to make me feel better about something." She sighed and rocked back against his arm. "It hurts so much that she's gone."

She swiveled away from him suddenly, shrugging off his arm. "But we're going to find out how this happened, you understand? You have to promise me you will help. You know more about Arcannen than I do. I don't think Isaturin is strong enough to do what's needed. I don't think he even cares. He hasn't said a word to me since Karlin died."

Paxon was astonished. "Well, he's probably in shock. He's lost his entire delegation save for you. He'll come around. He knows how you feel."

"Maybe," she said distractedly. Then, fixing on him, "I can depend on you to help me with this, can't I? I need to know this, Paxon. I need to be sure."

"You can depend on me. But just to be clear, I don't know for sure that Arcannen is behind this. I only *think* it might be him. Still, I want whoever did this to be punished as much as you do. We just have to be sure who it is before we act."

She kicked at the foothills earth, looking determined and angry. "I know that, Paxon! Don't treat me like a child." She steadied herself. "I just want to make clear that this isn't something I'll forget about later. I won't. I will find who's responsible, no matter what stands in my way. I won't rest until then—even if I have to leave the order to achieve it. Even if I should die trying."

Paxon held up his hands in a warding gesture. "Stop talking like that. I understand how you feel. And don't worry. We'll get at the truth. And I'll stand with you when it matters."

They lapsed into silence again, a long slow stretching out of time and space that seemed much longer than it actually was. Within the next half hour the sun rose, the sleepers woke, and the new day began.

The members of the little company were almost out of food, so they ate only a bit of what remained before setting out. They knew this was likely all they would get for nourishment for the rest of the day unless they foraged or hunted game, and no one really wanted to take time for that. Instead, they needed to find a Dwarf village, and there were plenty of those somewhere ahead. They did find a stream running down out of the mountains and stopped to drink and to fill the two remaining aleskins. Thirst was more of an issue than food.

The difficulty with what they were attempting was apparent from the geography of the Lower Anar. Had they been able to continue through the foothills to get past the carnivorous plants before descending once more to the flatlands, things might have been different. But the Battlemound Lowlands were studded with dangerous plants and trees of all sorts, including the treacherous Sirens and Stranglers. So they couldn't descend onto the flats when the foothills disappeared but instead were forced to climb into the mountains. The presence of sheer cliffs and jagged outcroppings severely limited the choice of trails and left them much higher up and deeper into the Wolfsktaag than they had intended. The way forward was rugged and treacherous, and even after they had gotten down out of the cliffs and onto the foothills once more, they were swallowed by heavy forest-land that fronted defiles, and caverns big enough to swallow entire buildings, which hid who knew what sorts of dangerous beasts.

They kept far enough away so as not to find out, but the presence of those black holes was a constant reminder of how close to the ra-zor's edge they were walking.

The forests they now traversed were equally disturbing. They con-sisted mostly of conifers grown so closely together that even walking single-file they could not pass between them without the branches brushing their shoulders—an unpleasant reminder of the plants they had barely escaped before. The darkness and silence were pervasive and ominous, and after a while all of them began to hear noises where there weren't any. If there were birds nesting in those trees, there was no evidence of it. They never saw a single winged creature. They never saw squirrels, chipmunks, or mice, either. They saw nothing living besides themselves.

Their progress was also mind-numbingly tedious and slow. Their surroundings never changed; the claustrophobic feel of their path never varied. Thousands of trees came and went, all looking exactly the same. The absence of other living creatures was a troublesome and disconcerting constant. They talked a little among themselves sometimes, just to break the silence, but mostly they concentrated whatever strength remained on moving ahead. Paxon passed the time replaying the events that had taken place in the Assembly over and over in his mind, trying to conjure a recognizable scenario that would explain the reason behind the attack, but the effort defied him. Even if Arcannen was to blame, why would he go to so much trouble to disrupt their peace talks with the Federation? What did it gain him? There must have been a reason. He must have thought there was something to gain.

The day passed, and once again it was nightfall. Still deep within the thickly forested foothills, they found a place sufficiently wide to stretch out and sleep while at the same time offering a modicum of protection from predators. After eating the last of their food and drinking a small portion of their water, they sat together in the darkness and silence for a short while, then set a watch schedule and lay down to sleep.

Before doing so, Paxon sat with Fero Darz. In the cool darkness of nightfall, the latter's face was streaked with sweat and grime, and his lean features were strained. He had barely spoken all day, keeping to himself as they traveled. It almost felt like Darz was avoiding him.

"You've been quiet," Paxon said.

Darz looked at him. "What is there left to talk about? We are just marking time. Just waiting for the inevitable." His eyes filled with mistrust and dark expectation. "You understand. You know what's going to happen."

He was waiting to die. It was so odd to see this side of him that it caused Paxon to hesitate before responding.

"Another day or two and we'll be fine. The worst is past."

"You don't know that. You don't even know what the worst is. We have miles to go. We're on foot and everything in these mountains is hunting us. So don't pretend otherwise."

"I'm not trying to. But I trust in our ability to fight off anything that comes at us. We're not helpless."

"Oh, like the other night? When that thing came out of the girl? Are you trying to tell me you had everything under control when that happened?" He shook his head. "We're dead, Paxon. We're just walking around waiting for it to become official."

"The Sleath." The Highlander pulled his knees up to his chest and hugged them to him. Time to change the subject. "Why do you think it came out of Karlin when it did? Why did it feel the need?"

"It was protecting itself, of course. What are you talking about?"

"But it wasn't in danger. Karlin wasn't under attack. Neither were you and the Trolls. You were all standing off to one side, safely out of the way. It was Miriya and Isaturin and myself who were surrounded by those plants. When the Sleath came out of Karlin's body, it felt random, unmotivated."

Darz grunted. "Maybe."

"And why was it hiding in her in the first place? Why did it use her like that?"

"How would I know?" Darz was angry now, confused. "And what difference does it make? I just want out of this. I want to go home."

"We all do."

But Darz wasn't listening, and he talked right over Paxon. "I believe what you told me. I believe the Druids didn't create the—what is it called? A Sleath? I don't know what happened back in the Assembly, but you couldn't have intended it to come to this. So maybe it was Arcannen or some other madman. Or maybe it was another sect of sorcerers or enemies of the Federation. Maybe anything."

"I appreciate hearing that. You should tell Isaturin."

"Should I? I tried, earlier. I couldn't get him to look at me. He just nodded and kept walking. Like it didn't matter. Like *I* didn't matter." He shook his head, his eyes fixing on Paxon. "He seems broken to me. You should watch him closely. He's your leader, but he seems like he's lost his way."

Paxon had to agree. Earlier, after they had stopped for the night, he had suggested to the Ard Rhys that he should say something to Miriya. After all, she was hurting from the loss of her partner; a few words from him would provide her with a little comfort.

Isaturin had looked at him as if he didn't even know who he was. "What can I say to her?" he had replied. "What is there *to* say? She will have to find her own way through her grief. I can't help her."

The bluntness of his response was so unexpected that Paxon had just stood there. Isaturin had dismissed the idea out of hand. He didn't seem to understand the importance of it. Again, the Highlander had told himself that it was the shock of losing the others, of failing to save them, of being driven out into the wilderness and left with only the tattered remnants of his delegation to find a way home again, that influenced him.

But now he was thinking it might be something more. It might be that Isaturin—who had no real experience with disasters of this sort, and who had not been trained in the field—was beginning to fall apart.

Paxon slept that night with the specter of this possibility gnawing at his confidence. For the first time, he found himself questioning the ability of the Ard Rhys to lead. Why had Isaturin entrusted their fate to him? While he was the High Druid's Blade and delegated protector of the members of the Druid order, he was neither a tracker nor a survivalist. His experiences made him no better qualified than the rest of them to find a way to survive in the wild or to avoid the creatures that lived there. Even the Trolls were better equipped for that responsibility than he was.

He woke at dawn more doubtful than ever, his eyes bleary and his brain fogged. He had slept badly, restless and dream-racked. The others shuffled around like the walking dead, as well. Because there was nothing to eat, they set out almost immediately. The day was dark with storm clouds, and within the first hour it began to rain. They turned back into the mountains because the foothills ended at a deep, wide canyon that ran east and west for as far as the eye could see. A river flowed along its floor, but it was so far down it appeared to be little more than a slender thread. Trees and brush clung to the cliff faces with roots dug into the rocky surface like grasping fingers, but there were no paths leading down and no indication that attempting a descent was a good idea. The shortest, quickest path was through the mountains where, farther up, the cliffs met, allowing for a way to cross.

But the climb was slow and arduous, and before long they were breathing hard, their muscles strained and their heads light. They paused to rest close to what appeared to be a shelf of rock that would serve as a bridge. Behind it, the cliffs split apart once more, opening into a vast, high, impenetrable darkness in the rainy gloom. Higher up still, the peaks disappeared into the clouds. The tree line ended just below this misty canopy, tapering off into scrub pine and fir, the tiny trunks gnarled and twisted as they hugged the rugged surface of the rock.

"When we get to the other side, we're going back down onto the flats," Paxon announced while they collected their breath. He couldn't tell if his companions heard him or not. No one was looking at him; no one responded. "Those plants can't have grown this far north. We must be almost to the Silver River by now. We should find some Dwarf villages not too far away."

He said it without knowing if it was true and mostly just to offer some small bit of encouragement. He said it as much to convince himself as them. But he meant it nevertheless. He was determined they would get through this.

When they rose to move on, it was raining even harder—hard enough that it was virtually impossible for Paxon, who was in the lead, to see the Trolls, who were acting as rear guard, as more than vague shadows. He would never have attempted to continue if there was any sort of shelter to be found, but there wasn't. The rock face was bare of everything but scrub; the conifers that warded them the night before were nowhere to be found.

Miriya moved up beside him. "We can't go on like this much longer, Paxon. Are you sure about those Dwarf villages?"

He shook his head. "I'm not sure about anything at this point. But we might as well assume the best. We can't stay up here. We can't stop. We have to keep going."

She gave him a look, nodded, and dropped back again. She couldn't be pleased with his answer, but he didn't want to lie to her. She would understand. Miriya was a warrior. Yet he wondered what would happen to her now that Karlin was gone. The seer had been her whole life these past few years. Her passing would leave a hole that would be hard—if not impossible—for Miriya to fill.

They summited the ridgeline and found themselves face-to-face with mountain walls that rose into the clouds. They stared upward in awe for long moments, thinking of what it would mean to try to climb those towers, then turned toward the stone shelf that formed a bridge over the canyon cliffs bracketing the river. Its flat-layered surface was broad and open, but the split behind it was a scary-looking crevasse that might be hiding almost anything.

Or nothing, Paxon told himself. Nerves weren't a good idea at this point. He glanced back at Miriya and Isaturin as he drew his blade. The Trolls were already moving up, placing themselves between their charges and the split. Paxon took a moment to let everyone settle in place, then nodded to the others and started ahead. In single file, with the Trolls fanned out toward the cliff face, they edged out onto the shelf.

The rain continued to fall, and their rocky bridge, carpeted thick with lichen and moss, was dangerously slick. Paxon motioned for them to remain spread out, to create enough open space between them that they couldn't all be swept away if anything went wrong. He thought belatedly he should have had them roped but then remembered they didn't have any rope. They barely had anything left by now; most of their supplies had been lost or consumed along the way.

Lightning flashed across the sky ahead, jagged streaks of blinding white fire that arced from horizon to horizon before lancing down to strike the peaks atop their perch, exploding with such force it felt as if the whole mountain might come down. Paxon, halfway across the bridge, dropped to one knee. Behind him, the others hesitated as well.

Miriya moved up in a hurried crouch. "Keep going! We can't stop out here! There's no protection at all!"

She was right. The wind was picking up, whipping over them with tremendous gusts. Lightning was still fracturing the black sky. He rose, motioned to the others, and started ahead once more. By now the Trolls, acting as a buffer, had caught up to them and begun to move ahead.

It was their undoing.

They were a little more than halfway across when a monstrous apparition, obscured by sheets of rain and heavy gloom, burst from the dark opening in the cliffs. It gave no warning save for the scuttle of claws against rock and a sharp hiss that managed to rise above the howl of the wind. Paxon caught only a momentary glance of their attacker before it was on them. *A giant lizard! No, a dragon!* It had the thick, scaly hide and horned spine of both, but its neck and tail were long and sinuous, and rows of teeth jutted from its open maw. There was no time for anyone to act. It caught up the Trolls—one snap, two snaps—and they were gone. It kept coming, right at Paxon, who squared away, sword in hand, facing this juggernaut as it bore down on him like a landslide. The Sword of Leah blazed to life, fire ripping through it, green snakes climbing its length, brilliant light filling the darkness. The dazzling suddenness of it was startling. Enough so that it caused the dragon to shy away.

Which did not slow its momentum but did cause it to lose its footing.

Claws scrabbling futilely at the slick surface, it careered into Paxon and Miriya. And, as it slid over the edge of the rock shelf, it took them with it.

Fero Darz saw it all. He was trailing with Isaturin, barely able to lift his head he was so weary. His night had been long and sleepless, plagued by nightmares and repeated waking. One of those nightmares had apparently come looking for him. He heard its claws rasping against the rock ledge at the last moment and looked up in time to see it emerge from the darkness—a horror that dropped him to his knees in a huddled ball. He reached for his weapon, but it was still in Paxon's hands. He fell backward into Isaturin in his frantic efforts to escape as the dragon disposed of the unfortunate Trolls, lost its grip on the stone surface of the rock shelf, and slid into Paxon and Miriya, sweeping them away as it disappeared over the edge.

"Paxon!" he managed to scream.

"They're gone!" Isaturin grabbed him by his shoulders and hauled him to his feet. His face was an unreadable mask—stark, flat, and empty of expression. "Perhaps you should join them."

Then he seized the hapless Commander of the Ministerial Watch and flung him into the void.

Once alone, Isaturin continued across the uneven ledge, fighting wind and rain, trying not to stumble, intent on finding his way down off the mountain.

21

THEY FLEW OUT OF GRIMPEN WARD EARLY THE next morning—Leofur, Imric, and Olin—the three of them crammed into the Druid two-man. It was an uncomfortable squeeze at best, but flying was the only reasonable choice, for the Murk Sink was at least two days away by foot and one by horseback—and all of it through rugged country populated by very dangerous creatures. This was the Wilderun, after all, and everyone who knew anything about the history of the Four Lands understood its perverse and treacherous character.

Leofur flew their vessel, with the boy seated next to her to provide directions. A taciturn and introspective Imric Cort rode in the rear with the supplies, listening but adding nothing to the conversation. He had said little to Leofur after their conversation the night before and even less since rising. It seemed to her he had retreated into a place of his own choosing, one to which he went when he required privacy. His mood wasn't outwardly dark, although within his carefully spun cocoon it might be. But it felt more complex than that, and she could sense the wheels turning and the gears shifting as he watched and considered. There was a marshaling of strength and a determination reflected in his lean features, a kind of gathering up of resources to face what he suspected lay ahead.

Her own demeanor was scarcely less off-putting. She had risen that morning vaguely unhinged and thoroughly out of sorts, a different young woman from the one who had gone to bed the night before. She could not explain it, but there was a seismic shift in her regard not only for herself or her razor's-edge rescue mission, but also for the direction her life had taken. It came over her so quickly it left her disoriented, infused with dark and troubled emotions. It demanded her attention. No, it screamed for it. The flight gave her time and space to let it have its say. She had always been honest about herself, in large part because of the nature of her childhood. When you were the daughter of Arcannen Rai—a child of one known parent only—you learned quickly how to separate fact from fiction and avoid pretense in favor of truth.

Over the course of her life, she had found this to be a good and necessary principle, and had always embraced it willingly. And so it was here.

So what, exactly, was she doing here?

What was she doing with her life?

What sort of life had she found for herself?

These were the core questions she grappled with in the cool, damp light of the new day, off on what might turn out to be a fool's errand or a pointless exercise in self-indulgence. These were the questions that would not be banished until she had satisfied herself with answers. She considered each in turn, found them inextricably connected, then set about trying to discover the reason they had surfaced so abruptly, in the middle of this quest, at a time when such questions were highly intrusive and unwelcome.

She was miles from Paranor, her home. She was farther still from Wayford, where so many of her years had been spent before that. She had wandered away from everything she knew, and what sort of reason did she have for it? On the surface, the immediate answer was simple. She had come to save her friend, Chrysallin Leah. But she had come a long way, and to an extremely dangerous place, with no assurance that her friend was even here. What did she really know of Chrysallin's whereabouts and condition, after all? She was relying on the skills and abilities of a man who was not entirely human, but something so foreign and mysterious she might never come to understand more than a little about him. She was relying on the words of thieves and kidnappers—words forced from their lips by her threats—to guide her. She was trusting to instincts and hunches where both were highly suspect. She was taking a risk no sane person would take because she felt a responsibility to do so. If she was wrong, she might die. If she was wrong, her friend might be lost.

Worst of all, Paxon had not come with her.

She understood why, and she knew she shouldn't blame him for his absence. And yet she did. Because at the root of her questions was the fact that Paxon was never there when she most needed him. No, that sounded selfish. And, besides, it was worse than that. He was never there, period. He was a paladin, a Knight-errant in service to the Druids, and so was always off on some quest or other. It was in the nature of his duty—and to Paxon, duty was everything.

She had not thought it would be like this. She had thought, when he had appeared on her doorstep all those months ago, that he had come back to her because he needed her. And in the beginning, he had. But now he didn't seem to. Oh, he loved her well enough, and he valued her. As she loved and valued him. But the fire that had been there in the beginning was gone. The need and the want and the pure, unadulterated passion—there was no time for it now. You had to be together to have that, and they were always apart.

This had to change. They had to find a way to change it.

Beyond that particular concern, however, she was questioning her life in other ways as well. She found again a lack of purpose since she had moved to Paranor with Paxon. She had enjoyed a busy life in Wayford as a trader of goods and a procurer of hard-to-find artifacts and weapons. She had friends and acquaintances with whom she did business on a regular basis, people from all over the Four Lands. She loved traveling for her work, loved the constant changes in her life, the challenges, the shifts in fortunes, the ebb and flow of trading and procuring.

Every bit of that was now lost to her.

And there was nothing to replace it.

She didn't think she could continue like this. The lack of anything to do in Paxon's absence was beginning to tell. She couldn't accept a life of just sitting around. As much as she enjoyed Chrysallin's company, her friendship, she needed to have something that belonged to her and her alone. She needed a purpose.

She needed so much, but she had never asked for any of it. She had never told Paxon of her unhappiness, or demanded more of him. She supposed she had been waiting for the right time. She supposed she had thought him too busy, too occupied with responsibilities, to be further burdened.

So she had kept everything to herself and carried the burden alone. Not realizing, until now, that there was never going to be a right time.

But without him, who was she? Who had she become? It felt as if her entire identity had been stripped from her. Everything she had become could be defined by her relationships to other people. Paxon's life partner. Chrysallin's best friend. The Druids' special guest. Imric's tether.

This last was particularly galling because it suggested that she was only there to serve his needs, that the tethering was not a true sharing on any level. It required one to serve and one to be served. She was his link, but she was there for him and not for herself. Was this also true of her relationship with Paxon? She wondered if maybe it was. Certainly, she did not feel as if she had any other purpose in his life.

And what, exactly, did that require of her?

And where, exactly, were the attributes and characteristics of her identity beyond that?

She was still mulling this over, her dissatisfaction evolving into a resolution to act, when Olin said, "You should set down over there." Pointing. "By the big cedar. We have to walk from here. There's no other solid ground after this on which to land an airship."

Leofur did as he instructed, finding an open piece of ground in the forested surround and descending safely. As she did so, she noticed what lay ahead for the first time. She had watched it as they approached without really seeing it, so absorbed in her private thoughts she had paid no attention to what it meant. A vast, sprawling wetlands stretched before them, a dank and fetid smell rising from its watery surface, which was dotted with islands of cypress and mango and swamp grasses of every variety. Trees were halfway toppled, drowning by inches as they were swallowed whole. Logs that might have been something else lay motionless in a miasma of gloom and mist. Birds flew through this endless haze, big and predatory, hunting. Now and again, a solitary splash was heard—a swamp dweller surfacing, perhaps, or a victim being dragged to its death. Now and again, a scream could be heard, something on the order of a screech or a howl. Hard to tell if it was hunter or hunted; the sounds all seemed the same.

All Leofur knew for certain as she climbed from the two-man and stood staring into the unchanging face of this damp, misted monstrosity of a landscape was that she wasn't meant to be here. No sane person was. But here was where she was, and there was where she must go.

Into the Murk Sink.

Olin was already beside her, and Imric beside him. Neither carried a weapon. She had her short-barreled Arc-5 strapped across her back and the smaller flash rip strapped to her waist. The boy was smiling uncertainly.

"You can take those with you, if you want," he said, indicating her weapons, "but they won't help you if you get into trouble. Not in the Murk Sink."

"Still, it makes me feel better to have them," she said.

Imric gave her a small nod. *Good for you.*

"Just stay close to me," the boy said. "Walk where I walk. Walk in my tracks, if you can. Keep your eyes open. Be aware of everything— especially the water. It's the things that live there that you most need to worry about."

"Do you have any idea where you're going?" Imric asked abruptly.

The boy shrugged. "I've navigated the Murk Sink before, so I know a few of her routes. As to where Melis is? Your guess is as good as mine. But you're the one who insisted I come. So how do you think I should do this?"

"Just start walking," Imric said. "Don't overthink it. Trust your instincts. I'll be right behind you, picking up on whatever trail I can find. We'll find something."

Olin stared at him. "Sounds a little vague, don't you think? But it's your decision. I just don't want you blaming me if nothing turns up."

The shape-shifter nodded. "No one's going to blame you. Just take us where you think Melis might be. Let your memories open up and guide you as best they can, and I'll do the rest."

The boy looked doubtful. "If you say so."

They set out into the swamp, and within a dozen yards the mist and gloom closed about them so thoroughly that the way back vanished. Ahead, the mists created a constantly shifting curtain that opened to reveal long stretches of swamp and then just as quickly closed again to seal them off. The boy seemed untroubled by this. His footsteps were quick and certain, his sense of direction apparently unaffected by the whims of the brume.

No one spoke.

What was there to say, after all?

But their otherwise silent passage was constantly broken by the movement of the swamp waters, the shrieking of birds, the screams of animals, and the occasional crack of limbs and deadwood being broken. Leofur stopped thinking about her life, about her worries for the future, about everything but what she was doing. If she didn't, she might find herself in trouble or dead. She watched the boy, the placement of her feet, and the water. Once, she saw a shadow pass just beneath the languid surface, a monstrous apparition fully fifty or sixty feet in length. It passed slowly, smoothly, and she found herself momentarily hypnotized by its fluidity until Imric placed his hand on her back to move her along again. She blinked in confusion, then in fear. It was so easy to lose focus.

Once, while they walked through a grove of cypress, the heavy mists above them suddenly opened and sunlight streamed through in long, hazy shafts that were stunningly radiant. It was magical—and so unexpected and foreign to this place that she could scarcely believe it. She smiled at the wonder of it. But in the next instant it vanished, the mists descending once again.

As the streamers of light were replaced by shadows, her smile faded.

They walked for hours through this strange world, deep into the gloom and stench and deadness. The Murk Sink seemed a place where things went to die, and all that could be found in the aftermath of their passing was the lingering smell of decaying bodies and a profound sense of loneliness.

I don't want to die here, Leofur thought suddenly.

It surprised her, the forcefulness of it. This was no random thought. This was a plea to whatever forces governed the fates of men. It came from somewhere deep within, a response to fears and doubts she had tamped down but could not dispel. She was at risk here, and not in any familiar way. There was a sense of impending doom about the Murk Sink, a whisper of death that wafted in the air. She was not normally the sort who frightened easily or lacked the courage to stand and fight whatever might come against her. But today, in this place and time, she had reached her limit.

She wanted to turn back but fought down the urge. She reminded herself of the shame and cowardice of abandoning Chrysallin, and the urge was quieted, at least for the moment.

Ahead, the swamp opened up to reveal something quite extraordinary, and she stepped up her pace to get a closer look. At first it was only an unexpected brightness, and then she saw beams and struts and cross-bracings. And curtains made out of fabrics so thin and transparent they shimmered in the pale swamp light as if they were woven of the swamp's mists. The structure emerged from the gloom, sitting open and empty in a clearing amid giant cedars that ringed it like sentries.

A bower.

Out here, in the middle of such desolation. Built by human hands, but for what purpose? And who maintained it? For it was in perfect condition, and someone must care for it or it would have fallen into ruin long ago.

But no, she thought suddenly. Even caring for it wouldn't be enough. The elements and the passage of time would erode the finishes, no matter how much care was provided. Something else was at work. *Magic.* This bower was cocooned in a shell of brightest sorcery, layered over so that nothing would change it. It was preservation of the purest sort.

Olin walked under the canopy and into the bower without a word and stood there, awe reflected on his ravaged face.

"You know this place?" Imric asked him.

The boy nodded. "She built it. She brought me here afterward to witness her wondrous accomplishment. She remade me that day in ways I will never fully understand or even try to speak of. I was hers, and it was the best thing that ever happened to me. You cannot imagine the joy I felt. You cannot believe how new and wonderful I was!"

"But you've never been back here?"

"Never." He was crying now, barely able to speak. "I couldn't find it again! Not until now. Not until this very moment. I searched for it as I searched for her cottage and could find no trace of either. But here is the one, so perhaps this time I *will* find the other, as well!"

Leofur stood next to him, gazing upward through the rafters to the low-hanging clouds and wondering at the structure's purpose. It was impressive, but so out of place here that she could not imagine a use that made any sense. She glanced questioningly at Imric, but he only smiled back and shook his head. His eyes were bright and there was an odd sense of happiness about him.

"Is this not the most amazing anomaly?" he said softly. "I have this feeling I could stay here forever."

In fact, she thought, maybe she could stay here, as well. She felt a strange peacefulness in this place that seemed so contradictory to the rest of the Murk Sink. How was it that it could shut out the otherwise dark feelings the swamp generated in her?

"We should go," Olin said suddenly. "We don't want to be out in the open at sunset."

They began walking again, with the boy leading, moving ever deeper into the Sink. Leofur went back to paying close attention to her steps and the surrounding swamp. Once, she saw fresh movement below the surface of the water, but nothing after that. It was past midday, and the diffuse sunlight was now brightest directly overhead. They still had not encountered anyone, only glimpsed birds in the air and shadows in the water. She wondered what else lived in the swamp. There would be moor cats, wouldn't there? There would be snakes and swamp rats and iron herons, at the very least.

And much worse things within the murky waters, if those shadows were any indication.

She noticed some hesitation in the boy's progress, as if he were casting about for a direction. He never lingered long, but she wondered anyway. He seemed more than a little unsure, even though he pushed ahead.

Finally, after perhaps two hours of what seemed a decided lack of progress, Imric brought them to a halt and faced the boy. "Your instincts aren't telling you anything, are they?"

The boy stared at him with something approaching fear. "No. It's not that. It's just, I'm a little—"

"You're lost." Imric cut him off dismissively. "I've been watching you. You don't know where to go. You don't have the vaguest idea."

Leofur frowned. "Did you plan to just keep us walking around in circles?"

"I didn't . . . I just wanted to . . ." Olin was stumbling over his words, unable to frame an answer. "I just didn't want to give up! I need to find her as much as you do."

"We'll find her," Imric said. He reached over and touched Leofur's arm gently. "I've found something." He knelt, his head lowered to the ground. "No mistake. It's there. A scent. A human scent."

"Chrysallin?" she asked at once, forgetting all about the boy.

"I can't tell whose scent it is without knowing more. But a scent is what we've been looking for, and this one's worth tracking." He straightened, then looked around the confines of the swamp and frowned. "Though it's not a good place to be tracking anything on foot."

"What are you talking about?" the boy asked. "You won't be able to find anything without me! You have to keep me with you!"

Leofur knew he was asking not to be sent back, but she really didn't care one way or the other. She looked at Imric. He shrugged. "The boy can come if he does what we tell him."

"You're going to shift?"

"If I can find the right shape. I'd be safer in the air, but the scent is on the ground, so let me think. Maybe a moor cat would do. Good trackers, great instincts, not many predators would go after them."

"Just be sure you stay in control after you change." She took hold of his arms and positioned him so he was facing her. "I don't want you losing contact with me again. Not for any reason. Do you understand? Promise me, Imric."

He nodded. "I'll manage it. Are you ready?"

She shifted her eyes away, a kind of resignation settling in. "As ready as I will ever be. Go ahead."

She was looking at the boy, who was looking at Imric. From the gasps he emitted and the look on his face, she could tell exactly when Imric began to change. It all happened quickly, and then he was inside her mind. She could feel his catness intruding on her thoughts, his feline instincts taking hold, his sinewy power as he flexed his claws.

Don't leave this spot. Wait for me here so I can find you. Keep an eye on the boy. He's not entirely trustworthy.

He isn't? She laughed. *Thanks for the warning.*

I will try to be quick. And keep myself safe. For you.

Then he went silent. When she turned around there was no sign of him. She gazed out into the swamp, but it was as if he had vanished completely.

For you? What did that mean? An attempt at irony, she supposed.

She looked at the boy. "Let's find a place to sit while we wait."

They decided on a small clearing where a log offered them a seat and the trees and swamp grasses were not right on top of them. They were positioned where they could look out across of the broad stretch of water they had been skirting. They could not see very far because trailers of mist hung over the surface, shifting this way and that but constantly moving. She was surprised. It felt like a windless day to her.

"Do you really want to see her again?" she asked Olin after a few minutes of silence. "Is it that important to you?"

"That and more." He didn't look at her, his eyes on the swamp.

"But what if she doesn't want you back? What if she sends you away again?"

"I won't go."

"But if she makes you? If she threatens you with harm?"

"I will accept whatever she does to me. Even dying is better than living without her."

She could not imagine this was so, but she was seeing in this boy a devotion that went beyond reason, a blind commitment to an ideal that in all likelihood did not exist. She wondered what that was like. She loved Paxon, but her commitment to him wasn't blind, and she didn't think she would choose death over life should something happen to him.

Still tracking. The scent is strong and repeats itself. Whoever uses the trail must use it often.

Imric? She quit thinking about the boy. *Are you all right? Did anything try to come after you yet?*

A chuckle. *Stop sounding so hopeful! Most things avoid moor cats, you know.*

His humor was unexpected. She liked it. *Stay alert.*

He made no further response. She glanced at the boy again. He was watching her curiously. "What are you doing?" he asked.

She shrugged. "Thinking."

She left it there, and they were quiet for a time. She stretched her legs and arms, sighed, and watched the swamp. The mists continued their pointless meandering, the shadows coming and going like wraiths. A squall appeared far out on the water, then moved away. A huge splash sounded from somewhere off in the gloom, but there was only silence in the aftermath.

"Why did Melis take your friend?" the boy asked.

"My friend has a brother. A sorcerer wants to hurt or manipulate him, I don't know which. The witch is helping by taking his sister hostage."

"You won't get her back, you know."

"I'll get her back."

"You don't know what Melis is like."

"It doesn't matter what she's like. Now stop talking."

She was angry at him for saying she would fail, but mostly she was irritated by the inactivity. She wanted to be doing something. Even knowing there was nothing more she could do until Imric finished with his tracking, she was looking for a way to help him.

She rose and walked to the edge of the lake, noting the layers of scum and grasses that choked it, her eyes drawn to the slow movement of its waters the farther out you got. Something was down there, she thought. Something very big and probably very hungry. It wouldn't do to get caught out there without a way back. Or even to think about wading in a few yards to test the waters.

Leofur! Imric was speaking again. *I think I've found what we're looking for. A cottage, right in the middle of the swamp, set back from a lake in a stand of cypress. A very deep lake, I might add.*

Do you see anyone?

No. I have to get closer to the cottage. I'm shifting back now. Just long enough to work my way along the shoreline and up to a window.

Come back and get me first. I don't want you doing this alone. You might need another pair of eyes.

Not yet. I don't want to take the time. Be patient. I'll only be a little longer.

Imric!

Silence. He was gone. She stared out at the lake, suddenly worried. Why was he so insistent on doing things by himself? What was the purpose of the tethering if he wouldn't let her be part of what was happening?

I'm back. I had to make the change. Are you all right?

Am I all right? Stop cutting me off like that! How am I supposed to know what's going on?

It was just to make the change. We can talk now. I'm walking the shoreline. Creeping along it, really. I have to be careful. I can't tell what's in that house. It's facing right toward me. I thought I saw movement in the front windows . . .

You come get me right now!

All right. Maybe that would be best. There's something out there on the lake . . .

Imric!

More silence, and then, *I can't make out what it is. It's coming this way, though. I'm moving off the shore and back into the trees. It's safer back there. Oh, oh, wait! This thing is huge! I can't be sure where it starts and stops. I'd better hurry now.*

Fear surged through her, sudden and overpowering. His, not hers.

Imric!

I'd better run, in fact! It's awfully fast for something that size. What . . .

Imric! Shades, hurry!

I'm doing that already. But I think . . . Oh, oh. Leofur, I've got to . . .

Silence.

Imric! Say something!

She waited, breathless. No response.

Imric? Imric?

When again there was no answer, she screamed his name out into the gloom and mist and felt the silence like a vast immovable weight pressing down.

22

CHRYSALLIN WAS SITTING BY THE WINDOW AGAIN.
The light was beginning to fade from the hazy sky, and
the day was winding down. She had been given lunch
and subjected to more of the little girl's revolting game, made to pretend at things she knew weren't true. They were back to watching the
swamp lake and the huge creatures that swam in its depths—an ac-
tivity of which the little girl never seemed to tire. She sat primly next
to Chrysallin, her knees together under her frilly dress, her hands
folded in her lap. She wore this same outfit or some version of it
nearly every day, having no apparent concerns about the dictates and
challenges of the place she was living.

Just once let her go outside and see what happens, Chrysallin
thought. *Just let her try walking the swamp in those ridiculous clothes.*

But maybe it wouldn't make any difference. If you were a witch
and you could do magic, you could wear whatever clothing you
wanted. You probably didn't have to worry about much of anything.

Chrysallin tried not to look over at the witch. Looking at her only
encouraged her. So there they sat, two bumps on a log, staring straight
ahead, saying nothing. Chrys watched the swamp—not to see the
swamp dwellers surface like leviathans to snatch something in their
jaws, or even with any expectation that something interesting would

happen. She watched it because most of the time the Murk Sink was peaceful, its waters smooth and still, its mists a gentle swirling that lulled and calmed her. She could think in those moments. She could let her thoughts wander where they would and remember better times. Always, she could picture those who were coming to her rescue—an army of them, led by Paxon and Leofur, who would never abandon her, never leave her in this horrid place . . .

She couldn't help herself; she started crying.

Every time she was reminded of what she was missing, she cried. She despised herself for it. She tried to hide it from the horrid little girl, but she knew the other was watching, enjoying her suffering. It would have helped if she could have stopped thinking about home and her friends and loved ones and rescue, but she couldn't. It was pretty much all she had to fall back on. She comforted herself with the knowledge that before, when the witch Mischa was trying to subvert her, she was in an even worse situation. At least now she could sort through what was what without drugs or mind control dulling her senses.

She steadied herself and the tears stopped. When she got out of this mess—however long it took her to do so—she hoped to never again have anything to do with witches. Two in one lifetime had turned out to be more than enough.

She found herself smiling. Good. If there was humor to be found, she could survive anything.

She caught a glimpse of movement out on the swamp. A sudden flash against the landscape off to her left, away from where the little girl was sitting. Chrysallin fought to keep from looking at it more directly. But she could see, even if just out of the corner of her eye, a man, naked and unarmed, creeping along the shoreline of the lake. She blinked in spite of herself. She must be seeing things, because he had come out of nowhere. But no, there he was. And still without clothes. How in the world had he gotten this far in *that* condition?

He was moving toward the cottage. Clearly, he had seen it and was coming to investigate. If the witch didn't see him first, he just might . . .

"What does he think he's doing?" the little girl said softly, a sly tone to her voice. "Does he want to attract the things that live in the deep swamp? Does he think he will escape Mr. Teeth?"

Chrysallin's heart sank. Of course the little monster would notice. How could she help but notice? All she did when not tormenting Chrys was stare out into the swamp, waiting for some unsuspecting creature to provide entertainment for her pet, Mr. Teeth. It was the biggest beast of any kind she had ever seen, so huge she didn't even know how the lake could hold it. Somehow, the girl had control over it and could get it to do what she wanted. If it didn't act fast enough on its own.

It didn't seem to be paying much attention this time. The man was getting closer, and the swamp dweller was still nowhere in evidence.

The little girl winked at Chrysallin conspiratorially, made a few quick gestures with her hands, and abruptly something splashed out on the waters, causing the man to hesitate and look back over his shoulder.

"That should be enough to make sure we don't get bored," the little girl announced happily.

Chrysallin was stunned. Now there was no hope for the man, none whatsoever. He was still trying to reach them, but she could see the surface of the lake swirling where Mr. Teeth rested—a clear indicator that he was awake and moving to intercept his prey.

She watched the ripples swell to a small wave and then a larger one as the swamp dweller picked up speed. It was less than fifty feet away from the man now, and coming on so swiftly that it was already too late for him to run. And with her voice gone, Chrys couldn't even scream to save him. Maybe he would sense the danger. Maybe he would still have time to . . .

Mr. Teeth broke the surface of the water, a surge that carried his front half right onto land and through the trees, his massive jaws sweeping up the man as if he were no more than an insignificant insect. The man disappeared into the creature's maw without a sound and was gone.

Slowly, languidly, the monstrous swamp dweller slipped back into the swamp waters and disappeared from view. Chrysallin closed her eyes in despair.

"Wasn't that exciting?" the little girl enthused. Then, with a crest-fallen look, she added, "But I guess it's over." She sighed as if disheartened, then brightened again. "So, Chrysallin, what should we do now?"

Leofur stumbled a few steps forward in shock, screaming Imric's name over and over in her mind, trying to reach him. But it was pointless. The tether was broken. *He* had broken it. There would be no answer. She stood there in shock, staring out into the layers of brume.

When she turned back again, Olin was standing there with the Arc-5 pointed at her stomach. "Don't move."

She didn't. She couldn't believe she had been so stupid. She had unslung the weapon when they sat down together on the log, as the weight of it across her shoulders had been wearing on her. She had set it on the other side of her, keeping it away from where he was sitting. But in the stunned aftermath of losing contact with Imric, she had forgotten all about it.

"Take out your other weapon and lay it on the ground," the boy continued, gesturing with the black barrel. She saw that his hands were shaking. "Then step away from it."

She hesitated, unwilling to give up both weapons, trying to think of how she could distract him for long enough . . .

"Do it right now!" he screamed, his voice cutting at her like a knife-edge, sharp and penetrating.

So she did, pulling the handheld from its sheath and setting it down gently. She moved away a few yards and looked back at him. "What are you doing, Olin?"

"Taking advantage of an opportunity." He picked up the handheld and tucked it in his belt. "I'm closer than I have ever been to finding Melis, and once I find her, I have to give her something so she'll let me come back. A present. An offering. Your friend might have been a nicer treat, but with him gone, I think I'll give her you."

Leofur tried to relax, to keep the emotions roiling inside her from revealing themselves. *Keep him talking,* she thought. *Wait for your chance.*

"Imric will be back soon," she said.

"Will he? It didn't sound like it to me. When you called his name, it was clear he was in trouble." He paused. "He's a shape-shifter, isn't he? You can communicate with him somehow when he's not with you. Wasn't that what he was doing just now? Telling you he was in trouble?"

She shook her head. "No."

"You could have fooled me. You looked worried enough. Calling out his name like that, you sounded scared. I think he found Melis, and she made him pay."

She ignored him. "Melis banished you, didn't she? She sent you away. That's why you have to bring her something she wants. But how long will she let you stay this time?"

The boy suddenly looked irritated. "You should be worried about how long *you'll* get to stay once she has you. Now start walking. Go the way your shape-shifter friend went. If he found her, so can I! Go on. Move!"

She did so, conscious of him following, the Arc-5 pointed at her back. She picked her way over swampy ground. Once, she tried to change direction, intent on leading him another way, but he called her back immediately.

"Don't try to be clever. I can read a trail better than you can."

They walked for a short distance before reaching a vast lake that sprawled ahead of them until it disappeared into a horizon of drooping tree limbs and mist. On its shores, he brought her to a stop.

"I *know* this place! This is the lake where she lives! We're close to her cottage. I've found her!"

He was so excited he was practically hysterical. She tensed, listening to him babble. This was her chance to disarm him. She was stronger, quicker. She could do it.

But then he prodded her with the flash rip. "Turn around. Walk over to that tree and sit on the ground."

He pointed to where he wanted her, and she moved over obediently. He was about to make a mistake. She was good with ropes and locks. She could get out of anything. He might bind her, but she would be free of her restraints quick enough. Then she would go after him.

Because she had to accept that Imric's admonition to stay where she was until he returned for her might not mean anything now. The boy was right. Imric's words had been cut off abruptly, as if he had been attacked. As if Melis or one of her creatures had found him. She had to assume the worst.

She sat quietly, her back against the tree, and waited. Olin moved behind her and dug from his backpack an odd-looking cord with metal cuffs attached to each end. He snapped the first metal cuff on one wrist, the lock closing with a sharp *snick,* maneuvered the cord around the tree trunk, then snapped the second cuff to her other wrist. The cuffs were firm and tight. There was no give to them at all. The cord, however, hung loose.

The boy moved back around in front of her and stared down wordlessly for a moment. Then he swung the Arc-5 over one shoulder and tucked the handheld into his belt.

"It's best if you wait here. She wouldn't want me bringing you to her home. Just sit there and be quiet. You don't want those big dwellers out in the lake to come looking for you. You've still got your knife, though, if they do. You're pretty good with that knife, aren't you? You'll need to be."

Then he turned and walked off into the gloom. He didn't even bother to look back.

She went to work on the cord and the cuff locks right away, turning about so she could see what the boy had improvised. The cord consisted of woven metal strands. It was too thick for her to break, but it was loosely draped about the trunk of the tree, giving her some freedom of movement. She glanced at the tree. The trunk was three or four feet thick—too thick to cut through by herself even if she'd had the proper tools.

But the cuff locks were a different story. The cuffs were joined by a clasp, which contained the locks and could be opened by a key. She didn't have that key, but she had something equally useful.

Inside her belt was a pocket, and inside the pocket were her picks, given to her years ago by Grehling Cara. Grehling had taught her this skill while she was still living in Wayford, the boy already an amateur thief and scrounger, accomplished at getting in and out of locked places. Deeply enamored with her, even at the age of twelve, he had shown her how to use the picks—possibly to demonstrate how clever he was, or possibly to impress her. That was all over and done with once she had met Paxon. The boy was still a friend, but grown up enough to realize there would never be anything more between them. Still, she had kept the picks.

This seemed like a good time to discover how much she remembered about using them.

Since she was free to move her hands and arms, she was able to extract the tiny pouch from her belt without difficulty. She opened the pouch and dumped out the picks. A quick glance at the sky warned her that darkness was coming on rapidly, so she would not have all that much time to free herself. She set to work, trying the first of the picks.

Fifteen minutes later, she gave up on that one and moved on to a second. Another fifteen minutes, and she wondered what was happening. No amount of coaxing would budge the locks. The longer she worked, the more worried she became. She was having no success whatever.

As twilight edged toward full darkness, she felt her hopes fade with the light. Clearly, something had been done to the locks to prevent them from being opened by anything but the key the boy had taken with him. Or would the key even work? What if the locks were magic-infused? There was no way of knowing. What she did know was that if she stayed where she was for much longer, she would be inviting every creature living in the lake to come up for a snack. She had to find better protection.

She looked up at the tree to which she was chained. If she couldn't get away from the tree, maybe she could use it instead. She stood, pulled the metal cord tight against the trunk, and began to climb. Inch by inch, she shimmied her way upward, her boots planted against the tree, using the cord to leverage herself, progressing a little higher with each step.

It was slow, arduous work, but she got as far as the lower branches before she was stymied. There was no way to get the cord past even the smallest limbs. So she found the biggest branch available to her, climbed onto it, took up the slack in the cord, and settled herself in place. Here, at least, she would be off the ground, and maybe not so easily spotted by predators.

It was the best she could do.

She tried to keep the panic at bay, but she understood well enough the precariousness of her situation. The boy would return with the witch. They would find her and take her away with them. She had no idea what would happen then, but she did not think it would end well.

Her only chance was Imric. She needed him to return.

She tried repeatedly to link to him, to re-form the tether, but there was no response. It left her dispirited and frightened. Whatever had happened, he could no longer reach out to her. The silence in her mind was deafening. Maybe he was dead. Maybe he couldn't come to her.

Whatever the case, she was helpless without him.

And alone.

Inside the witch's cottage, Chrysallin had been returned to her crate for the evening. It was night now, and sitting at the window and playing the stupid game were over for another day. Memories flooded her thoughts, particularly of the naked man being swallowed by Mr. Teeth. She could not seem to dispel it or even to push it away from her. It haunted her relentlessly.

She was sitting in a corner of the crate, waiting to grow tired enough to sleep, when she heard a knock at the door.

A knock? Who would come knocking on the door of this place?

She heard the little girl's footsteps, and then the cottage door opened. "You," she said in a voice that somehow suggested both irritation and surprise. "What are you doing here? How did you find your way back?"

Chrysallin moved over to where she could peer out through the mesh-covered airholes and see the little girl facing the newcomer. *A boy.*

Her impression was confirmed when she heard him speak. "I brought you something wonderful—a young woman who claims to be a friend of your guest."

"You have her manacled and ready for me?"

"Yes."

Chrysallin went cold. Leofur? Was the young woman Leofur?

"There was also a man, a shape-shifter," the boy was saying, "but I think you may already have gotten him . . ."

"A shape-shifter? Describe this man!"

The boy did so, and the little girl gave a disgusted snort. "He's been eaten. Mr. Teeth took him. A single gulp and gone. We watched it happen. Hardly any entertainment at all. He was naked, so that fits with your description. It must have been him." She paused. "So, you've only brought me the lesser of two treats. Did you not understand what it meant when I sent you away?"

"I am so sorry, Mistress! I just had to see you again . . ."

He blubbered on awhile about how he had done his best and how much she meant to him and some other nauseating stuff, until Chrysallin wanted to get out of the cage and strangle them both. The little girl kicked the boy at some point, telling him he was a worthless fool and should be fed to the swamp creatures and to get out of her sight and never come back.

The boy was on his knees, arms reaching out to her, beseeching her all the while to remember how much he wanted to please her and how wonderful it was just to be with her, but she ignored him and pulled away.

Then suddenly she seemed to remember the other captive, the one still waiting on her pleasure, and she asked for a description of her, too. It was clearly Leofur. A rescuer had come after all, but Leofur was obviously no better off than Chrysallin and in every bit as much danger.

"That's the girl our guest was walking with when those thieves took her. Too bad for her she thought to come visit. I could just leave her where she is and let the swamp creatures have her."

"Yes, you could," the boy agreed quickly.

"On the other hand, not seeing her die is sloppy. And no fun at all." She was musing to herself, her voice lazy and contemplative. "I do so like watching them die. And I want to know how she found her way here. She shouldn't have been able to do that. She must have found out from those fools I let live back in the Kennon. No good deed goes unpunished, does it?"

She walked over to the cage and peered in. Chrysallin moved back quickly. "Listening, are you? I see your little face pressed up against the mesh. Nothing for you to worry about, my dear. It will all be taken care of. If this young woman is your friend come to save you, I'll bring her back here and let her share your crate. You can tell her how much fun we have together, and she can play with us, too."

A pause. "Of course, if she isn't your friend . . ."

The girl pulled away from the airhole and unlocked the crate door. Chrys pulled back from her. The little girl knelt, looking at her as if examining an interesting bug. Then she held out a piece of the bitter root that stole Chrysallin's voice. "Eat this. Chew it and swallow it down. Then open your mouth and let me see."

Chrysallin did as she was told. She took the root, chewed until it was broken up, and swallowed. Moving forward, she opened her mouth and let the little girl feel around inside. It was loathsome and degrading, but she had learned early on what happened if she did not obey.

The little girl nodded, rose, and resecured the crate door. "We'll be back before dawn. Why don't you try to sleep? And don't do anything foolish. Remember where you are."

Then she was out the door, the boy following like an obedient puppy, and Chrysallin was left alone.

23

WHEN THE DRAGON TOOK PAXON OVER THE cliff, sweeping him away like debris from a pathway, he fell a long way, but not as far as he might have. At two hundred feet, a thick-limbed hemlock clinging stubbornly to the side of the cliff face arrested his fall. As he came to a bone-jarring stop, he instinctively grabbed for the branches he was already starting to slide out of, catching himself and holding fast.

It took another few seconds for him to realize he was still holding on to the Sword of Leah and was keeping his perch solely with the strength that remained in his free arm. All about him the rain continued to fall—a torrent that wrapped him in a dark, wet curtain and limited his visibility to less than a dozen feet. He had no idea what had happened to Miriya and the dragon. There was no sign of either, and no sounds rising up from farther down. He looked to see if there was any sign of the beast, but in the heavy rainfall he couldn't begin to see much of anything below the base of the crooked tree. He noted broken branches, torn-out shrubs and grasses, and assumed the dragon had continued down.

He closed his eyes with relief. Somehow, he was still alive. It had all happened so fast. One minute they were crossing the stone bridge and the next the dragon had launched itself from its hiding place and was on them. He remembered watching the dragon devour the Trolls and then rush for him. He remembered Miriya being close when the beast lost its footing and careered into them, carrying them off the ledge and down into the abyss . . .

A body plummeted past him through a screen of mist and rain, screaming and thrashing, and for a second he was certain it was Miriya. But then he caught a glimpse of the other's face, and realized it was Fero Darz. And there went the last hope of persuading the Federation of their innocence.

He closed his eyes until the screaming stopped. What had caused Darz to fall off the ledge? And what had become of Isaturin?

Taking his time, he managed to sheathe his blade. Then, using both hands, he righted himself within the limbs of the hemlock and looked about. He judged he was closer to the top than to the bottom of the canyon, so in order to reach safety he would have to climb back to the ledge. He tested his limbs and checked his ribs and found himself bruised and sore all over but with his bones intact.

He was just rising from his perch to try to find a way up the cliff face when he saw Miriya. She was hanging limp and unmoving in a cradle of branches farther up, head and limbs hanging down, water running off her still form. She looked as if she was dead. It was easy to imagine she had broken her back in the fall. He all but resigned himself to the fact that she was lost.

But he would have to get to her to be certain.

He began to climb through the branches, moving slowly so as not to disturb those boughs that held her momentarily safe, trying to stay directly underneath her as he progressed. He could not tell how securely she was wedged into her perch, and if she began to slip free he wanted to be in a position to catch her. Easier said than done, he discovered; the thickly clustered branches severely limited his route.

He was within six feet when he did something that jarred her loose. Without warning, she slid clear of the branches. Still unconscious or dead, she did nothing to slow herself as she bumped through the tree limbs on her way down. Bracing himself, Paxon grabbed the closest branch with one hand and snatched at her limp form with the other. He caught hold of her tunic as she tumbled past him, jerking her to a stop. But then the fabric began to rip, a slow rending of cloth, and he was forced to use his other hand, as well. With his legs locked around the branch on which he was sitting, he grabbed her arm and swung her toward him. He almost lost his perch, her weight yanking him away from the tree. But at the last moment he managed to gather her in, dragging her close as he steadied himself once more.

They were face-to-face now, and he could see the deep purple bruise at her temple. Her eyes were closed, but she was alive, though her breathing was slow and shallow. She'd suffered a concussion and was unconscious. He pressed her against him, feeling the coldness of her body, knowing he had to wake her. Swinging her over the branch on which he sat so that she straddled it, her back against the trunk, he slapped her cheeks, gently at first, then harder.

"Miriya!" he snapped. "Wake up! Look at me! Open your eyes! Listen to me, Miriya! Wake up!"

He repeated his efforts several time, then her eyes fluttered. "Stop it," she whispered.

"Look at me, and I will!" he shouted at her.

Her eyes opened. "Paxon? What happened?"

He took a quick few moments to tell her, then added, "You've been hurt. You're concussed. You have to stay awake. Don't close your eyes again."

"Sleepy," she murmured, her eyes beginning to close.

"No!" He slapped her hard—once, twice, three times—and her eyes opened.

"Quit hitting me, you idiot!"

"Just look at me. Does anything hurt? Does anything feel broken?"

She shook her head. "Only my face, thanks to you." She experimented with her arms and legs, felt her ribs, and shook her head. "No. I don't feel anything else. Where are the others?"

He straightened her on the tree branch. "Gone. Maybe Isaturin's still up on the ledge, or maybe trying to climb down to us. But probably he's left, thinking us dead."

She snorted, and the look she gave him was ironic. "Maybe we are and we just don't know it yet." She glanced around, a doubtful look on her rain-streaked features. "How do we get back up? Or do we climb down?"

"It's too far to climb down, so we have to go up. But you rest first. You'll need to regain your strength."

She nodded, yawned, then looked at him wordlessly for a few long moments. "Thanks for saving me."

"Yeah, well, save it for when we're both really safe again and not just hanging from a tree." He still had his water skin slung over one shoulder and handed it to her. She drank thirstily, taking deep swallows, then handed it back.

"That dragon was big," she said.

He managed a shaky grin. "The biggest thing I've ever seen. At least it's gone. After a fall like that it must be dead . . ."

A roar sounded from down in the canyon abyss—huge and ferocious and unmistakable. It rose out of the gloom through the howl of the wind and the steady rush of the rain. It shook the air.

"Okay, I'm rested," Miriya announced. "Let's go."

With the dragon's voice still echoing in their ears, they began to climb. Though the cliff face offered clusters of roots and tangled scrub along with deep crevices and rocky projections to which they could cling or on which they could stand as they worked their way up, it was slow going. The rain had soaked everything, leaving it damp and slippery. Footing and handholds both were treacherous, and the wind blew in a steady whistling howl, each fresh gust threatening to shake them loose. They had to climb separately; there was no rope to tie them together, and perhaps that would not have been something either of them would have wanted, anyway. Paxon watched Miriya carefully at first, worried that dizziness or exhaustion, coupled with her injury, might confuse or impede her. But when it was clear she was able to continue, he quit worrying and concentrated on his own efforts.

It took everything just to accomplish that. It was one foot, one hand, over and over, each time searching for a place to grab hold and dig in, the risk of falling always present. Paxon did not dare look down after they started. He knew it was a long way to the bottom. The cliff face, while not sheer, was steep enough that any slip would send them tumbling away. Plastered against the damp rock, trying to keep the wind and rain out of their eyes, the Blade and the warrior Druid pressed on.

It was an endless climb. Paxon was never able to tell how long it took, although he was aware of a darkening of the skies beyond what the storm was causing, as the day passed away toward nightfall. If they were caught out here in the dark, still trying to find their way, they were probably not going to make it. He couldn't do much about it, though. They were going as fast as they could, and doing anything more was too risky.

The only way he knew when they had finally reached the rock shelf once more was when the canyon wall began to slant gently away from him, and he was able to haul himself upward onto a horizontal slope. Together, Paxon and Miriya lay on the ground breathing heavily, faces turned toward each other as the rain beat down on them. Their fingers were scraped and bruised, their fingernails split, their hands raw with scratches and tears, and their arms and legs screaming with pain. Both were exhausted, their strength depleted from the climb. But they could not afford to rest out in the open, still on the wrong side of the rock ledge.

"Come on," Paxon said finally, hauling himself to his feet. "Let's go home."

They trudged on, crossing the bridge to the far side of the canyon. They walked all night, down out of the mountains and through the ancient trees of the Anar forests—a slog that left them emptied and mindless, able to summon just enough resolve to keep going, allowing the terrain and their instincts to guide them. The weather changed again at some point, the rain slowing but the temperature dropping as it did so. They were still in the mountains when this happened, albeit farther down the slopes and closer to the lowlands to the west. After a while, it started to snow, which caught them by surprise. Paxon wasn't even sure he knew when it began. It seemed to him, on reflection, that one minute it wasn't snowing and the next it was. He lifted his face to the soft touch of flakes falling against his skin and looked over at Miriya. She was smiling like a child.

Eventually, they reached a point where they could no longer go on. By now the snow had ceased and the grasslands were within easy reach. It was still several hours before dawn. Finding a place in the shelter of the trees bordering it, out of sight if not smell of predators, they lay down and slept.

The sun was fully risen when rough hands shook Paxon awake and a gruff voice said, "Come now, lad. Time to rise and shine."

The Highlander's eyes opened to find a Dwarf's bluff face peering down at him. Ginger beard and hair, startlingly blue eyes, weathered skin, and a touch of humor—Paxon's immediate impressions were not the sort to startle but to reassure. Nevertheless, he took a few moments to wake sufficiently to remember where he was and what had happened.

He sat up then, nodding to the other. "Well met."

"And you. Are you all right? You look rather ragged. What's happened to you and this lady, sleeping out in the open like this, with no blanket or supplies or apparently much of anything?"

Paxon glanced over at Miriya, who was still asleep. "We've had a hard time of it. Our airship crashed. We've been walking for four days, maybe more. We've come up from the Southland below the Battlemound."

The Dwarf puckered his lips. "You didn't try to come through there, did you?"

"We came through the mountains. Through the Lower Anar."

"That's even worse. Terrible things live there. You're lucky they didn't eat you."

"They tried." Paxon sat up slowly, holding his head, which was pounding. His entire body ached. "We're trying to reach Culhaven to find transportation home."

"It's a long way to Culhaven," the Dwarf said, giving him a look, "but I'll do what I can to help you. I can't leave you out here like this, that's for sure. Are you hungry?"

They woke Miriya and the three shared a portion of the food the

Dwarf was carrying. His name was Trond Ulkend, and he was a hunter tracking game for his village, which was only a few miles off. Hunting along the edge of the Anar was good, he told them. Animals tended to come down out of the mountainous regions of the Anar whenever possible for better foraging, which made things easier when you wanted to find them. He'd just set out on his hunt earlier this morning before stumbling on them.

"I haven't seen a thing since I started out, so I think I'll just see you both safely back to my village and try again tomorrow. Can you walk? I've no means by which to carry you."

"We can walk," Miriya assured him, eating the last crust of bread from her portion of the meal, washing it down with a long series of swallows from the water skin.

Trond regarded her solemnly. "This was Druid business that brought you here?"

She hesitated. "Why do you ask?"

"You wear the insignia of the order." He pointed to her breast.

She nodded. "Does it matter to you?"

He shrugged. "Just curious. Lots of talk about Druids and the Federation, even out here. It's none of my business, though, is it? Are you ready to leave?"

Paxon rose. "Is there transportation in your village that would get us back to Paranor?"

"No airships, if that's what you mean. But I could probably find you horses to get you somewhere there are airships." He looked up into the mountains. "Still, you might want to rest a bit longer first."

Indeed, Paxon thought. A longer rest would be wonderful. But he didn't think they could afford the time. Already, he could feel things slipping away from them. If Isaturin had escaped, he needed to be located and a decision reached on what was to be done to stave off the Federation. At present, the Coalition Council must still be convinced that Darz and the entire crew of his ship had perished, and that the Druids were to blame for that as well as the assassination of the peace delegation.

Things had to be set right quickly. If not, they would only get worse.

"Your offer is appreciated," he said, exchanging a glance with Miriya, "but we have matters at home that need our attention. We'll have to leave again at once."

Trond smiled. "Fair enough. I'll do what I can to help you. Let's be on our way."

24

As soon as the little girl and the boy were out the door and Chrysallin heard the lock click behind them, she began to count to one hundred. When she finished counting and neither had returned, she stuck her fingers down her throat and threw up the piece of voice-numbing root she had only pretended to chew and then swallowed whole. It was an unpleasant, disgusting effort at best, but she got the job done. The regurgitated root was essentially still whole. She had ingested almost none of its juices.

The next part was a little more difficult. She had to find a way to hide the evidence of her forbidden act. She took the piece of root and shoved it down between gaps in the crate floorboards where it couldn't be readily seen. Then she used part of the towel she had been given to wash with to wipe up the leavings and mute the smell. It wasn't an entirely satisfactory cleanup, but it would probably be good enough to fool the witch if she didn't climb into the crate for a look around.

Oh, that she would, and I was standing outside when she did!

Wishful thinking, but pleasant to contemplate. Chrysallin sat back, pleased with herself. She had found an opportunity to avoid allowing the hated root a further opportunity to work on her system. She had bought herself an entire day in which to recover her voice.

One or two more, and she might have it back—and with it, the wish-song's powerful magic.

She slept for a time after that, waking again when she heard the lock in the front door release. Upon peering through the mesh of the airhole she saw the little girl enter.

"I'm back!" came the cheerful greeting. The little girl walked over and peered into the cage, her eyes meeting Chrysallin's. "I wasn't gone all that long, was I? Did you miss me terribly?"

Chrysallin shrugged to show her disinterest.

"You probably want to know what happened to the boy who went with me, don't you?" The little girl smiled. "That's a rather sad story, I'm afraid. He risked himself foolishly and is now in several pieces in the stomachs of the swamp dwellers. We won't be seeing him again. Something you should be grateful for, considering. Because you won't be seeing your friend again, either. It was my intention that she come back here and join us in our games. I was looking forward to it. But Olin was careless and left her where she could be eaten. And she was. Every last bit of her. Now she's all gone, not a trace of her left."

Chrysallin fought back a scream and hurriedly wiped away the tears that followed.

"Are you dreadfully sad?" the little girl inquired with false concern.

Chrysallin refused to answer. She would not give the little girl the satisfaction. She would not let her see the extent of her dismay. She could practically hear the eagerness in the other's voice, in anticipation of her response. *No,* she thought. *I'll show her nothing.*

Instead, she pointed at the little girl, then ran her finger across her own throat in a cutting motion.

The little girl laughed merrily. "You are so funny! I love talking with you. Let's agree to disagree, and in a few days we'll know who's right, won't we? Let's just go to sleep and wake up fresh to a new day and another chance to have fun!"

She drew back, moving away to whatever part of the cottage she slept in, leaving Chrys to ponder her situation anew. But Chrys was done pondering, done with obedience and good behavior and pointless hope. Even if Leofur truly was gone, she was going to find a way out of this.

And when she did, she would make this weasel-faced little girl, this brain-warped witch, sorry she had ever been born.

How had things come to *this*? Leofur wondered.

The question burned in the discontented silence of her mind as she contemplated her situation. Of all the things she might have imagined happening, this was not one of them. It was so unexpected and out of her comfort zone (even as large as that zone had become since meeting Imric Cort) that it bordered on surreal.

She was lying in a depression perhaps fifty yards off the shores of the swamp lake where the boy Olin had taken her captive. She was naked, as Imric had confiscated all of her clothing before she was allowed to climb into her hiding place. Even her boots were gone.

"I'm sorry about this," Imric told her, "but I need your clothes to convince the witch there's no further threat."

The witch whom Imric was convinced was on her way to gather Leofur up and haul her away. Or worse.

She gave him what might charitably be called a withering look. "You want me to take everything off?"

"You've seen *me* naked often enough. What's the harm in me seeing you? But all right, I won't look. I'll turn away while you do it."

So he did, looking off into the distance, and she had reluctantly removed all her clothes. And then, at his further insistence, she walked to the edge of the lake while he turned away once more and rubbed mud all over herself, leaving no part of her body uncovered. The mud was slimy, cold, and stinky, but she forced herself to apply it; she understood its purpose. Once he was satisfied, she had lowered herself into the depression atop a bedding of soft moss he had gathered.

"You look comfortable enough," he said, looking down at her after she was settled in place. "I know the mud is cold, but your body will warm it up soon enough, and you'll feel better."

She nodded as she hugged herself, then winced as her eyes were drawn to the deep slashes across Imric's back and limbs, to the break in his wrist, to the way he shivered as if with a fever. It was cold in the swamp, but this was something more. He had fought hard to get free of the witch's creature, and it had cost him. With wounds like these— some of them open and bleeding—he lacked the strength necessary to travel, even if it meant reaching Chrysallin and setting her free. Rather than chance losing him, she had agreed to this substitute plan.

Hide and wait.

Rest through the night.

She thought Imric might climb into the shelter with her—a prospect she found truly troubling even though she was used to his nakedness by now, finding him as familiar this way as when he was fully clothed. But instead of joining her, he began covering her with grasses and broken limbs, leaving the ground surrounding the place in which she hid looking undisturbed.

Then he left, taking her discarded clothing with him and setting out into the gloom of the Sink.

Now she waited, and as she did so considered how strange all this was. The shape-shifter and herself both naked as they tried to become one with their surroundings. What would Paxon think if he knew? She couldn't say with any certainty, but she thought he would approve; Paxon was nothing if not practical.

But if felt odd anyway. The daughter of the sorcerer Arcannen Rai and a star-crossed shape-shifter had been thrown together by chance and need, companions as different as night and day. But how different, really? Certainly things were not the same as when they had started out together on this quest. The distance between Imric and herself had closed considerably. She found herself wondering at the obvious changes, particularly in herself. While he had always responded in pretty much the same way to her, ever since they established the tether, her own attitude toward him had been altered. She had started out not just reticent toward him but frustrated by his behavior. She had found him difficult and taciturn, his insistence on doing things his way irritating at best and dangerous at worst. She had not liked him much and had decided early on that setting boundaries and exercising a firm hand were required. She had managed to achieve exactly nothing with such an approach, yet somehow she had been drawn closer to him, had come to understand that their tethering had formed a complicated bond. She wasn't sure how this had happened, but it had changed her thinking about him. She liked him better; she appreciated and respected him more.

And it didn't hurt that he had come to her aid twice now in situations that might otherwise have left her injured or dead.

Tonight was an astonishing example of the commitment he clearly felt toward her. He had appeared as if by magic, emerging from the swamp just as she was ready to abandon hope. Her efforts at freeing herself from the tree had failed, and she had begun to hear things moving around in the trees and out on the water. The predators had smelled her; they were searching. Even perched in the tree's lower limbs, she was not safe. It would take little enough for any of those hunting to reach her and drag her down. She had no weapons with which to defend herself save her knife. She had no plan for what to do when something came for her beyond fighting as hard as she could.

Then, all at once, there he was—his lean body surging through the trees to reach her, a sort of manic need reflected on his face as he leapt from the ground into the limbs beside her, reached for the chain and lock, broke them as if they were paper, and lifted her from the tree.

"I though I'd lost you," were his first words.

She would never forget him saying this, as if she was the most important thing in the world to him, as if she mattered to him more than anything.

But then the moment was past, and he was telling her what had happened to him when he found the witch's cottage and moved closer to have a look inside. Apparently, the witch had seen him and had summoned a swamp dweller from the depths of the lake—a monster of enormous proportions. He didn't know it was there at first, but when he sensed its approach, a rising wave out on the water announcing its arrival, he moved quickly back into the trees, thinking to hide from it, to conceal himself in the gloom, to place himself within the protection of the huge old trunks.

But the thing that had come for him was enormously strong. The trees had provided no real protection. It had gone through them as if they were weeds, lunging out of the water and smashing them aside, propelling itself ahead by using its short, squat legs. Its head was all jaws and teeth and not much else, and it had snapped Imric up in a single bite.

Yet the shape-shifter had managed to perform one last, desperate change. In the few seconds between the jaws snatching him and the teeth grinding him to pulp, he had transformed into a bat and fastened himself to the inside of the creature's cavernous maw. When the swamp dweller tried to expel the irritating presence by opening its mouth and coughing, Imric flew free.

He had not attempted to remain there, torn and bloodied by his ordeal, and weakened to the point of collapse. Instead, he had flown back through the swamp to where he had left Leofur, seeing at once that both she and the boy were gone.

She told him then what had befallen her, and they agreed that if the boy had gone to the witch, he would bring her back as quickly as he could. So they must create a deception.

Which was why Leofur was lying naked in a hole in the ground, cold and damp, while Imric was off doing who knew what, hoping the witch would find her torn, bloodied clothing lying in the shallows of the lake and presume it was all that remained of her.

It was not a great plan, but it was the best either of them could come up with. Imric was in no condition to undertake an extended trek, much less engage in a battle with the witch; his strength was depleted and his exhaustion apparent. He needed to rest. How he would manage this—or even where he intended to hide—Leofur could not have said. Somewhere close by, she hoped. Somewhere his scent would not give him away.

She found herself thinking about how much a part of her life he had become. True, theirs was a temporary relationship and would last only until they returned to Paranor, but it was surprisingly intense nevertheless. As she huddled in her hiding place, waiting for his return, hugging herself against the night chill, she began to ask questions about him. After all, she knew so little. What sort of life had he known in the years after his parents' death? Had he found friends in those years? Could a shape-shifter make real friends when his secret was so strange and, to many, so abhorrent? Had he found others like himself, a surrogate family perhaps? What were his hopes and dreams? To become able to shape-shift again; she knew that one. Perhaps the most important one. But were there others?

The questions flooded her thoughts.

Questions about a man she did not begin to understand.

Questions she could not answer, or even ask him directly.

Because she had no right to ask. They were traveling companions on a quest, but not much more. She could not bring herself to pry, could not make herself intrude. She could not expect to know his secrets.

Though she wanted to know, so badly . . .

She was still pondering when he linked to her through their tethering and spoke. *Are you all right? Are you still safe?*

Are you?

Safe enough. I'm coming back.

Then he went silent again, but she let him be. She felt reassured by his promise. She did not require more.

Minutes passed, and she grew drowsy in spite of her discomfort. She began thinking of Paxon and Paranor. They felt like memories from another life—one lived so long ago that it no longer seemed real. She felt removed from it in the same way she had felt removed from her father and Wayford when she had moved to Paranor. The comparison felt odd, but there it was.

I'm here, Imric said suddenly. *Don't move. I'm coming in with you.*

Leofur held herself steady as she felt a burrowing in the earth down near her feet, then something small and furry was working its way along her legs. She worked hard to keep herself from flinching. When it reached her stomach, it curled into a ball and nestled against her.

She exhaled sharply. *What are you now?*

Don't know. I created it myself. A burrowing animal, a cross between several species. I made my fur soft so as not to scratch you.

So, not a hedgehog?

No, nothing like that. Listen. The witch and the boy are coming. I shape-shifted into a bat again and flew far enough up the trail to be certain of it, then returned. If anything goes wrong and she finds us, I will do my best to protect you.

She felt a surge of gratitude at the thought—even knowing he could barely take care of himself at this point. *I don't want anything to happen to you because of me.*

Are you cold?

A little. Turns out a coating of mud doesn't keep you very warm.

Then let's try something else.

She felt his furry form begin to warm, heat radiating out, filling the depression and chasing the chill. She reached down, grateful for the warmth, and pulled him tightly against her.

Better now?

Much. Thank you.

They were silent then—she curled around him, he pressed against her—sharing a small bit of comfort.

Until they heard the sound of footsteps approaching.

For a few long moments after the footsteps ceased, Leofur lay within her hideout without moving. She could feel her heartbeat increase as fear gripped her, triggered by a sense of being trapped beneath the earth, of being vulnerable to whatever was up there. And she was pretty sure she knew what that was.

"I don't understand!" she heard Olin exclaim in dismay, the sound of his voice penetratingly close.

Unable to stand the uncertainty, Leofur raised her head just far enough to peer through tiny gaps in the leaves and sticks to find Olin and a little girl standing just a few yards away, close to the lakeshore.

Stay still, Leofur, Imric whispered in her mind.

She held herself motionless, watching as the boy rushed forward, eyes sweeping his surroundings, settling on the tree to which he had left her bound. "She was right here!" he screamed in despair. "She couldn't have escaped!"

The little girl moved up beside him. "Although apparently she has. Are you certain she was securely fastened?"

Leofur felt a chill go up her spine at the way the question was asked. This wasn't any little girl. This was the witch. Without waiting for his answer, the witch moved over to the tree and walked around it, searching the ground. She found the chain moments later, discarded in a heap among a stand of reeds, the lock sprung. She found Imric's discarded backpack with his clothing piled on top. She flung both into the trees in fury.

Leofur kept watching, unable to look away. The witch was very close now. If she moved to her left even a dozen feet . . .

But instead she walked back to the boy and stood looking at him. "You've failed me, Olin."

"She couldn't have broken that lock! She wasn't that strong." He shook his head and gestured with his hands, desperate and pleading. "Someone must have helped her. Someone must have found her." His words were tumbling over each other. "We can track her! We can find her again! How far could she have gotten?"

He knelt hurriedly, scanning the ground for footprints. Nothing. He searched frantically, clearly hoping they had to be there, that she had to have left some sign . . .

"You can stop searching," the witch said from behind him. "I've lost interest."

When he turned to further argue with her, the little girl had disappeared and in her place was a loathsome specter garbed in tattered strips of moss and lengths of vine, hunched and twisted, features warped and riddled with cancers and covered in green scales. Olin recoiled—but one impossibly long arm reached out with whip-like swiftness, seizing his wrist and holding him fast.

"What's wrong, Olin?" As the creature's mouth moved, it made wet, sucking sounds. "Don't you find me attractive? Don't you want to be with me always as my pet? Don't you want to play with me until the end of your days? Isn't that your wish?"

"Please, let me go!" he begged. He seemed unable to look directly at the monster she had become. He writhed in her grip. "Please! Please, don't hurt me!"

"Oh, no, I wouldn't do that. Even though you have failed me. No, it is not my intention to hurt you."

She paused, glancing out into the waters of the lake. "It might be different out there, however."

And with a snap of her arm she flung him into the middle of those placid waters as if he weighed no more than a piece of deadwood.

The boy flew through the air, flailing wildly and screaming in terror, and dropped into the swamp with a night-rending splash. He rose to the surface sputtering and thrashing, still crying out for help. He tried to swim to shore, to gain its safety. For a moment, it seemed he might succeed.

Then the boy's screams reached a new level of horror as something began pulling him under. He fought as hard as he could, beating at the water, struggling to break free of the grip that was pulling him down. But his strength was no match for that of the swamp dweller that had gotten hold of him. Seconds later the boy disappeared. The water churned where he had vanished and then went still.

Leofur watched it all, lying on her side within her covering, head raised just enough to peer through the gaps, Imric's furry body pressed up against her. It was horrific and shocking, and she knew—*knew*—that the witch was coming for her next.

Standing at the water's edge, the witch changed back into the little girl. Then she turned and walked a dozen yards farther down the shoreline to where pieces of Leofur's clothing floated in the water. She knelt, picked them up, smelled them, and studied their torn and bloodied remnants. Then, as Leofur waited for the inevitable, she stood up again, dropped the clothing back into the water, and walked away.

Leofur lay back again, her eyes closing. Time passed. She pictured Olin's death, the images fresh and raw. She heard the heated exchange between the boy and the witch, the harsh words and fearful replies. She was a silent, invisible witness to the horror of Olin's demise. She relived all of it; she could not avoid doing so, even though she would have wished it otherwise.

Stay calm. Be strong.

Imric was speaking in her mind, quieting her thoughts. His voice could do that. His steadiness bolstered hers.

They waited silently to be certain the witch was gone. The minutes passed, but neither moved.

Leofur spoke finally. *We should look.*

There's nothing to see. We know what happened.

What do we do now?

Sleep. I'm not strong enough yet to face her. But I'm healing.

He did so quickly, she remembered. It never took him long to recover from injuries.

I'll be well enough by morning. We'll go after her then.

She did not reply. She was tired, too. She closed her eyes. It was warm and comfortable now, hidden beneath their concealment, wrapped around his small furry body. She was content to wait. The idea of sleep appealed to her.

In minutes, she had drifted off.

She dreamed that night, and her dreams were many and varied. She saw the witch fling the boy Olin into the swamp even as she rushed to help, trying to stop it from happening. But she was too late. She saw him die, torn apart. She fled into the swamp to escape the witch, who watched her go without making any attempt to follow. Once in the trees, she quickly became lost. She called for Paxon, but he didn't come, and soon she was so panicked she could barely think. She had no weapons with which to protect herself. The way forward grew denser and the footing less certain. She didn't know what to do. Her fear was palpable and insistent. She had lost all semblance of reason. All she could manage to think about was finding a way out before she was eaten.

Then the setting changed, and she was standing in a meadow. Sunshine poured down out of a cloudless sky, and wildflowers bloomed in profusion in every direction. She was alone until a figure appeared on the horizon. A man, but she could not make out his features. She was blinded by the sunlight, which in turn lit him with such radiance that he seemed surreal. But when he moved toward her, she could tell he was not a mirage and was coming to her. The urgency of his movements told her he was anxious, and she began moving toward him in response.

She was close enough to reach out for him, close enough to be certain she knew and loved him even though she could not seem to remember his name . . .

They came together, and he abruptly disappeared.

She stood alone once more, the field with its flowers and the sky with its brilliant sun the same, but the man nowhere to be found.

Another shift, and now she was in a dark place, lying on her side, curled up in a soft bed, safe and warm, drowsy and drifting, her thoughts scattered. Arms encircled her, pulled her close. She could feel the soft rub of skin on skin. It was the man she had lost in the meadow. He was back.

I love you. The words were a whisper in her head.

She slipped away again, back into dreamless sleep, and the moment was lost.

25

WHEN LEOFUR WOKE THE FOLLOWING MORNing, she was alone.

She lay within the depression, still covered with moss and branches and coated with mud, but Imric was gone. For a long time, she didn't move. She just lay where she was, her eyes closed and her body unmoving, letting her senses confirm what she had deduced.

The furry creature Imric had shape-shifted into and that had been curled against her stomach during the night was not there. Nor was Imric, reverted to his natural form, pressed up against her from behind, draped over her like a blanket. If, in fact, he ever had been. If it hadn't all been a part of her dreams. She couldn't be sure; the memory of it was a vague collection of impressions and possibilities rather than a clear and certain image. She tried to imagine it otherwise and failed.

Taking a moment to gather her wits and strength, she tried to determine if she was in danger from anything that waited just outside her shelter. She shifted her limbs, straightened her torso, and peered out through squinted eyes to find light filtering down into her hollow. She was ready.

She pushed her way up through the debris that hid her with small, cautious movements that allowed the world to gradually come into view. From the sun's location in the sky, it was well past dawn. She sat up and looked around. In the distance she could see shadows flying across the swamp, but beyond those few small indicators of life, everything was still.

She looked for Imric and did not find him. She reached for him in her mind, seeking a link, but found none.

Beside her, the clothes he had taken to decoy the witch lay in a pile. The rips and bloodstains were still in evidence, but a quick examination revealed that everything she had been wearing before could still be worn again. She fingered the garments inquisitively, making sure. Then she noticed her boots and backpack; they had been reclaimed, too.

She sat where she was for a few minutes more, almost persuaded that if she did so he would appear. When he didn't, she made herself rise and walk to the edge of the lake and use its waters to clean herself as best she could. A makeshift scrubber of interwoven tufts of moss scoured away the mud and grime, and aloe leaves helped soothe the places that were still sore. Afterward, she stood on shore again, brushed away the droplets of water that still clung to her skin, and waited for the air to dry her damp body and hair.

She had finished dressing and was sitting with her back against the tree when Imric reappeared. He was fully dressed, his clothes apparently retrieved from her backpack, and he was moving as if he was fully healed. He came over without a word and sat down bedside her, staring off into the swamp.

"You let me sleep," she said finally. "You should have woken me."

"There was no need." He looked over, a cool indifference in his gaze. "We won't be leaving here until midday. I don't want to arrive at the cottage before late afternoon. I want the witch to have the day to think she is safe. I want her placid and unsuspecting when we confront her."

Always thinking ahead. She nodded her agreement. "Then thank you for letting me rest. And thanks for retrieving my clothes. You seem much better today."

He shrugged. "Enough that I can continue on. We mend fast, we shape-shifters. I ache, but the wounds are closed. The wrist is another matter."

He lifted his arm and showed her the makeshift splint he had fashioned to protect the break. Formed of three short lengths of peeled wood and bound with strips of woven reed, it looked surprisingly sturdy. She reached out and took his hand, examining the fastenings carefully.

"It will slow me down, but it won't stop me from doing what I need to do. It might even heal by nightfall. The break was to a pair of small bones. I've set both and now they're being held in place by this brace."

She gave him back his hand. "Pretty resourceful."

"When you are alone as much as I am, you need to be." He looked away again quickly, as if realizing there were unspoken implications to what he had just said. "Mostly, anyway. Last night, it took both of us. Fooled the witch, though, didn't we?"

She nodded wordlessly. She badly wanted to ask him if he had shifted into his human form while she slept so that he could hold her. She wanted to know if he had said *I love you,* if he had spoken those three words or she had dreamed them. But asking such questions seemed impossible, an invasion of privacy she could not afford to indulge in. Especially when she could not reply in kind.

They sat in silence, looking out over the placid surface of the swamp, into the trees and through the mists and beyond to what seemed like forever. It was not an awkward silence, but a companionable one—the kind that makes you feel at peace because you are with the right person and talking isn't necessary. So odd, she thought. She had not felt this until now. She did not think she could have before. What had changed?

She glanced at him. "Do we really have any chance of getting Chrysallin back? Or even of coming out of this alive?"

He didn't look back. "That is a very odd question, coming from you. Isn't that the reason we're here? Wasn't this your idea?"

"Well, yes, but I made that decision in the heat of the moment and in ignorance of what we would find. Now I don't feel so confident."

She kept looking at him, searching his face for some sort of tell. "I'm not saying we should turn back. I wouldn't leave Chrysallin even if there were no chance at all. I'm just trying to . . . to gain some small measure of reassurance that you're not following me just because . . ."

She trailed off. Because what? Because all at once she was feeling differently about him? Because all at once she was uncertain of herself where he was concerned?

Now he looked at her. "We came to get your friend back and that's what we're going to do. We are strong enough together to overcome the witch, and to survive whatever she throws at us. We know what we are up against, and we know what's needed. That was true when we started out, and it's true now. Nothing has changed."

But it had. Something had changed. She couldn't define it yet, but it gave her pause and it made her want to understand its implications. A shift had taken place inside her. Perhaps nothing had changed for him, but it most certainly had for her.

"Do you have a plan?" she asked him.

He grinned. "Don't you?"

She laughed in spite of herself. "Not really. I just know I have to go in there and get Chrys back."

His smile broadened. "That sounds like a good plan to me. How can you improve on something like that?"

Impulsively, she leaned into him and kissed him on the cheek. "Thank you for being here with me, Imric Cort."

He had the grace to blush as he replied, "I can't imagine being anywhere else."

On a bright, clear morning, Arcannen Rai rose from his bed and, after washing and then donning the robes of the Fourth Druid Order, began walking the halls of the Druid's Keep. He was awake early, preferring to conduct his ongoing investigation of the Keep's layout while others slept, still wary of being surrounded by so many men and women who would like to see him dead. It was easier to move about when he didn't have to worry about someone realizing that he was not who he appeared to be. Both the success of his plan and his survival had relied on subterfuge and misdirection from the beginning, and nothing had changed in the interim.

He went high into the Keep's main tower, heading for the cold room, intent on having whoever was monitoring the scrye waters report any disturbances that might indicate the presence of a powerful magic. He had been careful to keep his magic hidden since being admitted to the Keep—a necessary protection against revealing who he was. He couldn't be certain that it would register in the same way Druid magic did. Before, when using his magic in the city of Arishaig and again while struggling to reach safety in the Battlemound, he had been able to rely on the confusion and stress besetting his companions to distract them from spotting any differences. But within the Keep, he was vulnerable. It would be all too easy here to recognize a foreign magic. He had to step lightly. Everything happening now was new and unfamiliar to him, a journey of discovery and revelation. He had never been inside Paranor's walls before, and its secrets were only just beginning to reveal themselves to him.

Even if it appeared otherwise to the Druids of Paranor.

He paused at a window that overlooked the courtyards situated just inside the east walls. He did this not to enjoy the scenery or attempt further measurements of the structure's parameters. It was not even to try to determine once again the location of the vault that hid the artifacts of magic the Druid order had collected and locked away. None of those mattered just now. Instead, he paused for no better reason than to consider his appearance. To judge how well he was maintaining his disguise. To take momentary pride in what he had accomplished. The sunlight was reflected off the glass as it streamed through windows situated along the hall in just such a way that it created a mirror effect.

And revealed not Arcannen Rai, who he really was, but Isaturin, Ard Rhys of the Fourth Druid Order, whose identity he had stolen.

His reflection made him appear a bit haggard, but that was mostly due to the unevenness of the mirror. Besides, the members of his unsuspecting flock would simply attribute it to what he had been through while escaping from Arishaig and fighting to get home again.

They would think it was the weight of the losses he had suffered in Druid lives. No one would suspect the truth. No one would guess he was not who he seemed or that the effort of maintaining his disguise was beginning to wear on him.

It was only for another day or two, and then he would have what he wanted and be gone.

His plans had been solid enough at the beginning, even though everything had begun to disintegrate right away. It had been easy enough to assume his disguise and infiltrate the sleeping quarters of the Druids in Arishaig. Easy enough to find Isaturin alone and dispatch him before he could even begin to understand why he was facing a mirror image of himself. Easy enough to burn his body to ashes afterward and hide the remains where they might never be found.

Arcannen smiled in spite of himself. Oh, the look on Isaturin's face! It had been priceless. For just a second, he had been completely confused by what he was seeing. For someone with Arcannen's lethal talents, a second was more than enough.

The others in the Druid delegation had suspected nothing—not in Arishaig, and not afterward during their flight north. His efforts at disrupting the Druid–Federation conference had gone well enough. He had brought the Sleath in earlier, during the night; it was a creature that could climb walls and did so. He had positioned it to come when he summoned it, and it had behaved as expected. A few dozen Federation guards were nothing to a wraith like that, for it was a demon of the first order, a monster of terrible power. It had taken him months to create it, to conjure it out of dark magic and subverted natural elements—months of physical pain and emotional agony of a sort he had not thought he could withstand. But the chance both to set the Federation against the Druids and to finally get inside the Druid's Keep was too enticing to abandon. He'd kept a low profile ever since the destruction of the Red Slash, but nothing was ever accomplished by hiding, and he'd decided it was time to reemerge.

His only miscalculation was in not anticipating the Sleath's disobedience. He had not expected it might refuse his orders. It had happened in the Assembly, right at the end, just as he was preparing to put the finishing touches on the matter. He was trying to steer the creature toward the old man because he was the most malleable member of the party. It had always been his intent to keep his creation close until he was safely inside Paranor—a hedging of bets in case things went wrong—but instead of the old man, the Sleath had chosen the seer in which to hide, the partner of the most dangerous member of their party—and one Arcannen worried would discover the truth more easily because of the nature of their relationship. Especially when his escape plan had failed so utterly that they had been reduced to walking home and fighting for their lives every step of the way.

Eventually, he had been forced to sacrifice the Sleath, as well.

Even the best-laid plans go wrong, and the more complicated the plan the more likely the failure. He was fortunate things had turned out as well as they had. After all, he was still alive, while everyone else who had gone to Arishaig was dead, and he was inside the Druid's Keep with his true identity still a secret. Considerable accomplishments, by any measure.

He turned away from his reflection and continued on. Sunrise was just breaking, and as yet only a handful of Druids were awake. The cold room was staffed twenty-four hours a day; he had picked up that bit of information from his aide, young Keratrix, who had been anxious to report to him. He knew of the scrye waters already, of course. He knew of the existence of many of the Druid secrets—knowledge gained over the years from one source or another, in one way or another. What he didn't know were the particulars, and that was turning out to be a bigger problem than he had expected.

But it was a problem he was working on and would soon solve.

He reached the cold room and entered. The Druid standing watch glanced over and nodded companionably. "Ard Rhys."

"Any disturbances?" Arcannen asked him.

The other shook his head. "All quiet. Small readings, nothing significant."

Arcannen nodded and left.

While he was all but certain that Paxon Leah was dead and his sister a captive of the Murk Witch, he didn't want to leave anything to chance. If a strong magical reading had occurred in either of the places where he believed the siblings to be, there might be cause for worry. Since it hadn't, he could go about his business.

The part of his plan that had been the trickiest was finding a way to get both Paxon and Chrysallin out of his way so they could not interfere. Paxon had been assigned to the delegation dispatched to Arishaig—which Arcannen had suspected he would be—so that had put the Highlander within easy range for elimination. Once they had fled the Assembly and tried flying back to Paranor—where Arcannen hoped to be welcomed—he had intended to isolate Paxon Leah and dispose of him the same way he had disposed of old Consloe and Isaturin, taking advantage of the first opportunity that presented itself. But when their airship went down and they were forced to walk through dangerous country while being tracked by the Federation, he had decided to wait. Anyone who could help him at that point was a bonus. He could have bolted and gone off on his own, but that would have defeated his entire plan to get into Paranor. With Paxon and the others beside him, no one would even think to question whether he was really who he appeared.

But the dragon had solved one problem and left him with another. Conveniently, Paxon and the female Druid had been swept off the ledge, but he still had to get into Paranor. A combination of pilfered horses and airships, however—along with minimal sleep—had finally gotten him as far as the Keep's gates yesterday morning, and everyone was so glad to see him back—to find even one member of the ill-fated delegation still alive—that there had been no hesitation about bringing him inside.

Of course, he had been forced to rid himself of the troublesome Federation commander, but by then he had revised his thinking on what he intended to accomplish at Paranor. Initially, he had thought to gain control over the order for the express purpose of destroying it. To compel the Federation to attack the Druids in retaliation for what happened in Arishaig, to undermine any attempts at peace between the two in his guise as Ard Rhys and bring the order down. But the danger to himself in doing so was enormous, and both that and the obvious complexity of what was required now suggested he change those plans. Instead of attempting a subversion of the Order by acting as Isaturin over the next few weeks, he had decided simply to pillage the artifacts vault of anything and everything he could make use of and go back into hiding while he decided how best to make use of his new acquisitions. The problem at present was that not only did he not know where the vault was situated but he also did not know how to get into it. Asking Keratrix or one of the other Druids would seem strange, to say the least, so he needed to get the information by other means.

That might take a little time and patience. But he had both at his disposal for the moment, having gotten rid of both Leah siblings.

Chrysallin's kidnapping had been arranged for that specific purpose. Whatever was to happen when he got to Paranor, he wanted her out of the way. The rumor was she had mastered the use of the wishsong, and if so she was dangerous—especially to him. If she had a chance to use it on him, she wouldn't hesitate to squash him like a bug. So a confrontation was to be avoided at all costs. Enlisting the aid of the Murk Witch to snatch her and hold her prisoner had been a stroke of genius. It removed her from Paranor and placed her on the other side of the Four Lands. It meant that for Paxon to save her, he would have to travel a long way. Maybe he would be successful and maybe not, but he would not be around to interfere with Arcannen.

Of course, none of that mattered now. Paxon was dead and gone. The witch still held Chrysallin prisoner, using the root with which he had supplied her to deaden the girl's voice, but now there was no reason to expect her back, either. Not once he sent word to the witch to do with her as she pleased.

A message he would send off by arrow shrike later today.

Only one loose end remained, and there wasn't much he could do about it. A casual conversation with young Keratrix had revealed that Leofur was at Paranor, too. She had become close friends with Chrysallin and was now searching for her in the company of some stable hand. His daughter stood not a chance in a million of succeeding, of course, but it was annoying to know she was out there blundering around. It was exactly the sort of thing Leofur would do; she couldn't seem to help herself from engaging in these pointless quests to aid other people. He had thought her still in Wayford, but apparently he was wrong. She had followed Paxon here, and now she was trying to prove her love for him by bringing back his sister.

It was just stupid, even for her.

He wandered down to Isaturin's offices and found an anxious Keratrix waiting for him. The scribe looked less than happy, his brow furrowed as he paced back and forth in front of the door. There were Druid Guard present, too, hulking creatures with impassive faces and slow movements. They stood ready and waiting for something, but it was not at all clear what that was.

Arcannen tried not to sound impatient, even though he was irritated beyond measure. "What's wrong?"

Keratrix shook his head. "Visitors. Federation warships. Almost a dozen in all if you count the transports. They're waiting just outside the south gates. For you, specifically. They've sent a demand for an immediate audience."

This was inconvenient. He had not expected the Federation to act so swiftly; usually, actions of such magnitude required days of debate and dithering by the Coalition Council. He would have to put his search for the artifact vault on hold.

Keratrix had already started walking down the hall. Arcannen, sensing his plans were in further trouble, reluctantly followed.

26

LEOFUR AND IMRIC HAD BEEN SITTING TOGETHER IN silence for almost an hour, waiting for midday to arrive before setting out for the witch's cottage, when the shape-shifter began to speak.

"I have something to tell you," he said. "I wanted to do so earlier, but I didn't think you were ready to hear it. Or maybe I wasn't ready to talk about it. It's difficult for me even now, but I think I have to."

He hesitated, as if still not sure of himself. "You remember how I spoke of Sarnya, who was tethered to me before you?"

Leofur nodded. "I remember. She was a Druid."

"Yes, she was assigned to me. She was instructed to work with me, to learn by practical experience how to control my shape-shifting tendencies. She was young, but she was very smart and sure of herself. I believed she could help me, even though she was a tiny thing physically, and emotionally she lived with her heart laid bare."

"But you were not lovers."

He had told her this earlier, so she made it a statement of fact, sensing there was something more and he was about to tell her what it was.

"No, we were not lovers, but she wanted us to be. Even though she never said so, I sensed it. And I was drawn to her enough through the tether that I wanted it, too. But I was afraid for her, so I did not let it happen. I thought that, by doing so, I could keep us both safe. This was my chance to conquer my addiction, and I was determined not to let anything interfere with that. Her interest seemed only an infatuation, in any case, and by ignoring it I believed it would run its course and that the tether would not be affected. I was wrong."

"So she persisted?" Leofur could hear the uncertainty in his voice, could read the pain in his eyes. "I think she must have been deeply in love with you."

"She insisted she was not once I felt confident enough to ask. She said it was her interest in finding a solution to my problem that intensified our relationship. When she was tethered to me, what I felt was her need to help—to stay close so she could be the safety line I required in order not to lose control. Still, I knew. Her emotional makeup did not allow for half measures. But I thought it safe enough to continue and did not report my concerns. Again, I was selfish. I was afraid if I said anything, they would take her away and not give me a replacement."

Leofur thought about it. "The Druids are unpredictable," she said finally.

His gaze shifted again toward the swamp as he continued talking, his features tense. "In any case, I could feel our relationship strengthening the more time we spent tethered, but she never once suggested we should be anything more than partners. So, thinking back, I suppose I convinced myself that she had managed to back away from her earlier attachment."

"But something happened?"

"It was inevitable, I guess. We were far out in the forests of the Upper Anar, practicing changes while tethered and some distance apart from each other. She felt it was safe for me to try changing in rapid succession, and she wanted to test my control. I wasn't sure, but she was so insistent about it, so certain. And I had come to rely on her judgment, thinking her better able to measure my progress than I was. After all, she had been right about everything else until then. She had monitored and controlled my efforts with such precise and careful steps forward that I had convinced myself I was close to cured."

He shook his head. "The truth of the matter is, I will never be cured. Not entirely. It isn't possible for me to ever be able to shape-shift safely and without fear of losing control. I was tethered to her when I discovered this. One minute I was changing effortlessly, from ground squirrel to shrike, Parsk wolf to moor cat, and she was urging me on—telling me to keep changing, to remember she was there for me, that she would bring me back again if I started to slip. I was doing everything she told me, and I was making the shifts without any problem. Not even a hint of one.

"Then all of a sudden—maybe on a whim, maybe because she truly believed I could do it, or maybe even because she wanted to experience it with me—she told me to try shifting into something imaginary, to become a creature I had never seen. I did it without thinking. I did it recklessly and foolishly. I didn't even stop to con-sider the consequences. I felt something slip inside me, but it was too late to stop. I had changed into a huge, loathsome creature, and in doing so I lost control. I knew it instantly. I screamed to her—a call for help and at the same time a warning. My mind was changing with my body, filling with dark and terrible urges, so repulsive I could barely endure them. I tried to back away from them, but there was nowhere to go. Hunger and rage and lust . . ."

He broke off, lowering his head, tears leaking from his eyes. "I was despicable in those moments, and I begged her to release me. She refused. She said that she loved me, that she would never let me go. She told me to hang on, to bring myself under control and change back again, but I couldn't manage it. I was thrashing inside my own body, fighting myself, maddened and terrified, and I needed her to get away from me. But she kept clinging on, desperately, and I could hear her screaming now—not at what she had felt me become, but at how it was affecting her. She was tethered to a monster, and she was finding out for the first time what it was like to be one."

Leofur listened without interrupting. She tried to give away noth-ing of how this made her feel, but his agony and regret were so pal-pable it broke her heart. He was reliving those last moments with Sarnya so vividly—and struggling with the same guilt and loss he had felt back then.

"In the end," he said, "I broke the tether myself; I was able to do that much, at least. It took everything I had, but I felt the tie snap apart with an audible crack that sent me spinning away into a mindless blackness and finally unconsciousness. When I woke again, I was back to myself. The monster I had created was gone. I didn't know if she had done this by hanging on to me for so long, or if the untethering had done it. I still don't know.

"I went back to find her. She was dead. Her eyes were open, and I could see the horror reflected in them. I could see from the way her face was contorted and her lips twisted that she had died from the shock of what had happened, and I imagine she died with the image of the monster I had become still fixed in her mind."

Leofur reached for his hands, took them in her own, and squeezed gently. "I am so sorry. I cannot imagine what that must have been like."

Imric's lips tightened. "I relive it every day. I was responsible for what happened to Sarnya. I killed her. It was my fault."

"I think you are taking too much on yourself. She was a Druid, Imric. She had Druid training and the use of magic, and she knew the danger she faced when she agreed to the tether. Just as I knew it. Yet even with all of that, she urged you to do something that was clearly risky and foolish. You might have contributed to her death, but she was the one who brought it about."

"I can't accept that. It makes me sound innocent of any wrongdoing."

She gave him an angry, impatient look. "And tell me, what is the nature of your guilt, exactly? Are you guilty of being born a shapeshifter? Are you guilty of being subject to that magic's unpredictable nature? Are you guilty of trying your best to find a way to live? Just like everyone else tries to live, coming to terms with their own demons and misfortunes?"

He shook his head slowly. "I am guilty of letting people get too close to me. First Sarnya, and now you. Because I am worried, Leofur, that our tethering will end as badly my first one did."

"Listen to yourself. You are trying to find reasons to fail! You are losing heart just as we are on the verge of saving Chrys. Stop it! I am not Sarnya. I am nothing like her." Somehow, she managed not to shout, but instead to keep her words calm and reasoned. "Look at me, Imric. I am an entirely different person. Sarnya's mistakes and failings are not mine."

She paused, then took the plunge. "And I do not feel the same way about you that she did."

His smile was bitter and sad—a jagged crease that changed his features so abruptly it caused her to flinch. "I know that." He took a deep steadying breath. "But it isn't your feelings I am worried about. It's mine."

What? Leofur stared at him in shock.

He seemed to realize what he had said and got to his feet immediately, snatching up his backpack and pulling it on. Leofur sat where she was, trying to make sense of what had just happened.

"It's time to go," he announced as he stood waiting for her.

She stared at him a moment and then rose, as well. Without another word, he set out along the shoreline of the lake. His stride was firm and determined, as if he sought to distance himself from her. He did not look back.

It isn't your feelings I am worried about? It's mine.

He had just admitted he was worried about his own feelings. And why? Was he saying he was in love with her? Was that what he was implying?

She caught up with him quickly enough, but for a time she didn't say anything. She was working it through, seeing clearly what she hadn't seen before. This strange, taciturn, withdrawn man had just voiced something so unexpected that she could barely make herself take it in. This was a man who kept his feelings closely guarded and his emotional state tamped down. He was a man who was used to being alone, and she believed that to a large extent he had chosen this path quite deliberately.

Still, he had revealed himself to her, whether on purpose or in an unguarded moment, and now they needed to talk about it. He might feel there was nothing more to say, but she believed otherwise—and was no longer content to tell herself that it was improper to intrude.

She moved up next to him, keeping pace. "What did you just say to me?" she asked quietly.

"I don't remember."

"Yes, you do."

"I was just talking. I might have said anything. Let it be."

She grabbed his arm and pulled him about. "Look at me."

His strange eyes fixed on her, his face an expressionless mask. He was trying to speak, but he couldn't seem to get the words out.

"You're afraid it's how you feel about me—not how I feel about you—that puts me in danger. You think your feelings might impact my safety during the tether. It was the opposite when Sarnya died— she was the one clinging to you—but you think it doesn't matter where the feelings originate, only that they are present and might compromise you in some way."

She took a breath. "Are you worried that, if your control was compromised, you might hang on to me too long, not let me go? Drag me down with you as you dragged Sarnya?"

He shook his head. "You don't understand. You *can't* understand if you're not me."

"Try explaining it, anyway. Try making me understand. We can't just leave things where they are."

"How else can we leave them? What else is there to say? I know the realities of my life—and yours. I'm not meant to be with anyone. Not now, and not ever. It will always be too dangerous. I am a dangerous person. A dangerous *creature*. I am only partly human, and sometimes I wonder if I am even that. And the tether only exacerbates this. How can I ever be sure what will happen to the person I am tethered to? How can either of us ever feel safe with the other?"

"We've done pretty well so far. I think we know what to expect. You had a terrible experience with Sarnya, but I've already told you several times I'm not like her, not given to the same impulses she was. And you've told me all along that either one of us can break the tether. So why are you assuming I won't know what to do should the worst happen?"

Imric frowned. "Because . . ." And he trailed off, seeming at a loss for words.

"Because you love me?" Leofur persisted. "Is that it?"

"I only said what I did because I am afraid for you. I said it to clarify that your participation in the tethering wasn't the cause for my fear—mine was. I couldn't let you continue to tether to me without admitting to it."

"But what you've said changes nothing. Haven't you been paying attention? I've understood the risks right from the beginning, from the moment you explained them—from the first time you went off on your own after promising not to, breaking the link between us and leaving yourself exposed. You must think I am pretty weak to doubt me now."

"I doubt *myself*, Leofur, not you. My feelings are complicating things to such a degree that I doubt my objectivity. I wonder how much judgment and common sense I can rely on when they're needed. Don't you see? I have become a risk to you that I never intended to become. It was bad enough being a shape-shifter with a decided lack of control. But now, feeling about you as I do, discovering that it's there and I can't make it go away . . ."

She shook her head. "How did this happen? When did you decide this? Are you sure about it? Maybe you're . . ."

He shook her off. "Don't treat me like I might be confused or muddle-headed. Or like I'm somehow unable to recognize the truth. I've known from the first time we tethered. I've been sure of it ever since . . ." He looked away from her. "But you're partnered with Paxon Leah. You already have a life. You're in love with someone else."

He quit talking and wheeled away. "This is pointless. I wish I'd turned you away that first day and let you find someone else to come looking for your partner's sister!"

There was real anger and regret in his voice now, and for a few moments Leofur didn't know what else to say to him. She stared after him as he walked away a few steps and stood looking down at his feet.

When it appeared he had nothing further to say, she went over to him and put her hand on his back. "I'm sorry you feel this way, but I'm not sorry you came with me. Without you, I never would have found Chrys. I will owe you that for the rest of my life, and I will never forget your courage and your determination. Besides, I think coming with me was important to you. I will never accept that this was a mistake."

He was quiet a moment, still not looking at her, his face turned away. "I don't regret being given the chance to shape-shift again," he said finally. "I didn't realize how much I had missed it until you gave me the chance to get it back."

She took hold of his arms and turned him around to face her. "Then let's leave everything where it is, Imric. We'll talk about it later. No more anger or pain or regret or guilt for now. For now, we have to remember why we're here. We have to think about Chrysallin. Can you just think about her?"

He looked at her as if the effort actually hurt. "I can do whatever you need me to do. Except for one thing, Leofur Rai. I cannot change the way I feel. Don't ask it of me. I am tired of pretending. I do love you. Even knowing it will come to nothing. Even knowing you don't love me back."

"Oh, Imric," she whispered, shaking her head. "I wish I could give you that."

The words came from her lips before she could think better of them—an admission of her own. She was surprised to hear herself speak them and even more surprised to realize she meant them.

Because she was admitting to herself, for the first time, that maybe she might love him, too. That she had bottled those feelings up and even denied them by pretending they were something else. That she had dismissed them as being nothing more than a response to the intensity of their situation and her own general unhappiness with her life.

But she wasn't sure she could do so anymore, now that it was out there. And she wasn't at all sure she wanted to.

When Arcannen reached the walls above the south gate and saw for the first time the number of warships ringing the Druid's Keep, he turned immediately to Keratrix and said, "Let them wait. Meanwhile, come with me."

There were already large numbers of Druid Guard manning the walls, readying for battle, bringing up defensive weapons to repel any attack. Not that Paranor required such things. The rumor—a rumor he knew to be true—was that the Keep had an infusion of ancient magic that made it capable of defending itself. No enemy had ever breached these walls through anything but subterfuge and betrayal.

In any case, the sorcerer had no intention of sticking around to find out. He was nothing if not practical, and he knew that now was the time for him to cut his losses and disappear. What he had come here for was to pillage the artifacts vault, and if he was able to manage that before the Federation attacked, he would have accomplished enough to pronounce his mission a success.

He waited until he was safely inside and out of sight before turning once more to Keratrix. "Listen closely. I have been keeping this to myself, but now I see it is impossible to do so any longer. The journey back to Paranor with Paxon and the others was harder on me than I have revealed. I was poisoned and injured internally during one of the fights in the Battlemound. As a result, I am much weakened—perhaps too much so to stand and fight with the others. I will try because I must, because it is expected of me—and, live or die, I will do what I can. But I will need your help."

"Master, we have healers who are skilled . . ."

Arcannen quickly put a finger to the young man's lips. "Shhh, shhh. There is no time for that now. Haste will help more. What I require lies in the artifacts vault, but I have lost all memory of how to open the vault. I keep thinking it is a temporary disability that will eventually subside, but perhaps it goes deeper than that." He paused, giving the other a rueful smile. "I was hoping you could help me to get inside long enough to retrieve what we need to protect ourselves."

Keratrix nodded at once. "Of course! I have memorized the codes that open the vault doors. In case you've forgotten, I do an inventory every other week. I know where everything can be found. We can retrieve whatever you wish."

Arcannen smiled and clapped him on his shoulder. "Lead on then, young man. You have proved your worth this day!"

Keratrix set off eagerly, with Arcannen following. They went down through the tower to its base, and then farther down into the cellars underneath. Below, there were rooms that might once have been many things but now were locked and abandoned. On the third level down, they followed one corridor deep into a maze of others, the intense darkness lit only by a thin spray of werelight that Keratrix had summoned to his fingertips to guide them. Their footsteps echoed in the silence, and the darkness closed in behind them like a wall. If you became lost down here without light—or perhaps even with it, Arcannen thought—you might never get out. This was treacherous ground, so he made it a point to memorize the way back as they proceeded deeper in.

Finally, they reached the end of a hallway and a massive iron door with multiple locks, and bars fed by gears into holes bored into the stone of the Keep. Keratrix stopped, passed the werelight to Arcannen, and turned to the door. Slowly, deliberately, he began running through a litany of words and odd sounds, addressing the barrier in front of them as he did so. It seemed to take him forever to finish, but when he did the bars slid back, the locks released, and the huge door swung open to admit them.

An entry chamber awaited them, small and claustrophobic, and again Keratrix stopped Arcannen from proceeding farther. "Careful," Keratrix cautioned. "You've forgotten the traps."

Arcannen shook his head in a self-admonishing way and smiled. "It seems I have forgotten a lot of late."

Again, the scribe began moving about, touching the wall in select places. Each time, Arcannen heard a click or snap or hiss from somewhere nearby as a trap was disabled. It took Keratrix a little longer than opening the door, but in the end he managed the task and beckoned the man he believed to be the Ard Rhys forward.

A section of the wall swung open and they walked into a sudden blaze of light. Here they found a cavernous room with dozens of smaller chambers opening off it like spokes on a wheel hub. Arcannen stood where he was for a moment, dazzled by the sight of what was arguably the most coveted and protected sanctuary in the Four Lands, amazed at how easy it had been to gain entry. Yet he knew that he never could have done so as anyone but Isaturin, and perhaps not even this disguise would have been enough if the threat of an attack did not loom just outside Paranor's gates. Still, that he had been able to persuade Keratrix to allow him entry was nothing short of a miracle, and he intended to make the most of it.

"What is it you seek, Master?" the young man asked.

Arcannen shook his head. "I am considering what will best serve our order," he answered, moving to the center of the room. "You say you inventory all the artifacts regularly? Then you must know where each one lies and what each one does."

He was eager to begin choosing, a malevolent child in a room full of dangerous toys. He could barely contain himself. What should he take with him? What would best serve him in the years ahead? For a moment he simply cast about aimlessly, euphoric and enthralled. He was in the forbidden castle of the Druids. He had gained access to their most priceless and ancient magic. How could he begin to choose?

"Where do you keep the crimson Elfstones?" he asked.

When he glanced at Keratrix for his answer, he caught just a glimpse of discomfort or maybe even suspicion in the other's eyes. The young man looked away quickly and moved toward the doorway. "Why don't you begin looking about, and I will summon men to help you lift and carry . . ."

Arcannen was on him in a flash, one hand fastened on his neck, the other on his arm. "Too late for that, I'm afraid."

He liked Keratrix. He was grateful for the help the young man had provided, even if he had been tricked into providing it. He might have found greater resistance in another man. He might have been questioned or challenged. Only because Keratrix was pledged to serve the Ard Rhys and considered it his paramount duty to do so had Arcannen been able to get this far.

He liked this young man, indeed.

So he killed him swiftly and painlessly by breaking his neck and then surveyed the room, wondering what he could find that would prove most useful.

27

UCH EARLIER THAT SAME MORNING, PAXON and Miriya rose from where they had spent the night near the merging of the Runne and the Mermidon Rivers, and set out to complete their journey back to Paranor. Much recovered from their ordeal, they were in possession of a little workman-like two-man lent to them by the dwarf Trond and his friends in return for their promise to return it as soon as possible. It was foggy as they followed the soaring cliffs of the Dragon's Teeth west toward the Kennon Pass. With luck, they would reach home before the day was out, even in their clunky little craft, which was efficient enough, if awkward, and labored like a horse run ragged.

But they had been inordinately lucky to get this far, so neither was complaining.

Trond had been as good as his word. He had taken them to his village, fed and clothed them, and provided beds for the night. They had gone to sleep in the late afternoon and not come awake until midday of the following day. Once up and about, they discovered that the Dwarf had managed to secure the hard-used two-man they now flew—a feat he claimed had been a work of Dwarf magic. Grateful beyond words, but anxious to get back to Paranor, they had thanked him profusely and set out at once. By nightfall, their endurance and concentration drained once more, they had decided to rest at the juncture of the Mermidon and Runne Rivers until morning.

There were questions that needed answering, of course, and as yet no answers to any of them.

No one had seen Isaturin after Paxon and Miriya had tumbled off the ledge. No one had heard anything of anyone else seeking aid in getting to Paranor. No one had heard anything at all about what had taken place in Arishaig. Admittedly, Trond's village was small and isolated, so word of what was happening in the rest of the world sometimes didn't arrive for weeks, if ever. But that didn't reassure either the Highlander or Miriya. The absence of news was not necessarily good.

The two spent what remained of that first day talking over what they knew about the slaughter in the Assembly. On some points, they were in agreement. Arcannen was likely behind it; he was the one who would benefit most from disrupting any peace talks. Sure, there were ministers in the Coalition Council—fanatics against all magic and magic users—who did not favor an alliance with the Druids, but it seemed a stretch to think they would go this far to force a split.

But if Arcannen was behind it, where had he been hiding during the attack? He couldn't have dispatched and then controlled the Sleath from afar. Didn't he have to be close enough to orchestrate the attack? Paxon wasn't sure, but Miriya, with years of training in magic's uses, had insisted that he had to be present to be certain only the Federation delegates were killed and to move the Sleath like a chessboard piece during the attack. The idea of pre-programming such a demon brought a snort of derision from her. Such sorcerous creatures couldn't be controlled if simply set loose. Arcannen had to have been there.

But if so, why hadn't they been able to see him?

There was the troubling fact of the Sleath's merging with Karlin Ryl, as well. Why had it bothered? Why hadn't it just fled once it had finished its work? And then, afterward, why had it reappeared during their battle with the plants in the Battlemound Lowlands? It had expended what remained of its strength defending the Druids, dying in the process. It had saved the lives of the Druids and their companions, but why would it do that?

Neither of them had been able to come up with an answer the day before. It wasn't until they were wending their way through the Kennon and Paxon found himself thinking about Fero Darz plunging to his death off the cliff ledge, wondering why Isaturin hadn't been able to save him and hadn't fallen himself, that he remembered something Aphenglow Elessedil had once told him. Something he hadn't thought about in years.

He looked over at Miriya with a confused expression on his face. "What?" she said.

"Did it seem to you that Isaturin was not entirely himself once we fled Arishaig? You said yourself that he seemed less than concerned about Karlin. I thought he seemed distracted, not really present."

She stared. "Well, his behavior *was* odd at times. Almost cold."

"Then listen to this. We've already agreed that, for things to have happened in Arishaig the way they did, Arcannen must have been present. What if he was, but we just didn't recognize him? Aphenglow once told me that Arcannen has a gift for disguise. He can make himself look like anyone. She told me he did it a few years ago in Arishaig when he pretended to be one of us and assassinated the Minister of Security Against Magic, a man named Fashton Caeil."

She nodded. "I don't think I knew any of this."

"Not many people did. There was good reason not to make it public. Relations between the Druids and the Federation were already bad. But that isn't what matters. What matters is who Arcannen was impersonating when he killed Caeil."

She stared at him. "Who?"

Paxon did not respond, waiting on her.

"Isaturin?" she guessed finally. "No! Is that even possible? Isaturin?"

They were quiet for a long time after that, thinking it through.

They were nearing Paranor when Miriya spoke again. "If what you suspect is true," she said, her voice rough and uneasy, "then Arcannen is inside the Druid's Keep with no one but us the wiser."

Paxon nodded wordlessly, his eyes on the land ahead as they flew above the treetops of the forest surrounding their destination.

"Someone will notice he isn't entirely right," she added after a moment or two. "Someone will suspect."

"We didn't," he said. "And we traveled with him for more than a week!"

"But in the Keep he has Druids all around him . . ."

"He will fit right in. Worse, he will be in a position of authority, meaning no one's going to question him." The Highlander glanced over and gave a dismissive shake of his head. "And any changes they might notice will likely be put down to the rigors of the journey he just survived."

Miriya gave a distressed grunt. "How did we let this happen? How could we have been so stupid? He was right there under our noses and not one of us realized it! We should have noticed something. We should have suspected. We are fools."

Paxon shrugged. "We are human. And, more to the point, Arcannen is a skilled wielder of magic with lots of practice at deceptions like this. He got past the entire Federation when he infiltrated their Coalition Council offices and killed Fashton Caeil. I guess we should have been thinking harder about the possibility that he would try something like this again."

He paused. "You have to wonder when the switch was made, though. At Arishaig? Even before? When did Arcannen become Isaturnin? And what happened to the real Isaturin?"

"I'm more worried about how we expose him once we reach the Keep," Miriya said. "We can't just accuse him. He's the Ard Rhys, after all. What if we're wrong?"

"What if we're not?"

She stared at him in dismay. "So what do we do?"

"Find him and surround him with enough Druids and Troll guards to stop him from escaping. Confront him. Someone in the Keep must possess a magic that will penetrate his disguise." He paused. "Anyway, that's not our biggest problem, Miriya."

She looked at him with fresh interest. "What is, then?"

"That he will disappear before we even have a chance to confront him."

He squinted into the hazy sunlight, looking ahead to where the tallest of Paranor's towers had just begun to come into view. Had he seen movement there, ships? He waited until they got closer, suddenly worried. Miriya was talking again but he wasn't paying attention, his mind on what he was seeing in the distance, trying to make sense of it.

"Paxon!" she snapped suddenly. "Have you heard a word I've been saying?"

He pointed toward the Keep. "Look there. What do you see?"

She did as he asked, peering ahead. "Airships," she said finally. "But they're not ours." She hesitated. "Shades! They're Federation warships!"

"Looks like they've decided on a response to the loss of their delegation. We'd better find out exactly what's happening—and quickly."

"We can't fly straight in. We can't let them see us. They'll shoot us right out of the sky." She was angry now, her face rigid.

Paxon banked the two-man away from a direct approach, choosing to angle north, away from the south gates where it appeared the bulk of the fleet was anchored. He took a swift count of the vessels hovering before the Keep and came up with ten. But there were also flits circling the walls, and transports hovering to the south awaiting instructions.

Paxon's brow furrowed as he considered the situation. How long had they been there? He descended even lower, almost skimming the treetops as he flew toward the west walls. When they were nearing a point where any Federation scout could not help but see them, he dropped their airship through the trees and set her down in a small clearing.

Together, he and Miriya climbed out and stood looking toward the Keep, which now sat about a mile distant.

"What now?" she asked, almost as if she were ceding the decision to him.

Paxon cocked an eyebrow. "Since we can't enter Paranor through the gates, we have to get inside another way. I seem to remember something about an underground tunnel from Allanon's time. A secret passage for just this sort of situation."

Miriya nodded thoughtfully. "I remember it, too. And I even know where it is."

As she walked through the dank gloom of the Murk Sink, following just behind Imric, Leofur Rai found herself thinking how strange it would be to share her companion's life. He was not an ordinary man. He was in many ways barely human. He could do things no other man could do, but doing them caused him constant doubt and fear. He risked himself each time he gave in to his compulsion—to the urgent genetic need with which he had been born. He must change to be complete, but he must also accept that the act was so dangerous, a rational man would have disdained to engage in it.

A rational man, one not addicted to the act of shifting, could manage to live a reasonable life by not giving in to the urge. But this was clearly a need so powerful it dominated Imric's every waking moment.

So it was asking too much of Imric to forgo the demands of his blood legacy. After all, he had not been able to withstand the lure once she gave him the chance to explore it. He had needed only a catalyst that would give him an opportunity to reengage in the act he had spent ten long years forsaking, and she had provided it. She had offered him a reason to begin shape-shifting again. No, more than a reason. Hope. She had offered him at least a reasonable possibility of maintaining control over the effects of the changing through her.

She felt a momentary surge of guilt. She was, in fact, the cause of his present dilemma. Without her to tether to, he would not have given in to the urgings of his body. Without her he would have stayed away from the dangers that shape-shifting presented.

And now he had compromised himself and his needs by falling in love with her. Had she given him cause to think she would respond? She was committed to Paxon; she had pledged herself to a life partnership. Yet even knowing this was so, Imric had allowed himself to become entangled by his feelings for her.

To become so entangled that he had been compelled to tell her of it. To bare his feelings in a way that completely contradicted his personality.

And now, suddenly, she was in doubt of her own feelings. In the aftermath of his revelations and the rush of her own confusion, she was wondering if maybe she felt the same for him.

Because where would all this lead if nothing between them changed?

She could guess the answer clearly enough. They would rescue Chrysallin. It would not be accomplished as easily as the words suggested. They might not come out of the effort intact—or even come out of it alive, for that matter. And if they died, her questions were meaningless. But if they lived to return to Paranor, then she would go back to Paxon, and Imric would go back to his stables.

Which meant he would go back to a life without shape-shifting because she would no longer be able to tether him. He would have to either ignore his body's demands or shift on his own, alone and untethered. And if the latter, he would return to risking his life and courting madness.

It was this latter choice she felt at that moment to be inevitable.

She had not considered this before. She had not bothered to think that far ahead. But by doing so now, she saw the extent of the problem. When he said he understood she would never be with him and loving her was pointless, no matter the strength of his feelings, he was telling her something else, as well. Or perhaps admitting it to himself. He was saying that when she left him to go back to Paxon, he would be left with nothing. Without her and without shape-shifting, he would go back to the life he had been leading before meeting her. He would go back to a life that held no meaning for him.

She wondered, too, what their parting would do to her. It was not as if it would leave her unscathed. It was clear that she was already changed from who and what she had been when they had started out on this journey. How was she to deal with that? What sort of resolution was possible?

She walked without seeing, keeping pace but staying back, not wanting to talk to him, needing to be alone with her thoughts. All around her, the swamp was alive with watery splashes and birdcalls and scurrying movements. Snakes slithered in the underbrush and hung from the trees. Now and then, one appeared along the shoreline, with a ripple of water and a glimpse of a searching head. Rumbles sounded from distant places, indistinct and unidentifiable. Overhead, fog swirled in thick curtains, masking a sun that lingered somewhere out of view, its brilliant light a diffuse and vague glow that barely penetrated the pervasive gloom.

. She experienced a moment of despair. She was wandering in a world where she didn't belong, and living a life she shouldn't be living. It had all seemed so clear when she set out. Rescue Chrysallin. Save Paxon's sister. Find her and bring her home for Paxon. Accomplish what she could while he was off fighting for his life and for those he was sworn to protect.

Do something to make herself feel worthwhile. Because, in truth, she hadn't felt that way for a long time.

"Watch the snakes," Imric said over his shoulder.

A pile of them writhed off to one side in a watery depression, folding and unfolding sinuously. She stepped away hurriedly.

"It's not far now," he added.

The light was beginning to dim with night's approach, but it was still at least an hour away. Leofur wished she had one of her flash rips—any diapson-crystal-powered weapon really—or anything other than the knife in her boot. A blade would be useless in a fight against the witch. She was unsure how Imric planned to take Chrysallin back, anyway. She thought he must have a plan, but she expected it mostly involved him undergoing a shift and her providing a distraction. The thought of it did not instill her with much confidence.

They had gone only a short distance farther when Imric signaled a halt. She crept up to where he knelt and bent close. "What is it?"

He put a finger to his lips, then pulled her down next to him and put his lips against her ear. "Her cottage is just ahead, beyond that stand of cypress."

She glanced at a thick grove of weeping trees that formed a barrier at a bend in the lake's shoreline.

"We have to leave the path here and go into the trees. Stay close to me, and watch where you step."

He rose and started off, and she was quick to follow. They wove their way through stands of scrub trees and heavy stands of tall reeds and clumps of brush that formed small islands among the waterways and quicksand. She was aware of something big moving off to one side, disturbing the foliage as it passed, apparently uninterested in them. She tried to step exactly in Imric's footsteps, but mostly she tried to keep from panicking.

Ahead, the limbs and brush parted just enough to reveal the first faint details of a cottage nestled in the swamp's watery cradle, set back from the shores of the lake and surrounded by ancient willows. Imric slowed again, then dropped into a crouch seconds later. He motioned for Leofur to do the same and pulled her close.

Mouth to her ear again, he whispered, "We can't go any farther until we've agreed on what happens next."

She shifted so that her mouth was now at *his* ear. "What *does* happen next, Imric?"

He pulled away and gave her a look. Then, leaning back in, he said, "I'm going to tether with you so we can talk about this without speaking. I'm worried out voices will carry. Ready?"

She nodded. Immediately she felt a pushing inside her head, a presence she recognized and allowed to enter.

Can you hear me?

Yes. What is the plan?

We wait until twilight, then I rush the door, break it down, and overpower anything waiting inside. You follow me in, only a second or two behind, look immediately for Chrysallin, and try to free her.

That's your whole plan?

I knew you would approve.

It's a terrible plan! What if Chrys isn't where we can see her? What if the witch has set traps for just such an attempt? What if I have to fight when I don't have a weapon?

There was a long silence. *Did you think this would be easy? Do you have a better plan? Because if you know of one, please tell me. I am happy to listen.*

All right. Change into something small and unnoticeable so you can have a look inside first. See if the witch took any of my weapons from the boy and kept them. If they are there, maybe I can reach them in case you need help. Be very sure you can tell where Chrys is so we don't hurt her by mistake.

He didn't argue with her. Instead, he stripped off his clothes and began to change into a tiny finch, its back and wings dotted with white spots, its head and breast orange. *Stay here. Wait for me.*

You don't have to tell me that.

He flew off, darting through the foliage, keeping close to tree limbs and leafy boughs, rising several times to vary his approach until he was perched on a branch that allowed him a peek through one of the front windows. He remained there for several seconds, and then darted to a different position with a different view. One time more he switched his location, flying around to the side of the cottage. Finally he returned, settling onto a branch next to her.

Chrysallin is in a wooden crate near the back of the room. A little girl is speaking to her through the slats. There's no one else in sight. The crate is locked, but I will smash it open when I go through the door so you can get to her.

He paused. *Both of your weapons are sitting on a table off to the left side of the door, maybe ten feet away.*

You're sure there's no one else there?

No one in sight, and the doorway to the back of the house is open and darkened. I listened for sounds of life. I didn't hear any. We have to hope the little girl is the witch and there isn't anyone else. Are you ready?

She nodded. *I'm ready.*

Swiftly, he changed into a huge brindle-and-gray moor cat, flexing his limbs and claws as he settled into place. They were perhaps twenty yards from the front door, which faced out onto the swamp.

His whiskered face turned toward her and his lantern eyes fixed on her. *I don't regret anything I've told you. I don't regret how I feel about you. I won't ever regret the time I've spent with you. Do you believe me?*

I do. I don't regret any of it, either. I will never regret it.

He hesitated and turned away. *I will try to keep you safe. Ready?*

Ready.
Then here we go.

The sun was directly over Paranor and the sky clear when the first of the flits flew overhead. Paxon and Miriya shrank back into the cover of the trees and waited for them to pass, exchanging a quick glance of shared understanding.

"They saw us land," Paxon confirmed. "We have to hurry."

They broke into a trot, moving swiftly toward the Keep. The flits might have landed, as well; they couldn't be sure. Whatever the case, a shuttle from one of the transports—the kind that carried troops— was setting down close by, and they could hear the sound of ramps being lowered.

"They're going to hunt us," Miriya said.

Paxon's expression tightened. "They can try."

It quickly became apparent they were going to try very hard. Paxon knew that if he and Miriya were trapped outside the walls of Paranor, they would lose any chance of reaching Arcannen. They had to find the underground tunnel and get into the Keep before the soldiers caught them. But he could already hear voices shouting to one another through the trees and knew that time was running out.

"How far to the tunnel?" he asked Miriya. He was breathing heavily, not yet recovered from their ordeal in the Battlemound and Anar.

She glanced over. "I can't be sure. Keep running!"

As if there was any other choice. He pushed on. More flits passed overhead, but there was no time to worry about them now. The Federation already knew approximately where they were. The soldiers on the ground would be on top of them shortly.

He had barely completed the thought before the first of them appeared off to their right, breaking through heavy brush. "Over here!" the shouts went up.

Miriya slowed and turned, bracing herself. "Get behind me!" she snapped to Paxon.

Then her hands came up and blue flames exploded from her fingers to form a wall of fire between the Federation soldiers and themselves. It rose thirty feet into the trees, a huge barricade that engulfed everything around it. Paxon flinched away in shock, then Miriya was running again and he after her.

"You set the forest on fire!" he shouted.

Where the flames burned through the trees, screams of terror filled the air.

Her laugh was harsh and sardonic. "Not really. It's just an illusion. Come on, Paxon! Run!"

They bolted through the trees ahead of those trying to catch them from behind and those trapped by the illusion off to their right. The trunks of the ancient forest flashed past them, an army of dark watchers. Paxon wondered how much longer he could keep up with Miriya, who seemed to possess inexhaustible amounts of energy.

Finally she called back to him, "Just ahead! Hurry!"

They entered a clearing of downed trees and large boulders, the debris of storms come and gone evident. She slowed and began casting about, hands sweeping left and right, seeking the entrance.

"Hah!" she exclaimed in glee, pointing.

Paxon couldn't tell what she was pointing at, but she hurried over to a grassy hummock, fastened her fingers in the thick tufts, and pulled. A section of grasses and earth lifted away to reveal the hidden door. It was a hatch of heavy iron that looked all but impassable. Paxon could tell at once that it was sealed against entry, and there were no hinges, handles, or locks in evidence.

Miriya knelt, summoning magic with deft gestures and words. What had seemed a door of iron disappeared entirely, leaving an open black hole into the earth.

"Inside!" she snapped, gesturing.

Already the voices were back again, this time coming from both sides. The Highlander went through the entrance quickly with Miriya right on his heels. Once they had begun to descend the set of stairs that waited, the iron door re-formed behind them and the ground quickly covered over the entry once more.

Now in total darkness, Paxon waited for her to tell him what to do. Instead, light flared abruptly, and she appeared with two flameless torches in hand. She gave one to him and immediately moved into the tunnel beyond. "They won't catch us now."

He was inclined to agree, but the difficulty in escaping the Federation was now supplanted by the difficulty in finding Arcannen. They couldn't even be sure that he was still at Paranor. If he was gone, their chances of convincing the Federation of his role in the disaster were minimal. Worse, their chances of undoing whatever damange he had done were smaller still.

They pressed on through the murky gloom, their torches providing just enough light to allow them to put one foot in front of the other. The tunnel was clearly very old. Roots had grown in through the earth, and parts of the ceiling had fallen away in large clumps. It could have been years since it had last been used; there was really no way of knowing.

"There should be a door ahead that opens into Paranor's cellars," Miriya offered at one point before going silent again.

When the tunnel took a sharp downward slope, she whispered back that they were about to pass under the walls. They descended a long way before the passage leveled off and continued on.

"Who told you about this tunnel?" Paxon asked at one point.

"Isaturin. The real Isaturin. Aphenglow Elessedil told him. I guess it is something that gets passed down. But you still need Druid magic to get inside."

They walked the rest of the way in silence until they reached another door, this one much bigger and much stronger than the one before. A huge, iron monster, it was clearly the door leading to the inside of the Keep and, as such, virtually impregnable. But again Miriya knew the magic that would open it, and they stepped into the interior of the Druid's Well.

This was not a place anyone wanted to be—not even a Druid. This was the dwelling place of the spirit that warded the Keep, protecting against attacks from outsiders. Paxon had heard from Aphenglow Elessedil about the last time the Federation had attempted a forcible entry. The Keep's spirit had risen up in fury and smashed the intruding ships to pieces, sending them broken and helpless back to where they had come from. That the Federation vessels outside had come no closer than where they were now suggested that perhaps that event had not been entirely forgotten.

Proceeding quietly, Paxon and Miriya climbed the circular stairway that led to the Keep's ground level. If they moved quietly enough, perhaps they would not call attention to themselves and wake the thing that lived at the bottom of the well. You never wanted that to happen. No one wanted that.

Once or twice, Aphenglow had told Paxon, members of the Druid order—mostly High Druids—had woken the creature deliberately to bring it to their aid. But the magic was not always discriminate and it was dangerous to be in its presence. Neither he nor Miriya wanted that now, so they stepped softly and did not talk.

There was a slight stirring at one point, a rasping and a hiss from the darkness far below. But then the sounds lapsed back into silence, and there was nothing further.

At the final level, a door opened into the main tower of the Keep. Paxon and Miriya passed through gratefully and secured the door behind them. They were in a lower hallway now, the smokeless lamps affixed to the walls at long intervals, the darkness pervasive in the spaces between.

They stood where they were until Miriya beckoned to Paxon and started ahead. They had gone only a short distance when she abruptly stopped and stood, listening. Then she stepped backward and leaned into him, her voice low and urgent in his ear.

"Someone's coming!"

28

CHRYSALLIN LEAH WAS LISTENING WITH HALF AN ear as the little girl ranted on through the slats of the wooden crate. She was locked away again, her captor having grown bored enough to want her out of sight if not out of hearing. Throughout this whole, interminable day, the little girl had been carrying on about Leofur and her awful fate, about the shape-shifter's disappearance and disposing of the troublesome boy, all of it horrific and disgusting. Chrys kept imagining what it would feel like to get her hands around the little girl's neck and squeeze. She kept picturing various scenarios of blood and exploding heads and shrieks of pain.

Finally she blocked all of it away, afraid she was going to drive herself mad with such thinking. It was bad enough that she had to live with the possibility that Leofur was dead, even if she couldn't quite bring herself to believe it. It was just too horrible to accept. But the little girl was so intent and eager to layer on image after image of what it must have been like for Leofur when the swamp things took her. She relished the telling of it, and while the Highland girl could rationally understand the other's motivation in making her listen, emotionally she was enraged. She had tried repeatedly and unsuccessfully to indicate that she wanted to talk about something else, but the little girl was having none of it. Today the game did not seem to matter to her. What mattered was making Chrys feel as terrible as possible, as if it were all her fault that any of this had happened, as if the inconvenience of having to dispose of Leofur was entirely on her head. Petulant, nasty, and derisive by turns, the little monster kept at her endlessly until finally she retreated to the far corner of the crate and sat there with her hands over her ears and her head lowered.

"He's coming for you, you realize! Arcannen Rai? He'll be here in another day, perhaps sooner! He sent me word, little pet. You will be his plaything before you know it. Can you imagine what he will do to you? You will be sorry you ever left me! You will regret the way you behaved toward me—pretending to play along or refusing to play at all. You missed your chance, foolish child! I might have kept you from him if you were more compliant and willing to be my companion. But no! Not you. Not the precious Chrysallin Leah!"

Chrys couldn't shut out the words entirely, and the weight of their vindictiveness was clear. She found herself wondering suddenly if the witch was losing her mind entirely, if something had taken her over the edge of sanity and toppled her into a black hole of madness. Certainly she was raging mindlessly, attacking relentlessly, attempting to stamp out any trace of hope her captive might still harbor.

"He wants to use you against your brother. He will do whatever he thinks necessary to make that happen! You are such a little fool. Why didn't you ask me to keep you safe from him? Why didn't you try a little harder to have fun with me?"

I hate your stupid game! Chrys wanted to scream. *That's why!*

But she couldn't use her voice, her vocal cords still paralyzed and her breath still weak and strangled when she tried to make any sound. She thought her voice might be starting to come back, just a little, but not yet enough to matter.

It was maddening, and it drove her to the brink of despair. She was so utterly helpless, and she hated it. The witch had not as yet given her the nightly piece of root to chew, but she would do so soon. And what could she do about it this time? Could she swallow it once more and then throw it up again without the other knowing? Could she manage to regurgitate it when the witch was right there in the cottage with her? But she had to. She had no other choice. She only had another day or so before Arcannen arrived, and she must do whatever it took to escape him. When they opened the crate door, she would have one chance to destroy them both with her voice, and she would have to make the best of it.

She was crying again now. The thought of Leofur dead was so heart wrenching she could barely hold herself together. But she was determined that if Leofur was gone, she would make sure the witch never did anything like this to anyone else again. She would put an end to it. She would put an end to *her.* She would use the wishsong against her the same way she had used it against Mischa, that other foul creature Arcannen had managed to dredge up out of the dark corners of humanity. No one would ever have to play the little girl's horrid game again.

Suddenly everything went silent. The little girl had stopped talking. She had frozen where she was, unmoving. The silence lengthened. Chrysallin moved to the front of the crate and peered out through the airhole into the room beyond. The little girl was standing with her head cocked, listening. Her nose twitched and a smile appeared on her lips.

"Something's creeping 'round my house; creeping, creeping like a mouse," she whispered in a singsong voice.

She went still again and turned to face the door. Her child's features hardened and began to twist into an ugly expression.

"Who's out there?" she hissed softly. "I sense you there. I've smelled you before . . ."

Then she changed in the blink of an eye into something so loathsome and repellent it was all Chrys could do to keep from gagging.

An instant later the front door exploded inward, disintegrating into jagged pieces of wood and metal, and a giant moor cat catapulted past the witch, knocking her aside as its momentum carried it across the room to crash into Chrysallin's crate and reduce it to splinters.

To Leofur, linked to Imric's moor cat by the tether when it broke from hiding and raced for the cottage door, it felt as if she were a thing of grace and beauty, speed and power, huge muscles rippling beneath her strange mottled coat of gray, brindle, and silver, sleek body stretched out so close to the ground she seemed to be gliding across it. Leofur felt herself surging ahead, experiencing the sense of freedom it was giving Imric, the sensations it was providing, finding her breath catching in her throat.

Then she broke the connection and was back inside herself, charging after him, her eyes on the cottage and her mind racing as she sorted through the list of things she must do once she was inside.

Clear the door. Reach my weapons. Run to Chrysallin. Or maybe to Imric?

Faster! Faster! I'm too slow!

She was falling behind. In his cat form, Imric was too swift for her. He was at the door and crashing through, the barrier simply disintegrating as he launched himself against it. Shouts and screams rose. Flashes of fiery light followed. A terrible battle was taking place, smashing furniture, walls, and windows in its fury. She bounded up the steps and toward the shattered entry but found it blocked by the moor cat and a thing composed of rags and ooze and rotting flesh that lacked either form or identity. She could not get past the combatants as they surged back and forth in front of the opening, tearing at each other, the witch as much an animal as Imric.

A glimpse of what lay beyond showed the room in a shambles. Stacked against the far wall were the remains of the wooden crate with Chrysallin sprawled at their center, half buried and motionless.

Seconds later the witch and the shape-shifter fell apart, the former rising up like a specter summoned from the Murk Sink's deepest, darkest mud, tentacles and feelers lashing out with barbs and razored edges in an effort to keep its opponent at bay. Imric's cat was slashed and bloodied, crouching in readiness for another attack, snarling and roaring as it feinted and lunged, claws raking at the wooden floor.

"Shape-shifter, do you think yourself a match for me?" burbled the witch out of a mouth Leofur could not even see. "Do you think I am some feeble human? I see you for what you are, but you mistake me completely!"

The moor cat made a sudden rush and was thrown back in a heap. It rose again instantly, but was further damaged and struggling.

"Is it shape-shifting you love, creature of smoke and mist? Is it the changing that gives you your freedom, your power, your life? I will provide you with all you want! I will feed you such power that you will choke on the pleasure of it. Is that not your deepest desire? So be it, then!"

The little girl was back, face twisted with hatred, a monstrous apparition, thin arms lifting and fingers pointing. "Shift until you die, you wretched beast!"

A kind of shimmer emerged from her body, unfolding like netting to enclose the moor cat in a cloud of sickly, glistening ichor. Imric reared up in an effort to escape, but the ichor formed a cocoon that would not release him. Ripping and tearing and roaring in fury, he could not break free. Leofur watched in horror as he struggled futilely, thrashing against a magic that held him fast.

Then he began to change, shifting from a moor cat into other shapes. One after another the shapes ensnared him momentarily and then released him to change again. He changed and kept changing, unable to stop himself. The little girl was screaming with laughter, a frenzied wildness consuming her until she was out of control. Imric was changing faster and faster, the shifts coming so rapidly they were almost a blur within the shimmering light of his prison.

Stop! Leofur begged him, reaching out through the tether.

He called back to her, his voice approaching a wail of despair. *I cannot! Her magic is too strong!*

The little girl stepped forward then, raised both hands, levitated him off the floor, and flung him back through the doorway, barely missing Leofur who stepped away just in time. Imric, still caught up in his kaleidoscopic shifting of forms, flew out into the swamp.

But in Leofur's mind, he was still calling to her.

Release me! Sever our link! Do it now!

She would not do it. She would never do it.

Then she thought of Sarnya, who had held fast to Imric until she had perished, and of her own promises to Imric not to behave in the same way. How often had she claimed to be stronger than Sarnya? Now she must prove it.

Her heart breaking, her eyes squeezed shut against further images of Imric Cort, she severed the link, and he was lost to her.

She watched in horror as Imric disappeared, helpless to stop it from happening. Only for a moment did she hesitate, but it was a moment too long. When she recovered sufficiently to rush back through the doorway and into the room beyond, the little girl was waiting.

"Oh, look," the other said, her voice sly and insinuating. "It's Chrysallin's friend, not eaten after all—another playmate for me to enjoy. What should we do first?"

The flash rips lay on the floor amid the debris, ten feet away. Leofur did the only thing she could think to do and made a rush for them, desperate to escape whatever the witch intended, but quickly found herself frozen in place. It was as if her feet were nailed to the floor, her muscles frozen, her body sapped of strength.

"A bit tired, are we?" the little girl said, the false sympathy oozing from her words. "Is there something I can do? Wait, I see what you want. Let me help."

She walked over and picked up the weapons, cradling them in her arms as she moved back again to stand in front of Leofur. "Would you like these?" she asked. "You can have them, if you wish. All you have to do is reach out and take them. Go on; just take them out of my arms. I won't stop you."

But Leofur could not move. Not even a twitch of her finger. She tried to say something, but even that proved impossible. The little girl waited on her, smiling and nodding encouragement. Then finally she gave up any pretense and backed away.

"I don't know how you and your shape-shifting pet escaped the swamp dwellers, but you should have realized that coming here was a huge mistake. You should have turned around and gone home."

The witch carried the weapons back to where she had found them and laid them on the floor again. "There. You won't be needing these, will you? What a foolish young woman you are! Did you believe yourself a match for me? In my own home? In a place where I have lived my entire life?"

She snapped her fingers and Leofur could move again. "If you make a single threatening gesture or move toward me, I will freeze you in place again. You are not to do anything. You are not to say anything. You are to listen to me and accept what I am about to tell you. Nod if you understand me."

Leofur nodded, her eyes searching for a way out of her predicament. Her gaze passed over Chrysallin; she tried hard not to look startled when she saw her friend looking back at her.

Chrys was conscious.

"I won't kill you if you'll agree to be my friend and play with me. We can all play—all three of us. You can stay here until it's time for you to go, and then you can leave unharmed. If you do as you are told. If you don't cause trouble. Do you understand?"

Not even a little, Leofur thought, but she nodded anyway. Whatever the witch was talking about didn't matter. Whatever she asked, Leofur was going to agree to. All she was doing was buying time, waiting for a chance to escape. If she could just manage to keep the witch's attention a little longer, Chrys might come all the way awake and together . . .

The little girl was looking at her strangely. "What are you thinking about? Because if I thought for one minute you were planning to deceive me, I would be very unhappy. You've already seen what that means. So maybe you ought to—"

She never finished. In a panther-like display of stealth and quickness, Chrysallin Leah rose from the debris of the crate and launched herself at the witch. Since she was only ten feet away, Chrys was on top of her before she could react. The startled look on the little girl's face just before her former captive slammed into her clearly reflected her surprise. Then the two tumbled past Leofur in a tangle of legs and arms, scratching and clawing. Leofur was racing for her flash rips when she heard a scream so chilling it brought her about.

The witch had broken free of Chrys and was changing back into her oozing, pulsating, tentacled form again. On seeing what the witch had become, Chrysallin Leah screamed in shock and rage, the sound so powerful it caused her attacker to lurch backward. But even then the tentacles lashed out and wrapped about the young woman's throat, cutting off all sound.

Leofur stared in momentary shock. Chrys had her voice back! Whatever magic the witch had used to silence her had been negated!

She snatched up the smaller of the flash rips as the tentacles fastened about her legs. Opening the parse tubes so that the power of the diapson crystals engaged, she leveled her weapon as she was being dragged toward the witch and pulled the trigger. A fiery charge exploded from the barrel, burning into her attacker's loathsome body, causing it to shudder violently.

But when she attempted to fire again, the flash rip failed. Whether it had jammed or had carried only one good charge to begin with, she didn't know. But its power was gone.

Another of the tentacles reached out and tore the weapon from her hands, flinging it through the window and into the night.

In desperation, Leofur reached for her Arc-5, barely managing to get a grip on it as the witch began dragging her across the floor again. Thrashing and kicking, she tried to trigger the weapon's release. By now the tentacles were tearing at her hands, attempting to pry the weapon away. Slowly, inexorably, she felt her fingers loosening.

But while the witch was preoccupied with subduing Leofur, she had inadvertently loosened her grip on Chrysallin's throat.

The Highland girl's voice erupted in a high-pitched cry that exploded the tentacles wrapped about her throat. Too late, the witch realized her mistake. She tried frantically to silence the young woman, to close off the magic of the wishsong. But Chrysallin had full use of her voice now, and the sound of her singing filled the room with fire and steel, the force of it strong enough to shake the cottage walls. The witch lashed out at her in a final desperate attempt to render her unconscious.

It wasn't enough. Across the room Leofur had regained control over the Arc-5. Releasing the safety, she pulled the trigger all the way back and a massive charge ripped clear of the weapon's barrel. The fiery projectile slammed into the witch and sent her skidding backward against the wall. Under attack now from two sides, ooze and rags and tentacles thrashed wildly. Chrys was focusing all of the considerable power of her newfound voice on the witch. She was seeing in this amorphous creature the faces of all her enemies—the hateful little girl, the insidious Mischa, and the nightmarish Arcannen— clearly reliving in those moments every monstrous wrong that had been done to her. Knowing from previous experience what it could do, she used her magic purposefully and without caution, ramping it up and expelling it in a single, concentrated blast of sound that hammered into the witch with the force of an avalanche descending.

The witch disintegrated, her body shattering, until all that remained were tiny pieces.

Leofur watched it happen—and even knowing the dual nature of the wishsong's life-and-death power, she was stunned by the result. One minute the witch was there, foul and fearsome, and the next she was reduced to bits of swamp matter. Even Chrysallin seemed shocked. In the aftermath of the witch's demise, she abruptly ceased her singing and stood where she was, staring. Then slowly she hunched over and began to shake, hugging herself and crying, tears streaming down her face.

Leofur went to her at once, took her in her arms, and rocked her gently. "It's all right, Chrys. It's over."

She held back her own tears, determined to be strong for her friend. They clung to each other as if that was all they had to cling to, as if anything else would cause them to fall apart as surely as the witch. They were safe, but they were not whole. Neither would be wholly herself again; neither would be able to put aside her memories of what had happened. And while Leofur could not be certain what Chrys's thoughts might be, she was thinking of Imric. But she could not speak of him now, not even to her closest friend. Later, perhaps, when the moment was not so raw.

"I knew you would come," Chrys whispered into her neck, still sobbing.

"Someone would have come, even if I hadn't."

"But it was you, Leofur. Not even Paxon came."

"I did not come alone," Leofur answered. "I had help. The man with me, the shape-shifter, was Imric Cort. He didn't have to accompany me, but he did." She was speaking of him without intending to. She could not help herself. "He was the one who tracked you, the one who found you in the swamp, the one whose shape-shifting allowed him to become the creatures he needed, and who could do the things I could not. When it was needed, when there was no other hope of finding you and even though it was dangerous and he knew it, he . . ."

She broke down completely, her determination not to cry shattered, reduced to tears she could not stop. Chrys was hugging her tightly, trying to soothe with comforting words, but Leofur knew she could not be consoled. Imric was dead. He had given his life for her. He had done so because he loved her, and now he was gone and she would never get the chance to tell him how much that had meant.

When finally she was able to stop crying and bring herself under control, she gently pushed Chrys away. "Enough. We have to go. We have to get out of this place. Right now."

Chrysallin nodded. "I don't want to stay here, either. I can't bear another minute of it. I don't care what we're risking."

More than if Imric were still with us. But Leofur let the thought go unspoken. They could leave. She knew the way back.

Armed with the big flash rip, she led Chrysallin from the cottage and back out into the night.

29

CROWDING BACK INTO THE DARKNESS OF AN ALCOVE,
Paxon and Miriya waited to see who was approaching. At
this point, every moving shadow suggested Arcannen, and
if anyone was to be caught off guard, they wanted it to be the sorcerer.

"Who is it?" Paxon whispered, already seeing something wrong
with the shadow.

"Someone too small for the sorcerer," Miriya answered.

Without waiting, she stepped from the shadows into the light and
let the person approaching have a good look at her. Paxon could tell
by now it was a man, but not a very big one. In fact, he looked very
much like . . .

"Oost Mondara!" Miriya exclaimed abruptly, extending an arm in
greeting.

The weapons master stopped where he was. "Miriya? Shades alive,
girl! Is it really you? I thought you were dead."

"Not yet. Not so you would notice, anyway. Come here, Oost.
Have a look at who else isn't dead."

When Paxon showed himself, the Dwarf gave an audible gasp and
lumbered forward eagerly, both hands reaching out to take the Highlander's own. "You are full of surprises, Paxon Leah! You and Miriya
both. We were told you fell off a cliff and into a canyon a thousand

feet down, thanks to a dragon. You were swept away like deadwood—or so Isaturin believes."

"He does, does he?" Miriya mumbled.

Oost didn't hear her. He released Paxon's hands and grinned. "It's hard to kill you two, isn't it? And a good thing, too. Whatever happened?"

Paxon gave him a quick overview, wanting to get on with the search for Arcannen as quickly as possible. "Where is Isaturin, Oost? Up on the gates with the Troll guard? Has he gone down to speak with the Federation commanders?"

The Dwarf shook his head. "Neither, as far as I can tell. That's why I'm down here, looking for him. He was seen going off with young Keratrix. I thought maybe when he told the order to stay put and not communicate with the Federation until his return that he had gone to the artifacts vault looking for a particular magic to use in defense of the Keep. But he's been gone long enough that I thought I ought to check on him."

"Why don't we go with you?" Miriya said at once. "We can surprise him." She gave Paxon a look that suggested her words had more than one meaning.

But Paxon wasn't quite ready to go anywhere. "Wait a minute. What happened to Fero Darz? Did Isaturin say anything about how he was killed?"

Oost looked confused. "He just said everyone was dead." He hesitated. "What's going on?"

Paxon looked at Miriya. "We have to tell him, even if we're not sure. He needs to know."

"Know what?" the Dwarf asked.

"That the fox is in the henhouse," Miriya answered. "And all the chickens are at risk."

Together, the two revealed everything they knew or suspected about Arcannen Rai, not holding back even the darkest possibilities, needing the Dwarf's support in ferreting out the truth but wanting to make sure he would keep their suspicions among the three of them until they were sure one way or the other.

"Do you see what we're up against?" Paxon finished. "We can't know for certain if we're right about this, but something is clearly wrong. The risk of Isaturin being Arcannen in disguise is just too great to ignore."

Oost looked worried. "Hmmm. He did seem particularly dismissive of the idea of talking to the Federation officials, and he's not usually like that. We'd better find him right away and make sure about this. Follow me."

He set off at once, navigating connecting corridors until they reached the door that opened into the cellars and started down. Miriya and Paxon stayed behind him as they descended one floor and then another. If Isaturin and Keratrix had gone to the artifacts vault, they would be on the next floor down.

Paxon was feeling an unmistakable sense of urgency, knowing what he did now about Isaturin's return. No mention of what happened to Fero Darz and no one left alive from the delegation to Arishaig but the Ard Rhys. Or not even the Ard Rhys, if their suspicions about Arcannen were correct. If Arcannen was inside Paranor's walls, he could do a great deal of damage. If he was inside the artifacts room, any theft could set the order back hundreds of years and allow him to pose an even greater threat to the Four Lands. If it was Arcannen for whom Keratrix was opening the vault, they had to reach him right away.

Paxon wondered suddenly what else might have happened in his absence. What of Chrysallin and Leofur? Oost had made no mention of them.

"Where is my sister?" he asked. "Where's Leofur? Are they safe?"

Oost looked back at him uncomfortably. "Long story. Neither of them is here, and they haven't been in days. Chrysallin disappeared the same day everything went wrong in Arishaig, and Leofur left the following morning to find her. We couldn't get word to you after you fled the Federation. This is the first anyone has even heard from you since that happened."

A part of Paxon whispered that this was more of Arcannen's doing and that he should get out there and find his sister and Leofur right away. A part of him screamed at him to do so. But he knew he couldn't. Not while there was a possibility that Arcannen was somewhere within the Keep. He would have to put aside his fears until any immediate danger to the Druid order was resolved. He was stricken with guilt, but he tamped it down. If he was to survive this day and the confrontation that likely awaited, he would need his wits about him. Arcannen had to come first.

At the bottom of the second set of stairs, they turned up the corridor that led to the vault. Paxon had been down here only a handful of times, and always in the company of Aphenglow Elessedil. Since her death, he hadn't had a reason to return. Not until now.

Oost continued to lead the way, a werelight at his fingertips as they passed into the maze of the underground cellars. When they arrived at the vault door, they found it ajar. Immediately Paxon knew they were too late.

They stepped inside, Oost lifting his light to spread a wider glow. When they saw Keratrix's body lying sprawled to one side, his neck twisted in an unnatural way, there was no longer room for doubt. There was also evidence that someone had been rummaging through alcoves and niches, leaving numerous discarded and empty containers strewn about. Arcannen had definitely been here. He had killed the young Druid, then taken a number of artifacts with him when he departed.

"We have to find him!" Miriya was looking around in dismay. "We can't let him get out of the Keep!"

Except he might already be gone, Paxon thought, but he kept it to himself. "Look, he doesn't have personal knowledge of Paranor and there are no drawings of the Keep's floor plans, so he might not know about the underground passageway. And he can't get through the gates with the Federation parked right outside. So how will he try to escape? What other choices does he have?"

"He might assume a new disguise," Miriya suggested.

Paxon shook his head. "Leofur says assuming disguises takes him a long time. He'd look for a quicker way."

"An airship!" Oost said at once. "One the Federation couldn't catch easily and might not bother with at all."

In the next instant an angry hiss rose through the stone floor, deep and insistent. Paxon had never heard it before, and he looked around in confusion.

"That's the Keep!" Oost exclaimed. "Someone other than a Druid has used magic!"

"Arcannen!" Miriya wheeled toward the door. "He's still here!"

In a rush they were out of the room and racing back the way they had come.

It was not often Arcannen Rai made a mistake, but he had made one this time. In his eagerness to get at the artifacts in the Druid vaults, he had let his desire to possess them overrule his usually clear thinking. Worried that Keratrix would escape him and sound the alarm, he had employed the quickest and easiest solution to the threat and had killed the young Druid. He should have thought it through a little better, because his precipitous act had now come back to bite him.

To begin with, he quickly discovered that the most vital and powerful artifacts were sealed away so thoroughly that it would take him hours to break down the magic keeping them safe. Clearly he did not have hours—he would be lucky if he had minutes—so he had to abandon any hope of adding them to his collection. He had to settle for taking lesser treasures, ones nowhere near as powerful. He left the Elfstones behind, and the Stiehl—Druid magic he had gone to great lengths to learn about over the years, and magic he greatly desired.

So he settled for what was easiest in order to assure himself of a swift and untroubled departure from Paranor. His plan was to return through the cellar passageways following the route they had taken coming in, which he had memorized, then locate the underground tunnel he had learned about that would lead him out of the Keep. It was useful having spies in his employ; not even the vaunted security of the Druids was enough to protect what he needed to know.

All well and good, except that once he began to make his way back through the tunnels, he discovered that his memory wasn't quite what he thought it was—or perhaps this was yet another Druid magic at work, obscuring the way out. But the result was the same. He quickly became lost, wandering down various corridors, unable to find his way clear. Again, if he had thought ahead, he would have kept Keratrix alive at least long enough to provide him with a map.

But he hadn't done any of that, and as a result precious time was being wasted as he stumbled blindly through the passageways, growing ever more confused. After a while, he began to mark his way so that he could tell if he was going in circles, but even that didn't seem to help because he never saw any of the marks again. Either there were hundreds of passageways down in these black depths, or else magic was erasing his efforts the moment he left them behind.

He also realized he probably wouldn't be able to find the underground passage out of Paranor in time to make use of it. His entire plan was going up in smoke.

Eventually, he gave in to his frustration and used magic to escape. He realized this might very well alert someone; the Druids would certainly have wards in place to let them know when an intruder was using a foreign magic. But he had no choice. He had no use of Druid magic. He might take Isaturin's form, but he could not assume his powers.

Sure enough, the moment he used his magic, a deep hissing sounded all through the passageways about him. The Druids had been warned. They would begin searching immediately. He would have to hurry now if he was to have any chance of getting clear.

From somewhere in the darkness behind him, he heard voices, quick and insistent. A pursuit had been mounted already. Frustration bloomed within him, driving him ahead more swiftly.

Don't panic. Just keep moving away from them, whoever they are.

The problem with staying calm, however, was that he thought he recognized the voice of Paxon Leah. How that could be, he didn't know. And he didn't want to find out. He just wanted to put as much distance between them as possible. If Paxon was still alive, there was every reason to think he knew about his sister. If so, he would come after Arcannen—and not stop coming after him until he was dead. The sorcerer did not much care for that idea. He would prefer to save the confrontation for another day, in a place and time of his own choosing. The Highlander had already proved himself entirely too dangerous to be taken for granted.

So he moved quickly along the escape route his magic had mapped out for him, not hearing the voices anymore, leaving whatever was back there safely behind. He found the stairs and went up them swiftly and silently, then reached the door leading back into the Keep and went through. The hallway beyond was deserted, but as he made his way along its length, Troll guards began to appear, inquiring in their deep, scratchy voices if he had seen or heard anything odd. Smart enough to recognize that a denial would look suspicious, he directed them toward the cellars and passed on.

Everything was happening too quickly. All his plans were falling apart. Yes, he had possession of stolen magic, but he didn't know what use it would be, if any—and the really important magic had eluded him. Plus, he was about to be discovered if he lingered even a moment too long. The Federation was camped outside Paranor's walls, waiting for him to emerge as Isaturin and confess his complicity in the assassination of the members of the Coalition Council.

It was time to find an airship and get out of there.

He had settled on this mode of escape while fleeing up the stairs. It was the best choice left. The likelihood of the Federation taking the time and trouble to come after a lone vessel was small. They might send a flit or two to intercept him, but if he could commandeer a Sprint he would be able to outdistance a flit easily. He would be gone before they even knew who he was. He could fly to the Murk Sink, take Chrysallin off the witch's hands in payment for the magic he had promised her, and go back into hiding. Then he could bargain with the Druids to return Paxon's sister in exchange for a more important and useful magic. He had long since tired of trying to figure out how to make use of the wishsong, anyway. Better to just give it and her up. Commanding any assistance from that wretchedly difficult young woman was futile.

He maneuvered his way through the halls and stairs, climbing several levels of the Keep to reach the doors leading out onto the airship-landing platform. Troll guards were everywhere, but he simply summoned the closest one and ordered a Sprint brought out. Then he stood with his back to the airfield and his eyes on the doors through which he had come and waited.

No one appeared.

When the Troll guard returned, informing him that his airship was ready, he breathed a sigh of relief.

"Have you filed a flight plan, High Lord?" the Troll asked.

Arcannen almost laughed. "Young Keratrix has it tucked safely away in his head."

He hurried over to his craft and tossed his bag of stolen artifacts into the back. He was about to climb into the pilot box when the door from the Keep burst open behind him.

"Arcannen!" he heard Paxon Leah shout.

Without hesitating, the sorcerer wheeled back, summoning magic as quick as thought and sending a blinding sheet of fire toward the sound of the voice. The Troll guards closest to him were incinerated on the spot. Several aircraft went up in flames or simply burst apart. The Highlander would have gone up with them, but he had that infernal sword out, and the blade deflected the sorcerer's attack. Protected as well were the female and Dwarf Druids in his company, who dropped to their knees to shield their eyes, both instantly summoning magic of their own.

Sword raised, Paxon raced toward him.

Arcannen struck out a second time, this effort more successful than the last. He put down the Dwarf with a blow that took the other's legs out from under him and threw him back against the wall. At the same time, he flung up a wall of dense smoke and crackling fire between himself and his assailants.

It gave him the few precious moments he needed. He leapt into the Sprint and powered up the diapson crystals, parse tubes wide open and thrusters jammed all the way forward. He caught a glimpse of Paxon Leah rushing toward him. The Sprint shuddered and lurched as something struck it a shocking blow and then it shot away so quickly the fiery after-strikes launched by the female Druid missed him entirely.

Airborne and free, Arcannen flew west into the midday haze, the Druid's Keep and its dangers safely behind him.

Paxon had tried to use his sword to disable the Sprint so that it could not fly, but he was too far away. He broke through the wall of fire and got close enough as it started to rise to deliver a single blow from his blade, which exploded through the hull in a ragged tear that might have damaged the stabilizers but failed to prevent the craft from lifting off and racing into the distance. He wheeled back immediately to the Druid Guard.

"Do we have something that can catch her?"

The bluff, impassive faces remained expressionless as the Trolls considered. Then one said, "A Ghost Flare might get you close enough to use your weapons. We have one."

"Bring it up, then. Right now. We have to catch him!"

He rushed back over to where Miriya was kneeling by Oost. "Broken leg," she said, glancing at Paxon. "Did you damage his ship?"

"I think so. I'm going after him."

"Not without me." She was on her feet. "He's not getting away this time. Oost, you have to tell the others what's happened. If we don't make it back, they'll need to know."

Then she and Paxon were racing across the landing platform to board the Ghost Flare, its mooring lines already in the process of being thrown off.

30

LEOFUR AND CHRYSALLIN WALKED INTO THE MURK
Sink with the taste of smoke and ashes in their mouths and
the reek of death in their nostrils, free of the witch's grasp if
not her memory. The night was shrouded in deep mist but illuminated
by a strange glow that emanated from some hidden source within the
waters of the swamp. The gloom was alive with sounds. Everything had
gone still in response to the ferocious din of the battle, but returned in
its aftermath—as if the death of the witch had put an end to any need
for further silence. The calls of night birds, the splashes of the giant
swamp dwellers, and the cries of animals large and small flooded back
in a wave of sound that rose and fell like an incoming tide.

Before setting out, Leofur had taken time to retrieve Imric Cort's
discarded clothes and stuff them into her backpack. It wasn't that she
expected she would ever see him again to return them. It was just her
need to preserve something of him—something tangible to remember him by. Or maybe just a way to compensate for the shock of losing him so abruptly. They had come so far and suffered so much
together, and now that he was gone his absence was a black emptiness
in her heart.

She would keep his clothes not because they signified anything
special, but because they were all that remained of him.

Tears streamed down her face, and she did not bother to wipe them away. *Gone! He's really gone!*

The young women walked along the shores of the lake, navigating an uncertain course through mist that swirled and limbs that drooped within acres of sprawling dark cypress and willow. Leofur led the way, keeping them on a path she mostly, if not entirely, remembered, guiding them back to the lives they had left behind. It was not safe for them to be traveling in the Murk Sink at night, when they could see so little and predators were so plentiful. But the prospect of staying in the cottage until morning was unthinkable, and both felt that risking the dangers of the swamp was the better choice.

"What a miserable place," Chrysallin murmured after a long silence, her boots scuffing the soggy earth disdainfully.

Leofur looked over. "Are you all right?"

Chrysallin shrugged. "Are you?"

"No."

"Me, either."

"But we will be. As soon as we get out of here."

"Maybe. Maybe not."

"I'm sorry you had to go through this, Chrys. I should have done a better job looking out for you."

Chrysallin made a dismissive gesture. "You couldn't have prevented what happened. It was enough that you came to find me. That's all that really counts."

"It was my father's doing, wasn't it?"

"So the witch claimed. Something about getting back at Paxon. It seems to be an obsession with him."

Leofur looked out over the lake. "My father," she repeated softly. "When has he ever been that?"

All those years he had left her to her own devices, without a mother, without any sort of real family. All those years he had treated her the same way he treated everyone—with disdain, with barely disguised tolerance, with the intent to make her submissive to his whims, with complete disregard for their relationship. It all came flooding back in memories she had thought buried so deep they would never resurface. But clearly they were not buried deeply enough. She felt more tears come, and this time brushed them away hurriedly.

"I'm sorry about your friend," Chrysallin said suddenly. "He was very brave. He fought hard for me."

Leofur nodded. "He fought hard for everyone when it mattered. But he was so unhappy. He was conflicted and driven by what he was. He was the most tragic person I have ever known."

Then slowly, cautiously, she began to tell Chrys about Imric. She related the details of his birth, his parents, his upbringing, and the terrible set of events that brought about his flight into the larger world and the years of pain and sorrow that had followed. Much of it she still didn't fully understand and now never would. But she knew enough from what he had revealed to be able to imagine it, and that was more than enough.

She finished by recounting the particulars of what had brought her into the Murk Sink to find Chrys, but she kept to herself Imric's feelings for her, what he had told her that morning, and any part of how their relationship had begun as one thing and somehow evolved into another. She kept to herself, as well, her unresolved feelings for him. All this was her secret and hers alone, and she did not think she would ever tell anyone.

"I will never forget what he did for me," Chrysallin said when Leofur had finished. "I wish he were here so I could tell him that."

I wish so, too, Leofur thought. But she tamped her regret down quickly, unable to examine it too closely.

She shifted the big flash rip in her arms, keeping a watchful eye on the landscape ahead. Too many big predators lurked in the Murk Sink for her to let her guard down, even for a moment. Chrys was right; this was a miserable place. If she ever got out, she was never coming back. Where she ended up didn't matter as long as it wasn't here.

She glanced back at her friend, following close behind. What sort of life would Chrys have now? Would she continue working with the wishsong, her newly rediscovered magic? Would she remain with the Druids and perhaps become one of them? It was an option that was not available to Leofur, who possessed no magic and had nothing to offer the Druid order. Going back to Paranor no longer felt right. Her time with Imric had changed that. It had caused her, even without fully understanding why, to rethink the course of her life. All she could be at Paranor was Paxon's life partner, and she knew now this wasn't enough.

She realized suddenly she had not yet told Chrys what had happened in Arishaig. She had not spoken of the assassination of the Federation delegation. She had not spoken of Paxon's flight with the Druids. Chrys knew nothing of any of this.

She wondered if she should tell her friend now.

She decided against it. Chrysallin had endured enough. The news about Paxon could wait until they were safely out of the Murk Sink. It could wait until all this was behind them.

Silence descended, deep and prevailing, the noise of the swamp drifting away. She listened to Chrysallin moving behind her. She listened to her own breathing as it punctuated the steady cadence of her steps.

Leofur.

She stopped short, her head snapping about in shock. Her breath caught in her throat.

Imric!

Can you . . . come for me?

Where are you?

The bower.

She tried to think what he was talking about, then she remembered. The framework construction they had passed on their way in, a sort of decorative collection of beams and cross-bracings draped with gossamer curtains.

"Leofur! What's wrong?" Chrysallin was at her elbow, shaking her. "What is it?"

"It's Imric, Chrys! He's alive!"

Leofur.

I'm here.

You did the right thing . . . letting me go. I was able to gain con-

*trol . . . without dragging you in. I've stopped changing . . . but I don't
know for how long. I am fighting hard not to give in . . . to the urges . . .
but the witch . . . turned me inside out. I can barely hold on. It was all
I could do . . . to link to you. Stay with me. Come find me!*

I'll find you. No matter what!

Don't let me . . . go!

He was weak and having trouble breathing. It was reflected in his
thoughts as he reached out to her. Fear bloomed within her like a
poisonous flower.

"Chrys," she said to her friend, "I have to go to him. I have to try
to save him. He's hurt. He's still in danger of changing and not being
able to stop. Will you come with me?"

Chrysallin gave her a withering look. "Don't be stupid. Of course
I'll come."

They picked up the pace, practically running along the lakeshore.
But the going was hard. They tired quickly and were forced to slow
down again, their strength depleted from their earlier struggles. Even
so, Leofur kept moving ahead steadily, refusing to give in. She understood what was at stake. Once Imric started changing again, he might
not be able to stop. He might continue changing until he destroyed
himself. If she lost him now, knowing he was still alive, she didn't
know what it would do to her. She had to make things come out right,
to find him and save him.

Leofur?

I'm still here.

Talk to me. It helps me . . . steady myself.

*We fought the witch, Chrys and I, and she's dead. We're safe, both
of us.*

That's good. You . . . weren't hurt?

*No. Banged up a bit, but not really hurt. And you? How bad is it?
What happened?*

*The changing. It just kept . . . I couldn't stop it. I couldn't even slow
it. One form after . . . another.*

He coughed—a kind of gasp. *I couldn't . . . do anything to control
it. I was flying into things . . . slamming into them . . . trying to stop . . .*

but nothing helped. I shape-shifted over and over . . . a thousand times. I was fighting just to . . . to keep from drowning in the lake . . . or being eaten by . . .

More coughing. *I think I have bones . . . broken. I'm hurting so bad . . .*

There was a pause, then: *I feel like it . . . might happen . . . again soon. The changing. Don't know . . . how to stop it. Leofur, I'm afraid.*

Don't be. I'm here. We're coming for you.

It's so . . . awful. I'm trapped in . . . my own body. I'm helpless.

Listen to me. You've stopped the changing. You're tethered to me now. Just stay calm and listen to my voice. Just . . . She hesitated. *Just think about us.*

Chrys was looking at her strangely, brow furled. As if she had heard Leofur's unspoken communication. Leofur made a dismissive gesture and turned away.

Are you there?

Did you . . . just say . . . ?

Never mind what I said. You don't need to repeat it. Just know I meant it. Keep talking. Stay calm. Wait for me. Talk to me. Tell me about yourself. Tell me everything.

He began doing so, revealing things he had kept hidden until now. He talked about his childhood and then the years after the deaths of his parents when he was forced to go out into the world and make his way while hiding his secret life. He held nothing back, confessing everything. He opened up to her about all that had happened, all that he had endured before he became afraid for himself and his use of shape-shifting and sought help from the Druids.

His voice was growing weaker, a coarseness settling into it that was troubling. All the while he had been talking to her, she had pushed ahead, Chrysallin at her heels, trying to reach the bower. They had passed all the most familiar landmarks, including the place on the lakeshore when she had hidden and listened to the boy Olin die at the hands of Melis. Now she was frightened she was bearing witness to another death. It made her more determined, more insistent on pushing back against her weariness.

Imric, we are getting closer.

Perhaps it was the truth, perhaps not. How could she be sure? But he needed to feel she was near, that help was at hand. What sort of help she could provide once she reached him, she wasn't sure. What difference would it make to his debilitated condition if she was there in person as opposed to being there by virtue of the tether? This race against time could easily be for nothing.

His voice broke into her thoughts, ragged and sad. *I feel the change . . . coming on. The witch. Her magic. So strong. Overwhelming. I don't know . . . what else to do . . . to stop it.*

Push back against it! I just need a little more time, Imric! Just a little!

Don't think . . . I can give it. Don't think . . . I can . . .

Silence. *Imric! Answer me!*

Good-bye, Leofur. I . . . love . . .

No! You can't do this! Imric!

The silence lengthened. Leofur screamed into the dark emptiness of the swamp.

They found him less than an hour later, sprawled within the bower, masked by the curtains and the darkness. Leofur slowed as she neared, afraid she would find what she already suspected to be true. She pushed aside the curtains and her heart stopped. He was still in his human form, still recognizable as himself, but he was not breathing. She knew at once he was dead.

She knelt beside him, leaning close. "Imric," she whispered, reaching out to touch his face.

His skin was cold, his body lifeless. She reached down and took him in her arms, pulling him against her. "It isn't fair! I came for you!"

She felt him stir, and it nearly undid her. "Imric?"

"Still . . . here."

"I thought . . ."

"Almost . . . but your . . ."

"Don't talk. Chrys! Can you find something to wrap him in? He's freezing!"

". . . your voice . . . kept me . . . from giving in . . ."

She held him tighter, crying hard now. "Shhhh. Shhhh."

Behind her, she heard Chrysallin ripping down one of the curtains, tearing it loose from its fastenings. Working together, the women wound the fabric about his body. Then, while Leofur continued to hold him, cradling him against her, Chrys set about rubbing his hands and feet in an effort to bring life back into his chilled body.

"Better," he murmured to Leofur, nuzzling into her. "Always was . . . with you."

"I thought you were gone. I was so sure I couldn't reach you in time."

". . . waited for . . . you. Hung on . . . until . . ." He coughed roughly. ". . . knew you would . . . reach me . . ."

She kissed him impulsively. Full on the lips, passionate, needful. She had crossed another bridge, and she wasn't coming back. "You had more faith than I did."

"I . . . don't . . ." Another cough. "No one has . . . more faith . . . in me . . . than you."

"Don't die, Imric. Please, don't."

"Won't . . . now."

"Promise?"

"I . . . promise."

She held him for the remainder of the night, refusing to let him go, unwilling to take the chance that by doing so she would release him from this life into the next. Chrysallin sat with her for a long time before eventually falling asleep. The hours slipped by as Leofur held Imric and listened to his breathing, assessing his condition from his movements and sounds, on guard against anything that suggested he was getting worse. She kept telling herself he was returning to her, that he wasn't letting go, that death would be pushed back by life. Her thoughts drifted in the long, slow hours of predawn, replaying in hazy snippets the times they had shared, the hardships and struggles they had met and overcome. She thought about how willingly he had given her what she needed, even at repeated risk to his life. She was stunned by the enormity of what he had sacrificed for her, and she knew she would never be able to repay that.

And then, in an unexpected flash of understanding, she knew she was looking at it in the wrong way. This wasn't about repayment. It was about his feelings for her and hers for him. What would she do, now that she had him back safely? The answer had been there all along, yet she had not recognized it or perhaps simply had not been ready to embrace it. But the tether had revealed it clearly, its truth born out of the closeness that link had entailed. She understood for the first time the consequences of the one risk she had dismissed in agreeing to his help, the same risk that Sarnya had ignored in her own tethering. Without trying and even without knowing what she was seeking, she had found with Imric Cort what she had been searching for all along, from the time she was a little girl until this very moment.

She had found where she belonged.

When he woke, it was nearly dawn. He opened his eyes to find her still cradling him, blinked away the last of his sleep, and gave her a wan smile. He glanced over at Chrysallin, sleeping nearby, her breathing deep and even, and then back to Leofur.

"I knew . . . you wouldn't . . . leave me," he whispered, soft enough so that only she could hear.

She felt herself smile in response. She bent down and kissed him gently—on his forehead, his cheeks, his lips, everywhere. "No," she said, as she continued kissing him. "I won't ever leave you."

31

THE DAY WAS ALREADY WELL ADVANCED WHEN
Paxon and Miriya set out in pursuit of Arcannen Rai,
tracking him south toward the Kennon Pass and then
west along the Mermidon River and out into the grasslands of the
Streleheim. Miriya used her magic to search the air currents for traces
of thruster exhaust from recent vessels on the air currents, thereby
determining the direction of any airship passing down the corridors
they were following. It was simple enough to find Arcannen's craft
within Paranor's boundaries because, once past the Keep, it was the
only vessel that had departed the area recently. Even down through
the Kennon Pass to where it veered west, the airship was easily traced.

Only after it moved out into the open spaces of the Southland
below the Dragon's Teeth and then west did the trail begin to fade
more quickly. The vessel's heat and particle displacement grew less
stable the more exposed it became to wind and weather, so there was
some danger they could lose the trail entirely. But the cruiser they
were using was much swifter than the one Arcannen had taken, and
they were able to make up ground so quickly they soon had him in
sight.

"Look at his ship," Miriya said. "Look at how it's flying. You must
have done some damage to it after all."

"Another hour, maybe less, and we'll be on top of him," Paxon muttered.

The vessel's thrusters were seated all the way forward, and the parse tubes were wide open. Their efforts at gaining on the sorcerer were measurable by eyesight alone, so estimation by other means was not required. All they needed to do was keep flying at the same speed and without interference from another aircraft and they would catch him.

"What do we do when that happens?" Miriya asked, leaning in to be heard above the rush of the wind.

Paxon looked at her. "I know what you're thinking. But we need him alive to prove to the Federation that he was responsible for what happened to their ministers, so we try to keep him that way."

"Just so you know, I don't intend to let him get away again. No matter what. This stops here, whether he lives or dies."

Paxon nodded. "Don't worry. He won't get away."

The sky ahead was clear, empty of clouds, a bright backdrop against which Arcannen's airship was clearly outlined. Behind them, the horizon was turning dark as night began to creep out of the east, swallowing what remained of the daylight. Paxon judged they had another hour before darkness began to set in, but even in deep twilight they would be able to find Arcannen easily enough.

He thought about what it would take to bring the sorcerer to bay—a daunting prospect. He had faced him before, once by himself and a second time with Avelene. Both times, Arcannen Rai had gotten the best of him. And both times, friends had died. He knew better than to take anything for granted on this third attempt, even with the vastly more experienced and skillful Miriya to back him up. Arcannen would fight back using every weapon he could call upon and every trick he could conjure. He would try to kill them; he would not hold back. He had no reason to keep them alive, as they did him. He would try to find a weakness and exploit it. But Paxon was not the youth he had been before. He was mature and experienced and had far better command of his magic. No matter what Arcannen tried, he would find the Highlander ready.

"What's he doing?" Miriya asked suddenly.

Paxon shifted his gaze to a direct focus on the airship they were pursuing. At first, he couldn't be sure what she was talking about. But then he realized the airship was fading away. It was growing steadily less distinct against the sky, losing shape and color. It had begun a slow sweep north, dropping earthward in a way that suggested something was wrong.

"Is he out of power?" Miriya snapped. "But then, why is he disappearing? What's happening to him?"

Paxon didn't know, but it was apparent they were going to lose sight of Arcannen in the next few seconds. "Start tracking his exhaust again," he told her. "Find him the way you did before."

He tried to draw further power from the diapson crystals, but they were already giving everything they had. No matter what he did, they were still too far away to close on the sorcerer before he disappeared entirely.

Seconds later, he was gone. The sky ahead was empty, the airship vanished.

"Shades, his magic is dark, indeed!" Miriya hissed. "But an airship leaves a displacement residue, dark magic or no, and I can track it!"

Brave words, Paxon thought, not at all certain she could.

They continued their search for what was now an invisible presence, Miriya giving directions as she read the air currents and measured heat and particle disruption with a sure and steady application of her magic. Paxon worried aloud that, now that he was invisible, the sorcerer might swing back around, turn his airship's weapons on them, and knock them out of the sky. But Miriya assured him Arcannen couldn't manage such a trick; keeping the airship invisible would require all of his power and concentration. It was possible he might use his invisibility to try to get behind them, but since she was aware of this chance she would be watching for it. He would not catch them unprepared.

Again, Paxon wondered.

Below, the land turned rugged and barren, a mix of broken earth and shattered rocks dotted with isolated patches of scrub and small stands of trees. To the east, the Mermidon rolled through the countryside, broad and swift.

Ahead, a large island came into view, the river flowing past it on both sides, leaving it marooned midstream.

"Slower," Miriya said suddenly.

Paxon pulled back on the thrusters, eyes searching the sky's dark blue sweep, finding it empty even of clouds. There was nothing to see. He glanced over at his companion but she was engaged in a series of intricate hand movements. Her eyes were closed. It gave him pause.

"Can you actually tell anything that way?"

"More than you can with your eyes open. Now stop talking."

He held the airship steady, leaving her to it but scanning the sky on his own nevertheless. Night was creeping closer. East, it had swallowed the Dragon's Teeth and was advancing at a steady pace.

"He's gone all the way down," she said quietly. "He's landed."

"Where?"

"I can't be sure."

"What do you want to do?"

She shook her head in frustration, her eyes opening. "Find him, of course. He's down there somewhere."

Paxon searched the landscape, his gaze settling on the island. "I know this place. That's where the city of Kern stood hundreds of years ago, before the Warlock Lord destroyed it. All that's left are ruins." He looked over at her. "That's where he is. In the ruins."

He couldn't explain why, but he sensed that Arcannen, who had lived so long in the ruins of Arbrox, would find a certain comfort in seeking protection from the ruins of Kern. It was the sort of refuge where he could make a stand and feel he had an advantage.

He swung the airship toward the island, drawing the thrusters back even farther to slow their approach. "He'll be waiting for us."

She laughed. "Do you think so?"

"He'll watch us land and know where we are. He'll be able to come at us from any direction he chooses."

"You aren't afraid, are you, Paxon?"

"I'm wary. I've fought him twice. I don't relish doing it a third time. But that doesn't change what's going to happen."

"You can be certain of that. Just remember what I said about him. He doesn't get away, no matter what."

The way she said it left no doubt about what she intended. She wanted Arcannen dead, and Paxon wasn't sure he could prevent it from happening, her promise notwithstanding. Her rage over Karlin Ryl's fate was too intense to be contained, her need to sate it too strong. She would spin out of control at some point, and if it happened at the wrong time it would doom them both.

But he let his opportunity to caution her pass. It was too late now to say anything further and expect that it would make a difference. He had already warned her what was at stake. Either she would do what was needed or she wouldn't. Miriya could be volatile, and she had no particular reason to pay attention to him. Certainly not here, where her anger burned white-hot.

They rode the air currents down, and just as they reached a point where they could make out the tumbled walls and collapsed towers of Kern through the encroaching darkness, they spied Arcannen's craft. It was settled in the center of the ancient city, in an open space between a pair of shattered buildings. They set down next to it, looking everywhere as they did so, waiting for the expected attack.

But it did not come. Arcannen was nowhere to be found, and the city felt empty and abandoned. Everything was silent in the hush of twilight. Once on the ground, Paxon locked down the controls to prevent tampering, and they climbed out of the pilot box and stood amid Kern's remains.

"How do you want to go from here?" Miriya asked him quietly, deferring to his experience.

He paused, considering. "Can your magic help us?"

"I don't think so, not with finding him. He will have countered already any attempt I might make." She hesitated, glanced over. "But maybe he will have failed to erase all physical signs of his passing."

"Maybe." It was possible the sorcerer might not have thought to disguise those since it was almost dark and he was more worried about Miriya's magic than leaving tracks. "It's worth a look."

He walked over to the sorcerer's airship and circled it slowly, searching for prints. He found them almost immediately, heading off into the ruins at what appeared from the length of the stride to be a swift pace.

He beckoned her over and pointed. "Ready?"

"Just worry about yourself."

He took the lead, following the small signs of Arcannen's passage into the rubble, searching the dark corners and layered shadows, worried that darkness was coming on too fast and would soon leave them blind. But there was no help for it. They had to be cautious in their efforts, aware of the peril if they acted in haste. Arcannen was too dangerous.

They wound through the crumbling walls of the dead city. Paxon kept one eye out for signs of the sorcerer's passage and one eye on the ruins surrounding them. Miriya was doing something new with her magic, using hands and words to summon it. The Highlander guessed she was setting up a shield to try to protect them against a surprise attack—her way of giving them a chance to respond.

Then even the smallest traces of Arcannen abruptly ended, and his trail vanished.

Paxon slowed, hesitated, then quickly took them off the trail they had been following and into the shelter of a half-formed wall.

"He's deliberately hiding his trail now," he whispered. "Likely because he's decided to make a stand."

She looked around. "Why here?"

As if in answer, the ground where they had just been standing erupted in a forest of long, thin spikes, which then dropped away into a black hole. Had they still been there, they would have been skewered.

Paxon was already moving. He threw himself on top of Miriya, bearing her to the ground. An instant later a bolt of fire slammed into the wall next to them. The Highlander rolled one way and Miriya the other as they tried to find shelter from the attack. Earth and stone exploded all around them as Arcannen lashed out from his concealment. Paxon brought up his blade to deflect the sorcerer's fire, and Miriya wrapped herself in her shielding magic.

In seconds both were pressed up against the remains of walls that offered some small protection from their adversary.

They couldn't determine where he was. There was nothing to indicate where the attacks had originated. Paxon scanned the ruins unsuccessfully. He brushed dirt and grit from his head and shoulders and looked over to where Miriya was crouched. He gave her a searching look and she shrugged. She couldn't find the sorcerer, either.

After a few moments, they rose cautiously. When nothing happened, Miriya moved over to study the blackened marks the fire had left and then backtracked their trajectories. There were no footprints to be found, but a series of small scrapes and crushed weeds marked their assailant's escape route.

"We'll never catch him at this rate," Miriya hissed angrily. "He will hold us back long enough to find a way clear if we don't force him to turn and fight."

Paxon nodded. "I'm open to suggestions."

Her eyes narrowed. "I was hoping you might have one."

"One of us goes ahead. The other hangs back. When he attacks again, the one trailing slips around behind him before he can run off."

She made a rude noise. "Not very imaginative. Why don't we separate and come at him from two sides? Then we'd have twice the chance of catching him off guard."

"And twice the chance for him to catch us off guard, too. Besides, if we separate, we might not be able to find each other again."

"All right. Your way, then." She looked disgusted. "Just remember to keep your guard up."

She left him to go on alone, and soon she was out of sight. He followed at a steady pace, searching for sign, spying out enough small details to suggest Arcannen was somewhere ahead.

His suspicions were confirmed when he heard a series of explosions. He rushed ahead, managed several dozen yards, and then abruptly encountered a massive wall where the way had been clear only minutes earlier.

He used his sword on it, thinking it a mirage, but the wall deflected his blade easily. Beyond its twelve-foot height, he could hear further explosions erupting. Miriya was under attack, and she was alone. His temper and frustration boiled up. He had to get through. He peered down the wall's length in both directions. It seemed to go on forever. But that wasn't possible, even for Arcannen. There was more than one sort of magic at work here—a merging of reality and appearance. He reached out to feel his way along its rough surface, hoping to find a weakness, but his hand passed right through the wall. He stood staring in surprise, then shoved his whole arm through and walked all the way through himself. The wall repelled magic, but not flesh and blood. A trick to slow him, and it had succeeded.

He rushed toward the sound of the explosions, which had ceased by now, but when he came upon piles of newly created rubble and blackened stone he found no sign of the sorcerer or Miriya.

Just a single scorched Druid's boot.

Arcannen moved silently through the ruins, Miriya's body slung over one shoulder. He could have left her for Paxon Leah to find, but the troublesome Highlander would be more unsettled if he couldn't find her at all. Let him retain hope that she lived. Let him think she was a prisoner. It would make him more likely to be careless and thereby more easily dispatched. The Druid had been the more dangerous of the two. Now Paxon was alone, the only obstacle left in Arcannen's path, the only one that could prevent his escape. Paxon would see it as his duty to stop Arcannen, but he would fail this time just as he had failed every other time.

The sorcerer reached a collapsed building where the cellar level lay open to the sky and threw the Druid down into it. She had been strong, that one, her strength fueled by rage over what had happened to her partner. But she had not been strong enough to defeat him. No one man or woman was that strong.

He studied her remains for a moment, thinking suddenly of Leofur, lost to him forever. While at Paranor, he had learned of her foolish decision to go searching for Chrysallin Leah. She would already have fallen into the hands of the Murk Witch if she wasn't already dead, and Melis would not treat her kindly. Leofur had always been an impulsive child, never obedient, never rational. She had doomed herself years ago when she had decided to forsake him and abandon his protection.

He moved away, already thinking of how he would go about ridding himself of Paxon Leah. He had stashed his treasures in the hold of the airship, certain his pursuers would not pause to look for them, too intent on finding him to bother. Once the Highlander was eliminated, he could return to his vessel and set out for home with his treasures intact. He had already decided not to bother with either Chrysallin Leah or his daughter, both of whom were more trouble than they were worth. He would leave them for the witch to dispose of. She would be more than happy to do so once she tired of the little games she was obsessed with playing.

What he would do instead was spend uninterrupted time studying the artifacts he had stolen from the Druid vault, determining what each one did and how best he might make use of it. His time for hiding within the Druid order and sowing dissension while disguised as Isaturin had been cut short by the arrival of the Federation, but it was more important that they be at each other's throats. If he could keep them warring with each other for long enough, he would eventually find fresh opportunities to bring them both down.

Ahead, he sensed movement. He slowed his approach and listened. Footfalls, slow and cautious. It was the Highlander, come looking for him.

He smiled.

Time to let his adversary find him.

Paxon had only just stepped out from between the walls of the two collapsed buildings when the familiar green fire lanced out at him from above. His blade was ready, and he deflected the attack easily, finding the window of the tower in which the Druid was hiding. He rushed toward it instantly, attacking rather than waiting, his patience exhausted. There was no sign of Miriya, so he had no choice but to go after Arcannen Rai on his own.

No choice but to corner and put an end to him.

Because he was no longer thinking about taking him alive. He knew now that this would be impossible. Better to forget such a lofty ambition and just make sure the sorcerer could never trouble anyone again. Better to rid the world of him once and for all.

He reached the door and charged inside, blade at the ready, green fire racing up and down its length, the snakes of magic that inhabited it alive with anticipation. Dodging left and right as the sorcerer's magic struck out, he gained the stairs and charged for the second floor.

But Arcannen Rai was no fool, and if Paxon had stopped to consider, even for a few seconds, he might have wondered why his enemy had allowed himself to become trapped in a building when there were so many more sensible choices. But he was eager to reach the sorcerer, so he was reckless and unprepared when a section of the stairway beneath him gave way and sent him crashing twenty feet to the rubble below.

He lay stunned, the wind knocked out of him. He had managed to hang on to his sword, but the magic had gone dark during his fall. Before he could recover, the sorcerer's magic found him—and this time without his defenses in place. It slammed into him as he tried to roll away, and pain ratcheted through his body. Ignoring all thoughts of the damage he might have suffered, he brought up his blade. The Sword of Leah flared awake, blocking Arcannen's next attack and providing a momentary respite.

The sorcerer came down the stairs, stepping carefully past the section he had weakened, the green fire burning at his fingertips. By the time he reached the bottom of the stairs, Paxon was on his knees, trying to rise.

"Let's finish this, boy," Arcannen said quietly.

He expelled a fresh surge of magic from his fingers and knocked the Highlander backward once more, pinning him up against the wall. Then he advanced slowly, clearly watching for a response. Paxon was disgusted with his inability to act more quickly, angry that he had failed to recognize a trap that should have been obvious, thinking that maybe this time he wouldn't be lucky enough to escape the sorcerer, let alone subdue him. In those few seconds he found himself remembering the many tells he should have recognized when he was traveling with the man he had assumed to be Isaturin.

How Arcannen, masquerading as Isaturin, had instantly known the name of the Sleath—the demon he himself had conjured.

How the demon had come out of Karlin Ryl to save them from the plant creatures when there was no clear reason for it to do so—unless at someone's command.

How the man he believed to be the Ard Rhys had been acting so strangely, never acknowledging Karlin's death or attempting to take command.

These memories and others flashed in rapid succession and were gone—a brief kaleidoscope of images. His vision steadied. Arcannen had stopped approaching and was looking down at him. His enemy, waiting to strike the killing blow, and he did not think he could stop it from happening. He did not believe he had the strength.

He readied himself in anticipation. His sword came up, the fire dim but still potent enough to respond.

Then he threw himself at Arcannen. It was a final desperate effort, and it failed miserably. The sorcerer deflected his attack, throwing him aside. Paxon stumbled and fell against the stairwell wall, gasping for breath, beaten.

But in that instant of angry despair and lost hope, a shadow appeared in the doorway behind Arcannen Rai, a ghost backlit by the light of moon and stars, a wraith emerged from the afterlife. It was a terrible apparition, blackened and bloodied—a mauled and ragged thing, its clothes in tatters and its skin streaked with dirt and ash. How it managed to walk even the few steps it took to reach the sorcerer was impossible to imagine. Sheer will, Paxon would tell himself later. Enormous determination.

Incandescent rage.

Miriya, upright and alive, moving with stiff, awkward steps, came up behind Arcannen Rai, lifted the jagged steel rod she was carrying, and drove it through his back with such force that the tip emerged from his chest, covered in his blood. The spray showered Paxon as he bore witness at last to the death he had envisioned for so long, finding it in the sorcerer's shocked, furious expression.

In response, he dragged himself to his feet, swung the Sword of

Leah with strength dredged up from a place he didn't know he had, and cut off his enemy's head in a single sweeping blow.

In the silence that followed, Druid and Highlander staggered toward each other and fell together like rag dolls before sinking then to the floor in exhaustion. Neither spoke. There were no words for what they were feeling; what they shared in those moments went beyond words. They held on to each other, heads bowed, lost in a mix of relief and weariness and something that approximated joy but also felt like sadness.

Long minutes passed, and then the good feelings dulled and were eclipsed by pain and an urgent need to find a way out of the moment. Miriya said quietly, "When you try to kill someone, it's a good idea to make sure you finish the job. You shouldn't take it for granted."

They trudged back through the ruins to their airship and collapsed in the pilot box, treating each other's injuries as best they could, putting healing creams on burns, splinting broken bones, and sewing closed deep gashes. Then, exhausted, they slept until morning, their bed open to the sky with its canopy of bright stars and moon, their sleep uninterrupted.

And in the morning, they talked in low, reassuring voices about what they had experienced and how it had left them. Most of what they said Paxon would forget over time, but not all. He would always remember Miriya's fiery determination not to give in, even after being tossed in the pit and left for dead. He would always remember how she cried again for Karlin Ryl. He would always remember her praise for him as she insisted no one else could have done what he did to hold the sorcerer at bay until she could reach him.

He wasn't sure it was true, but her words stayed with him.

They retrieved the stolen artifacts from Arcannen's Sprint and flew back to Paranor on a day as clear and blue as Paxon could possibly imagine a day being. Only once did he think of the Federation army that waited and the threat it presented to the Druids. Only that once did he glance back to where the head of Arcannen Rai rested on the pilot box floor, tucked inside a canvas sack.

P AXON WAS BACK HOME WHERE HE BELONGED, AND his life was slowly returning to normal. Arcannen Rai was dead, and the Federation was appeased, if not fully convinced that he had acted alone. It had taken a delegation of Druids meeting with the commanders of the Federation airships besieging the Keep to settle matters. At that meeting, the Druids had provided a detailed account of everything that had happened as related to them by Paxon and Miriya upon their return. Both the Highlander and the Druid had wanted to be included as members of that delegation, but they were in such bad shape that wiser heads decided it would be best if they were placed under the care of healers immediately. Yet whatever the Druids who ultimately spoke to the Federation commanders said, it proved sufficient to break the siege. It probably hadn't hurt that they ended up handing over Arcannen's head in the bargain, providing at least that much in the way of physical proof. Probably not everyone would be convinced of what had happened, but those of the Federation who listened to what the Druids had to tell them had been happy enough to haul anchor and fly home.

All of the stolen artifacts recovered from Arcannen's airship had been locked away again, back in their niches and cubicles and boxes in the artifact vault, tended now by a new keeper—a Druid of long and trusted service who had stepped in to fill the void left by Kera-trix's death.

Chrysallin and Leofur were safely returned, too, although almost as beat up and ragged as Paxon and Miriya. The women had returned a day after Paxon, accompanied by the Keep's stable manager, who had gone with Leofur on her quest. Why this had happened was something of a mystery, and as yet no one had heard the full story behind his involvement.

Paxon had been given only a brief overview by Chrysallin, and neither Leofur nor the stable manager was saying anything at all.

The Highlander had gone to Leofur on her return, but she had said little, and since then had secluded herself in the healing center, permitting no visitors save Chrysallin—and even his sister had been allowed only a single visit. Whatever had transpired during that visit left his sister looking troubled. She refused afterward to talk about it, and when he asked her to speak to Leofur about making an exception so he could visit, too, she was quick to say no.

His efforts at getting further details were unsuccessful. He was worried Leofur might be more badly hurt than he knew. He even considered the possibility she might be dying. But Chrys told him this was not the issue and to let things be. Leofur was not ready for other visitors, and he should wait for her to come to him.

Which earlier that morning she had sent word she was ready to do.

He glanced up to see her arriving as promised. It felt odd even now to have waited for her to come to him. But he didn't know what she had been through or how it had affected her, so he was willing to allow her almost anything. Perhaps now, at last, he would find out what was troubling her.

He smiled as she drew near, squinting against the sunlight that backlit her slender form, noting the familiar tousled hair, cut short and looking a bit ragged around the edges, the brilliantly sharp eyes with their steady gaze, and the sure, firm stride. She seemed the same as ever, except for the serious expression that sat uncomfortably on her sculpted features.

"Sit with me," she said, and taking his hand she led him farther into the gardens to a bench deep within overlapping stands of fuchsia and hydrangea, both of which provided a concealing screen of kaleidoscopic colors.

"How are you feeling?" she asked him as they seated themselves next to each other.

"Much better than my caregivers think. What about you? I was worried when you refused all visitors. I was imagining terrible things. You're not badly hurt or ill, are you? That's not what's wrong, is it? Because I can tell something is. Are you all right?"

She gave him a wan smile. "That's hard to say. I'll be better after we talk, I hope. I asked not to see anyone—especially you—because I wasn't yet prepared to talk about what happened. Maybe I'm still not ready. But I don't think it is right to put it off any longer."

"Put what off?"

She leaned forward and took his hands in her own. "Just this. I love you, but I've realized that I don't love you enough. I have to leave you, and I am doing so now. I am releasing you from your vows. And me from mine."

He stared at her, a sense of the unreal overriding any chance of accepting what he was hearing. "This seems awfully sudden. Why would you do this?"

"The short answer is that I met someone else. Someone I love more than I love you. More, I think, than I ever have or ever will love anyone."

"You met someone? How?" He paused, understanding flooding through him. "The stable hand. Is that who you're in love with? I don't understand. How can you be in love with a stable hand?"

He felt her hands tighten on his. "Don't try to diminish him, please. It's beneath you. He is much more than what the word suggests. He is a shape-shifter, and his abilities are the equal of your own. How I fell in love with him isn't what matters. All that matters is that I feel strongly enough about him to want to leave you. That required more than a little self-examination and some very hard consideration of what I was giving up and why. I found it strange myself at first, but now I know I am doing the right thing. There are reasons for why this is so, and they are very good reasons. Reasons why I should be with him and not with you."

She paused, and he said, "Go ahead. Tell me. I want to hear everything. I want you to make me understand."

"I don't know if that's possible, Paxon. But I will try my best." She sighed deeply. "It's such a strange world we live in, where I can give you up for anyone else. You've been kind and generous to me. You've loved me and me only, and you've never lied to me or misled me."

She leaned toward him. "But you don't *need* me, Paxon. You haven't since those first few weeks when you came to me in Wayford. Once you became strong enough to return to Paranor to look after Chrys, that was the end of your need—your *real* need—for me. After that, I became your bedmate and your companion only. And I was starting to feel like my identity and my life were slipping away.

"Then I met Imric, and he really *does* need me. Enough so that if I am not there, I think there is a real danger he might die. It is difficult to explain. There is a connection between us that transcends any ordinary bond. A mental connection called a tether binds us together when he shape-shifts so that he will not be lost to himself. Without me to steady him, he cannot do it safely. And if he cannot shape-shift, life means nothing to him. There is more to it, but that is the part you need to know. How we feel about each other is what matters. We are not complete without each other. We are not whole."

"But you and I complete each other, too," he insisted.

"No, Paxon, we don't. We are companions and friends, but we do not complete each other. What I discovered about myself on my search for Chrys was that what I really require is a partner who needs me. I have missed being needed for some time now. It is not something you can give me. Promise what you like, but you can't. For you, the Druid order and your position as the High Druid's Blade will always come first. It is your calling in life, your mission. You are driven to be special, the one and only, the person others will always depend upon. I want someone who depends on *me* in that way. I've never had it—not with my father, not with those who have been my friends, and not with you. But Imric can give me that. And that's why I am choosing him."

"You've already told Chrys, haven't you?" Paxon said. "Even before telling me."

She nodded. "I'm sorry about that. But she was there while it was developing, and she watched it happen. I wasn't ready to talk to you yet, but I needed to talk to someone. So I talked with her. She was very upset and sad, but she understood. She is a wonderful friend, and I will miss her greatly."

He closed his eyes against what that meant. "You're leaving Paranor." He could barely speak the words. They seemed to signify an irrevocable end to their life together, a decision made that could not be altered.

"I have to. I don't belong here. I haven't belonged for a while now. Without you as my life partner, I have no place at all. We have talked about it, Imric and I. We want to start over somewhere new, somewhere neither of us is known. Somewhere he will be accepted for who and what he is, and where I will have my chance to do for him what I think I was never able to do for you."

She rose, releasing his hands. "I've told you what I came to tell you. I am sorry, Paxon. I will never forget you. I will always care for you. I wish you happiness and success, and I think you will find both. But try to be happy for me, as well, and don't be angry with Imric. Just remember you and I were happy once and good for each other, too. Maybe we can be good now for other people."

She stepped away. "Good-bye, Highlander."

He rose and faced her. "I can't accept this, you know. I will wait for you to come back."

She turned away. "Don't. It would be pointless. I'm not coming back."

Then she was gone, and he was left feeling empty and broken, all thoughts but one driven from his mind.

How could this have happened?

As Leofur walked away she was thinking of the things she hadn't told him. Paxon was kind and understanding, but he didn't need to know the entirety of what had gone into her decision to leave him. It wasn't as if he could change her mind. She wasn't the kind to make decisions that required revisiting. And she didn't have to wonder if she had thought it all through quite thoroughly. She had done that, and more.

Besides, he might not even be able to understand or accept what it had taken her so long to realize.

So while she had made it plain that their partnering wasn't working, in large part because she had become superfluous in the relationship, she had not talked about why she was so drawn to Imric. It required a complicated explanation, one she was not prepared to give. She felt a deep satisfaction in knowing that someone depended on her in a way that no one else ever would, and that this dependency was conceived not just in her ability to facilitate his shape-shifting but also in her clear understanding of what that gift meant to him. Because after experiencing what it felt like to be inside him when he changed, she now craved it as much as he did. It was a pleasure shared, a pleasure no one else could know, and it provided her with the gateway to the identity she had been searching for.

He had once told her that she provided him with the strength necessary to buttress his weakness, that she was steady where he was mercurial, that she grounded him where he was prone to losing himself in his need for shifting. But she understood now that he provided strength to buttress a weakness in her, as well. He gave her the freedom to expand and grow where she had felt constrained and inert for so long. He had allowed her to escape the feeling that she was serving no purpose in her life. In their differences, they were more alike than she had realized, and it was this that had helped bring them together.

She understood this now, but she did not think she could explain it to Paxon in a way that would allow him to accept it.

She had not told him, either, that she believed her tethering with Imric worked in large part because they were so much alike. They came from similar backgrounds, from families that were far from normal and parents who were dead or absent entirely from an early age. As a result, they had grown up on their own. They had both been forced to become self-sufficient and directed; they had both learned early to rely on themselves and themselves only. What this meant to the tethering wasn't immediately apparent to Leofur, not until after she had found Imric in the bower and stayed with him through that first night of his recovery. He had told her then that she had saved him simply through being there for him. She had no reason to doubt him, but it was a revelation. It demonstrated not only that she was strong enough to experience the most rigorous demands of sharing his ability to change shapes, but also that she was strong enough to steady him in situations where he was in danger of losing control. Even when there was a dark spell causing it, even when a witch had infused him with a magic designed to cause his shape-shifting to kill him.

This meshing of personality and character was a large part of why she was drawn to him, why she felt so close when they were linked. It wasn't quantifiable or even completely understandable. But it was there, and it was real. Who she was and how she had lived her life was why she and Imric loved each other.

But Paxon didn't need to know of this.

Nor did he need to know that she had decided that one day she would bear Imric's children. It wasn't that she had talked openly about it with Imric. It was more of an unspoken promise. Right from the beginning of her agreement to be with him, she had understood that a family was important. For both of them—deprived of family at an early age, left parentless and rootless as they had grown—a stable family was both desirable and necessary. Yes, Leofur found hints of it in his words and looks and knew it was there.

Nor did she tell Paxon where she would go or what she would do when she left him. She did not want him to know. She wanted their separation to be complete so each could begin a new life unencumbered by the old. Her decision to leave Paranor was easily made. Her choice of a new home was the Westland, where the prospects for creatures like Imric to lead normal lives were not limited by the prejudice and distrust so prevalent in much of the Southland. Leofur did not know exactly where in the Westland they would go, but it would be somewhere that would give them a reasonable chance at starting over, at fulfilling the promise of a shared love, and at experiencing the happiness that had been so long in coming.

As she reached the elevated airship platform, she saw him standing by the two-man she had piloted back from the Murk Sink. His possessions were piled next to hers, and he bore the look of expectant resolve that had become so familiar. He smiled on seeing her, and she felt herself go warm in response.

When she reached him, he took her in his arms and pressed her against him. "Is it settled?" he whispered in her ear.

Her answer was wordless. She turned to face him and kissed him hard. "Time for us to go."

Paxon spent most of the rest of the day trying to figure things out. He stayed in the gardens long after Leofur had gone, thinking it over, still stunned by the suddenness of her decision, still trying to make sense of it. Afterward, he walked the parapets, the hallways, the courtyards, and the forest beyond the Keep. He walked wherever his feet took him. He kept to himself, not stopping for those who tried to engage him in conversation, not able to talk to anyone feeling as he did. He skipped his meetings with his healers and his therapy. He did not eat. He could barely think of food.

When twilight approached, he went to his room and shut himself in. He was still sitting there, the room growing dark around him, when a knock on his door signaled a visitor.

"I can't talk right now," he said. "Please go away."

The door opened anyway and Miriya walked in.

Actually, she hobbled in, her splinted leg giving her a stiff shuffling gait, her body swathed in bandages and her face still blackened and bruised. She was balancing a plate of food in one hand and using a staff to support herself with the other.

"I carried this all the way from the dining hall. So don't tell me to go away."

He was surprised to see her moving around. "I thought you were confined to bed. You are supposed to be healing."

"I thought the same of you. The difference between us is that when I'm in pain, I prefer to share it with someone."

The way she said it told him everything he needed to know. "You've heard. Who told you?"

"Chrysallin. She can't bring herself to talk to you about it yet, but I have fewer reservations. Here, eat some of this."

She hobbled over and set the plate in his lap. Then she sat down next to him. "That wasn't a request, Paxon. It was an order."

He realized he was hungry and began to eat.

There were already rumors going around that Miriya would be tapped as the next Ard Rhys. She sounded as if it were already an accomplished fact. "Practicing for your new position, are you?" he asked, aware that she was watching him. "Getting used to the idea of ordering people around?"

She snorted. "Don't believe everything you hear. I would make a terrible Ard Rhys. Too much sitting around, not enough action. I need to be out and about, not just sending others to do the work for me."

"Maybe your approach would be a welcome change. We've had leaders in the past who actually led by example, leaders who didn't sit around letting others do things. Leaders who did things themselves."

"I'm doing something right now. I'm spending time with you. Why is it so dark in here?"

She flicked her fingers at the smokeless lamps and they lit instantly. "I haven't lost my touch," she muttered.

"So you've come to comfort me, have you?" Paxon said.

"I've come to feed you. And drink with you."

She produced a black bottle from beneath her robes and set it between them. He studied it a moment and then picked it up, uncorked it, and drank deeply. The cool liquid burned on the way down to the pit of his stomach, and his eyes watered. "That isn't ale."

"No, it isn't. That's pure sket, and hard to come by. Good for everything that ails you—especially heartbreak."

He nodded. "I hope so. I could use a little of that sort of healing."

Her features crinkled in an attempt at a smile, the mottled skin giving her a somewhat gruesome appearance. "There's an old saying. If someone doesn't want to be with you, then you probably don't belong with them."

"Very insightful. Exactly who said that?"

"I did. Just now. She loved you once, but now she doesn't. If she doesn't, she needs to let you go. Which she's done. Now you need to let her go, too."

"Don't think I'm not trying."

She paused. "Let's you and I make a bargain. Let's agree to spend this evening commiserating with each other. I will tell you why you are better off without Leofur Rai, and you will tell me how I will eventually get over losing Karlin. We will lie to each other, but we will do it in a kindly way. We will promise to be there for each other in the days to come. You and I, we've shared something that neither of us will likely ever share with anyone again. It binds us, that sharing. We should celebrate it."

She took the bottle from him and drank several long swallows. When she finished, she wiped her mouth gingerly with the back of her hand. "Here's to the end of days gone past—some good, some not so good. And here's to the beginning of new days."

She passed the bottle back, and he drank from it again.

"Here's to both," he agreed, blinking as his eyes watered.

"We'll always be friends, Paxon," she said. "Bound by bandages and bottles of sket, if nothing else."

He nodded his agreement. "Friends always."

They drank some more and were silent for a time.

"Friends share secrets, you know," Miriya said finally. "So you start. Tell me something about yourself. Something personal. I don't really know much about you. Go on. Tell me something."

So he proceeded to talk about his early days in the Highlands and about Chrysallin and his mother, and then she told him about her childhood and how she had become a Druid. After a while their talk segued into tales of artifacts and magic hunting and from there into stories of unusual people they had met along the way. Somber tones and reluctant words gave way to laughter and jokes. The bottle of sket gradually emptied.

Midnight came and went, and by sunrise they were still talking, and the new day was looking a little brighter.

Terry Brooks is the *New York Times* bestselling author of more than thirty books, including the Dark Legacy of Shannara adventures *Wards of Faerie* and *Bloodfire Quest*; the Legends of Shannara novels *Bearers of the Black Staff* and *The Measure of the Magic*; the Genesis of Shannara trilogy: *Armageddon's Children*, *The Elves of Cintra* and *The Gypsy Morph*; and *The Sword of Shannara*. The author was a practising attorney for many years but now writes full-time. He lives with his wife, Judine, in the Pacific Northwest.

www.shannara.com
www.terrybrooks.net

Find out more about Terry Brooks and other Orbit authors by signing up for the free monthly newsletter at www.orbitbooks.net.

ABOUT THE TYPE

This book was set in Minion, a 1990 Adobe Originals typeface by Robert Slimbach (b. 1956). Minion is inspired by classical, old-style typefaces of the late Renaissance, a period of elegant, beautiful, and highly readable type designs. Created primarily for text setting, Minion combines the aesthetic and functional qualities that make text type highly readable with the versatility of digital technology.

SHANNARA
the
FOUR LANDS

ARTWORK BY RUS